TORTURE
TO
BLISS

PUBLISHED BY SIENNA GYPSY 2022

Angels of Fury

TORTURE
TO
BLISS

BY

SIENNA GYPSY

DEDICATION

T hank you to everyone who encouraged me to write this book. First, a special thanks to Anita writer to writer, love ya, girl. To my sister-in-law, Lee, thank you for spilling the beans and being my first cheerleader from the very beginning. And Dani Stevens, your pep talks and honest feedback were truly invaluable.

To my incredible beta readers LB, Jess, Cherice, Amanda, Kate, Megan, and Carol your insights were essential during the final edits. And to Mama Bird Jess, you've been amazing. Thanks for introducing me to Nicole Kincaid she was truly a godsend.

Each of you has played a unique and special role in bringing this book to life. I've learned so much from you all, and this book wouldn't be what it is without your unwavering support.

TRIGGER WARNING

This book contains references of child abuse, violence, sex, abuse and trafficking, and alcohol.

ANASTASIA FRAZER

PROLOGUE

ANASTASIA FRAZER

With a sudden jolt, I bring myself back into consciousness. The chaos around me rips through the darkness. Something is happening, there isn't usually this much yelling. The ropes are still pinching into my skin where they are tied. I hear a big commotion towards the front door and my breath catches in my throat. As I teeter on the brink of unconsciousness, the room empties out. Abandoning me in my vulnerable state. Naked, bound, and bloodied…

Voices surround me, whispering through the air. Keeping my eyes closed, I try to listen to the man and woman. I stay as still as possible. My hands are beside me, and warm from the blanket covering me.

Searching through my memories. Seeing if I can remember the last things that happened before everything went black. An icy chill runs through my body. What if these people are worse than my father? I remember pain everywhere. But I can't feel any now. I decide to stay still and hope they think I'm asleep. At least no one is touching me. God, I hope they don't touch me. I tune into what they are saying around me.

"She was there. Naked, tied up and beaten. I wasn't leaving her there. She looks between ten and twelve... I can't even let my mind think what was happening to her." The man says.

"Jesus Cobra, what are you going to do with her? She can't stay here. The club is the first place they will look." The woman says.

"I know. I've got some ideas. I'm leaving for the Western Australia charter in five days."

What? My whole body freezes at what he said. *Western Australia. I have no money. W-what... How am I going to survive? What if they're like dad? I can't go to Western Australia. OH MY GOD. How am I going to get out of this?*

I silence my mind, unsure if I said anything out loud.

"Look, she's waking up." Oh, no. Don't look at me... Then, someone is stroking my arm, which is so foreign to me.

"Honey, you're safe. Open your eyes, Little Bird."

I shift a bit, then moan in discomfort. There's that pain that I couldn't feel before.

When I finally get my eyes to focus, I panic at the sight of the enormous man looming beside the bed. I frantically curl my body into a ball and press myself against the wall so intensely that I fear

2

I'll break through it. He slowly gets down to my level, as if he's approaching a caged lion, speaking to me gently.

"Little Bird, we won't hurt you. We've saved you. You are pretty banged up, sweetheart. Where are you hurting?" I open my mouth and no words come out. My mouth won't work. I don't know what hurts. In a daze, I nod my head, hoping he understands and stays true to his word.

The lady next to him states, "You go get the doc, I'll stay here and keep her safe." As he's walking out, he looks back at me with... I'm not sure what's in his eyes. I've not seen it before.

As the door closes, I hear loud noises and I jump with every sound. The lady comes and sits close to me and tries to pull me into her. I resist her at first, but something inside me ends up folding. I relax into her body. Before I know it, I'm sobbing. I faintly hear her say, "He just hit the wall, honey, it's not you. It's the men that hurt you."

I'm not sure when I started or when I stopped crying. Can this be real? Am I saved? Is Frazer, my father, dead? God, I hope he's dead. I don't care if that's wrong. I calm down after what felt like forever, with the lady shushing me and stroking my hair from the top of my head, down. It feels nice, really nice. Then she pulls back and gives me some tablets.

Panic rushes through me, looking at the tablets. The lady soothes me, "Little Bird, these are only for the pain. Doc and Cobra put them in here for you when you were crying. Honey, I'm not going anywhere. Cobra asked me to stay till you're ok."

I take a shuddering breath and nod, still staring at the tablets. I'm not sure about them, but I take them anyway. Then she introduces herself. "My name is Savie, short for Savanna. We are at a motorcycle club. Cobra is V.P. at one of our other charters. He won't let anything happen to you. He has a kid, so he will protect you like his own. Trust us, honey."

She's stroking my head to soothe me, and it seems to work. I simply nod and relax into her shoulder, allowing the tranquillity to seep into every fibre of my being.

The next time I wake up, Cobra is back in the room and Savie's lying down with me, cuddling me. The warmth of her chest beneath my head as I listen to her conversation with the man she introduced as Cobra.

"She should come good today. I'll get her up and walk around the compound, then you can tell her about your plan." There is silence for a bit before he replies.

"Savie, I'll be telling her as soon as she wakes up this time, you can't keep her. You said so yourself, but I'll make sure you can keep in touch." I feel movement above me, like Savie is nodding. I open my eyes slowly. Seeing Cobra first, he smiles at me, which is strangely comforting.

"Morning Little Bird, how are you feeling, any better?" I nod again, lifting my head to look at Savie for reassurance. She smiles at me, then sits up, pulling me into her arms more.

"Honey, Cobra has something to tell you. Don't worry, ok, it's for the best. I promise." I look at Cobra, and he tells me his plans.

"In a couple of days, I'm going to Western Australia, Esperance. My mum lives there and it would be the safest place for you to live. She can't wait to meet you. How do you feel about that?" I take in everything he says. Confusion is spiralling through me. Will I really be safe? I try for the first time to talk, but it comes out as a whisper.

"F-Frazer... where is he?"

"No one knows where he is now. But you're safe and he doesn't know me or who I am, so he'll never guess you're in W.A., or I'd find somewhere else for you." I'm looking at him as he winks before saying the next part.

"Besides, my mum is good with a shotgun, so you are safe with her." I nod, but I don't want to leave the safety of Savie's arms.

She squeezes me slightly and I hold on to her tighter as she asks me, "You hungry? Let me up and I'll get you some food." I'm not, but I nod anyway. When she gets out of bed, I regret saying yes. I feel lost without her next to me. The safety is gone.

Cobra stands and sits on the bed next to me. I shift back, not meaning to. He reaches out and rubs my right foot. I don't know why, but I don't feel scared. He is huge, like two, maybe three of me. And wide too, but he's gentle. He takes a deep breath and begins.

"Little Bird, I need you to tell me who else was at the party, so I can keep them away from you." Like I'd know. But I don't want to say that to him, he's big. Gathering all my courage, I clear my throat.

"Um, I- I'm not sure. I know my father was there an-...."

"What! Your dad was there? And what? Watches?" I flinch, pulling my foot from his hold and retreating from him. The feeling of safety didn't last long. I scurry to find somewhere safe.. The corner of the bed next to the wall isn't big enough to hide me. God, why did I upset him?

"I-, I'm so sorry. Please don't ask me. I, I c-can't."

"Jesus," He stands up and starts pacing, "Sweetheart, it's not you I'm mad at. It's everyone else in that room letting you be in that situation, and now your dad."

"H-He told me I was born for that." I say in a whisper

"Well, you weren't. Jesus, you're a kid. Okay, names, do you know any?" I'm shaking my head looking down at my fingernails. "I only know one, h-he's always been mean to me," Cobra stays quiet, so I keep going.

"Frankie. He tells my father that I'm his."

"Like fuck! Ahh! No, you're not his, honey! Is that all you can remember? Anything will help."

Shaking my head, I say, "N-no I don't remember anything else." I wasn't sure what else to say.

Without warning the room shakes from a gigantic explosion from somewhere close.

Cobra turns in my direction saying, "Stay put. Me or Savie will come for you, okay? Don't go with anyone else." As he opens the door, another man comes barrelling in. He's younger than Cobra.

"Cobra! The explosion has hit Prez bad. We gotta get him to a hospital, Savie's with him. The threat is gone, I don't think they thought we were all here." Cobra rushes out the door. He stops still, turns, and looks at me. Then glares at the man who barrelled in. "This is Krip. Don't leave his side. I'll be back."

It seems like forever before anyone enters the room. The door bursts open, Cobra barges in and I jump out of my skin. For a minute, I'm not in that room with Krip and Cobra. I am back in my bedroom and my dad is beating me viciously. I feel my body shake and try to hide within myself. Backing into the wall, I hit it hard, which brings me back to the present, as Cobra walks towards me. I'm trying to stop shaking like a leaf but my body has a mind of its own. I can't seem to stop the uncontrollable tremors, no matter how much I try.

"Little Bird, we need to get you out of here. Can you stand yet?"
I try to speak. The words are in my head, but I can't say them. My
eyes are so wide it feels like my eyeballs are going to pop right out.
I look at the ground and nod my head.

Cobra moves my blankets back, trying to help me out of bed. I
try to move with his hands guiding me. He seems to be on a
mission. He turns his head to Krip.

"Prez is gone. Savie's coming whether she wants to or not."
Then he looks at me.

"Krip get her to the truck."
Is he leaving me now? Oh, my god. My heart feels like it stops. I
don't know what's going to happen to me now.

I go to stand, but my legs won't carry me. I fall, but Krip is the
one who catches me. He picks me up like I'm a puppy. Warmth hits
my cheeks. We are out the door, going down a dark hallway. Krip
kicks open a door that exits outside. He runs across the dirt until we
get to a truck. He opens the back door, checks inside and puts me
in. Leaning around me, he grabs the seat belt and buckles me in.
Grabbing my chin gently, he looks into my eyes.

"You good?" I'm finding it too hard to talk. Even thinking is not
working. He must realise this because he looks at me tenderly.
"Just nod, Little Bird. I'm okay with that." I nod. He races to get in
the front seat of the truck, starts it up, and drives.
This jolts me out of the fear that's been suffocating me.

"W-what about Cobra and Savie?" He turns to look at me.

"They're coming. I'm making sure he doesn't have to carry her
far."

"What? Carry her? Is she okay?"

7

He nods and replies, "She's distraught but she's not physically hurt." Oh, God. I feel tears running down my face as I stare out the window. These people are going to hate me. I just met Savie, and she has given me more comfort than anyone has my whole life. God, she can't hate me.

Bringing my knees up on the seat, I rock back and forth. My sides hurt, but I don't care anymore. God, I hope this isn't my father looking for me.

I jump when the door opens. Cobra jumps in with Savie, she is curled around him. He looks at Krip in the mirror, and with one nod, we pull away. Cobra is rubbing Savie's back but asks if I'm okay. I nod and lean my head on the window, watching the trees go by. After a while, it seems to lull my mind. Eventually, I fall asleep.

As the truck stops, I notice the smell of the ocean in the air. It is close. So close. When I get out of the truck, I grip hold of the door like no tomorrow. My legs are weak and it's hard to bear my weight. That's when I see it. The ocean is straight across the road. Eventually, my body takes my weight. I find my balance and let go of the door, but Krip picks me up. He's picked up on my new nickname as well.

"I got you, Little Bird, just hold on." I can walk now, but decide not to fight it. He walks me through the front door, then I hear a lady's voice say.

"Her room is on the right. I set Savie up across from her."

"I'll sleep with Little Bird for a bit. I need the company." No one questioned Savie. Cobra brought in the bags full of clothes, and some personal hygiene items we stopped to get on the way. He put them on the table, kissed us both on the top of the head, then left the room. Savie got some clothes out for the both of us and we started to change. I knew the exact moment she noticed my marks from Frankie. The room fell into an eerie silence. With a racing heart, I hurriedly put on my clothes

As she relaxes in, she asks, "How long have you had those scars, Honey?" She reaches her arms around me and cuddles me tight, making me feel safe. It's nice. I wonder if my mum would have done this for me when I was sad or hurting.

"The first one was when I was ten, and it kept happening." I shake the automatic tremors that claw at my skin, not wanting to talk about it anymore. She rubs my arms and my back.

"Get some sleep, Little Bird." That's all the encouragement I need because it finds me straight away.

Over the next couple of days, I get to know Nana Sally. I've still been jumpy, so most of the MC has kept their distance, including Cobra's son. Soon, they will all be going back for the Prez's funeral, but Cobra says I'm staying here with Nana Sally. Reminding me I'll be safe here, and that my father and Frankie won't be able to find me. I don't have any other options, and so far, they seem to have kept their word. Maybe I am finally saved.

I've been here for a year, and I love it. The beach is awesome, and so is Nanna Sally. She's taught me so much. She got me to go to counselling to help with my fears, but it doesn't seem to work. I've found a place to hide in my dreams at night.

Every few weeks, Cobra passes through to check on us. He became the Prez of the Melbourne Club. Sometimes Krip would come with him, wanting to catch up with me to see how I was doing. He's like a watchdog. He takes me places but makes sure no one gets too close.

Nanna Sally and the guys have become what a family should be.

I hope it will stay this way, but one thing I've learned in life is that nothing good lasts forever.

Sienna Gypsy

STASIA JONES

I

STASIA JONES

Six Years Later…

Beep, beep, beep, beep! I stretched out while listening to the noise I hate so much.

"Omg, argh! Shut up!" I turn over with my eyes still shut and begin swinging my arm in my clock's general direction. *Tap, tap, tap, bang!*

"Shitty alarm clock," I growl when it finally goes off. Every night the nightmares from my past come to visit, I hate them. When is this going to stop? The same thing every night reminds me of that bloody movie, Groundhog Day. I'm ready to be done with this shit.

So many lives are broken, and some even died because of me. I always thought that it wasn't my father that came to the club that night, but I found out on my last night with Nanna Sally that it was. And the more I think about it, the more I wonder who the hell my father is.

"Grah!" I shake those thoughts away while I roll off my bed to take a cold shower. Yes, cold, because I couldn't pay for the gas. Thinking about a cold shower causes me to shiver like it's minus six degrees.

Stepping into the bathroom, I psych myself up to get in the shower. Shit, I hate this! One more week, then I can pay the bill. Taking off my clothes, I continue with my internal pep talk. I jump into the cold running water and immediately regret not paying the bill. "Oh shit, that's cold." So glad no one can hear me. Washing as fast as I can. Scrub, rinse, and out.

Drying quickly, I brush my teeth, and get dressed for work. I return to the bathroom to put on some simple makeup. Brushing mascara through my long lashes and dabbing a bit of gloss on my lips. Taking one last look at myself, perfect. Now I'm ready to walk to work. No sense in wasting money on petrol when other bills need paying. I double-check that I have my phone, walk out the door, lock up, and then off I go.

My life is like Murphy's Law. If it can go wrong, it definitely will.

When I get to the crosswalk, I wait for the green person to blink, but there are no cars, so I cross the road. What I don't hear or see is the bike coming. Next thing I know, I'm on my ass looking at... I'm not sure what, or who.

Tall, muscles, tattoos, and light brown skin. Mmm, I'm internally fanning myself and praying like hell I don't say something stupid.

"Um, sorry, I ..." I'm still looking at him. Trying to kick-start my brain, I don't even notice at first how pissed he looks.

"What the fuck are you doing?"

"I... I don't know. W-What are y-you doing?" I knew I was going to say something stupid.

"What the fuck does it look like? Could you not hear my Harley, it's loud enough? And why the fuck were you crossing the road at a red light? I could have hurt you." Yep, still staring at me like I'm an idiot. Trying to ignore him, I attempt to stand. Pain shoots down my leg. I'm not sure what's wrong, but I hit the ground again, so I say the only thing I can say.

"I'm hurt." Shit. Okay, hold it together. No crying or he'll hate you more.

"Fuck! Now what am I supposed to do?" He asks like I want him to do something. All I can feel is the pain. I mentally kick myself.

"Don't worry, I'll be fine. It happens all the time." When will my mouth stop talking?

He snaps back at me, "What, are you serious?" Argh, can he leave now?

"Y-Yep pains going s-slowly. I'll be good s-soon. You can go now." Making eye contact with him, a shiver washes over my body. I shake it off, not wanting to think about anything but getting away from this guy. Shit. He's getting off his bike and taking his helmet off. Oh my god! He needs to put it back on. Yep, put it back on so I can concentrate on not saying anything stupid again. Shit! The look on his face has changed now. Concerned? I'm confused.

He asks in a nicer voice, "Where does it hurt?" He has to stop looking at me because I can't think.

"I'm fine. You need to go." Yep, subtle, that's me.

"Sorry, not goin' anywhere. What's your name?" This is where I need to think straight. You can do this, I pep talk myself, don't look at him and talk.

"Look, thank you for stopping. I'm fine. It's just a bruise. Please, if it still hurts tonight, I'll get it looked at, okay?" It's like he didn't even hear me.

"Where were you going?" he asks.

"Work," I snap back, trying to get up again, slowly this time. With his hands on me, I can't feel any pain, only sparks where his huge hands hold my hips steady.

"You good to stand now?" Stumbling a bit, I manage to gain my balance as he lets go.

"Yep, I'm fine. Thanks again." I muster a faint smile, despite the excruciating pain shooting through my leg. I wanted him to leave me alone. Trying to escape without more talking, I walk away. Well, limp, really. Okay, I will get checked out later.

Before I can get away clean, he asks, "You going to tell me your name?"

Feeling like an idiot for falling, I reply, "Oh, I'm Miss Hit-the-Dirt. Nice to meet you, biker dude." Original, I know, but I've never been cool before. I turn away from him again, carefully walking on my hurt leg, thinking I'm getting away clean

Then I hear him yell, "I'm Drew. I'll be seeing you around, Miss Hit-the-Dirt." Did he think that was my name? Rolling my eyes at my stupidity, I hobble to my job.

Getting closer to work, I look behind me to see if he's gone. Nope, still there, all gorgeous and masculine, staring back at me. It's only then I notice the leather jacket with no sleeves and patches over it. Memories of my past hit me as I walk. Cobra, Krip and Savie. Then I remember Krip's word about bikers, "Always your brother, never your lover, Little Bird." I shake my head to brush away the memory. Yep, bad to the bone. Not going to see him again.

Pushing through the doors of where I work, I see my good friend, Sophie, serving a customer. I give her a wave and limp to the back to put my stuff away. By the look on her face, I know she notices something is wrong. Walking back out to start my shift, Sophie glares at me.

"Honestly, Stasia, you need a padded bubble to walk around in. What happened?" Still feeling the pain of my stupidity, I agree with her, but didn't let her know. I decided to give her a bit of the story.

"Well, the non-complicated story is I got run over by a motorbike."

"And the complicated?" I looked away from her concerned gaze. "You don't want to know."

"You, okay?"

Am I okay? Let me think. *NOT AT ALL*, I scream in my head.

"Yeah, I'll be fine. Just need to walk it off." Hopefully, she moves on to something else.

"Didn't you walk here?" She asks. I roll my eyes again. Why couldn't she leave it alone?

"Yes, but it just happened, so chill out. If it's not getting better by lunchtime, I'll leave and get it looked at, okay?" Before Sophie can give me any more shit, the bell rings over the door, and in walks biker dude, Drew. *Shit. Shit. Shit.* Sophie gives me a look that tells me she's not finished with me by a long shot.

She then turns to biker dude with a smile and asks, "How can I help you?"

He looks straight past her, focused on me, and says, "I followed Miss Hit-the-Dirt here to make sure she was okay. She landed hard on her ass and her leg was giving her trouble." My face goes red, and Sophie can't help but laugh.

"Miss Hit-the-Dirt?" Sophie looks at me, raising her eyebrows.

"That's what she told me her name was," sexy Drew replies. Sophie laughs again. After a bit they are both staring at me, waiting for an answer. I'm not sure what answer Drew is looking for, but I'm sure Sophie wondering how I became Miss Hit-the-Dirt. I wanted this day to be over and to get the hell out of here. So insanely embarrassed, I pretend not to notice they are staring at me.

"Did you say something?" I ask. Sophie burst out laughing again. What was so funny, I have no idea. Sophie walks over to me and whispers, "Now I know why it's complicated. Damn girl, is he the one that ran you over?"

Trying my best to look unaffected by him, I reply, "I told you I'm fine."

"And I told you I would see you around." He says, still staring at me like he wants to taste or kill me. I can't decide which.

"Well, I didn't think that would be today.... or ever," I say the last part as a whisper, hoping he didn't hear me.

"Well, I didn't give you my number, thought I better, seeing as I hit you. Need to make sure there's no permanent damage. Ring me tomorrow and let me know." Well, he heard me, and he doesn't seem angry. He walks across the room and passes me a card with his number on it.

He turns to walk out, but stops and says, "If you don't ring, I'll find you myself to make sure you're okay. You hear me?" Oh my God, bossy much?

I can't think of anything to say, so I say, "Okay." He gives me another long scowl and walks out the door. Thank God he doesn't know my name.

DREW

2

DREW

Swinging my leg over my bike, I sit and stare at the cafe window thinking about what just happened. How the fuck did I not see her walking across the road? I watch her wipe the bench, thinking… and that's the problem. I never think about girls. They are there for fun, nothing else. Here I am thinking about how I'm going to see her again. I have no idea why I should care. She better ring me tomorrow. Shaking my head, I start my bike and head out to the clubhouse. I can't wait to hear the shit the boys are going to give me when I tell them what I've done.

Pulling up to the clubhouse, I see a few of the guys standing around the garage. The garage is one of the businesses our club owns. Most of the time I work here, and the rest of the time I'm on a run for the club. All the boys take turns on the runs. Some guys have a wife, kids, or old ladies. With us taking turns, it makes it easy for everyone.

Taking off my helmet, I get off my bike. I need to see what is on the agenda for the day. Walking towards the President of this charter, I put my hand out as he passes me a clipboard with jobs for today on it. "Drew, you got three tune-ups today." Looking at the clipboard, I see two smaller cars and one bike. Awesome, simple day today. "Cool. Thanks, Prez. I'll get on it." I make a move to get started when he stops me in my stride. "How come you're late? You're never this late." I look at my watch to see how late I am. Forty-five minutes. Fuck.

"I got held up," I say while shrugging my shoulders.

"That's obvious. You going to tell us why?"

I sigh heavily, irritated at telling them, but I think better of it, and began my explanation.

"I sort of collided with someone at the lights on the main road."

I see Prez and the guys looking at my bike, checking it out. Prez looks at me.

"There's no dent on your bike. Was the other vehicle, okay?" I cringe at what I have to say next.

"Well, it was… a person. But yeah, she's fine. I'm checkin' in with her tomorrow, just to be sure. She only had a slight limp when she went to work." Well, that sounded better in my head.

Bullet and Knight laugh. I grind my teeth. I know what they're thinking.

"Yeah, yeah. Just shut it. I feel bad as it is."

Prez looks serious and I'm not sure why.

"Why didn't you take her to get checked out if she's hurt? It's only going to get worse by the end of the day."

Of course, he's right.

"I was thinking of getting these jobs done, then going back to check on her, so I'll just get started." Walking off, I look back at the guys. Prez looks concerned, but Bullet and Knight look smug. I wonder what the fuck is going through their minds.

One job down, two to go. I still can't get that girl out of my mind. Miss Hit-the-Dirt. How is she holding up? She must have felt worse by now. I hit her pretty hard.

Looking up at the clock, I want to get back before she knocks off, so I start to pick up the pace with the job at hand. The faster I get this done, the faster I get back to her.

Finishing up on the last bike, I call Bullet over.

"Hey man, are you good to go? Maybe we can grab a beer after I check on this chick."

He walks over, wiping his hands on a rag, narrowing his gaze on me.

"What makes you think I want to get in the middle of whatever it is you got yourself into this morning?"

"Man don't act like you're not interested in coming so you can get the dirt. I know you guys have been talkin' about it all morning. Now shut it. Pack up and let's go."

Locking up my toolbox, I change my shirt with the spare I have in my saddlebag. I jump on my bike and rev it a bit while I wait for Bullet to pull up next to me. We give each other a knowing nod before revving up and driving off. Riding normally puts me at ease. A sense of freedom that is hard to explain. The wind in my face, nothing holding me back, but right now it doesn't help how anxious I am feeling. Let's see if Miss Hit-the-Dirt is still on her feet. Something tells me she doesn't stay on her feet for long.

Pulling up to the café, a chill runs up my spine. Something doesn't look right. It's too quiet. I squint my eyes to try and focus as I look through the window of the cafe, there is no movement inside. My gut is telling me something is wrong, but I can't put my finger on it. I turn off my bike, and so does Bullet. We both get off and look around. Bullet nudges me. I look at him and then look in the direction Bullet is focused on. He thinks something is off as well.

Still not sure what it is exactly, we check it out. Bullet leans in close and tells me, "Going around the back."

As he heads that way, my gut is still churning. I walk towards the front door, and I realise what's going on. Both girls are as still as statues. Neither of them is talking or moving. I keep walking, pretending not to pay attention to what's going on inside, but then I see him. A guy with a gun pointed at both of them. Fuck, she's had enough shit today. Clenching my fists, I keep walking, ignoring what's happening inside. As I open the door, the gun swings in my direction. That's better, it's off Miss Hit-the-Dirt. *Bullet, I hope you are nearby mate, cause here we go.*

"What the hell, man, put that away!" I say loud enough so, hopefully, Bullet knows this guy has got a weapon. I try to get him to talk.

"'Sup man, what are you doing here? You're scaring the customers. Why don't you come over here and tell me what's up, and maybe I can help you?"

I hope he looks at my cut and thinks I can get whatever he's looking for, but he just starts getting jumpier. I watch as the gun is going back and forth between me and the girls. Fuck! I need to get that gun, so no one gets hurt.

Looking around to see how many people are in here. One family and two couples, thank God. Examining the area again, I see that Bullet is in and he shows me he's armed. Good to know.

I try again to get the freak to talk, but he's staring at the girls.

I turn to the girls and boldly ask, "Ladies, do you know what he wants so we can get this over with?"

I hope it's not a suicide mission. Miss Hit-the-Dirt looks pale, and I don't know if it's because of what I did earlier today, or what this guy is doing. "He hasn't said anything other than, don't move," she breathes. Fuck, he's back to pointing the gun at the girls.

"WHAT THE FUCK DO YOU WANT?" I yell loudly. "Because I'm tired of watching you point that gun everywhere!" The guy turns all the way around to me, which is great. Now Bullet can slip in and sneak up on him. So, I keep going.

"Why the fuck you in here with a gun, mate? Who the fuck are you, bringing a gun in here? In our town?" This seems to get him thinking. Now he's looking at my cut.

"This is not your business, or your clubs'," he says. Now, to keep him looking at me. If he spots Bullet, he might shoot someone.

He starts to turn slightly. Sweat pebbles at my temples, waiting for his next reaction. His eyes glimpse at Bullet, and his panic is instant. Shit, now the gun's pointing everywhere. Bullet gets my attention, as if to say he's going to shoot. I fuckin' knew it.

BANG! BANG! BANG!

It happens so quickly. I do a quick look around to see who's hit. It's like watching a movie in slow motion as Little Miss Hit-the-Dirt hits the floor. Fuck! I run to her. Her work friend is trying to hold her up, but I think she's going to faint. I swoop in, hoping Bullet has his part covered. When I look around, I note he must have let the other shots off. Because the guy's hand is bleeding, and I know Bullet doesn't miss his target.

I lift her up and take her over to the bench. Once I've got her settled and as comfortable as I can, I look her over. There is blood on her leg seeping through her pants. I look at her friend, demanding, "Call 000 and get an ambo here ASAP!"

She responds with a shaky but quick, "On it."

Turning back to Miss Hit-the-Dirt I add pressure to where the blood is, hoping I can clot the bleeding. Looking at the friend, I ask, "You hurt? Any blood on you?" She looks around, then at herself like she can't believe what happened.

"She bloody jumped in front of me and stopped me from getting hit." Fuck, of course she did. As if getting hit by a bike isn't enough for one day. My eyes scan more of her, I can see it's only her leg. The same leg she was limping on when I hit her this morning. Poor girl can't catch a fuckin' break.

26

Looking at her friend, I say, "Hold her leg here. I need to get a towel or something." She takes over without question, also telling me where I can find some towels.

Bullet comes over after he's got the guy tied up and ready for the cops. He looks at the wound, then at the other girl, and says, "Hey Honey, you okay? What's your name?"

"I'm Sophie," she whispers. "I'm fine. Stasia got hit, not me. What's wrong with her?" she snaps. I go to say something, but Bullet beats me to it.

"Settle down, Sophie. She's fine. It's just a leg wound. Hurts like a bitch but won't take her life. She's in shock right now. But look at her chest, she is breathing, see? You lookin' Soph?" Wow. Who would've thought Bullet had the touch to calm a girl down? I'm speechless, but it's working. So, when I get there to put the towel on the wound, Sophie slides down the counter. Her shock is setting in.

Hearing a commotion at the front door, I see the attendants coming in, looking at whom to go to first. I wave my hand to get their attention when they spot the idiot on the floor tied up, which makes me see red. As I'm about to say something, Bullet gets their attention.

"Oi, over here! That scum can wait. He won't die on anybody, trust me. It's a through and through. No bullet in his hand. Leave him for the police." The medical team takes a quick look at both injured parties and decides my Hit-the-Dirt is first. Like I'd let them choose different. One attendant pushes everyone away to get through. I'm standing close to Miss Hit-the-Dirt, and I'll be damned if I'm moving. We seem to have a bit of a standoff. His eyes glare, "I can't help her with you in the way, mate. Move." So, I reluctantly shuffle over to make room. No way in hell am I letting go of her. He can get fucked if he thinks that.

Meanwhile, Bullet is silently watching it all go down. Asshole! God knows what he's thinking.

Looking back at Miss Hit-the-Dirt, she's passed out, but breathing fine. The medical dude tries to get her attention. "Miss, can you hear me?" I'm hoping it's not worse from the fall this morning. Fuck. Come on, girl, open your eyes.

After what feels like hours, but who knows, she moans quietly. Relief washes over me straight away. Hoping it's not short-lived. The medical dude looks at me.

"What's her name?" I'm fucking mute at this point. Her friend jumps in and screams, "Stasia. Her name is Stasia. Is she going to be okay?" The medical dude keeps his attention on Stasia until she opens her eyes. Yes, perfect deep blue eyes. Wait, what? *Shit, Drew, get a grip.* Next thing I know, they're bringing in a stretcher for her.

I think they asked all the questions while I zoned out for a bit. Freaking the fuck out about how to absorb why I am next to this girl. Is it the girl or the shit that's just happened to her? I have no fuckin' clue. I try to stop them from putting her on the stretcher, but Bullet pulls me back. The medical dude glares at me as if I am stopping him from doing his job.

"She's going to be okay, but she is in a great deal of shock. There's no exit wound, so she needs to go to the hospital. Is there anything I need to know?"

"Yeah, she hit her head this morning, well actually she fell and hurt her leg too." The medical dude glares at me. It takes me a bit to realise he wants me to elaborate.

"Well, I sort of hit her with my bike at the traffic lights. She walked on a red. I was on a green. I didn't see her until the last minute." They pick up the stretcher and start walking to the ambulance.

"I'm going with you!" I do not want to accept a no, right now. Lucky for the ambo, he responds with the right words.

"I don't see a problem with that." When they get Stasia inside the ambulance, they direct light into her open eyes.

"She may have a concussion." As I'm about to jump in the ambulance, her friend comes out of nowhere and jumps in ahead of me.

I look up at her inside the ambulance and ask, "Who's looking after this place?" I feel like an asshole, but I need to be with her right now, and I don't care that her friend needs her too.

"Ernie. He's the cook. He's gonna close the café for me. But I'm going with Stasia. She has no family. I need to stay with her." I look at Bullet, who is already on his bike, ready to go. Feeling defeated, but not wanting to show how messed up I am by her; I take a quick look around. That's when I noticed the police have arrived and are taking care of the guy Bullet shot. Looks like he'll be waiting for a different ambulance. Fucking scum bag.

One cop walks over to me and informs us, "I need to ask you and your buddy some questions, but you can go see your girl first. We will be there when this is all squared away. Is that okay with you, Sir?"

Looking back at the scum bag I reply, "Yes, and he better not be getting let go, either." I want to say so much more but get on my bike instead. I take off fast after the ambulance, with only one thing on my mind. Stasia. Man, I hope she will be okay.

STASIA

3

STASIA

T he doors to the ambulance close, and I have no idea what just happened. My mind is still on the gun. When I saw it pointed at Sophie, all I could think about was, who was going to look after Keata?

I just jumped in front of her, and that's the last thing I remember. I turn my head at Sophie getting into the ambulance. My eyes connect with the bad boy I was not supposed to see again.

When did he get to the café? Looking back at Sophie, I ask, "Why is he here?"

She looks at me strangely, then rambles. "What the hell were you thinking, jumping in front of me? When you got shot, you passed out. I thought you were dead. Bloody hell, Stasia, why did you do that?"

I take a deep breath. So, she's freaking out. Oh God, my leg hurts. I try to focus on Sophie, but I'm seeing black dots all the time.

I take another breath and ask, "Soph, are you okay?"

The medic tells Sophie to move out of the way so he can see how much pain I'm in. I tell him I'm about a six out of ten.

Sophie looks at the guy and says, "In our language, that's a twenty. She has a high pain tolerance."

I'm trying to focus again on what's going on but suddenly more spots appear in my vision. I'm seeing them everywhere and before long my sight is gone and the darkness pulls me under.

Before I even open my eyes, I can hear beeps and whispering. Who is that? Trying to open my eyes, I moan and slur at the same time.

"Argh, too bright."

Sophie is the first one to me.

"Oh, my God, Stasia, you scared me. One minute you're talking like nothing's wrong, then you say you're a six out of ten. You say a fucking six, then nothing. I thought you died. Shit, Stasia, don't you do that again, you hear me?"

I'm trying to process what the hell she's saying when a deep husky voice comes out of nowhere.

"Hey now. Slow down Sophie, she's just woken up. Give her some time, then you can yell at her."

Oh, who is that? I like his voice, must be the doc. Trying to adjust my eyes from blurry to... *holy shit, what the hell?*

"Um, why are you here?" I ask the incredibly good-looking guy standing at my bedside. I continue to look around and I see another guy I don't know. I rub my eyes and squint as I open them again; just in case I'm seeing things. No, definitely not seeing things.

"Who are you?" I say as I'm staring at the other man in the room. Looking back to Soph, I ask, "Why are they here?"

"Honey, they saved us. You ended up getting shot, and Drew here looked after you till the ambulance got to you. You passed out twice. Once at the café and then again in the ambulance. As soon as we arrived, they rushed you in. They had to take the bullet out because it was still in your leg. They also think you might have had a concussion from earlier today. Which, I told you to get checked out."

Holding my hand up, because I can't keep up, "Soph, stop, too much." Looking at the guys, I realise I need to say something to them. Maybe then everyone will go home.

"Thank you for..." I start but decide that the fewer words, the better. "Just thank you." I close my eyes. Not because I'm still tired, well, I am, but not sleepy tired. I need to rest them.

Listening to everyone in the room while my eyes are closed is great because they think I'm asleep. I hear Sophie say, "I've got to get going, but I'll be back in the morning after I drop my daughter off." One guy talks. I'm pretty sure it's Drew. Why is he still here?

"You said she has no one, so I'll stay. Got nothing else to do until tomorrow, anyway. Bullet, tell Prez what's up, he will understand."

Then I hear the other guy say, "Alright Soph, I'll give you a lift." Sophie protests, but it falls on deaf ears.

"I'm not askin', Honey. You got no ride, and you're not taking a cab. I'll take you to get your car, then I'm following you to get your daughter, and also following you home."

She must try to say something, but he says, "Stop. That's how this is going to go. You had a freak of a day. I'll be happy and feel better if I know you got home safe. Please?"

Well, that shut her up. Next thing I know, Sophie is next to me kissing me on the forehead and whispering in my ear.

"These dudes don't take no for an answer. Sleep, Honey. I'll be here in the morning after I drop off Keata, okay? I'll give her kisses from you."

I think she hears me thank her, but I just hear the door close. Then I'm drifting off again.

Waking up, I look around and see Drew is still here. He's playing on his phone or something.

"Um, can you please pass me the water?" He gets up straight away, filling my glass and passing me the water with a straw. As I grab the glass, our hands touch, and we stare at each other for a bit. After I take a drink, he puts it back, still looking at me.

"Thank you," I say while I try to avoid looking at him. He smiles.

"How are you feeling?"

"I'm good for now. I think my head hurts a bit, but my leg hurts more."

He looks concerned, I notice he runs his eyes where I told him I'm hurting.

"Yeah, you had a rough day. How about mentally?"

"Mentally?" I say with my face all screwed up.

"You know, your feelings."

Feelings about what? Him? Surely not. Then he must see the confused look on my face.

"After everything that happened today, are you feeling jumpy? Scared?"

Oh, I was way off. So glad I didn't say anything. That would have been awkward.

"Nah. I'm fine, I think. Things don't bother me that much. I tend to just deal. Anyway, you don't need to be here. I'm fine. Soph is coming back tomorrow."

He doesn't take the hint. He sits back in his chair, puts his hands behind his head, and says, "I'm fine. Comfy too, so I'll stay." I look at him from the corner of my eye and breathe in deeply. Gathering some sort of mental strength to get my point across to him.

"Look, I don't need you to stay. If you feel guilty, don't. It's not your fault. I'm fine, promise."

Now he's staring at me like he's pissed, making me squirm. Shit. Just when I think he's going to leave, "I'm going to tell the nurse you're awake, get a coffee, and I'll be back soon. You want anything?" Okay, he's staying.

"No, but thank you," I reply, as he walks out.

Oh God, I didn't want to get to know him. I keep saying in my head, bad boy. Over and over again until a nurse comes in.

"How are you feeling, honey? Any pain?"

"I'm fine, thanks. It's not too bad at the moment." She observes me for a bit, then glances at the chart, and says, "Let's get a look at your leg. Make sure you're not still bleeding." Pulling back the covers, she unwraps my leg and cleans the wound. Before I know it, I have a new dressing.

"They got the bullet out in surgery nice and clean. The scar won't be huge. It will be a cool story to tell in a few years."

And that's when the dam breaks. Tears stream down my face, the nurse hugs me and rubs my back, and tells me it's going to be okay.

I know this, but shit, what the fuck happened today? And why did this bring back so many memories that I put to rest. It's like I can feel them starting to come forward in my mind. Its times like these I need Nanna Sally, or even Savie, they both would make the darkness go away.

Furthermore, I can't afford a day off. I'm going to be kicked out of my place. All these thoughts keep rushing around in my mind while the nurse is rubbing my back. What am I going to do?

Wiping my face, I apologise, "Sorry, I think everything just caught up with me. I'm fine now. Thanks for that."

The nurse pulls away, Drew walks back in with two cups of coffee, some chocolate, a packet of chips, and some biscuits. I'm trying to hate this guy.

Watching him take a seat, the nurse walks out and says, "Buzz if you need pain meds, honey. Otherwise, I'll be back in an hour to check on you."

I smile as a thank you, then I look at Drew. He passes me my coffee. I hope he didn't put any sugar in it.

"I only added milk. I wasn't sure, but I brought sugar with me just in case." I smile at him and take a sip.

"Thanks, it's sweet enough."

Showing the rest of the goodies, I give him a bigger smile and go to reach for some chocolate.

He smiles back and says, "So, did the nurse change your dressing?" I nod my head while putting some chocolate in my mouth.

"You're not in much pain or anything, are you? You want to talk about anything?"

Looking at him again, I shake my head.

"No, I'm fine. Thanks for the chocolate and coffee."

"You want to watch TV? I just got it put on for your room. Maybe a movie?" he says as his eyebrows lift in question. I don't want to seem rude, so I agree, even though I can feel sleep pulling me back again. Allowing him to pick the movie. We end up watching Fast and Furious, but I don't last long before I'm asleep again.

DREW

4

DREW

I t didn't take long for her to fall asleep. So, I get comfy and watch the movie.

When the movie is over, I turn off the TV and push the recliner back to see if I can get some sleep. As I'm drifting, my phone vibrates. It's Prez. He wants an update on how she is, and why I'm still at the hospital. Ha! Like I know, but I just can't leave her. Something is making me stay. Wish I knew what it was. So, I give him the only answer I can at this point.

ME: *She's good. In pain. Has a concussion, so should be out tomorrow. She has no family.*

I'm sitting like a kid, waiting for my father's approval. For what, I have no idea. I hope Prez gets it.

A text comes straight back.

PREZ: *Okay, just keep me updated.*

I exhale, thank fuck he gets it! I stretch into the recliner. It's not long before I drift off to sleep as well.

Noises wake me. The grunts and moans are obvious to me. I've completely forgotten where I am. Blinking my eyes and giving them a rub, I look around, seeing the hospital bed with Stasia in it. Everything comes back. Me hitting Stasia with my bike, then the shooting, and the hospital. Startled, I look left to the door and then right, towards Stasia.

She's thrashing and moaning, "Stop! Don't touch! Please don't!"

What the fuck? Panic washes over me. I push out of the recliner to stand straight away. It only takes me two strides to settle next to Stasia. Hating that she is stuck in a nightmare, I bend down to get eye level and call her name in hush tones, trying to wake her. She's having a pretty fucked up nightmare.

"Stasia, honey, wake up girl. Come on, now, you're safe. You're in the hospital."

Putting my hands in both of hers, I keep talking to her gently. She jolts awake. She's breathing fast and I can feel how clammy she is from the palms of her hands. What the hell has happened in her past? Why can't she be touched? Hearing the noises causes rage to rip through me. My gut's telling me it's not good. I'm struggling to control myself. I try again, keeping my voice gentle, rubbing my thumbs over the top of her hands softly.

"Hey, you okay? You're safe. You're at the hospital. Can you hear me?"

She nods her head, taking deep breaths, with a look of horror on her face. As she makes eye contact with me, she says, "You're still here. Shit, what time is it?" Not going to lie, it disappoints me that she didn't confide in me. Because I'm positive it's something different from the noises she was making. Not wanting to push for the answers yet, knowing it's going to be hard for her. I'll leave it for now. I go with what she has told me.

"You're fine now. The guy who shot you ain't getting out of jail any time soon, so try not to think about him, okay?" I watch her nod, but she is not looking at me. She is looking intensely into the blanket, like it might bite her, or vanish if she looks away. I'm not ready for her next question.

"Are you going home soon? I'll be fine."

Again, with going home? Gee, I don't even want to leave when her friend gets here. Shit. Especially after seeing her in that nightmare. I'm becoming obsessed with her. Maybe I need to go. I'll wait for her friend, then I better give us both some space. Rubbing the back of my neck, trying to ease the tension. Fuck! This shit is messing with my head.

"Nah, not till your friend comes back. Hey, you need some pain relief?" I press the button anyway. I know she needs it, whether she thinks she does.

The nurse tops her up with meds with no complaints from the patient. I watch silently as she takes her meds and talks to the nurse. All while I'm getting back in my chair, reclining back, and putting my back to her to get some more sleep. As I'm drifting off, I hear her say to no one, "Why are you here and when will you leave? I'm not ready for any of this. Why can't you see that?" It's silent for a bit and I think she is asleep, then she says one last thing.

"I'm so scared my monsters will come back and fight me to the death if you and your friends stay."

I hear a sob, like she is wiping her nose. Something inside me pulls again towards her like an invisible string that connects me to her. All this does is convince me she needs slow and steady. My head wants to run, yet my body refuses to cooperate. I'm bizarrely attached to her, like our souls are connected despite all logical reasoning.

Waking to someone shaking my shoulder, I see her friend. She must have just gotten here. I take my time to get up. Rubbing my face with my hands and then looking at Stasia. She's still asleep. I look back towards her friend Sophie, saying, "She had a nightmare this morning. Not sure what it was about, but it wasn't about yesterday. You know anything about that?"

Sophie shakes her head.

"Not really, but she has them a lot. Thanks for staying with her, but I got this from here. They're releasing her today and I'm making her move in with me, so she will be okay."

So that's it then. Squeezing my hands into fists, I tense up. Oh, hell no, I'm not leaving it here. Trying to keep my voice from sounding panicked, I breathe out and say, "Sophie, can you give me her number, please? I would like to know how she's doing, and maybe come by and check on her too, if that's alright."

Fuck, I hope she won't deny me.

Sophie shakes her head and my heart just about stops. "I can't give you her number. But your friend followed me home yesterday and knows where I live, so you can come to check on her."

Now my heart is beating so fast it doesn't know what to do. Fuck, I'll probably go into cardiac arrest. Looking up, trying to hide what's going on inside my body, I reply, "Thanks, Sophie, I'll be around later today if that's okay."

Sophie nods, "That's fine."

I turn to leave and think of something else.

"Hey, do you need me to get some stuff from her place to bring to you?" What the fuck am I saying? I need to stop.

Sophie again shakes her head.

"No, we should be fine. Thanks for the offer."

Walking out the door, I'm feeling different. Fuck if I know what it is. I've never felt like this before. It's scaring the shit out of me.

STASIA

5

STASIA

I'm sitting on the hospital bed waiting for the nurse to come in with the discharge papers. Soph is still quiet, quieter than usual.

"Sophie, are you alright? You're not saying much. It's freaking me out a bit."

"I'm fine, Stasia, just a big day yesterday. What about you?"

What about me? Shit, between getting hit by Drew, then held up at gunpoint and shot, and then Drew staying with me all night, which I'm still processing. Blowing out a big breath, I respond, "Yeah, Soph, I'm fine. I could be better, but I'm fine."

Thank God. As I finish my sentence, the nurse walks in with the discharge papers. She stopped me from lying to my friend. I sign the papers and Sophie helps gather my stuff. I feel a little weird getting put in a wheelchair because of the hospital regulations. Once I'm settled in the wheelchair, we make our way to Sophie's car. To be honest, I can't wait just to get in my bed and sleep the week away.

Getting into Sophie's car is painful. It takes a lot of moving around in awkward positions until I'm comfortable in the car for the drive home.

It's not long before we're at my place. I can see something attached to my front door from the car. My gut churns with what it could be. I mentally try to prepare myself for what happens now. As I hobble closer, I see it's a letter stuck to the door.

"Great," I mumble to myself. Sophie's the first one there, so she takes it off and reads it.

"Soph, spit it out, please. I need sleep." Knowing exactly what she is waving around, I blush and try not to make eye contact. I try to speak confidently, hoping Sophie doesn't see how embarrassed I am.

"Is that what I think it is?"

"Maybe. Well, how about you move in with Keata and me? We both love you, and it would divide the bills, and I have the extra space. What do you say?"

"What's on the paper? Am I getting kicked out?"

"Yeah, honey, you are. You have twenty-four hours to remove your stuff." Shit, I didn't think I was that far behind in rent.

"Stasia please, it will be great. Come on, lets grab some clothes. We can plan to get your stuff later today. I know someone who would love to do it." She says way too excitedly for me, but I'm too defeated to care right now.

Shrugging my shoulders, I realise I don't have a choice right now. I hate my life.

"Sophie, I can't make this permanent, but thank you. I'm drowning, and now I don't even know how long I'm going to be out of work. Shit."

Sophie smiles sympathetically at me.

"Look, let's not dwell on it. We don't need to figure anything out yet. Focus on you getting better, then we will figure the rest out, all right?"

Arriving at Soph's house, I just can't wait to get some rest. I just want some time to process all that has happened in the past couple of days and sleep.

Once we get inside, Soph walks straight into the kitchen. She puts the coffee maker on and gets out two cups.

She turns to me and says, "I need to pick Keata up by three. So let's have coffee, and talk about these not-taking-no-for-an-answer men. And do not tell me no. Neither of those guys will go away, and one thinks I'm having some kind of breakdown, which I could be. I haven't decided yet. And the other one is hot for you."

She takes a deep breath. Holy crap, she is never like this.

"Soph, no one is hot for me, and I hope you're not having a breakdown. Jesus, what a shit show yesterday was. And what do you mean they won't take no for an answer?"

Sophie puts my coffee in front of me and continues. "Well, Bullet, the one who took me back to my car from the hospital last night, followed me home to make sure I was alright. He even came with me to get Keata. Then, before you woke up, Drew wanted your number and, well…"

I do a double-take and scream in shock, "YOU GAVE HIM MY NUMBER!"

Holding up her hands like she's herding off cattle and shaking her head, she squeals, "Hell no, I'd never do that. But I told him I wanted you to stay with me, and his friend knows where I live. And if he wanted to see you, then his friend knows the address, so... hesaidhemightberoundlatertoday."

She said that last bit so fast I missed it.

"Say that last bit again."

She rolls her eyes like she is a teen or something, repeating her last sentence, "He said he might come around today."

Well, shit. She's looking at me like I might blow up Ha! I can feel the colour drain from my face. I can't deal with seeing him again. It confuses me. I don't see guys, ever. I don't have relationships either. It's too hard.

It brings up too much from my past. I can't go there. So, I do what I always do. I push it down deep and lock it up. I take a deep breath.

"Okay, well, I'd like to get some rest first, and maybe we can talk later. Sorry, Soph, I'm just overwhelmed."

Agreeing with me, she gives me a half-smile.

"Sure, Stasia. I get it. Give me your keys and I'll organise as much as I can today, okay?"

I want to say no, but I have no choice. My leg is killing me, so I pass them over and start walking to where I usually sleep when I look after Keata.

Sienna Gypsy

Seeing the look on my best friend's face, I know she knows I'm beat in more ways than one.

Curling up in bed, I try not to think of you-know-who, or anything else that's happened in the last twenty-four hours. Now I'm praying for a dreamless sleep.

DREW

6

DREW

Trying not to think about Stasia, looking around the club house, I see Mira talking to the two prospects. Once she has seen me, she bounces my way. The girl is like a baby sister to me. I'd do anything for her.

"Hey." I say.

"Hey." She smiles at me like she has a secret and blurts out, "Word has it, you got a girl?" *What the fuck?*

"Where'd you hear that?" I sense her scrutiny, probably trying to figure out how much to tell me.

"Well, you know me. I hear everything, Drew. So, is it true?" Argh! She's right, she hears everything.

Out of the corner of my eye, I see her dad and Bullet walking my way.

So I flick her ear and say, "Nah, just a new friend." Hoping that stops her from snooping. Prez cuts into our little conversation, which I'm thankful for.

"Drew, how's your girl doin'?" I do everything I can not to smirk. No wonder Mira thinks she's my girl.

Bumping fists with Prez and Bullet, "Prez, not my girl. Just a friend. She's good and going home today. She's probably there now."

Prez chuckles, "You keep telling yourself that, boy. That's good to hear, though." I turn to Bullet.

"Hey, you know where she lives, right?"

"Nah, but she's going to her friend's house till she's on her feet. Well, that's what her friend said." Prez pats my back and walks off with his daughter.

Bullet nods, "Dropped Soph off last night and met her kid. Those girls have it hard. They're on their own, from what I got out of her. I gave PC their details to see what he can find."

"Why?" Bullet looks me in the eye without missing a beat.

"Guessing they're going to be around a while. Wanna make sure nothing is hiding in their background, and no one comes looking for them. Club first brother."

"When are we leaving to check on them?"

"Not for an hour or so. That good for you?"

"Yeah, got some shit to do. I'll meet you out front in an hour."

Time went by fast. I'm pulling up at Sophie's house, not sure what to expect. I must have been dragging ass because Bullet didn't even wait for me. He's knocking on the door already. Shit. Sophie opens the door with a smile on her face.

"Hey, just the people I want to see." I am watching them converse as if I'm not even here.

"Yeah, why is that?" i watch as Sophies expression changes. Does she think we won't help?

"Well, Stasia agreed to move in here permanently, so I need your help getting the rest of her things." she says looking at the ground.

I cut in and ask. "And when does this need to happen?" She looks guilty, glancing at Bullet and then at me.

She shrugs and says, "It's no big deal. I can do it with my daughter's help. It would be an adventure for her. Don't stress."

Bullet glances at me and replies, "Hey, we didn't say we wouldn't help. We will. Just tell us when and where. We will be there, and you can let your daughter off the hook." It looks like Sophie is upset by Bullets Sttement. She shuts down and tries to close the door. Bullet's foot stops the door from closing and walks in after her. I, of course, follow, but I'm not interested in what Bullet got himself into. He can fix his own shit. I try to find Stasia's room, which doesn't take long. Opening her door, I see her laying down. She stirs a bit, so I walk over and sit on the side of her bed.

Stasia's eyes open and she sits up. Once she is comfy, she opens then shuts her mouth and shakes her head, so I cut to the chase.

"Stasia, I needed to see you. Not sure why, but I'd like to start as friends if you're okay with that?" Thought I'd lay it out and see where I stand because I can't get her out of my mind. She looks at me for a while, like she's thinking about what to say. It feels like forever, so I chew on my bottom lip for a bit, ready to say something else when she speaks first.

"I'm not sure what to say to that. I'll be honest. I can't stop thinking about you, but I don't know you, and I only spend my free time with my female friends. Please don't take that the wrong way. It's just something I can't talk about." I was curious.

"Can't or won't?"

She's fiddling with the blanket, then says, "Can't!" I grab her hand as gently as I can and start rubbing the inside of her wrist with my thumb.

"How about we get to know each other and slowly become friends, go from there? If it's too much, I'll back off, I promise." As she's about to answer me, Bullet and Soph come through the door. Bullet looks at me and nods towards the house entrance.

"Let's get this sorted." I figure he means the move. They look like they already sorted their shit out, whatever the hell that was. When I get around to it, I'm gonna make him spill.

Stasia holds my hand tighter, so I turn to look at her. She's smiling, then says so quietly, I almost miss it.

"I'm not promising anything, but I will try, okay?"

I bend forward and kiss her cheek and whisper in her ear, "Thank you." I get up and walk out.

Sienna Gypsy

As I make my way through the front door, Bullet says, "I sent a text to the prospects to meet us out there with Knight with a truck to help us. Sophie says there's not too much there, but that's all she has left in her life, so let's make sure she has it all." Fuck, I love my brothers. Getting on my bike, I nod my reply.

DREW

7

DREW

F inishing up at Stasia's house, we could see the last notices on the fridge. Knight found most of them, passing them straight to me. I put them in a folder so I can deal with them later. Once they're paid, she won't have anything to stress about. The boys take care of her front room furniture, and I do her bedroom. No way those assholes are going through her private stuff.

I come across some things I'm sure she would hate even me looking at. I smirk. Fuckin' vibrators. I packed them in a box with her panties. I'll be finding the right time to bring that up. Smirking again, I close up the last box when Bullet and Knight come in.

"All done out here, ready to roll?"

"Yep, let's go," I reply, picking up and taking the last box with me.

On our way back, I can't stop thinking about the little conversation we had and the feel of her skin. Fuck. Why did I let her put me in the friend zone? But something is telling me I need to tread with care. And if I'm honest with myself, I know I want to, because she's so much more.

When we get to Soph's house we unpack the van and head inside, there is a little girl with some sort of walking frame. I'd say she's about three or four years old. She's cute as hell. I notice she is different from other kids. She watches us with interest while we finish unloading and putting everything where Sophie tells us to put it.

I put all of Stasia's clothes and bathroom stuff in her room quietly, careful not to wake her. She can unpack when she's ready. Leaving her bedroom, I walk out to the lounge area and take a seat. The little girl comes over to examine me.

Bending down to her level, I ask "Hey what's your name, sweet girl?" She gives me a shy smile. I ask again, but she scoots away to find her mum.

Soph comes around the corner saying, "Who were you talking to?"

"Your daughter, but she's too shy to talk to me." Soph looks around and smiles at her daughter. Picking her up, she brings her back over to me.

"Keata, this is Drew. Drew, my daughter Keata." I put my hand out to shake hers, but she slaps it.

Sophie laughs and says, "Stasia taught her how to high five and knuckles. That's what she's doing."

I smile and say, "Okay Keata, let's try this again." I put my hand up, ready this time. She high-fives me with the biggest smile ever, which would make the biggest beast melt.

I look at Sophie, who says, "She is deaf, but she reads your lips. There's more, but I'll tell you another day." I have no words. Sophie walks away with Keata, and I see Bullet give her the same high five, plus knuckles. Then he looks at me and shrugs. She is something else, no fear of us, just curious. Knight comes over and sits next to me.

"Anything else, brother? I got something I need to do." He's looking at his phone, so I reckon he has pussy on-call, lucky fucker.

"Nah, all good brother, just check that Prez doesn't need your ass before you go M.I.A., we clear?"

"Eye, eye captain, catch you later, boys." The prospects follow Knight out the door, giving a wave to us as they leave.

After about an hour, I go back in and check on Stasia. As I'm walking into her room, she's standing up from the bed in her white PJ's with pink love hearts on them. She looks cute in them.

Instead of asking, I go straight to her and help, "Toilet or lounge?"

She smiles and says, "Both, but toilet first. I'm fine though, I'll meet you in the lounge."

Yeah, not commenting. I follow her. As soon as she finishes in the toilet, I get her settled in the lounge on the double couch. Once she's comfy, Sophie walks in with some food.

Stasia tenses and takes the food.

"Soph, I'm capable of getting my own. Please let me."

Just being around Stasia these past days, I see she hates relying on people, period. Trust must be hard for her.

Before I know it, Keata scoots into the room in her walking frame. She goes straight for Stasia and the smile she gets is huge. This little girl means something to her, and vice versa. I watch them interact, and it's different than she would talk to other children. Stasia makes sure there's eye contact with every word, and Keata seems to understand.

Bullet's phone rings. I didn't even notice he was in the room. Getting up, Bullet nods, and I know that's our cue to leave.

I turn around, lean forward, kiss Stasia on the cheek and whisper in her ear, "I'll visit tomorrow. Will you be up for that?" She blushes and nods her head.

I run the back of my fingers down her cheek and say, "I'll be here in the late afternoon, okay?"

"Sure, I'll see you then." She smiles shyly as I follow Bullet out of the door.

Sienna Gypsy

STASIA

8

STASIA

Listening to their bikes leave sends a chill down my spine. Sophie comes in, sits next to me, and looks with a smile on her face. I wait a minute to see if she's going to say something, but she doesn't.

"What?" I ask. Soph continues to smile. "What is it?"

"Well, I was going to say spill it, but I don't think you even know what's going on, yourself. So I'm going to wait, and then, when you're ready, you're going to spill, you hear me?"

Mortified, my cheeks burn, but I agree because I don't know, myself.

Torture to Bliss

The next day, Soph went to work, and I offered to look after Keata because she's never any trouble. She's fallen asleep on my lap halfway through her movie. I move her, with great difficulty, so I can start dinner. Looking in the fridge, I decide on curry.

She has chicken ready to use and has all the ingredients.

Getting lost in my thoughts, thinking about you-know-who. God, I can't believe he kissed me, and I didn't freak. Well, I freaked, but in a good way. Not like I always do. God, his lips on my cheek sent a jolt to Never-Neverland. Oh my God, what am I going to do? What if he thinks I'm a freak because I can't go there, or maybe I can? Shit. What am I going to do?

Dinner is ready, and I conclude I'm going to let things work themselves out. If it's just friends, I will be fine with that.

I walk into the lounge to check on Keata. She is so cute, asleep on the couch when there's a knock at the door. My leg still hurts, but nothing like when it first happened. I limp over, forgetting to look through the window and check who it is. I open the door and stare. Why is he back. He said in a few days. And look at him, sexiest, dark tattooed, beast of a man that is standing there in jeans, biker boots and a light blue t-shirt that's tight enough to see his muscles. He's ripped. Oh God, he makes something inside me just..
.

"Um, are you going to ask me in, Stasia, or would you like me to strip? Up to you." He winks at me, and I'm so hot, I'm burning. I go to fan my face and realise, shit, he'd love that. I turn, not even asking him in, hoping he will follow, which he does. As I reach the kitchen, I turn around and he invades my space, slowly coming closer. I think he's going to kiss me on the cheek again when he's lips are near my ear. Goosebumps tingle all over my body.

"I couldn't get that kiss out of my head last night. I'm going to kiss you on the lips again. If you don't want that, tell me now."

Pulling back, his gaze is locked on my eyes, waiting for me to say something. I can tell he's trying hard to read me. Shit, I'm trying to read me. But he must sense I'm okay with it because he comes in slowly and I close my eyes, waiting. It feels like forever before he makes contact. Oh God, soft, warm and delicious. He licks my bottom lip and I open my mouth to let him in. Keata cries. Shit. Pulling away, I hobble to her side.

"It's okay, honey. I'm here." I grab her softly and make sure she's looking at me, so she understands. She stops crying and hugs me tight. God, I love this girl. I limp back into the kitchen where I left Drew, and he's smiling big at me.

"Sorry, she was asleep on the couch."

He shakes his head and says, "Nothing to be sorry about." I don't know what to do now.

"Sophie will be home soon. Do you want to stay for dinner? There's plenty."

"Sure, what'd you make?"

"Curry chicken." Walking to the cupboards, I pull out the plates to set the table. I do everything to not look at him. Shit, why did I ask him to stay for dinner? He startles me by grabbing the plates from me.

"Just tell me where everything is. You have your hands full." Not long after he sets the table, and Keata is settled with her food, Soph walks in.

"Damn girl, you made curry chicken. Yum! I knew you would make my favourite." As she steps into the kitchen, she stops dead in her tracks and looks at all of us. I hurry to explain.

"Sorry, Drew just arrived. I made heaps, thought he could stay. You don't mind, do you?" Oh God, what if she didn't want him around Keata?

"Stasia, it's fine. You don't have to ask. You live here now. It's all good, just shocked me, that's all. Hey Drew, how have you been? I'm starved. Let's dig in." Drew nods in a hi, then we eat.

After dinner, Sophie takes off to bathe Keata and gets her ready for bed. She is gonna kill me because she already slept and probably won't go to sleep again easily. Drew helps me pack up and do dishes. We chat about anything and everything. He's so easy to talk to, nothing like the beast of a man I thought he was. He's a teddy bear. A giant one. Like Cobra was to me, and Krip. The memory comes out of nowhere. It pulls at my heart how much I miss them.

When everything is done, I put the dishtowel in the wash and turn around to see Drew coming in close again.

"I can't resist touching you. Just say stop if it's too much." With that, he's kissing me again. His hands come to my hips and slide onto my back. My tongue is already in his mouth. My mind is numb, but I can feel his hands moving, with light touches on my back. Up to my bra line and back again. While I'm getting lost in the moment, he pulls away.

"I've wanted to do that for a while now. I hope it's okay."

"Oh God, yes!" Shit, did I say that out loud? Oh God, how embarrassing. I pull away, he reaches for my chin with his pointer finger and thumb and makes me look at him.

"Don't be embarrassed around me, girl. I've got you." He takes my hand and starts walking to the door. Once we get there, he says, "Thank you for tonight. I've got to go, but I'll see you again soon, okay?" In a daze, I have no idea what he's saying as he leans in and kisses me again. Slow and soft. Before I know what's happening, he's gone. My door is closed, and I'm sliding down the door with my head all over the place.

For the first time in forever, I have pleasant dreams. Dreams about my biker man.

DREW

9

DREW

W ell, I'm fucking starving, and it ain't for food. I wonder if I can get PC, our computer tech guy, to get her number before we head out in fifteen minutes? I'm not even worried about what he or anybody thinks. Heading down to PC's room, I groan inwardly. I can't believe I'm going on this two day run with Knight. Fuck, I love my brother, but he just fucks himself into trouble. Knocking on PC's door, he opens it pretty quickly. I give him the piece of paper that has all I know about Stasia on it and hope it's enough. PC snatches it from my fingers. "I'll send it to you when I'm done." He slams the door and I stride purposefully out to my bike.

We're on our way down to Albany, which is a two-and-a-half-hour ride south. All I can think about is Stasia, wondering what she's doing. She'll be back at work tomorrow on light duties, which pisses me off, but I can't say shit. She's not mine, yet. I'm on my way to making it happen. It's just going to take time. I know something is there, in the dark of her mind. That nightmare in the hospital, that was my first clue. Then, the way she tries to stay invisible, so no one notices her, but she puts others before herself. It's like she doesn't feel worthy. Something tells me once I gain her trust, she'll be mine for good, which is the plan. I don't know when my brain decided to take claim, but I'm not fighting it. I've mucked around and had plenty of chicks, enough to know a good thing when it's there. Good thing PC got her number for me. I'm going to text her as soon as we pull over at the service station up the road.

There are five of us on this run. Me, Knight, Nova, and Cory are on our bikes, and Tommy is driving the van for the swap. We have drugs to swap for guns. It's the last of our illegal deals, this is supposed to be the last run, but something is making me nervous about it. I'm in charge since I'm in training for Dad's old position as VP. Which has been the story ever since I was patched in after being a prospect, which will be soon. This means I'm trusted with the hard shit and can make decisions.

Looking up ahead, I see the servo coming into sight. I give the hand signal to make sure they're all aware we're stopping. Once we are all parked and fuelling up, I look around. I take that moment to walk out of view so I can shoot off a text.

ME: *Hey beautiful it's Drew, just checking in. I'm out of town for a couple of days. Save this number and text me whenever.*

After it's sent, I go to use the restroom. The guys are hungry, so we grab some pies and sit out at the picnic table. We run through what's going to happen. Feeling my phone vibrate, I grab my rubbish and walk to the bin. Pulling out my phone, I see it's from my girl.

STASIA: *Hey, I'm good. And how'd you get my number? I know Soph wouldn't do that?*

ME: *I have my ways of getting what I want. A little birdie told me you're working tomorrow.*

STASIA: *Is this the same little birdie that gave you my number? And yes, light duties. Can't wait!*

ME: *Maybe. Well, take it easy, please.*

STASIA: *Oh, does the big bad biker worry about me?*

Oh, I see my girl has sass when we're not face to face.

ME: *Maybe.*

Let's see if she will open up a little.

STASIA: *Maybe? That's not an answer!*

ME: *Well, what sort of answer do you want?*

STASIA: *Mmm, I'm not sure.*

ME: *Girl, you can tell me anything. I want you to tell me everything.*

Here's hoping she will tell me everything.

STASIA: *Well, that's huge, Mr Biker. We just met! Lol. Let's just start with the basics, I'm glad u care. Xoxo.*

Nova calls out to say he can't find Knight. Shit. Bet that fucker found a piece of ass.

"Tell Tommy to check both toilets, male and female, probably got some chick somewhere." Looking back down at my phone, I text her back.

ME: *Babe, I gotta go. Be careful. Text you later.*

I put my phone away and start walking to my bike. As I get close, I see Knight almost tripping over his jeans, trying to drag them up his legs and running at the same time. Looking around, I see Tommy coming from inside, but Knight was around back.

Shaking my head, I get on my bike, then look at Knight and say, "Everything alright man?" His face is red as hell. He avoids my gaze.

Looking back to where he came from, I see this tall chick walk out slowly, with a smile on her face. Knight starts his bike and takes off.

The chick yells, "You could have sucked me off too, ya bastard!" The problem with that is the chick has a deep voice. I look at Nova and he cracks up. Knight just got sucked off by a dude. Fuck, that's gold. Laughing hard, we start our bikes and take off with Tommy in the van. I bet he's already sent a text to someone back home. Poor bastard, but he won't learn.

We arrive at the destination where we are doing the swap. I notice Frazer isn't here yet. He's never on time. The fuckin' ball bag never is. He's a slimy piece of shit that I hate working with. I can't wait till this business is done. Looking over at Knight, I see he's not making eye contact with anyone.

I walk over, but before I have time to rib him, he glares at me and says, "NOT. A. FUCKIN'. WORD!"

I smirk, shake my head, and then say, "How could you not tell, brother?" But I get the same reply.

"I'M WARNING YOU. NADA. YOU HEAR ME?" Nova chuckles, ready to say something, when a couple of vans come in and we all change our mindset. It's all business now.

I yell, "Look alive, and keep ya eyes open, boys."

Frazer gets out of his van and walks up to me. Nova is looking around, being my eyes, to see who else is here, then his eyes settle on me to give the okay.

Frazer asks, "Why did so many guys come? You don't trust me now? I thought we were the best of friends, Drew?"

Fuck no! I don't trust the ball bag, but I can't show him my disdain, so I smile and say, "Nah Frazer, it's only two more. We're showing them the ropes. You got everything we need?" he crosses his arms in front of his chest looking defensive.

"Why wouldn't I? Have I failed you yet?"

Inwardly, I roll my eyes and decide to get to it. Opening up the van, I show him the merchandise. He always checks it. The way he licks it off the knife makes me feel sick. This guy is not stable. He walks over to his two vans and opens one of them. It only looks like half of our stuff is there. I chin lift Cory. He knows he needs to do a proper inventory, so he gets to it.

I hate small talk, so I say nothing till Cory says, "Drew, you better check the second van." I'm not sure what he wants from me, but I know that look. As I come around to the open door, I see the girl bruised, battered and bloody. Shit, the fucker did this! I try to keep my cool.

Turning to Frazer, I say, "What the fuck is this? Did you bring some bitch to our swap? What the fuck are you thinking?"

Frazer's beady smile makes me want to punch him. It takes all my control while I wait for him to speak.

"Just a bit of fun. Can't wait to take her again. You want a sample? Bitch was a virgin, but not anymore." This girl looks no older than fifteen or sixteen. I could be wrong, but I'm pretty sure. I know I can't leave her with him; I gotta try to get her out. Seeing he's off his face, I'm hoping it's going to be easy.

I look at Nova, he lifts his chin at me, so I know he gets it, and I push on, "Well, if I get a sample, so do all my boys. How about we get her for free? This would make us even with all the fuck ups I've covered for you, Frazer."

Which I haven't. Prez knows every one of his fuck ups. Being in an MC, you don't keep things from your Prez, but he doesn't know that because he's a fool.

Frazer only looks nervous for a second. If I looked the other way, I wouldn't have seen it, but I did. I've got his attention.

"Fuck no, I'm not doing that. You all can use her, but she stays."

He's lookin' side to side to see if we're going to push it, which we do.

Nova takes that as his cue, "The way I see it, she doesn't get to live, so we get our fun, then we kill her, and no one knows. You were stupid enough to bring a bitch here. But if you don't agree, Frazer, she dies now, and we get to tell Prez you fucked this deal up!" Frazer is pissed. He walks past us, grabs the girl by her hair and drags her to our van, throws her in, then snarls at us.

"Have fun, you fuckers. I'll just get me another one."

Fuck, that pisses me off more! I hope he doesn't. We got the girl, so now all we have to do is get her to safety.

Once everything is packed and done, we get on our bikes, Cory swaps with Tommy and starts the van. He leads the way and we follow. As we hit the highway, Nova and I pull at our throttles, speed past the van, and lead the way. Knowing there are no problems with Tommy and Knight bringing up the rear.

We'll need to stop in the next town to check this girl out and make sure she's okay. Fuck, Prez is gonna be pissed.

Nothing worse than guys like him. Motherfucker!

DREW

10

DREW

We stop in Forest Hill, which ended up being two towns over. Being a small country town it's less likely anyone would see us or the girl. Once we are all parked, we get off our bikes and walk towards the van. Cory gets out, shaking his head. He opens the door, but I can't see her. Cory gets in the van and picks her up. She is shaking like a leaf.

He's murmuring, "It will be ok," to her. He looks at us, defeated. "She thinks we're going to use her, too. I've told her the deal, but she doesn't believe me."

I shrug, knowing it's for good reason she doesn't trust us. I shake the thought out of my head, trying not to think about what she has been through. Poor girl.

Stepping next to Cory, near the front passenger door, I keep my voice down.

"Hey, honey, we're not going to hurt you, but we need to take you back to our clubhouse with us, which is another hour drive north. Then we can get you help."

She's shaking so badly that I yell out to Knight, "Get a blanket from the back!" I notice the girl slowly nod her head. Good, I grab the blanket from Knight and wrap her up tight. Cory puts her in the van and asks her if she's hungry or thirsty, which she declines. But he tells Tommy to get her some stuff and to pick up some pain relief as well. Without a word, Tommy takes off. I walk off and send a heads-up to Prez, informing him about everything. I'm shocked at how fast he sends one back.

PREZ: *Don't do the drop tonight. Bring the girl back here asap.*

I knew he'd say that. I text back:

ME: *Only one hour out, see you soon.*

Seeing this girl makes me want to send a quick text to Stasia, needing the peace in my mind to know she is ok.

ME: *Hey beautiful you good?*

I see Tommy come out with everything Cory asked for. He passes it all to Cory and then heads to his bike. Cory jumps out of the driver's seat and goes to the back of the van to give her some meds. He's in there for a while before he is getting out and heading back to the driver's seat.

"Cory, did she take the meds?" I ask. He nods, starting up the van. I feel my phone vibrate, so I check it as I walk over to my bike.

MY GIRL: *Hey, I'm good. Quiet day. Just getting ready for bed. What about you?*

ME: *Fuck, I'd love to wrap you up in bed, girl!*

MY GIRL: *I bet you would. Sorry, no invite. Lol!*

ME: *Oh, you hurt my feelings babe Lol! Sweet dreams! xx.*

Too much shit going on right now, and probably too soon for Stasia. I wanted to take that further. I keep reminding myself, slow and steady. Feeling my phone vibrate, I get another text.

MY GIRL: *Be safe.*

Smiling, I throw my leg over my bike, and I see everyone is waiting for me. Nova gives me a chin lift as I start my bike up and we hit the road.

The drive seemed long, and I know all the guys are as anxious as me. As we pull in, I notice Doc's bike is here. Prez must have called him in. Thank fuck for that. I'm sure this is going to be bad. We all park and head over to the van as Cory gets her out without too much fuss. She is wrapped around him with her eyes shut tight. We head inside with Cory in the middle and all of us guarding her like a fortress as we walk. Once we get inside, we pass some club members. There are also men and foolish women who are always here to keep the guys happy. We walk down the hall to the infirmary. The fortress we held while walking separates as Cory puts her on the bed. As he lets go, she reaches out and grabs ahold of Cory like her life depends on it.

"P-please don't leave me!" She whispers, but it was meant for Cory. Prez nods at Cory, chin lifts to me, and walks out. Cory stays with the girl and I follow Prez out to his office.

As I enter, he says, "Take a seat."

He walks over to the window, stands for a bit before he growls, "What the fuck happened?"

"He was late, as usual. When we checked out the second van, that girl was in there, and I couldn't leave her. I reckon she is fifteen, sixteen at the most. Fucker raped her and was telling us he took her virginity. She has been beaten good too. You would have to ask Cory if she said anything. She's been in the van with him. She must trust him a bit, seeing as she wants him around."

Shaking his head, he responds, "So, how'd you get her out? Something tells me he didn't want to let her go."

"Yeah, you'd be right." I tell Prez what happened.

Putting his hand through his hair and pulling at the ends, he sighs, "Thank fuck he bought it. But what now?" Fuck, I've been thinking about that all the way home.

"Yeah, Prez, I'm not sure."

"Okay, let me think about it. Church, first thing in the morning. Spread the word." He dismisses me. Walking over to Nova at the bar with some bimbo trying her luck. I take a seat and tell her to beat it. When she's gone, Nova takes a sip of his whiskey.

"Good call today, brother."

"Yeah, thanks, but I was backing you up. I saw that girl and I was ready to gut that fucker." I knew this would hit Nova hard. He lost his younger sister to a similar thing. She went to Paris on holiday, but we couldn't find her. Shit, we're still looking. Finishing my beer, knowing there's nothing more to say, I clear my throat.

"Right. Well, I'm out brother, you know where I'm at if you need me." I slap his back, then head to my room. Then I realise I need to tell the boys what Prez said. So I turn around, put two fingers to my mouth and whistle loud and yell.

"Church in the morning, first thing! Don't be late, and spread the word!" I'm over today.

Once in my room, I hit the shower to rinse off the day. Stepping in, the hot water feels so good. Grabbing the soap, I wash my hair, rubbing my hand through it. While the water washes the soap from my hair, my mind wonders about the sexy little Miss Hit-the-Dirt. I wonder what she's sleeping in. I grab the soap again, washing my body all over when I come to my hard-on. Fuck, I'm hard as a rock for her. Using my palm firmly, I rub up to the tip, using my thumb to spread my pre-cum over the head.

"Fuuuccckkkk!" I let my mind wander to Stasia's lips, as I bring my hand up and down. I'm thinking about her hips and her luscious ass. Fuck! Her ass is… I let out a moan as the relief of my orgasm washes over me. Fuck, that was quick. Leaning against the wall, allowing the hit of the orgasm to relax my mind and soul. I can't believe how hard and fast I came.

Turning off the shower, I dry off, then jump into bed. I want to text her, but I know she's asleep. Closing my eyes, I put one hand under my head. As I fall asleep, I think to myself, I'll text her tomorrow.

DREW

11

DREW

I wake up early to go to church. I look at my phone and see I still have an hour. So I decide to look through the messages we sent to each other yesterday. Ha, when did I become such a love-struck idiot? It's fuckin' hilarious how I can't wait to hear from her now.

ME: *Mornin' Beautiful. What time do you leave for work?*

Getting out of bed, I get dressed so I can get a coffee and maybe something to eat. I know it's gonna be a long day, and I'm hoping I might get time to see Stasia at some point.

Heading into the kitchen, I see Knight and Nova sitting and chatting. I get my coffee and toast, then go sit with them, hearing the last bit of the conversation. I smirk.

"So that was a dude, hey?" Knight rubs his face hard. Nova tries to stifle a chuckle. While I'm still smirking.

"Fuck, that was fucked up, man. I swear I didn't know, but as soon as I shot down her.... *his* throat, they stood up, pulled down their pants and whipped it out. I fuckin' ran, brother. Dry heaving all the way to the swap."

Trying not to laugh too much, I slap his back, "What the fuck were you thinking? Wait, don't answer that! How about you figure out who they are before you let them blow you? Fuck man, you're lucky you haven't picked up a disease yet."

"Yeah, I know. No more pussy for me, man. I'm taking a break. Just finished telling Nova, here. Fuck, I need to recover from that shit."

"Yeah, brother, I bet you do." Leaving Knight's deviant lifestyle alone. I ask about the girl we've all been wondering about.

"Does anyone here know how that girl is?" Nova shakes his head.

"Poor girl has gone through it all. If I see that son of a bitch, I'm killing him. No questions." I knew this would be hard for him.

"How much sleep did you get last night, brother?" The look on his face says it all.

"Haven't yet, been sitting in her room with Cory. She won't let him go, so he hasn't left her. But she came out with most of the information around 2 a.m, after a nightmare. Strong girl. I've also told her she ain't leaving here. She has my protection."

I look at Knight, then back at Nova. Fuck.

"Nova, she ain't your sister, and she's safe now. There's nothing you can do for her. If she wants to leave, you can't stop her." He looks at the cup he's drinking.

I slap his back to get his attention, "After church, you need sleep. Voice your thoughts, because I know Prez has no idea about this. Sleep on it, and talk to Cory and the girl. Then we can decide. You okay with that?"

He nods his head. I see Prez already walking into church. He gives me a chin lift, so I follow him in.

After closing the door behind me, he says, "How's the girl, any news? Does she want to go anywhere?" He leans back in his office chair, crossing his arms, waiting for my reply.

"Not too sure, Prez. Mostly, they found out about the abuse. The shit that happened to her, and she was a virgin. She's in a lot of pain right now. She's talking to Cory and Nova, but the boys didn't leave her side last night."

Prez juts his chin, asking, "What's the story there?"

Shrugging my shoulders, "Nova wants to protect her. I'm thinking it's because of his sister. He's already told me she's under his protection. As for Cory, don't know, he is still in the room with her."

"Alright, get Nova and Cory. I'll find out what's going on before we take it any further. You and the boys are riding out for the drop by lunchtime, so don't make plans." Walking to the door, I hear him call me back.

"Drew, you did good. Now go get those two and get back in here." Nodding, I head out of the office and back toward where Nova is.

"Nova. Go get Cory. Prez wants to meet with you two. First, he needs all the intel about the girl, then we're all going in." Nova says nothing. He gets up and goes towards the room where Cory and the girl are. I watch as he enters the room, calls Cory, and then heads in the direction of the office.

We both walk into Prez's office. I take a seat in front of Prez's desk, waiting for Cory to arrive. My phone vibrates. Pulling it out, I see she's awake now.

MY GIRL: *Hey, just woke up. You're an early bird. I need my beauty sleep.*

Shaking with silent laughter, I type back:

ME: *Babe, you will love waking up next to me. The morning will be your favourite time! Lol!*

She takes a bit to respond. I watch the three blue dots appear and disappear, then appear again. I didn't even notice I'm smiling at my phone like an idiot. The next text arrives:

MY GIRL: *Too early for this. I need coffee. Talk later.*

I burst out a chuckle and put my phone away. As I do, I look up to see everyone looking at me. When the fuck did they all get in here? Shit. Prez shakes his head.

"You still talking to…?" he clicks his fingers together like it will jog his memory."What's her name? Uh, Stasia?" I stand firm with my decision, no matter what bullshit it brings.

"Yeah, will be for some time, Prez. You good with that?" The winning smile on his face makes me uncomfortable.

"Just keeping up with what's going on. Bring her around for lunch one day. You know Mira would like to meet her." Then he looks at the other two. "Fill me in." Cory goes first.

"Well, she says she has no family, but a cousin up north that she doesn't know. Don't want to explain what happened, just know that it wasn't good. He had her for what she thinks was two weeks, I'm thinking more. The timeline doesn't make sense." He looks at Nova, then back at Prez.

"But Nova and I want her under our protection. We've talked. He's gonna move her into his place, and I'm going to make sure she gets what she needs. Therapy, docs, whatever it takes."

"You taking claim to her?" Prez asks. Cory shakes his head and looks mad as hell.

"No!" He snaps, "Bell is sixteen, so hell no. Nova seems to want the parent side. I'll be the big brother of sorts."

Nova then interrupts, "Izzy's been through enough. So, she's going to be my daughter, if anyone asks. Thought about it all night, and I'm not changing my mind, Prez."

Shaking his head, Prez asks, "Which is it then, Izzy or Bell?"

Nova and Cory answer in unison, "Izzy." "Bell."

Prez holds up his hands, saying, "Okay, okay, well, I'm not going into the next meeting with the brothers with that." Shaking his head, he stands up and stops their questions. "I will tell the club that while she's here, she has our protection. Give you boys some time to make sure you're prepared for what you want. Nova, it's not a light decision to make. Think hard about it. Then we will make it legal as soon as you're sure." He turns to me.

"Call everyone else in and tell Mira to go sit with Izzy, or Bell, or whatever. Figure it out, but she can stay with her till we finish up. Prospects are in this meeting because they were there."

I call out to Mira, but she already knows. She waves at me and says, "On it, Drew!" And all I can think is Mira is the best little sister I could hope for.

We head into church with all the boys and the prospects, and go through what we need to cover. When it's finished, Prez brings the hammer down. Church is finished. Me, Knight and Tommy head out to do the drop-off, and then it's time to see my girl.

STASIA

12

STASIA

Waking up to a text from Drew put a huge smile on my face. Who would have thought a big bad biker would be so sweet? Getting up to take a shower, I notice how awesome the hot water is. It's funny how people take things for granted when they have them. Smiling while I get dressed, I think back to when Nana Sally was helping me to get back to my normal. Without her and Savie, or even Cobra and Krip, I don't think any of this would be possible. Every time I look at Drew, it reminds me of how protective Krip and Cobra were of me. I wish I knew where they were now.

I walk out to the kitchen. Keata is still asleep, but Sophie's up and getting her breakfast ready so she can wake her up.

Smiling at me, she says, "Coffee machine is on."

Walking over, I make myself a coffee, then turn back around and ask, "What's going on today?"

"Keata has school. We go to work, then home." She says, smiling at me.

"I'm not too sore from yesterday's shift, I hate sitting around." Soph nods, knowing I hate doing nothing.

"Stasia, do you want to ride together, or are you driving your car?" she asks as she is finishing with Keata's breakfast.

"I'll come with you. Seems silly to take two cars. Most of our shifts are the same, anyway."

"Okay, well, we're leaving in twenty. Gotta drop Keata off first."

We both take off to get ready. Taking turns with Keata so she is ready on time. It's crazy how efficient we are, like we've done this a million times before.

Getting in the car, I sit in the back with Keata. She's still tired. Keata has been deaf all her life, so I like to entertain her while Sophie drives. I know Keata doesn't care either way, but I've always made sure I sit with her if Sophie drives.

Halfway to school, she giggles as she watches me dance to the music and pull faces. Hearing her laugh is my favourite sound in the world. I pull out my phone and record both of us, so I can watch it later. Before I know it, we're at her school. Sophie takes her into class while I stay in the car and playback the video. Without thinking, I send our video to Drew. I hope it puts a smile on his face as well.

I spot Sophie walking back towards the car from Keata's class, I tuck my phone into my pocket at the same time as it vibrates. Bringing it back out, I see it's Drew.

BIKER BOY: *She looks happy today. Where are you two off to?*

Sophie gets in the car and looks at me, asking, "Who has you smiling so big?"

I look down to flick a text back to Drew and reply to Soph at the same time, "It's Drew." I say as I'm pressing send and look back up at her.

"So, you gave him your number, hey?" she asks, shaking her head with a huge smile on her face.

"Nah, he got it somehow. But he won't tell me how. He's been texting me since yesterday. It's nice." I can feel my cheeks burning while she's smiling at me.

"This is your first, hey? The first boy ever to be interested in you, or maybe the first boy you have ever looked at?" Man, she doesn't realise how close she is. I can't be around men at all, but for some reason, he makes me feel safe, like I can be myself around him.

Pulling up at work, I see another text from Drew.

BIKER BOY: *What time do you finish today, babe?*

I read it as I leave the car and send back the time I'm finishing up.

ME: *Three.*

BIKER BOY: *Don't work too hard.*

The smile on my face is enormous as I walk into work. My boss comes over with a gigantic bunch of flowers. I take them and inhale deeply, savouring the scent. When I glance at her she asks, "Are you sure you're going to be okay? You can take some time off. Whatever you need." I smile sincerely at her generosity. I really do have an amazing boss.

"I'm good Joan, honest. I'm sick of sitting around. When it hurts, I'll sit. I promise." Joan has always looked after us, ever since I got the job. All the staff are great and helpful, no bitchy days at work, just fun all the time. She knows Sophie has a daughter with disabilities, so if Keata is sick, she can take the time she needs, and Joan will fill the shift herself. She nods at me and then turns to head to the office.

"I'm hanging around for the next couple of days anyway, so if you need to go, it's fine, Stasia. Don't even hesitate to ask, okay?"

"Thank you, Joan, but I know I'll be fine." Heading to the back, I put my stuff in my locker and come back out front to the counter. If I take most of the orders, I don't have to walk around much.

By the time lunch is over, I'm feeling sore. Sophie monitors the café so I can go into the kitchen and take my pain relief. After swallowing the pills, Joan comes out of her office.

"Stasia, take a break for fifteen minutes. I'll tell the cook to make you something." Normally, I would decline, but I'm buggered and starved. I'll tell her to take it out of my pay check.

Sitting in the booth in the back corner, I decide to call all the people I owe money to and disconnect all amenities. But when I get off the phone with the last one, I'm stumped. They are all paid up. I know they made a mistake, so I've asked them to investigate and get back to me. I'm deep in thought, wondering what the hell happened to my bills, while I'm playing with the last part of my Shepherd's Pie. The bell above the door causes me to look in that direction. I freeze and my heart stops for a second. Drew and his friend walk in. I can't remember his friend's name. He spots me and comes straight towards me. I can feel my heart beating out of my chest as he approaches and leans in to kiss my cheek. He then sits next to me. Man, he needs to stop doing that. My face is burning up now. I absentmindedly watch his friend sit down on the other side of the booth.

Trying to play it cool, I dip my head, play with my food and say, "Hey." Oh, my God, is that all I got? I can't think when he's this close to me. His friend lifts his chin at me.

Drew looks at my food, asking, "You finished, or are you gonna eat some more?"

I shrug my shoulders, not really sure what I want to do with my food right now and take a minute to decide. "Nah, I'm finished. You want to finish it? It's still hot." I ask without even thinking about what I'm saying. As he says no, his friend grabs my plate, puts it in front of him, and starts eating. Drew turns his body more towards me so he's looking at me. I turn to him as well.

"What's going on after work?" he asks.

"Nothing. Just picking Keata up and going home. Why?" My eyes are hypnotised by his lips and the way they move as he talks, then that lopsided grin.

So hot…

Oh shit, did he say something? I shake my head.

"Pardon?" He has a full-on smile now. Yeah, he knows I was daydreaming. Oh God, kill me now.

"I said, would you like to spend some time with me? Then I'll drop you home." I shake my head, trying to wake my brain up from my Drew fog.

"I'd love to, but I came with Soph and we need to pick up Keata from school." As I finish talking, Soph cuts in.

"Hey guys." She waves at both the men.

"Stasia, you go ahead. I'll meet you at home. I'll be fine."

Smiling at Soph, then looking at Drew, I respond, "I'm too sore to go on your bike, Biker Boy."

He smiles big and leans in, saying into my ear, "Well, lucky for you, I brought the car." Shock is all over my face at this new turn of events.

"You drive a car?" Oh, my God, of course he drives a car. Argh!

He is still leaning in my ear as he answers, "Yes, Beautiful. I drive a car. So, what time do you finish?"

Sophie butts in and says, "Glad you asked. The boss told me to tell you goodbye. She's worried you overdid it today."

I blow the hair in my face away as I answer, "I didn't. It was easy taking orders. You even gave me a stool. So how did I overdo it, Soph?" She smiles, waving goodbye.

Sliding out of the booth, Drew tells me to go get my stuff. But I only get halfway there when Sophie runs to meet me with my bag and purse.

She whispers in my ear, "Have fun, honey," with a big smile on her face. Turning, I walk towards Drew. As we exit the café he turns to Bullet, "See you at the club house later." Drew points me toward a nice black car. It's a Holden V8.

"Oh, I love this car!" he even opens my door, which shocks the shit out of me.

"Thank you," he nods, then walks around to his side. I put my seat belt on and wait for him to say something, but he doesn't. He starts the car and pulls out.

"Are you going to tell me where we are going?"

Using that sexy smile that makes butterflies erupt in my stomach, he says, "It's a surprise! I'm hoping you'll like it."

Feeling excitement run through my body, I push for more information. "Give me a clue," I say, trying my hardest not to put that lovesick smile on my face. He probably thinks I'm an idiot.

"We will be there soon. So, sit and relax, Beautiful. Won't be long now." I put my head back on the headrest and close my eyes to try to keep my excitement at bay. The quiet between us is nice. Not an awkward silence, just peace and quiet. Pulling onto a dirt road, we drive slowly. It's like a big windy hill.

Once we're at the top, I see it's a lookout point. There's a picnic table and a manmade swing. Turning off his car, he opens his door and gets out. He runs around, opens my door and helps me out.

"This is my favourite place to come. I thought with everything that's happened lately, this would help." Wow! Looking around the view is amazing. Looking down at the green paddocks, I can see the town in the distance. Horses running free to one side and lilies growing wild in singular spots all over the place. Just beautiful! I turn to him.

"Thank you. It's beautiful here. I just don't know what to say."

"Take a seat." He helps me to the table, then runs back to the car and grabs some stuff out. When he comes back, I shake my head.

"If I didn't know any better, I'd say you're trying to wine and dine me." Putting the bag on the table, he gives me the blanket. He's still smiling.

"Maybe I am. It gets cold up here fast, so we might need to share this." I'm sure this was his plan but I'm not complaining.

"So, what's in the bag?" He undoes the bag and pulls out a chocolate cake and a coffee thermos.

"Chocolate cake and coffee. I thought we could share."

"Oh, this is a date, is it?"

"Not if you don't want it to be."

"Mmm, maybe I would like to try, but..."

"But what, Stasia? Because I'd like that too." Biting my bottom lip, I try to come up with an answer. But how do you tell a bad boy that he's your first kiss? That I may never do more than that.

"It's complicated. I don't know where to start and some parts I just can't talk about." He grabs my hand gently, closing his fingers around mine. He then rubs his thumb on my palm.

"I'm willing to figure it out with you, Stasia. Why don't you start with what you can talk about, then? We can get to the hard stuff later." Nodding, I use my free hand to put a piece of chocolate cake in my mouth. Running through my thoughts, I wonder how to start. Okay, just like ripping off a band-aid.

"You were my first kiss." Closing my eyes tight, I wait for his reaction. God, that's embarrassing. It feels like forever. Oh, God, I knew he would think I was stupid. He probably wants to drop me home and stay the hell away from me. Shit, shit! Then I hear movement. Yep, he's going to leave me here. Great! Suddenly, his lips on mine. Oh, God, that feels good. Before long, I feel his tongue slide along the seam of my lips, and I open up, I let out a silent moan. His hand comes to my neck and something in my head freezes. I stiffen. My eyes shoot open and I'm eye to eye with Drew, which immediately puts me at ease. He's looking at me. Studying me quietly.

"You, okay?"

Nodding my head, I say, "Yeah, I am now." He puts one arm around me, and with his other hand, he grabs the cake and puts more in my mouth. I can't help myself, I lick his fingers. By the look on his face, I shouldn't have.

"Don't start what you can't finish, girl... Now, tell me. What just happened? So next time I can make sure it won't happen again." Nodding, I try to figure out how to tell him without telling him.

"My neck. When you went to grab it, it scared me."

"Okay, but I would not hurt you. You know that, right?"

Nodding, "Yeah, I was fine when I opened my eyes and saw you."

"Good. Then we do that part with your eyes open till you're used to my touch, okay?"

"Yeah." He leans in and kisses me some more. Just pecks to start with. Some are wetter than others. While he's doing this, his hand goes up to my back, and at the same time, he's talking me through it.

"Now I'm going to rub the back of your neck while I kiss you deeper." Nodding, I let him take control, and a bolt of lightning goes straight to my lower gut. Well, even lower than that. Oh, God. That's nice. Then he growls and feasts on my mouth. Not with his teeth, but with his tongue and lips. Before I know what's happening, he picks me up, so I am straddling him. He brings his hands down to my hips, then moves my top up slightly. So he can feel my skin, where the edge of my pants starts and my top ends. It feels like heaven. My hips move without my mind telling them to. Drew pulls away.

"Easy, Beautiful. How was that?"

"Oh, God, you are good at this." He's still rubbing the skin around my front hip, making my mind scramble. That's my excuse for my stupid response. He chuckles and grabs the rest of the cake for both of us to eat. Shaking out the blanket, he puts it around my shoulders and grabs the warm coffee so we can finish it. When there's nothing left, he pulls my hips in really close and snuggles into my neck, so I do the same. He holds me firmly, rubbing his nose up my neck.

I think he's smelling me, so I ask, "Are you smelling me?"

He chuckles and replies, "Guilty."

"Oh, God, I have work sweat on me, and I need a shower. I smell gross!" He's still smelling me, but now he's shaking his head while doing it.

"No, you smell good. I bet you taste just as good." He then gives me an open-mouth kiss on my neck. Just as I'm about to combust, he pulls away.

"Don't worry, Beautiful. I will get to taste you all over soon enough." He gives me a quick kiss on the lips, then turns me around so we are both watching the sunset. It's magnificent.

I must've drifted off because I feel him gently trying to wake me with more kisses on the top of my head. I open my eyes and smile.

"What are you doing?" Giving me one last kiss, he stands up gently. Still holding me in his arms.

"Time to go," he says as he waits for me to get my balance.

"Oh, ok." As I'm about to fall over, Drew grabs me by my hips to steady me.

"So... Miss Hit-the-Dirt still comes out to play." We both laugh and head back to the car.

When I get home, I fall asleep in no time. All I think about in my dreamy state is:

BEST DAY EVER!

DREW

13

DREW

S itting at the bar in the clubhouse, all I can do is rub the top of my bottle of beer over my lips remembering how Stasia's lips felt on them. Fuck! My shoulder moves like it's not attached to my body. I turn to my left and see Bullet trying to get my attention.

"Drew, you in there, bro?" I nod, not sure how long I've been in dreamland.

"Yeah, what's up?" Bullet shakes his head.

"Sure, you are! I've only been talking to ya for like fifteen minutes. Any ideas?"

Not hearing what he has been saying and not wanting to look like a dick, I respond, "Sure." I don't know what's coming, but so be it.

Bullet shakes his head, "So, Stasia? You two getting serious?"

"Well, not sure what you mean, but as far as I'm concerned, she's mine."

"Yeah, that's what I mean. So, no more side pussy or...?"

"FUCK, NO!" I snap, looking him straight in the eyes and continuing, "She's it for me. Can't explain it. But I can't look at any of this," I say, throwing my arm around the room and gesturing to all the loose bitches around here. Fuck, I've barely touched them anyway. I always went out of the club to get what I wanted. One-night stands were all I ever wanted. Right now, I'm happy I was like that, cause when I bring her here, there is nothing to make her uncomfortable. Well, except Kim. I used her last month, but only her mouth. She became a leech. It took a bit to get rid of her. But you would think she would know better.

"Well, good for you, man. Glad you know what you want."

Pulling myself from my thoughts, I answer, "Yeah, I do." Silence fills the air for a second. I'm curious about Sophie. I've never seen Bullet act the way he did in the café on the day of the holdup.

Searching my thoughts, I ask, "Hey, so what did you do after I left the café today?" He has this small smile on his face, but he's not letting anything go. Bastard!

"I ate, ordered some more food, and offered Soph some help around the house when she needs it. Why? What about you?" Ha, sure he did.

I reply with, "About the same. Cake, coffee, a drive, then took her home." We both look at our drinks for a bit and chuckle to ourselves. Yeah, bonding and discussing our feelings here at the clubhouse, not happening! We enjoy the rest of our drink before Knight comes over with fucking Kim wrapped around him.

Bullet doesn't even look when he asks, "So, the spell over, Knight?" Knight's trying to peel her off of him so he can take a seat. I am tired of it.

"Kim, why don't you fuck off." She lets Knight go, rolls her eyes at me, and walks away. Wise choice.

"How's the dry spell, brother?" I can't help it. I had to ask.

"It's fine. I'm giving myself till my blood tests come back." Bullet coughs some of his drink out of his mouth, half choking. I slap his back to help him out. Laughing to myself, I look at Bullet, who's shaking his head. Fuck, Knight's a dick sometimes.

Finishing the night with the guys and having a few drinks is good. Taking the mickey out of each other. Good times.

"So, how're things with Nova, Cory and the girl?" I ask. I'm not sure where this girl is going to take this club, but my gut is telling me something. I don't think it's bad, but who knows?

Bullet shakes his head, saying, "Nah, but Nova and Cory are determined to help her. I hope she's ready for it. She's safe, that's all that she needs right now." Yeah, I agree with that.

Before I'm ready to hit the sack, Bullet brings up the girls as Mira comes over.

"I was thinking we could bring the girls here for a night off this Friday."

I like the idea because I want Stasia to meet everyone, but both girls won't happen. He's forgetting about lil' Keata.

"Won't happen. Keata needs a sitter, and something's telling me they don't know many people. I don't think they will leave her with just anyone." That's when Mira puts her two cents in.

"Hey, you two remember we have our family day this Saturday, right?"

Bullet winks at her and says, "Can you get close to little Keata so the girls can let their hair down?" Then he points at me and shakes his head.

"Not what you're thinking, brother. Both girls have had a lot happen. I'm only lookin' out for your girl and her friend." He gets up and walks off.

"Yeah, sure ya are," I mumble under my breath as he walks away.

Sienna Gypsy

STASIA

14

STASIA

Waking up in a cold sweat, my heart is nearly pounding out of my chest. I look around the room, stunned at first. How could he find me? I look around without moving my head. Scared that if someone is there, they will know I'm awake. Once, I'm sure no one is in the room, I sit up. It takes me a moment to grasp that I'm in my new room at Sophie's house. I try to control my breathing. Repeating to myself over and over. *In through my nose, out through my mouth. In through my nose, out through my mouth.*

Eventually, my heartbeat slows down. But I can't get rid of the stench of him and the feeling of his touch on my flesh. Chills run down my body in waves. I feel like there's a layer of dirt and grime covering my body. I need a shower immediately.

Scrambling out of bed, I rush to the bathroom, turn on the shower, and get in. I scrub like crazy. I haven't felt like this in years, and I need to get him off of me.

After my skin is screaming that it's clean, I fall in a heap at the bottom of the shower and cry. I cry for what I was. I cry for what he did. What hurts me the most about my escape and new life, is being without Nana Sally and Savie. In these moments I need them.

By the time I get out, I'm frozen. The water ran cold ages ago.

I'm getting into bed when Sophie knocks at my door. I cover myself, trying to hide what had just happened.

I attempt to yell with confidence, "Come in." She enters cautiously.

"Hey, you okay? I heard the shower." Breathing in deeply, knowing Sophie knows me so well, I gather she heard me crying.

So, I nod and say, "Yeah, all good, just a nightmare." I watch her tilt her head to the side as her silent answer. She sashays in and sits on the bed.

"Want me to stay?" Thinking about it, I still feel raw, so I nod. She smiles, "Scoot over, girlfriend, and don't hog the blankets!" I'm so relieved that she's not pushing me to talk because I am not up to it. Snuggling in together, I'm asleep in no time.

I wake to a noise. I can't quite figure out what it is. Rubbing my face with my hands, I realise it's my phone. Reaching for it, I answer without looking at the display.

"Hello?"

"Did I wake you, Beautiful? You sound like you just woke up."

"Yeah, I did… Sorry, what's up?" Rubbing my face again, I sit up.

"Just want to know what you, Soph, and Keata are up to this Saturday?" Searching my mind, I can't think of anything.

"Nothing I can think of, but my brain's not working yet, so can I get back to you? I'll check with Soph too, because I'm pretty sure they'll do the park, now that I think of it."

"Okay. Well, we have a family BBQ this Saturday." After a moment of silence, he continues. "I'd like you there to meet my brothers."

"Oh, okay. So just me then?"

"No, I want you comfortable. So, bring Sophie and Keata, it's always fun. There are some other kids at the club, so Keata will be cool."

"Yeah, no Keata will stay by us. She doesn't venture much."

"Stasia, when's the last time you went out?" Oh, okay, I get where this is going. Little does he know I don't go out. Ever. Sophie and I might have a get together at the house, or I'll let Sophie go out for the night with her friends. But for me, no way.

"I can't remember. But I don't enjoy going out, Drew. It's something I've never liked." Hoping he asks nothing else, I go on with, "So, if we are available, what do we bring?"

"Nothing, just yourselves." He pauses, but I can tell he has more to say.

"Oh, and Stasia, I'm going to make sure you all have a great time, okay?"

I bite my lip nervously and I'm not sure what to say.

I reply with the easiest answer, "Yeah, that would be good. I'm looking forward to it."

"Good. Now, you working today?"

I can hear the smile in his voice, which causes my lips to lift in a smile as well, helping me forget the night I had.

"Yeah, I'm on afternoons today. Sophie left earlier."

"You driving?"

"Well, how else would I get there?"

Drew chuckles, "Smart-ass, you have been known to walk before!"

"Well, yes I have, Mr Biker Man, but it seems it's a bit too far now, so I drive."

"Can I drive you, Miss Hit-the-Dirt? I would like some time with you." Wow, what's a girl say to that? I can't believe he wants to drive me.

Biting my bottom lip again, "Um, yeah. I mean yes. Is that okay?" squeezing my eyes shut, bringing my fist to my forehead, gently hitting it a few times. I curse myself for sounding needy, argh.

"Yeah, Beautiful. I'll be there in an hour, okay?"

"Wait, what?" I look at my phone and see it's way later than I thought.

"Shit, I gotta go. See you soon, okay?"

"Yeah, Babe, I'll see you soon." The phone goes dead. I've still got this stupid smile on my face when my phone vibrates and it's him.

BIKER BOY: *Get moving girl. You're going to be late!*

Laughing, I run to the bathroom and wash away my sleepy brain, as well as the leftover grime that is still lingering. Then, I get ready as quickly as possible.

Exactly an hour later, there's a knock at the door. Excitement running through my body, I run and slide in my socks to the door and I stumble over my own feet. As I'm about to reach the door, I fall forward to my knees, and my head hits the doorknob. I don't get time to process it because pain erupts in my head.

"Stasia. Honey. You okay?" I can feel pain throbbing around my eye. Argh, shit, my eye hurts.

"What the…?" Groaning, I try to sit up, but my hands are being held down firmly, and I panic. First, my breathing picks up fast and short, then I shake uncontrollably. It's hard. My heart is telling me I'm safe, but my brain is short-circuiting, trying to tell me to get up and get away. I hear Drew trying to settle me. It's only then that I slowly calm. His hand is softly stroking my hair.

"Babe, I heard the bang. I shoved the door open." Drew picks me up and puts me on the couch. I try to open my eyes. One is fine, but the other isn't. He turns to leave.

"Where are you going?" I ask as he strides towards the kitchen.

"Just getting ice, Babe." He's back with some ice wrapped in a towel. He places it on my eye where the pain is.

"Ah, shit!" I blurt quietly in pain.

"Shhh, it's okay, Beautiful." He is staring at me, checking out the damage, from the look of it. His intense gaze is giving me chills.

"Fuck, it looks sore, you want some pain meds or anything?"

"Nah, I'm fine. That all happened so fast. Not good, not good." I say out loud. I look up slowly as I hear him chuckle.

"Babe, I don't think you're going to work. Who can I ring for you?" Oh, my God, Joan is going to get sick of my sick days and sack me.

"Use my phone. Ring Joan and tell her what happened. I'm not on till Monday now, so I should be okay by then." I smile weakly. He walks off to make the phone call. I get comfy on the couch because I don't want to move my head. It's killing me. Shit, how embarrassing.

When he walks back in, he tells me everything is all sorted. Then he sits down next to me, grabs the ice pack from my eye, puts my head on his lap, and replaces the ice pack. Groaning, I tell him I'll be fine, but he cuts me off.

"Stasia, don't start. I'm staying unless something important comes up. Now lay back and relax and I'll put a movie on."

"Movie it is, but I don't care what. Use that control next to you. The hard drive has plenty of movies on it."

DREW

15

DREW

Hearing keys jingling as the front door opens, I look towards it to see Sophie carrying Keata inside. As she closes the door behind them, she walks over to look at Stasia. She's been asleep for the last hour.

"Ouch, that girl is in the wars. What the hell happened? Joan didn't say much."

"Well, I heard a bang like she fell, which she did. When I opened the door, she had slid straight into the door handle. She was in pain, I've been icing her eye, but her knee seems okay. She says there's no pain, but I don't believe her."

Sophie replies with a bit of a chuckle, "Good for you. She always says she's fine. Drives me nuts."

Sophie puts Keata down by her toys and says as she points to her daughter, "She'll be fine down there. She will play with her toys, I'll start dinner. You staying or leaving?"

Shaking my head, "Yeah, I'm staying, but I'm supposed to meet up with Bullet. Do you mind if I call him to meet here?" Looking down at Stasia, I stroke her hair and shake my head in disbelief at all the things going wrong for her.

"I sort of feel responsible." Sophie laughs out loud.

"Yeah, well, you sort of are. Anyway, yeah, that's fine, I can make extra. I can freeze it if no one stays." Sophie steps into the kitchen as I reach for my phone to ring Bullet.

Before Bullet arrives, the girls chat in the kitchen for a while. As usual, Stasia is persistent, so I found a compromise, she's sitting at the table while Sophie is cooking up a storm. I walk out to meet Bullet and we shoot the shit till Sophie comes and tells us dinner is ready.

Sitting at the table together isn't too awkward. Considering Bullet has Keata eating out of the palm of his hand. Who knew?

Next thing I know, Bullet says, "Hey, we have a family BBQ on Saturday. You girls should come." Sophie looks at Keata and then at Stasia, shaking her head.

"Nah, I'm good. I don't take Keata out unless I know it's safe for her. On Saturday, we go to the park, anyway, but thanks." Bullet shakes his head.

"She'll be safe. I'll make sure of it. And there are a few club kids about her age that will be there. It will be good for her, and I'll stay sober so you and Stasia can have a couple of drinks if you want. Drew too. We'll watch her. Besides, you both need a break, and we'd like to give it to ya."

Nodding, I add. "Yeah, Bullet and I can play with Keata. You two can relax. And Stasia, I want you to meet my family. Please?" I give her some serious puppy dog eyes, trying to convince her without saying more.

Stasia looks at Sophie and says, "Soph, Drew asked me before, but I told him I'll get back to him after we talk. Up to you, honey."

After about a minute Sophie responds, "Look, Keata stresses out easily. She also has seizures. You two don't know what you're asking and even if I say yes, which I haven't, it's not that easy with her. She will need her walker. The other kids might not like her and-" Bullet stops her before she can continue.

"Sophie, I'll personally take you there and back again. If she doesn't settle, I'll drive you home, no questions asked. Just see what happens. We might surprise you." Sophie is nibbling on her bottom lip, hard. I can see how stressed she is.

Leaning in her direction, I say, "Soph, sleep on it and you can tell us tomorrow, okay?"

She still looks uneasy, but she answers, "Okay, I'll let you know." I'm satisfied with her answer for the moment. I look at Bullet, he nods, and we get up to clear away the dishes and clean up. When we finish, Sophie is nowhere in sight and Stasia is sitting with her eyes closed. I go back into the kitchen, find some Panadol and a glass of water, and bring it back to her.

Entering the lounge room, Bullet is sitting on the single recliner. I move Stasia's head so it's on my lap, then make her take the

Panadol. She's so stubborn. When Sophie comes out, she looks around and finds that there's nowhere for her to sit. So she goes to the floor near the single recliner. Looking at us, she lets out a gigantic sigh.

"Okay, but Bullet, you promise? Straight back here no matter what? If I say let's go, we leave?" Bullet stares straight into her eyes as he answers.

"No question, straight back." I smile, then I see Stasia smile when she turns her head to look at Sophie, then groans.

"I don't think I'll be drinking if I can't lift this headache."

After we settle the primary plan, staying over, and Bullet will pick us up on Saturday, we all have a bit of a laugh and shoot the shit. Fuck if I care what we're talking about. Having Stasia's head on my lap is the best feeling ever.

As soon as Bullet says he's leaving, I whisper to Stasia that it's time to go to bed. Picking her up, with her protesting, I wave to them goodnight and I take her to her bedroom.

After I put Stasia in bed, I take off my cut and hear Stasia stutter, "W-what are you doing?" she asks in a panic. Smiling, I keep undressing.

"Don't worry, I'll leave my boxers on, and I promise I'll just hold you." She mutters something under her breath.

Something like, "God, help me."

I pull my side of the bed back and ask, "Anything you need? Your nightie? Drink?" She shakes her head and pulls out her nighty from under her pillow. Who the fuck does that nowadays? Sliding under the covers, she gets undressed and then puts on her nighty.

Sienna Gypsy

When she's settled, I pull her over to me, spooning her from behind. Putting my arms around her and kissing her under the ear.

"Night, Beautiful."

As she snuggles back into me, she mumbles, "Night, Drew." Feeling the warmth of her skin on me washes a sense of calm over me and helps me to dose off fast.

STASIA

16

STASIA

I *feel cold. The room is pitch black. I try to look around me but I can't quite make things out. Is this my old bedroom? I sense they're coming. I rock in the corner, trying to get warm. My head is throbbing like crazy. I search my memories for why my head hurts and they're just out of reach. Listening to the slightest sound, I hear a creak above me. Oh, God, they're coming. "No, no, p-p-please don't!" I whisper to no one. I try to concentrate on listening harder.*

I hear, "Stasia, wake up, wake up." They sound so distant. But I know they're just upstairs.

Something's not right. Pushing back into the corner of where I am, I try to find comfort. I watch as the door swings open and bounces off the wall.

"Stasia, Stasia, wake up."

"Stasia, come on, girl. It's a dream, I got you." I startle, waking up with sweat dripping everywhere. My lungs are screaming for fresh air, and I can hear myself wheezing badly. My mouth waters and my gut is turning. I pull free and race to my bathroom, hit the toilet with no control, and vomit out everything in me. My body is shaking while I'm heaving. There's something cool on my neck and my hair is being pulled away. It doesn't matter, because I've already got most of my puke in it.

By the time I'm finished, I can't handle the feel of my skin. His stench is washing over me.

"Get off me." I say. Not to who's in the room pulling my hair back, but to the memories that are clawing at my mind to come back. Stripping my clothes from my body, I jump into the shower. I try to scrub everything away. The smell of his stench, the weight of their bodies on top of me, the pain from the beatings. I claw at my skin, hoping to rip it off just to feel clean, but I can't. I camouflage my tears as they mould with the shower water that races down my face. My body remembers it all as I shake violently. I'm trying to gain control and make everything stop. My legs get weak and give out as I drop to the floor. Landing on my butt, I pull my knees in and hold them tight. Making myself as small as I can, the scalding water steams off my skin. *He can't hurt me*, I tell myself.

"I'm ok. He can't find me!" I scream the last part at the top of my lungs, hoping that the water and bathroom door drowned out my cries of pain as I sit there in the shower, alone with the disturbing memories that creep upon me.

"Beautiful, you need to calm down." A familiar voice breaks through my memories of pain. It's so soothing, my heart slows like it knows I'm safe. Why? Why does his voice do this? My dreams are back, with the fears and feelings that rip my soul apart. My nights and days are drowning with the thought of my old memories and clash with this new biker man. I can't figure out if Drew's my saviour or my kryptonite.

Before I have time to think about what's happening, he's behind me, pulling me close to him. Smothering my thoughts. Taking away the bad and dirty and making me feel warm and clean.

I'm not sure how long we were in the shower, but the water has turned cold. I felt nothing until my body is being pulled out of the water. He wraps the towel around me and takes me to my room. He sits me on the bed and tries to dry me. I flinch and shake every time he blots the water with the towel. Places that remind me of my ugly past. My neck, even my arms. I watch him silently walk over to my drawers and find my night dress. He walks back and immediately puts it on me. I hate that I can't control the way my body reacts to him.

Drew helps tuck me into bed. I pull my legs close to my chest to make myself as small as possible. I'm unconsciously waiting for the door to close, but I don't hear it. The blankets move on the other side of the bed. Then I feel the bed dip with his weight..

He gets in the bed, pulls me close and whispers in my ear, "I got you." His arms come around my body and embrace me tighter, so every part of my body is touching his. He whispers again in my ear, "We will beat these monsters, Beautiful. I promise."

I whisper back, "Just don't let go."

I wake up feeling great. Stretching out, my body stills as flashes of everything last night come flooding back. Oh, God, Drew.

I turn to see if he's still here and embarrassment creeps through me when I realise he's gone.

Relief starts to wash over me. I feel the tension leave my body, exhaling deeply as I realise that I'm content. At least I don't have to confront him and endure his pitying gaze. After going to the bathroom and washing my face, I walk into the kitchen and Drew is drinking coffee.

I swear under my breath, "Shit, you're still here." He must have heard me because he makes his way toward me. I turn my back to him to pull a cup out of the cupboard, but he doesn't let that stop him.

"Morning, Beautiful. That's no way to treat your monster killer." He wraps his big, strong, muscled arms around me, squeezes tight, and kisses me under my ear. Which is becoming his spot, or my spot, or… hmm.

Shaking my thoughts out of my head, "Morning. I thought you left." *For good.* I don't say that part out loud, secretly hoping he won't go anywhere.

"Not going anywhere, babe. Now, I'm not going to ask you about last night, but you will tell me in time. Yeah?" his brows lift with a genuine gaze that will be my undoing.

Shit, double shit. He can't know. He'll never understand. Denial is probably best, so I don't lie, only agree till it comes up again. Turning in his arms, I put my head on his chest. God, he feels so good and smells yummy. Mmm, just the right amount of aftershave and coffee. I hear him chuckling.

Looking up, I ask, "What?"

"Did you just smell me?" Shit, totally busted. Going into denial, I turn and shake my head, grab my coffee, smell it, and sit down. Feeling my cheeks burn.

Being Friday, it's my day to pick up Keata. Needing a distraction, I pretend Drew's not here, and I clean up. I start all of our laundry and tidy Keata's room. When I'm finished, Drew wants

126

to take me for lunch. He got a text earlier, and told me we'd be going together, and then we'd go get Keata. I'm still trying to figure everything out. Keeping busy helps me not think about what happened last night. Not feeling any pressure from him is helping. He still feels close and I don't understand why that comforts me.

We are pulling up to a petrol garage, or what looks like one. Drew drives around the back where there are a lot of bikes. He parks his car, gets out of his door and comes to my side to help me out. I stare at him nervously.

"What are we doing here? What is this place?" He smiles at me, puts his arm around me and squeezes me tight.

"Easy, Beautiful, Mira cooked lunch, and she said to bring you. Promise I won't leave your side." Who the hell is Mira? Knots form in my stomach.

I walk with Drew towards the front door reluctantly because I hate crowds. Drew strides through the front entrance and holds it open till I walk through. It takes a while for my eyes to adjust from being outside, in the bright sun, to a dark room. We walk toward what looks like a bar, I see it's an open-plan, similar to a school hall. As we get closer, I see four good looking men. There's also a girl sitting facing the kitchen bar area and a girl behind the counter who spots us first.

She smiles big and blurts out, "Drew, you brought her. Stasia, I'm Mira. Drew's sister, of sorts." I'm sure I look like a deer in headlights. She points at everyone and introduces them.

"This guy here is my dad, everyone calls him Prez, and that's Nova, Cory and Knight, but this in the middle is Izzy." I shake their hands as I go. All the men respect my personal space and keep their distance. Which brings a familiar feel from the day I first met Cobra. When he brought me back to the club in Melbourne and changed my life.

My eyes scan all of them carefully but when I get to Izzy, I notice she has similar bruises on her face as I do. I try to break the ice and divert my uneasy feelings in this environment.

"You look like you hit the same door I did." She gives me a small smile and shakes her head.

"Nah, no door, but I'm good now." She retreats a little, looks towards Mira and smiles ever so slightly, then stares at her lap again.

Hoping these guys saved her from something horrible, like I was. I leave it. I hate nosey people, so I don't ask.

Looking back at Mira, I say, "You need a hand?"

Shaking her head, she says with a beautiful smile that beams with kindness, "Nope, take a seat. Everything's ready." Someone grabs me. It takes a minute to realise it's Drew. He pulls me between his legs and it makes me feel uncomfortable. I try to move, but he holds me close.

With his breath on my neck, my body relaxes, and he whispers, "Stay where you are, Babe. I need you close. Okay?" I nod, but feel the other people looking at me, which makes it harder for me to settle.

As time passes, we're all eating, and I end up on my stool next to Drew, but the conversation is flowing. Mira is so nice. She has dark hair with glimpses of gold or blonde through it. She is young with an old soul and stands up for herself. She reminds me so much of Savie. I can see these guys respect and love her like a sister. Just like Savie has the respect of Cobra and Krip. She can cook too! The food is so delicious, I scarf it down like there is no tomorrow.

Just as we're ready to leave, Drew gets asked by Mira's dad to chat in his office.

Looking at me, he says, "You good? This won't take long." He looks at Mira.

"Stay with her." He says. Mira nods, and Drew struts towards what must be the office. After the guys leave, Izzy joins our conversation. Updating us on her recovery progress, but she expresses a desire for them to give her some space. I can tell she feels a little smothered. She says nothing about why she's all battered up, and I don't blame her. My memories are still too consuming.

"So, Izzy, you coming tomorrow?" I ask. Hoping she knows what I'm talking about.

"I'm not sure. I have good days and bad, but I'll be there if it's a good day. Nova wants me there, but Cory doesn't want me to have panic attacks, so he would rather I be away from all the activity."

Without thinking, I reply, "Sometimes you need to push through them, or you get stuck in the darkness which will consume you. I'd know." I whisper the last bit, realising I said too much.

"Okay, ladies, we gotta go. Time to pick up a young princess." I didn't know Drew was finished and standing behind me. I turn, expecting him to look at me, concerned, but he smiles one of his sexy smiles and grabs my hand. Goosebumps wash over me, and I can't help but beam at him.

Izzy grabs my hand and squeezes it with a slight smile on her face.

"Sometimes people meet for reasons that are beyond our knowledge." I beam at her, knowing she is right.

"You might be right Izzy." Drew pulls harder on my hand and guides me out of the bar and kitchen towards the exit.

Getting into Drew's Truck, I noticed there is a car seat in the back. That makes me smile even more. I fasten my seatbelt, and he jumps in and starts the car up.

He looks over at me and says, "Let's go get that princess, Miss Hit-the-Dirt."

Walking through the daycare, I pick up Keata, she is so excited to see Drew. I think she has a crush on him just like me. Little flirt. Thinking we're going home, I'm a little confused when we stop outside a Baskin-Robbins ice cream shop instead. Bullet is out front as we pull up. This is quite unexpected. Bullet comes straight for Keata taking her out of the car , and she is lapping it up! I get my phone and take a few shots because who would believe me anyway? Bullet takes her to choose her ice cream. I'm shocked at how she gets him to notice what she wants.

When we've finished eating, Keata is babbling big time, so I video it for Soph. It's not often she does this, and normally it's only with Soph or me. But the boys have her so at ease.

Cleaning her up, we all say bye to Bullet, and head home. I'm hoping for another early night.

Arriving home, Drew opens our doors and picks up Keata out of the truck he used.

As we walk to the front door, I say without even thinking, "I need to process. Lots happened today and I need time for my brain to catch up." My cheeks start to flush. I hope he understands. Not waiting for an answer, I put the key in the door and open it. Drew strides in and places Keata at her toys. He watches her for a minute and leaves her on the mat. Keata giggles, waving back.

Turning to me, he smiles, "Yeah, I get it, but I'm not gonna lie. I don't want to go." He walks into my space and his hand gently touches my cheek, then his fingers slide down to lift my chin.

He kisses my lips so softly and whispers, "Bye," at that moment I hate myself because I'm at war with my feelings. I clenching my fists, shaking off this unease. I must have been in my own world longer than I thought after that kiss because Drew is already leaving. I lean on the front door frame as he waves goodbye.

DREW

17

DREW

Getting the club organised for a party isn't that hard with everyone helping. When church starts, I tell all the brothers about my girl coming to the BBQ night. Making sure they know her friend and daughter are off-limits. Telling the guys that Keata is different from other kids but is cute as hell, wasn't as hard as I thought it would be. I think I've turned into a pussy.

Then, Prez reminds everybody it's family night and to keep it that way. Loose women are to be kept behind closed doors and not get out of hand, which I'm glad about. Stasia might run. Fuck, I hope not.

Walking out, Bullet gets my attention.

"Prez wants us out back. Didn't say what for." As we walk out the back, there's no one else around. Prez looks pissed.

"What's up?" Bullet asks. Prez shows me his phone. I see why. It's a picture of Izzy tied up and passed out with bruises on her face. I pass it to Bullet, and he doesn't like what he sees either.

"Who the fuck sent that?".Knowing the dipshit who sent it thinks we didn't tell Prez what's going on. Speaking up, I shake my head.

"Must be Frazer. Looks like before we took her. Fuck, don't show Nova. He's on the edge, waiting for a reason to take him out." Prez shakes his head.

"Yeah, that's my thought, but the number shows up as unknown. Keep a lid on it. I'm not sure if this person knows we have her or is trying to tell me something. I'll get PC to track the number and see what we can get. You two are the only two who know. Understand?" We both give a reassuring nod, and turn to walk off. Taking a few more steps, I turn and remind Prez where we are going.

"We'll be back. Going to get the girls. You need us to pick anything up?"

"Nah, you know Mira. She has everything in its corner. See you soon."

Picking the girls up was easy, but driving them back to the clubhouse, well, you could cut the tension with a knife. No one is talking. At least Keata fills the silence with her chitchat to anyone who listens, which seems to settle me.

Arriving at the clubhouse, I help Stasia out, and Bullet helps Sophie. Once Sophie is standing next to the car, Keata has her arms in the air, reaching for Bullet to pick her up. He smiles, and lifts her in his arms, keeping her on his hip. Sophie looks nervous. She occupies herself, getting everything out of the car. I call a prospect over.

"Tommy, grab that stuff Sophie has, put it where Bullet set up for Keata." Sophie looks at Bullet with a strange look but says nothing. Bullet leads the way with Keata in his arms. Looking around the picnic area, I see Mira is all set up. There's an esky under a tree with a blanket, chairs and a portable table. I turn to look at Stasia, and she looks stunned. Mira, being Mira, comes straight up and hugs the girls for a hello, and introduces herself to Sophie and Keata. Keata seems so excited to get Mira's attention. Sophie smiles and looks a little relaxed, then turns to Mira.

"This is just the way she is. If she likes you, it's for life. And she will be loyal and love you forever. So, I hope that doesn't scare you." She says the last part, looking at Bullet. Fucker has something going on. I just know it. Mira pulls out some drinks for the girls.

"Okay, so now the boys are on driving and kid duty, you girls can relax and see where this party takes us." Sophie goes still. I look at Bullet and we both look like we are holding our breath. I'm about to go explain but Mira adds, "By that, I mean enjoying a few and having a few more if you want." With a wink, she passes out the girly drinks. They are several colours, pink, yellow and green. Fuck that! Screwing up my nose at the drinks, I kiss Stasia on the temple and tell her I'll be back. Bullet nods to Sophie as well.

We both eye each other as we walk to get some more stuff.

When we're out of hearing distance, I say, "Fuck, that was close to Sophie leaving!" Bullet's reply is a knowing smirk and a nod.

As the others arrive at the family BBQ, we go make sure there's nothing more to do. The faster it's set up, the faster we are back on Keata duty.

After finishing up on the BBQ, Tommy organises a quick game of touch rugby. We always do this. We mix it up with the ladies and kids. Once the teams are picked, Soph freaks out when Bullet comes for Keata. We had it planned to put Keata in the game with me and Bullet tagging, making sure she gets the ball. We put Soph on the other team as well, the same as Stasia.

My team is winning but I call my guys over because I want this next try to be Keata's.

"Bullet, you need to get her down to the try line. This one is for Keata, okay guys?" They all give me the nod when I look at the other team. I see Mira's got Stasia laughing. She's shaking her head. When Stasia sees me looking in her direction, she nods at Mira while still looking at me, and her eyes seem to drink me in. I feel my face soften. Stasia winks at me seductively. I have to do a double take. She is never this obvious. Scratching the back of my head, argh, they have something planned, I just know it. I let the girls know that I know.

"Bring your best girls!" We have the play all set up. I look at Stasia one last time before I play the ball. One of the club kids, Johnny, grabs it and passes it off to Tommy. I run up behind Tommy, waiting for the right time to get the ball and pass it off. As Tommy passes it to me, I'm in mid-air, drifting. I crash into the ground with a thud. And Stasia's weight is on top of me. Sitting up on my elbows thinking, that little minx set this up. Mira took out my legs and Stasia tackled me to the ground. I lose the ball and watch Sophie pick it up. Stasia is giggling on top of me. I watch Stasia taking in the game while I'm memorising her face. After about a minute or so, I hear them all screaming. Even Stasia is looking and cheering at where they got their try. I grab her hips and give them a gentle shake, then I groan. She's right on my dick. She glances at me, but I hold her firm. Enjoying the feeling of my dick getting hard. Fuck!

"I'm sure this is called holding," I say, stuck in a trance looking into her gaze. Realising how dark blue her eyes are.

"Well, let go and you won't be holding me," she replies, giggling, as she tries to get up. I tighten my hold on her and pull her closer. Staring for a bit, not giving her the chance to pull away, I press my lips to hers and kiss her hard. It's like a match being lit, my soul awakening, a burning I can't seem to control. I've been holding back all day, so this comes across as desperate. Thinking it might be too much, I go to pull away when she bites my bottom lip. Then licks over it with her tongue to soothe the pain. I'm surprised when she says, "What took you so long, biker boy?"

Shit. I get us both up, smack her butt playfully, and tell her, "Oh, you're going to finish that, but first Keata is getting the next try." Kissing her quickly this time, I walk back to position.

Bullet looks at Keata and says, "That was Drew's fault. We got this girl. Our turn now." He looks at me and laughs. "You let girls take you out."

Bastard! I know this is going to be an ongoing joke. We play the ball and I get it to Bullet, he helps Keata put down the winning try. She is so excited that she claps her hands, high-fives the guys and gives them knuckles. I see Sophie watching with watery eyes.

"You okay Sophie?"

She nods, "Yeah, for a long time, it was only us, and now we have Stasia. Keata misses out on this sort of interaction. I suppose what I'm trying to say is, Bullet was right, we needed this, and he knew it."

I rub her back and tell her, "This is our family Soph, and I want Stasia and her family to be a part of mine." Her body stiffens and her eyes slowly come to mine, like she understood something. Not sure what I said, but she wipes her face and pushes her tears away, nodding.

"I understand, Drew, and thank you. That helps immensely." She walks off to grab her daughter, puts on a smile, and takes her to get a drink.

Something tells me I'm missing something.

I was hoping to sweep Stasia away for a bit after the game, but she's having fun with the girls and she looks reluctant to leave Sophie. I look over at Keata and notice she has fallen asleep.

Bullet and I both walk over to talk to the girls.

I point at Keata, "Hey, you want me to put her to bed? She can use my room."

Bullet looks at Sophie and adds, "I set my room up for both of you. I've got a swag on the floor for me. You two get the bed." Sophie shakes her head.

"Thank you so much, but I'd like to go now, please. Stasia, stay, but I need to take her home." Sophie gets up, passes Keata to Stasia and starts packing up Keata's stuff. Bullet scratches his beard looking confused as hell, and I've got to say, so am I.

Getting all the stuff in Bullet's truck, Sophie tells Stasia, "Stay, enjoy yourself. You've never done this. It's always me out for the night. Now it's your turn." Then she turns to me.

"Promise both of us that if she needs to come home, you'll bring her." I turn to Stasia.

"Stasia, let me know when you are ready, and we'll go. Okay?" Stasia nods and hugs her friend. Sophie gets in the truck, Bullet starts it up and we watch them drive off.

Sienna Gypsy

I pull Stasia into me.

"Now, you little minx, you are going to finish what you started." Stasia giggles. She struggles playfully, then breaks free, and runs off. I take off and chase her. As I get around the corner, I see Stasia looking shocked, staring at Kim, who shouldn't be here. Kim has a horrible smile on her face and when she sees me, she starts her shit.

"Oh, there you are. I was waiting for you as you told me to." Stasia looks at me, backing away. I point to Stasia.

"You wait and listen." Damnit, I turn my attention back to Kim.

"What the fuck are you talking about? I never talked to you. Get out of here. It's a family night. No whores allowed." Turning back to Stasia, she's shaking her head from side to side in slow motion. Her next words are not what I wanted to hear.

"I'm going. Where's Mira?"

"Mira can't drive you. She's been drinking all night. Stasia, I have nothing going on with this girl. Ask anyone." Kim opens her mouth to say something, but Mira stops her.

"Who the fuck invited you here?" Mira pushes her toward the gate and yells again.

"Who, Kim? I need a fucking name!" I know what she's doing. Mira's been trying to get Kim banned for about two months now. No one knows why, but she knows if she lies or dobs a brother in, she's out.

Kim looks around, looking for help, but the brothers are all sick of her cling-on ways.

So, she yells, "Tommy wanted me here!" I'm looking around, not seeing him anywhere, but Mira seems to know different.

"Well, that's a lie, Kim, because we had that conversation, and he has been trying to get rid of ya. Now get out and don't come back." On the last word, Mira boots her up the ass, but Kim seems to think she knows better.

"You can't kick me out Mira, you're only Prez's daughter and you don't give him what he needs. So, I'll be staying, bitch." Mira is furious. As she's about to grab a hold of her and punch her, Prez comes out from behind Nova, who is smiling big time.

"Mira, stand back. Kim, you're out! You disrespected my daughter and my brother by lying to his woman. And then you bring a prospect in on it. Mira is right. Grab your shit, you're done!" He then heads toward Izzy.

Everyone is getting on with their business as if nothing happened, and Mira turns to Stasia.

"My brother has been hanging by a string with you since the day he met you. Trust me when I say he wouldn't step out on you with that. Hell, he wouldn't step out at all. Kim always does this. She has split up a lot of the men from their partners, and trust me, they don't touch her. The new guys do and the hang-rounds." Stasia nods. I walk towards her, but she is still stiff.

I try again to explain, "Mira's not lying, Babe, but if you still want to go, I'll take you." Stasia looks around and sees Izzy with Prez, then looks at me.

"I'd like to go sit with Izzy. Mira, you want to come?"

Fuck if I know if I 'm in the good books or the bad, but I'll take more time with her. And if she thinks I'm not going with her. Well, fuck that.

140

Sienna Gypsy

STASIA

18

STASIA

Walking over to Izzy, I smile and wave. I knew Mira was walking close behind me, but I was unaware that Drew was following as well. I thought he might have left after the situation with that girl, Kim. I mean, I believe Drew and Mira, but she was so convincing. The thought of someone else touching him had my mind racing furiously with jealousy. I don't know why it hurt so much to think he used me like that. It's been a minute, not even that long, and my feelings for him have grown so much. I keep telling myself, Mira wouldn't have responded the way she did, or Drew. And what Mira's dad did? Well... Shaking my head, I know I need to get it out of my mind.

Reaching Izzy, I pull out the stool and she gives me the biggest smile.

I lean in and cuddle her, and she whispers in my ear, "Wish these guys would leave me while I'm talking to you guys. I just need to breathe a bit,"

Mira must have heard, because she tells the boys, "It's girl time. Move out of hearing distance."

But Drew looks at me and says, "I'm not going anywhere, Stasia." My heart warms inside. He opens his mouth to say something else, but I cut him off.

"Give me time to process the last thirty minutes and I'll be good. You don't have to go far. Just let us have girl time. Okay?"

He looks at me sheepishly, but treads over to me. Wrapping me in his arms, "I'm so sorry. She lied. I promise you." He looks so defeated I almost feel bad for him. I decide to put him out of his misery. I put my arms around him and hold him. I nod, then pull away.

"Go chat with your boys or mates or whatever you call each other."

He winks at me and says, "My brothers, Babe. They're my brothers." I giggle a bit because I knew that. But I wanted his correction, to put both our minds out from what Kim did. The guys move away, but Nova and Cory don't want to leave Izzy's side.

She gives Nova a kiss on the cheek and cuddles Cory, telling them, "I'll be fine, and I will call out if I need you." My gut tightens from my own personal experience, I know this feeling is forever.

Eventually, they leave. Izzy then begins to share. "My nightmares are getting worse and I'm spacing out, or as Cory puts it, freaking the fuck out." Izzy rolls her eyes at the last part. I rub her back, knowing how she feels, so I try to comfort her.

"You don't actually get over it, but you find somewhere to put it in your mind to keep you safe. Counselling helped me. I hope it helps you." Mira's soft smile confuses me. I'm not sure if she's worried, or if that look was understanding. She wraps her arms around us both providing encouragement. Not wanting to bring down Izzy and keep the mood light, I jump up and grab some drinks for us. Izzy shakes her head as I look at her. I know she's too young, but I wouldn't have cared . Then again, it could make things worse too. It did for me.

Shaking that memory away, I start up some girl talk about the game we played today and the way Drew's been my shadow lately, which I can't lie, I love! The girls don't say anything when I ask about their love lives. I understand Izzy not wanting anything like that, but I wondered if she's ever had a relationship before. But Mira, she must have someone, but the big question is, who? She is so tight-lipped about it, I reckon her dad would never allow it.

We talk about everything under the sun, makeup, hair, clothes, shoes, and music.

As we start up about music, we can hear the music pumping inside. Mira and I are bouncing in our seats.

Izzy smiles at us both and then asks, "Mira, can you take me to my room? I'm buggered, but don't tell the boys till later. They will want to stay with me. I don't need them to stay. I'm good tonight. Let them enjoy their night." I know she's not, she wants to survive just a little on her own. Mira nods and we all stand together.

She smiles, saying, "Follow me, ladies".

We all head inside.

As we enter the back entrance to the clubhouse, I'm shocked. There are heaps of people here now, far out! Where did they come from?

We are walking through the crowd when I get pulled by the arm and yanked back.

I go stiff when an older man is in my face, saying, "Where do you think you're going, missy?" I shake. The old horrible feeling washes over me, and I try to fight the memories. He looks mean, and there's a scar under his left eye. I start to answer him, but someone grabs my hips and I freeze. More memories flood through me and I fight my mind for control. I close my eyes and search for a happy place.

I hear Drew's voice "I got you, Beautiful." He turns me to look at him, searching deep in my eyes, knowing I'm fighting my demons.

He brings me in closer, looks over my shoulder and talks to the man, "Spud, see you've met my girl, Stasia. Stasia this is Spud, one of the brothers."

I force a smile because he is still freaking me out. He nods, then smiles this creepy smile back at me as he tells Drew, "Need to keep that one close, brother. Didn't know she was with you."
Drew changes positions to stand protectively in front of me. It puts me at ease, which helps my mind find more control.

"Well, she is. Spread the word. Will be for good, too. So don't get any ideas, Spud." Drew seems like he's ready for a fight, his hands have turned to fists and his body is tense.

When Drew turns his attention back to me, he relaxes and says, "Come on, Beauty, let's get you a drink." I can't see Mira anywhere, so I follow Drew. He puts me in front of him at the bar and cages me in. I'm facing the bar, standing, and he's sitting on the stool, legs open and arms on either side of me.

He leans in and whispers in my ear, "What are you drinking, Beauty?"

I lean back into him, loving the feeling and tell him, "What we were drinking outside will be good."

Mira shows up out of nowhere and yells over the bar, "Two B52's and a jug of illusions, Sandy." The lady winks at Mira and then gets busy with mixing the drinks.

She puts two shots in front of us and Mira looks at me, saying, "On three, one...two...three!" We both swing them back. As soon as I've swallowed the liquor, Drew turns me around and kisses me. I try to pull away, but he doesn't let me. After I relax and enjoy the kiss, forgetting where I am, he slowly pulls away.
"I'm not drinking tonight so I'll taste it through you, Beauty." I nod, then look at Mira and she is smiling.

"Another?" Mira yells.

Shaking my head at her, I say, "Let's try this green stuff here. Looks good." Drew reaches in front of me, fills our glasses, and gives Mira hers. He then gives me mine and reminds me, "You're still giving me a taste, Beauty, so don't think you're getting out of it."
Jesus, he's killing me here. Mira is bopping around to the music, leaning over to her, I yell over the music, "Did Izzy, get to her room, okay?"

Smiling at me, she replies, "Yeah, Nova was already there watching movies. He told her it's too bad, till he feels good with leaving her, it ain't happening." I nod, thinking it's a good thing, because my nightmares are a bitch to get rid of and having someone chase them away can only help.

Before I know it, Mira and I are up and dancing. I'm busting a move like I do with Keata at home, trying to get her to feel the beat. And then Jessie J's bang-bang comes on. I love this song, so I search out Drew and start teasing him with the words, by the time the chorus comes, he's walking towards me. When Nikki starts rapping, I'm going all out like it's me rapping the words. When I get to the part, "You need a bad girl to blow your mind." I'm in the air. He swoops me up so fast that I giggle with excitement. As I land over his shoulder, I see Mira, waving at me, laughing. Shit, I bit off more than I can chew.

He's taking me down the hallway, and then we get to a door. He opens it with a key, then shuts and locks it. I'm sliding down his body against the door. God, this feels so good. He kisses me, then pulls back.

"You say when, Beauty. I just want you to feel. Let me try to make you feel good." I nod, then he leans in and starts kissing me. My lips, my neck. His hot breath in my ear. His leg comes up between mine. His thigh hits my core, and it feels so good that I don't know if he's rubbing me or if I'm the one doing it. Between the alcohol I consumed tonight and the cloud nine feeling in my misted brain, I don't even register him unzipping my jeans. My body is burning for more.

Before I know what's happening, he's got his thumb on my clit, my eyes roll, and I moan. He puts his fingers close to my opening while his thumb is still blissfully circling my clit. My hips are moving with no thought when he slips a finger inside me. Oh, God, that's too good. I'm not sure what happens next because this feeling takes over, like a hard throb. It burns, and then it almost hurts.

My whole body is shaking, and my core convulses. I take in the feeling of these minor tremors that keep rippling through me. I've never felt this before.

Opening my eyes, I notice Drew is lying next to me, kissing my neck, and telling me how amazing I am. I must have passed out because I don't remember getting into his bed. Why is he smiling at me?

I feel his arms around me. He pulls me closer and cuddles me, whispering, "Get some sleep, Beauty. You've had enough tonight." Yawning, I stretch my body out. I'm enjoying the feeling running through my body, but I agree that I'm going to fall asleep. The last thing I remember is snuggling in tight and kissing Drew's neck.

DREW

19

DREW

As I wake up, I feel Stasia curled up against me, she's wearing nothing but my t-shirt. Right now, there's nowhere else I'd rather be. With her still in a deep sleep, I remain still, taking in every detail of her beauty. Etching her into my memory. Lifting my hand without thinking, I stroke her hair. A quiet moan releases from her soft lips. My dick twitches. Fuck, I need a cold shower.

Stasia is smiling, her eyes open slowly.

"What are you doing biker boy?"

Smiling back at her, I say, "Putting every mark, freckle, and dimple to memory. How'd you sleep, Beautiful?" Feeling her move, my eyes travel down her body. Watching as she arches backward, her breasts pressing against me. I reach around and gently grab her ass and squeeze a little.

Her moan sounds delicious. She nudges me back, "Gotta go to the bathroom." She whispers playfully. Shoving me gently, "Scoot over." She bounces out of bed and rushes to the toilet. I wrap my hand around my dick and squeeze firmly to take some pressure off. Argh! That feels too good. Getting up quickly, I try to keep busy to take my mind off of her. Hoping like fuck it will go away, but it's still standing as hard as a rock. I'm looking around the room for something to hide it. A cold shower is what I need right now. Stasia opens the door and stops in her tracks. It takes a minute before she leans casually on the door frame, watching me with a soft smile. Her eyes wander down, and I know the exact moment she sees my awkward situation. She seemed confident till her cheeks turn pink, and her eyes shoot to mine again. Her confidence is now gone.

"Umm, what are you doing?" She whispers. Her embarrassed pink cheeks have turned into a seductive look. Her eyes float down my body, not missing a centimetre, all the way to my dick. Her confidence is returning. My eyes stay focused on hers. My gaze follows her tongue, gliding along her lips. She can sense I'm losing self-control. Stasia sashays in my direction. I stumble over my words, not wanting to alarm her.

"I need to take care of this." Taking a quick glance down at my boxer briefs, I see I need that cold shower now. Raising my head, our eyes connect. Stasia is already in front of me. She's not saying anything, just focused on my hard dick. She drops to her knees and sits on her heels. I'm torn between walking straight past her, or letting her explore, knowing damn well this could go bad.

I don't get time to choose. She is pulling my boxers down. The anticipation is killing me, and she looks lost. Staring at it as if it's the first she has seen.

She puts her hand around me at the tip, and her hand moves down, feeling every vein, then back up to the tip. "Arghh ffuuuuuuck, that feels... fuck..." I close my eyes to enjoy the feeling. Trying not to scare her with my words. There is something warm

152

and wet around the tip. I slowly put my hand towards her head. At the last minute I remember what happened the last time I touched her there. It's a fucking miracle she's even doing this.. Everything is building. I'm gonna explode. I change the direction of my hand to gently glide the back of my fingertips down the side of her face. She pulls back and locks her eyes with mine and smiles.

"Tell me what to do?" This is another first for her.

"Babe, just keep doin' that." She smiles at me again, returning to what she was doing.

"Fuck... yes, that!" She puts the tip of her tongue around the head and then slides it through the slit of my dick. Holy fuck. I'm struggling to keep my hands to myself.
I watch her going back down my shaft and gliding her tongue underneath. The feeling becomes too much. I know I'm gonna cum. Shit, shit! I don't even get time to warn her. Cum spurts out. She must have known because she swallows and says something, but all I feel are the vibrations.

"Yes, fuck. Fuck!" I close my eyes, trying to rein it in and get some composure.

Once the ripples have stopped, I bend down, pick her up, and kiss her hard. Fuck, that felt good. Holy shit, I've never cum that fast! Pulling back, I look at her.

"Beautiful, you okay?" Nodding at me with a funny look on her face. I need to know what she's thinking.

"Babe, what are you thinking? Talk to me," I say, rubbing her back and soothing her as much as I can. Grabbing her chin to look at me, I see her cheeks turning pink. Why the fuck is she embarrassed? I'm the one who just came like a school kid seeing tits for the first time.

"Babe!" She's shaking her head.

"Drew, I've never done that. I mean, I've done some things, but you don't want to know that. They were scary. But I did it, I just did it! Wow, I did it and I'm feeling good. I think I'm good. Are you good? I mean, was it good for you? Wait... shit."

"Whoa, Beautiful, slow down." I chuckle. "I only got half of that, babe. Now, slow down and start from the beginning." I pull her over to the bed to straddle my hips. I want to make sure she's at eye level because half of what she said confused me big time. "Now, you asked, was it good? Babe, I wouldn't have cum that fast if it wasn't good, and I came fast like it was my first time, honey. So yeah, it was better than good.
Now, to the next bit. You haven't done it, but have done things and it was scary..." I'm stroking her hips with my thumbs, trying to keep her mind on me, but she buries her head into my shoulder, groaning.

"OH MY GOD, I can't believe I word vomited on you."

"Girl, look at me," she pulls back, looking at me. Studying her face for a minute. I notice the redness on Stasia's cheeks making her embarrassment more noticeable.

"I know we're fighting demons, and I know it's gonna be hard, but we are in this together, okay? Bit by bit, babe. Today's only about what you can give. But girl, I want something from what you said. We clear?

Nodding her head, she leans down again, saying, "I can't look at you though, okay?"

Allowing her to snuggle into my neck, I respond, "Yeah, babe, but I'm holding you. Deal?"

"Deal. Okay, well, a while ago I was sort of...no! Hold on. Okay, they forced me to do things a few times in my life, but that was a long time ago." Fuck, she has a death grip on me. Fuck. It takes all my control to stop my body from reacting right now. I know I need to keep calm.

"Babe, did you get help? Or did someone help you?" I know there's a shit ton more, I can feel it, but I can't push this or I'm gonna push her away.

"Yes. I bided my time. Eventually, one night, a group of people saved me." *Okay, Fuck!*

Searching my mind to figure out how to ask a question that will not push her too much, I come up with, "Can you tell me how old you were, Beautiful?" It feels like forever. I don't think she's going to answer. I'm about to change the subject and come back to this later, but she squeezes me and says, "The first time, I was ten. Can we talk about something else, please?" her voice is weak.

I hug her tight around her lower back, hoping like fuck it doesn't bring back any triggers. Shit. She pulls back, her eyes pleading with me. "I need a shower. Is that okay?"

I keep eye contact, but her gaze becomes glazed. "Yeah, babe, you did so good. That's enough for today. I'll go get us coffee." I watch her walk into the bathroom, and wait for her to close the door and turn the shower on. I grab the first thing I see and throw it at the door.

It breaks into a million pieces. I realise that she must of heard that. Shit. Stomping to the door, I swing it open. Prez and Mira are running my way. "Everything okay?" Prez asks, looking through the door and then back at me.

Shaking my head, I say, "We're good. Got some news, that's all." I don't want to tell people about Stasia's demons and lose her trust. Prez nods and turns back to walk toward the kitchen.

Mira asks, "Should I check on...?" She's pointing toward my room.

"Nah, Mira, this is for me. I've got her. Come help me make some coffee." Walking with me, we both follow the same way Prez went to get his coffee made.

Walking back to my room, Prez shouts out, "You and Bullet, two o'clock, in my office!" I give him a chin lift. He knows I'll get a hold of Bullet and we'll be there.

Stepping into my room, I see Stasia's all fresh now, fuck. What a sight!

"Baby, you are beautiful. Here, hope you like it. No sugar, just milk,"
Passing her the coffee, she smiles at me, takes a sip, then moans.

"That's amazing coffee. Yummy." Then she looks defeated, asking, "Um, Drew. I need to get home. I don't want Soph to worry."

I nod. "Yeah, Beautiful, we're gonna head out. You need food. We can pick it up on the way."

Nodding, she smiles, "Yes please, I'm so hungry."

"Ok then, let me take a shower, then we can get going." I lean over and kiss her head, then turn towards the bathroom to shower.

Sienna Gypsy

We pull up to Stasia's place with Maccas breakfast for everyone. We even got enough for Bullet, seeing as how I didn't see him at the clubhouse. *Lucky, 'cause guess what? There's his truck! Hah! I knew something was going on.* I'm smiling to myself.

Looking at Stasia, I see she is staring at Bullet's truck too, she turns to me and says, "Well, I wasn't expecting that." My eyes widen as I tilt my head. "What?" I shrug my shoulders. But the smile on my face gives it away. Stasia giggles, pointing at the truck like it's saying something. Which it does. With the smirk I can't hide, I'm sure she guesses correctly

"He took her home last night. Probably wanted to make sure she was safe. That's all." I shrug, then I get out of my truck, grabbing all the food we bought.

"Come on, Beauty, let's go see Keata!"

Walking in the front door, the place is quiet. We walk to the kitchen and put the food on the bench. There is no one in the living area of the house. No Sophie, no Keata, and definitely no Bullet. Moving to sit at the table I watch Stasia walking to her room.

She turns and looks over her shoulder at me she says, "I'll just get changed and see if Keata's awake." I nod, pull out my phone and send a quick text to Bullet, so he knows we are here.

I sit down and dig into my food straight away. I see Stasia coming back into the kitchen, looking a bit worried, "What's up, babe?" She's chewing on her bottom lip, which I've noticed is a tell for her. She does this a lot when she's unsure.

"Keata's not up yet, which isn't normal. She's always up by now. She looks peaceful, but I'm not sure. Something's not right." As she finishes her sentence, Bullet comes into the kitchen. He's alone, with his jeans on, rubbing his head.

"Thought you two would be out later."

"Nah, Stasia wanted to get back. She was worried about Sophie, so we bought breakfast for everyone." He's smiling then walks over to pick up his egg and bacon McMuffin.

"Cool. How was last night?" biting into his muffin and eying both me and Stasia.

"It was good. Things ran smoothly. How about here?" I'm smiling like I won the lottery, trying to get him to spill.

"Yeah, good. Soph was upset about something you said. I've fixed it, so all is good now." Wait, what?

Glaring at Bullet I ask, "What? What did I say?"

"Fill you in later. So, Stasia, does Keata normally sleep this long?" Stasia shakes her head no. We all go in her room. As we pass, Sophie comes out.

"What's going on?"

Stasia is the first to tell her, "Keata hasn't woken up yet. It's eleven-thirty a.m."
Sophie runs past us all, bursting through the door to Keata's room. Keata is shaking all over the place. Fuck, Sophie and Stasia run to the bed. Stasia puts her on her side and Sophie clears everything away that can hurt her. She looks at Stasia.

"How long you reckon?"

Stasia shakes her head, saying, "I came in about four minutes ago. She wouldn't wake up, Soph."

Sophie nods her head before saying, "Stasia, call 000." I grab my phone and give it to Stasia. Bullet is just watching patiently, seeing what he can do. I watch Stasia make the call to 000.

I wait for Stasia to finish and tell us what to do, "They're sending an ambulance. Should be here in twenty minutes." Bullet walks out. Before long he's back with a bucket. I'm wondering what the fuck that's for. Before long, the poor kid vomits. *Shit.* "Put her in a recovery position," He demands, as he walks towards the hallway to get a facecloth. He puts it on Keata's forehead, which is hard cause she's jolting everywhere.

Sophie sings a lullaby and Stasia joins in. Before I know it, Keata slows her jolting movements, and then she stops.

Bullet looks at his watch, saying, "Five minutes, is that usual, Soph?" Sophie shakes her head, and so does my girl. Stasia is the first to answer,

"No, only the bad ones last that long."

"Ok," says Bullet as he's walking out the door again.

I follow, "Hey, what are you doing?"

"She'll be staying in hospital after that, so I'm gonna get their bags organised so she can be ready to go." Blowing out a big breath, I walk with him to Sophie's bedroom and help him pack. When we're nearly finished packing, we can hear the ambulance coming down the road, so I head to the front door and open it.

The ambo's make their way directly to Keata's room, asking questions about what's happened as we walk.
Sophie answers them as we enter, knowing the drill. It all happens so fast.

Now I'm watching them load her up in the ambulance. My mind is racing with concern. Little Keata looks so helpless.

Bullet grabs the bag and asks, "You two coming with me, or are you driving there, Drew?"

"I'll drive. Come on, Stasia, let's go."
We all head to the hospital after the ambulance.

We're sitting in the emergency waiting room, no one telling us what's going on is driving me crazy. Stasia's rocking in her chair. I'm about to put her in my lap, hoping that will calm us both. Bullet is pacing, looking like he's going to murder someone.

I look at Stasia and ask, "This happen often, babe?" She nods. Then shakes her head. Then nods again. Jesus, which is it?

Sophie walks out.

"She'll be ok, she is comatose at the moment from the seizures. She must have had them all night. They're going to check for any infections, or other things that could cause the seizures. She'll be in a room soon, but you guys can go. I'm fine. We'll be fine, Stasia. I will need some clothes, though." As Stasia opens her mouth, Bullet says, "I've got them in the truck. I'm staying." Sophie smiles a half-smile but shakes her head.

"Honestly, Bullet, we're fine, thanks." Bullet walks over to her and puts his arms around her. Embracing her close, he whispers something in her ear and kisses her temple.

As he walks away, he tells me, "Come on, brother, we're on coffee and food." Well, fuck me!

After we grab the clothes, we head to the coffee shop in the hospital. I pull my phone out and send a text to Prez, letting him know where we are.

ME: *At the hospital, Soph's little one had a seizure, not sure how long.*

Looking at Bullet, I fill him in, "Prez told me before, he wanted us at his office by 2 p.m. I just texted him what's going on."

"Yeah, I'm not leaving till Keata's awake."

"Yeah, I figured." My phone buzzes, so I look down and read.

PREZ: *I'll be there at 2. Need to talk.... Hope the girls are good. I'll let Mira know.*

Bullet is reading over my shoulder, so he knows what's going on, it must be important if he's coming here.

Sitting in Keata's room, it takes about one and a half hours. Fuckin' hospitals.

I'm in a chair with Stasia on my lap. Sophie is on the bed with Keata, and Bullet is on the other side of me.
We are all waiting quietly for Keata to wake up. A knock at the door causes us all to turn. In walks Prez and Mira, with a big soft teddy.

Soph's the first to talk, "Oh, thank you guys, but no need to come. She'll wake when she's ready, then we'll go home." What the fuck? She must be in shock or something. Mira runs around the bed and wraps her in a big hug. That's when Sophie lets it all go. She sobs into Mira. Bullet goes to stand next to them, puts his hand to her head and whispers something in her ear. Sophie nods and Mira smiles, then she looks at Prez.

"Dad, can you get some coffee?" I stand up with Stasia in my arms, then place her on the chair and kiss her on the lips, soft and slow. Then, all us guys leave the room.

Prez speaks first, "How are the girls holding up and how is our new princess doing?"

"They're hanging in there, but they've only had each other since they met, and no one before that." Bullet nods his head, agreeing with me. He looks like he has more information, too.
I look at Prez.

"So, what's the other reason you came here?" Getting out his phone, he hands it to Bullet first. Bullet swears, then passes it to me.

"Fuck, when was this taken?" Prez is shaking his head. "I'm thinking the family BBQ, seeing as it's a picture of your girl." Shuffling through the other photos there is Izzy as well, I look at both brothers.

"They're planning something, and it has to do with my girl and Izzy." Fuck, my girl has enough demons to last a lifetime. Bullet looks at us, shaking his head.

"What if there's a connection? Maybe the girls know each other or something?"

Shaking my head. "Nah, they met for the first time the other day before the BBQ. Stasia does have demons and I'm only starting to understand them."

Both nod their heads in agreement. We arrive at the café and get the coffee and snacks for the girls.

As we are on our way back, Prez adds, "Drew, you need to find out if her demons are anything to do with Izzy's."

"Or, we need to find out who has it in for these two girls," Bullet adds.

Nodding, we push through the doors with unease in our guts and sit with the girls while they comfort Sophie.

STASIA

20

STASIA

W alking through the front door of my house, I can feel the weight of the day pulling me down. I'm ready for bed. I can't believe the weekend I've had, or the shit we've all gone through. And poor Keata's still not awake yet from her seizure. Hopefully, she will wake up tonight or tomorrow.

Hearing the door lock behind me, Drew walks up and wraps his arms around my waist. God, that feels good. He turns me around and kisses me senseless. I didn't think I was up for this, but my mind seems to shut down and I take in the feeling. And boy, does that make me feel better. Pulling back, he smiles at me.

"Better, Beauty?"

"Yeah, thank you. I need a shower and sleep." I untangle us and start for the bathroom. Getting lost in my thoughts of the day, I swing the door to the bathroom closed but it bounces off something. I turn around, stunned, to see Drew standing there.

"What are you doing?" He swaggers my way slowly, like he's scared I'm going to run. Shit, maybe I will. The butterflies in my stomach are flying around like crazy. A sexy as sin smile appears on his face, and I feel a throb down in the never-neverland.

"Babe, I've wanted you alone since this morning. Now, I want to enjoy you." Shit. We never talked about what we got up to, or what I told him. I'm shaking, but I can't tell if it's from fear or excitement. He must notice because he put his arms around me and kisses me.

"Babe, you've cum on my hand, and I've cum in your mouth, which is the highlight of our time so far. Now, beautiful, I want you to cum in my mouth." I can feel the heat rising on my cheeks.

"Jesus, is that even possible?" I shake my head, trying to think of something else. He chuckles, nodding at me slowly. Shit, I said that out loud. How embarrassing. I want to run away.

"Stasia, this is me and you, babe. Don't get embarrassed. Come on, arms up."

I feel his fingertips on my hips as he takes off my top. The sensation is hypnotic. His fingers slide up and over my body, to my head. Then it's gone. My eyes are closed, and I'm trying to predict what's next. As his fingers touch my waist, I jump, not expecting the skin-to-skin touch. His hands slide up to the edge of my bra and back down again. I'm lost in all the sensual feelings that are erupting in my mind. Then, his hands are at my shorts as he undoes the button at the front. I open my eyes and there he is, staring right back, beckoning my soul closer to his. In an instant, I decide his clothes are coming off. I fumble trying to undo the button on his jeans, fiddling with the zip till it jerks down. I jump back in shock.

I wasn't expecting him not to have any boxers on. Shit! I'm holding my chest, feeling like an idiot. Hearing his burst of laughter, great. I glare back at him.

"Look, let me have a shower, please." I've had it. I'm jumpy anyway, but with everything that's happened lately, no wonder I'm skittish. Drew says nothing, he brings me close and holds me for a bit, but I can still hear him chuckling under his breath. I don't find it funny.

Pulling away, I point at the door and say to him, "Out. I'm tired, embarrassed and uncomfortable. You know this is new for me and you are still laughing at me, so out." Trying to push him away, he pulls me closer.

"Beauty. I'm laughing cause only you would jump and get scared when my dick comes out, and the look on your face was priceless. I love that about you. Now come on, let me help." Turning my back to him, I'm not letting him see shit. I turn on the water in the shower then take off my bra, keeping my arm over my chest, so he can't see. When I'm naked, I jump in and grab the washcloth to cover my lower private area. I know I'm being stupid but so be it!

Drew doesn't seem to care, because he gets in and grabs the washcloth, which scares me, so I scream.

He grabs the soap, positioning me so that my back rests against his front, and begins to wash me. I'm not sure what to think, but it feels soothing.

"Is that nice?" he whispers with his lips at my ear, which is giving me goosebumps. He tells me what he's going to do.

"I'm going to wash you clean, Beauty, so I can dirty you up; just relax and enjoy." I lean further into him and let him go for it. Before long, I'm so limp in his arms that I don't even flinch when he washes or kneads my breasts. It feels right. My nipples pebble from his touch. The swelling of my breasts makes them incredibly sensitive. The urge to put my hands over his to play with them is uncontrollable. I can't stop the moan that comes from my mouth as he pinches the tip of my nipple.

"You like that, Beauty?"

"Mmmm," I'm at a loss for words, my mind is numb. Then, his hand gently travels downward, lower and lower. Oh, God, I'm throbbing so badly. Drew creates feelings that I never thought were possible. He finds my clit and starts rubbing in circles. I can't take much more. I can feel something strong pulling on the inside of me at my core.

"Shit, I can't... I can't.... oh, God..." Then everything goes white. The white turns into fuzzy colours that explode in my mind. My legs are buckling, and I feel like I'm going to collapse.

Drew's arms tighten around me. "I got you, Beautiful." In the next breath, he whispers, "Shit, you respond fast!" Before I know what's happening, I'm being picked up and placed on my bed and I'm dry. How the hell did that happen?

Looking up at Drew, my lips curling in a seductive way. "Oh, that was good. You have magic hands." I close my eyes and I'm drifting into darkness. I fall into a beautiful, blissful sleep.

I feel like I'm in a cocoon, warm, and restricted. Shit, where am I? Trying to get free, someone grabs my hips. I freeze. Please, no. I hear Drew's voice, and my panic subsides.

"Beautiful, it's me. I got you, babe. You good?" I tilt my head in agreement and sit up slightly. Letting out a sigh of relief, thank God!

"Babe, I need to ask you something." Looking at him, I nod to tell him to ask, but I'm worried this is going to hurt.

"Okay, so what you dreamt about just now, can the person that did this to you come back and affect you in any way?" Shit, of all the questions, he has to go back here. I look everywhere but him.

"Babe, look at me." It takes me a minute to build the courage.

Slowly, I look up, asking, "What?"

He leans in and kisses me on the corner of my mouth and says, "One day at a time, Beauty, but I've got to ask."

Nodding, I say, "Maybe, I'm not sure. He's not dead or anything, but I did change my identity, so if they find me...." He cuts me off.

"Babe, you're with me. No one is going to get to you. Please trust me, okay? I got you!" Not trusting the safety I feel around me, I reply with the truth.

"God, I hope so. I don't know what they will do if they find me." Drew holds me tighter.

"So, that's a maybe. It's a start. Do you have a name for me? Maybe a first or last or maybe a suburb? I know I'm pushing, but this will be the last question today, promise." I don't know what to tell him. If I tell him, and they show up... My heart starts to race from the fear of what could come. Breathe, you can do this!

"My fake name.... is Stasia Jones... My real name is.....
Anastasia.... shit I can't… Ummm… I come from... Melbourne... I
got away ... like I said before, people helped me… I was safe for a
bit. I got a fake ID. T-then I needed to run again." That's all he gets
today. I can't say any more.

"You did good, babe, really good. No more questions today, I
promise. Now, you want breakfast?"

Nodding, I say, "Yeah, but can we get it on the way? I need to
see Keata." Suddenly, I feel a slap on my ass. Shit, that stung.

"Hurry up Beauty, we got us a princess to wake," he says with a
genuine smile.

Arriving back at the hospital, I'm feeling rejuvenated. I don't know
if it's being with Drew, or just that I'm finding myself again. Or
maybe because of the feeling of someone knowing who I am for
the first time. Coming up to Keata's door, we hear chatter. I pick up
my pace and rush into the room, and the most beautiful little girl is
looking at me with a huge smile. My heart melts. I rush over and
give her the biggest cuddle, but she wants to look around me when
I pull back. She is reaching out to Drew, that little flirt. He smirks
at me and picks Keata up. He's careful not to move the drip in her
arm from the fluid they are giving her. They both breathe in when
he presses his nose to hers.

I see Sophie taking a deep breath and then she says, "She does
that with Bullet, too. She has taken to you guys." I can see the
worry in Sophie's eyes. Normally everyone leaves. She's been left
on her own, except for me. I've been with Soph since I came to
town.

Sienna Gypsy

It's been three years since Nanna Sally sent me away. Trouble was coming up the driveway and she sent me out the back of the house. She taught me for years how to get away. What path to take, who to contact, and where to head to. She always said, when she could, she'd come and find me. When it was safe. It hasn't happened yet. I worry, what if something happened to Nanna Sally? Is Cobra okay? I've been wanting to ask Drew if he knows Cobra, or of him. I never knew the MC's name. But what if they are enemies? What if they don't know each other? Then I'll cause more problems.

Shaking the thought out of my head, I realise my memories have crept up on me. I see everyone is packed up and ready to go. Shit, I must have daydreamed for a while.

Drew comes up and kisses me on the temple, then says in my ear, "You okay, Beauty?"

I nod and smile, and reply, "Daydreaming." He winks at me and squeezes my butt, then goes to gather what's left. Both guys take everything to the truck, leaving Soph, Keata and I. Sophie comes over and sits with me. I put my arm around her to comfort her. She has tears in her eyes.

She takes a deep breath, then says, "I don't know if I can do this, open me and Keata up to be crushed. Because, Stasia, I won't be able to pick up the pieces this time!"
I give her a big hug, squeeze them both tight, and tell her the truth.

"Sometimes you need to trust your heart, and trust the person holding it. 'Cause, honey, I can see he wants this for good, not just for the minute. He's not Keata's dad, honey, and he's not scared of getting his hands dirty. I've seen that, he takes control but lets you lead the way. Soph, promise me you will take it slow and see what happens. You will know if it's not right. So will Keata. Tell him you need time to learn to trust again."

She nods, then says, "How did you know? I haven't told you anything."

"Sophie, I wouldn't be a very good friend if I couldn't see what was going on. I know you, you're the closest thing to family I've got and I'm not going anywhere." She squeezes me back and dries her eyes.

"Come on, let's go before the guys think we need to be admitted." I giggle at myself. Soph hates attention and Bullet won't let her off the hook if he thinks she's upset. I love that about these two. They're both the same in that way. We both walk down the hall of the hospital, hand in hand. Making our way home.

Sienna Gypsy

DREW

2I

DREW

Arriving at the girls' house, my phone vibrates in my pocket. Reaching in, I pull it out and see a message from Prez.

PREZ: *Settle girls, then get back here. We have updates.*

ME: *Yeah, we'll be there soon.*

As we walk in the door, Sophie goes and puts Keata down for a bit. Keata fell asleep in the car and is still asleep now, poor kid. Stasia says this is normal. I can't help but think there has to be a new normal for this little princess. I watch Stasia put the coffee on.

Looking at Bullet, I walk over and say, "We have about fifteen minutes. Prez wants us ASAP." Bullet nods, heading down towards Keata's room.

I turn and see Stasia still in the same position. She's fussing with the coffee cups. I lean against the doorway, watching her quietly. She stops and starts banging her head on the cupboard. I can't stand watching her do this, so I walk up behind her, putting my arms around her. She's crying. I turn her around and look into her eyes. She's sobbing now. Using my thumbs, I wipe away the tears that stream down her face.

"Beauty, I got you. What's wrong?" holding her face in my hands I watch as her brows furrow and her lip's part slightly. Stasia's eyes convey a sense of struggle, but no words come out.

I keep soothing her with my hand running down her cheek. Until she replies, "I don't know. Everything is catching up to me, I think. It's not me though, it's Sophie and Keata. This is her normal. How has no one ever helped her? This is too much for her to do alone!" She blurts out.

"Stasia, honey, she has you. She is not alone. And she now has me and the club. I won't allow anyone that is a part of you to get hurt. She is family to you, Beauty, so I'm here to help, babe." She nods, wiping her face. I observe her walk over to the kitchen sink, her steps heavy with emotion as she washes her face. Feeling reluctant to part from her at this moment, but knowing I need to get to the clubhouse, I tell her I have to go for a while. She nods and smiles at me. Looking like she needs the space. Stasia turns away. I stop her by going in for another hug, and I kiss her on the lips. The kiss was supposed to be quick. Stasia turns it into a soft, sensual kiss. Now I really don't want to go anywhere. I want to stay in this moment, but I pull away, and we stare at each other. Lost in our bubble, unaware of how long we stood there, we're startled when Bullet comes in and says, "Meet ya out front?"

Giving Stasia another kiss, I tell her, "I'll be back later" I turn and strut towards the door. Walking through it, I close the door behind me.

Getting on my bike, I reflect on how crazy it is that my life has changed so much in such a short period of time.

Arriving back at the club, both Bullet and I go straight for Prez's office, knowing he'll be waiting for us.

Opening the office door, Prez is sitting, looking at something on his computer. Plus, there's a man in the corner who I haven't seen for a long time.

He gets up and comes to me, "Son, it's been too long"

"Dad, how have you been?" I walk to him. We embrace each other in an enormous bear hug. It's been years since we've seen each other, we talk from time to time but that's about it. Since he took over the president spot in the Melbourne charter, his visits have been limited. That position was supposed to be temporary until they found someone suitable. But they want Dad, or Cobra, as his brothers know him, and he's stayed there ever since.

"So, son, they say you've found a girl. Do I get to meet her while I'm here?" Well, shit! I guess he will.

"Yeah, Dad, but she and her friend have been through a bit. I'll talk to her. She might invite you to her place, or maybe I can steal her from home and we can do dinner."

"She doesn't come to the club? What? She doesn't like it here?"

"No, nothing like that. But you'll get it when you meet her. Her name is Stasia Jones." Now I know she has another name, but I don't know her surname yet, her hidden one, at least. She still hasn't shared, so I'll wait till she's ready to share. At the moment, she has a lot going on. She doesn't need me pushing any more than I have.

Dad accepts that and says, "Looking forward to it, son. Now, down to business. You filled them in yet, Prez?" My dad just shakes his head. Even though he's the Prez at his own charter now, he still respects our Prez, or Slash, which no one has called him in years. Prez just stuck when he took over, so the newer members probably don't even know that's his first road name.

"Nah, the boys have been with their girls at the hospital, so this is the first I've seen them, but they know about the others."

"This is about those pictures that were sent?" I ask. How the hell does dad know about this? Dad looks at Bullet, then at me, and nods.

"Yeah, I've been getting them too. The first girl that came through made no sense to me, but the other girl, I need to find her. Prez said you might know something about her?"

As I'm about to answer, Bullet's phone rings. He looks at me then answers, I can hear screaming down the line then Bullet cuts in.

"Sophie, calm down. Who took her? Okay, we will be there. Give me fifteen minutes. Sit with Keata. We won't be very long." He doesn't have to tell me who's been taken. I'm up and out the door with everyone in the room following me. Bullet is filling them in. I don't care what he's saying, I've got to get there.

I'm on the road, getting to the intersection, the one where I hit Stasia when we first met. This van does a total 180 and my gut tells me it's her. I roll the throttle back and everyone behind me follows. The van tries everything to get away from us, but I get up alongside the driver's side and see he's not alone. There are four of them in there, all with balaclavas on. Fuck.

There are only four of us on bikes. As I'm figuring out how to save her, Bullet shoots the front tire with his gun. The van swerves side to side. Bullet looks at me, prompting me to slow down and get out of the way. Then signals to the guys to do the same.

The van swerves to my side, then over to Bullet's, towards a T intersection. Everything goes in slow motion from there. Our bikes slow down, but the van doesn't. Before I know it, the van hits the sign at the T intersection and goes straight over the top into the bushes and flips. I skid to a stop at the edge of the road. I get off my bike and run after the van. Fuck, the only thing going through my mind is *nothing can happen to her.* Not now, NOT THE FUCK EVER!

Once the van stops rolling, I get in close and try to pull open the back door. The front door flies open and one of the guys who was inside the van fires at me.

My dad is there and shoots back at the guy that's shooting at me. Hearing a scream, I go for the door again, then another one comes out. His gun is pointed at me, but Dad and Bullet are there with their guns, pointing at his head.

Then, Prez points his gun at the driver. He's unconscious, and the guys in the balaclavas decide to give up. Dad and Bullet still have their guns on the guy in front of me, so I move him out of the way. I pull the door back and see Stasia. She's unconscious as well. So is the guy next to her. I don't care about him. I need her out of there. I grab her, with one arm under her knees and the other under her arms, cradling her closer to my chest.

Pulling her free of the van, I find somewhere to put her down and keep her head on my legs. My Dad comes over and looks at her. He crouches down and wipes the hair from her face, then his eyebrows lift, "This is your girl?"

"Yeah, this is my girl, Dad. Not how I wanted her to meet you, but yeah, this is Stasia."

Looking at her, she's breathing fine, but she's out of it like she's drugged or something.

Dad runs the back of his hand over her cheek and says, "Little Bird, you still getting into trouble?" If I wasn't sitting, I'd fall on my ass. It can't be. I look at Dad, then back at Stasia. FUCK!

"Dad, I didn't know!" Jesus, but I should have! All her nightmares and skittish behaviour. he's been missing for over three years, after what Frazer's guys did to Nanna Sally. Did she know, or did she get away in time and not know anything?

Dad smiles at me and says, "Chill boy, she's a good girl, you never met her, but your Nanna loved her. She'd be happy." I shake my head, not sure where everything is standing right now. She moans and I pull her tighter on my lap. I might not be sure what's happening, but I am sure about her.

She opens her eyes, whispers the name Cobra, then slips back into unconsciousness.

Prez calls it in to the club so they can get things under control before the cops show up. He's called a prospect to pick us up in a car and Knight to come and ride my bike back. Plus, another van for all these guys who took Stasia, so we can get some answers.

Sienna Gypsy

STASIA

22

STASIA

I thought I was dreaming.... *Cobra?* He can't be here. I fall into a haze where I can hear people talking, but my brain can't make sense of what they're saying. I drift back into a deep sleep.

I wake up in a room. I'm not sure where I am ... it looks familiar... is it Drew's room? My head is pounding. What the hell happened? I search my memories; a few images start to flash through. A man in a balaclava, Keata screaming, then Soph grabbing Keata. Oh, my God, what have I done? I can't be in Drew's room. Shit, did Cobra grab me? Oh, no. I try to get up, but my body won't cooperate. SHIT! I can feel a darkness in my mind that's pulling me back to sleep.

Hearing the door open, I try to open my eyes. It takes a minute, but I get them to open and see Cobra walk in with Drew behind him. Oh, God, I hope Drew is okay.

"Cobra, he is my... Shit, something.... but he's good to me! Please don't hurt him!" He smiles and sits next to me while Drew folds his arms in front of him, staring and shaking his head. They look so similar, but why?

Cobra bends down and kisses my forehead, then tells me, "Little Bird, I can't believe you were right under my nose and I couldn't find you. You might not know this, but you found my son. I can't believe you two found each other." I just stare at him. *Wait, what?* What did he just say?

"W-what?" The look on my face must alarm Drew. I'm freaking out right now. The man who took me in, looked after me and whose mother cared for me is my new... Oh, my God, what is Drew to me, my man? Boyfriend? Friend? I don't know what we are, shit.

"Beauty, calm down, you're hyperventilating. Breathe girl, in through your nose, out through your mouth." He does the action with me.

"That's it, Beauty. I got you."

I must have been out of it for a bit, 'cause I'm on Drew's lap and he's soothing me. I can't think when he's this close to me, but I need his words right now. Selfish, I know. So, I nod and hope for sleep to take me again.

I wake up curled around a hard wall of… I freeze, shit it's Drew. I try to unfurl myself from him, but he holds me firmly. I don't know how long I've been out for.

"Beauty, you're not going anywhere, now lay still. How are you feeling? Is your head still sore?" Nodding and having nothing else to say, I try to break free again. We can't do this, we are too close. He's my... shit… stepbrother of sorts. Shit… *Shit!*

Shaking my head back and forth, I tell him, "Drew, w- we can't do this. I- I'm like your stepsister... shit, you need to let me go." I am pushing hard against his chest, but he is not listening to me. Bloody men.

He chuckles, his strong chest moving and his deep voice owning me. "Stasia, we are far from being related, and we never knew each other. Dad is happy for us, Stasia. He's been looking for you since.. .." He pinches his lips together and stops speaking.

Curious, I ask, "Since what?" I need to know, so I push more. "Since I left? Nanna Sally, where is she? She said she'd come and she hasn't. Where is she?" He gathers me up and starts rocking me and shushing me. I'm a mess. Whimpering like a little baby. God, I'm so confused. Why me? *WHY?*

"Beauty, one thing at a time. Let's talk about what you remember. About when you were taken just now. How many men did you see?"

Not wanting to talk about this and wanting to know more about what happened to Nanna Sally, I answer, "Just one, he stabbed me in the neck with something sharp, then I saw Keata scream, and Sophie came to get her. Shit, are they okay? Where are they? Drew, they need to be okay. Shit, can't get any worse." I'm crying again, I need to get up, I need to find them. Oh my God, what have I done?

"Stasia, they're fine. They are here. Bullet put them in his room to rest. You guys are safe. I told you I won't let anything happen to you or your family."

"I need to see them, Drew." Feeling frantic, knowing I need to leave if this is about me. Jesus, if this is my father. Oh, God, no! I can't get these people hurt. I need to run again so no one will get hurt.

Drew is still rocking me and trying to comfort me, he's rubbing my back and I whisper this time, "I need to see them. Please." The last part comes out so desperately.

"Beauty, they will be in soon. I promise. Just hold me and cry, girl, let it all out and I will text Bullet to send the girls in when you're good, okay?" He's right, I don't want the girls to see me like this. I need to be strong! So, I do just that. I cry my heart out for everything I've found and for everything I'm going to miss, because I can't expect these guys to sacrifice even more for me. It's too much to ask of anyone.

I must've cried myself to sleep, because I feel small hands in mine. I open my eyes to Keata. She is staring at me with wonder.

Sophie speaks, "She has been so upset. When Bullet brought us here, she saw you, and now she won't leave your side. Drew tried to get her to bed, but she screamed." My gaze connects with Sophie's fingers while she's fiddling with them. Our eyes lock, she continues, "There is a meeting at the moment, but I'm supposed to knock on the door three times, so he knows you're awake. Fuck, Stasia, what happened? Did you know those men?"

"No, I don't think so," I say, shaking my head slowly. "I was in shock, but I only saw one guy. The one that stabbed me with something sharp." Shuddering, my hand goes to where I was stabbed with a needle. "I thought I was going to die at first, then this light headedness feeling took over." My eyes fill with tears, and I look away. "I'm sorry I brought that to your door, Sophie. Please forgive me," I plead, my voice breaking. "I would kill myself if something happened to Keata." Reaching out, I pull Keata into a hug and it doesn't take long for Sophie to join in.

We are still hugging when a bunch of people walk in. Prez, Cobra, Drew, Bullet, and I think Knight. He smiles and says, "Can anyone join in, or is it only girl-on-girl action today?" I turn to look at him and laugh because I know he's joking. He has to be.

Drew and Bullet both slap him upside the head and say in unison, "Off-limits, dipshit!" This makes Sophie laugh and pull away. I smile too. I can't help it, but the men look worried.

I turn to Cobra and ask, "What's going on? Tell me!"

Cobra moves forward, but Drew grabs him, "Dad, she's mine, I'll deal with this."

Cobra shakes his head saying, "Son, I know you want to, but this part needs to come from me. You can take the part where you come into her life."

Drew takes a deep breath then sighs, saying, "Yeah, but let me get next to her. She's gonna need me." Goosebumps wash over me as he picks up Keata and puts her on his lap. Then his arm comes around me and pulls me in, the comfort that he cages around me feels good. Feeling like I have some strength, I turn to look at Cobra. He is sitting on the other side of my bed, and he grabs one of my hands as well. Do they think I'm gonna run? Well, I might, but they don't know that, or do they? With that thought in my head, I hear Cobra's next words.

"Little Bird, I don't know what they told you about your father, or what Nanna Sally told you about him, but he was behind that explosion at the clubhouse that night we rescued you. I know Nanna Sally taught you stuff to survive if anything like that happened again. She didn't tell anyone, including me. Which is why I was still looking for you and hoping your father never got ahold of you again. I thought he had, till recently. I got a photo of you at this clubhouse, but I wasn't sure what you were doing here, so I made my way over here. Krip too. If you were a club girl, he was ready to kick your ass. He's eager to see you, been doing the back checks of all the club girls to see if he could find you that way. Anyway, Drew here won't let him in yet." Oh, my God, Krip is here? I need to see him.

So, I tell Cobra, "Bring him in!"

Drew growls, "Beauty, NO! He's not coming in here once you're up and about, you can..."

Before Drew can finish his sentence, Krip bursts through the door, saying," I knew you'd see me, Little Bird." Cobra moves out of the way as Krip barges over to me. I pull away from Drew and jump into Krip's arms, hugging him tightly. He was my overbearing security guard for years. If I'm honest with myself, he was my brother of sorts. Drew can't stop him from seeing me right now. Oh, my God, I can't believe he's here. All other thoughts leave me for now.

"God, I missed you!" I say, pulling back, but he's not looking at me. He's staring at Drew like he's going to rip his head off. Drew reaches forward and grabs my hand pulling me into him. Shit, these two are going to fight.

"Krip." I contemplate what I should say next. I don't know what to call Drew, but he's adamant about me. So I go for gold, hoping I don't get it wrong.

"He's my...." And then Drew blurts it out for me.

"Boyfriend, I'm her boyfriend!" Ok so I didn't have to go for gold, he did it for me.

"Yes, my boyfriend, we've been seeing each other for a while now. Well, it's fast, but it seems like a while!" I finish saying while shrugging my shoulders.

Krip nods, "My priority is you, Little Bird. If you're okay, I won't worry. If he treats you like shit, I'll kick his ass." I cringe at Krip's words and Drew laughs in my ear, then sizes him up.

"I don't treat her like shit."

Krip's lips kick up in a smirk, he bends down and kisses me on the top of my head, "Good!" When he goes to leave, he turns and gives me his parting words, "I'm not going anywhere, Little Bird, so you are safe with all of us by your side. I know you want to run, but don't. Trust us, okay?" With that bomb dropped, he leaves the room.

And I'm left wondering how the hell he knows I want to run. *Shit!*

DREW

23

DREW

K rip wasn't lying when he said they had history, but what sort of history did they have? I pull Stasia closer to me. I need her close now. Krip has pissed me off, big time! I told him not to come into that room. But no, he couldn't wait to see her. Maybe it's just me, but I can't stand the thought of anyone near Stasia. Even my dad is making me angry.

I know my dad has daughter or niece feelings for her because Nanna Sally had adopted her for a while, until she told Stasia to run. Stasia doesn't even know what happened to Nanna yet. Something is telling me this will hurt her more than anything.

I must have been in my own head 'cause when I decide to look up, only Dad, Sophie and Keata are in the room.
Keata is still curled around me, but Sophie bends down, picking

Keata up, "I'm going to take Keata to Bullet's room." Keata goes into her arms quietly, which pulls at my heart.

Dad stays, but he has something to say. I hope Stasia isn't faking sleep because I don't want her to know just yet about everything.

No such luck, Dad wakes her and says, "Stasia, wake up girl. I need this out before it gets too bad, and shit gets twisted." Dad always had a way with words. Shit, I don't want her to hear this, so I pull her even closer, if that's possible.
She nods that she's ready and I grind my teeth.

"So, Stasia, what do you remember about the day Nanna Sally told you to go?"

"Not much. She told me to do as practised, and that she would catch up or see me when she knew it was safe, so that's what I did."

"And when was that? Do you remember the day or the month, and what exactly did she tell you? It's important, Little Bird, it will help." Stasia takes a bit to answer, so I rub her back to comfort her. She clears her throat and starts.

"I can't remember the day, but I'm sure it was in May. She'd been teaching me to shoot and showing me safe places. She even gave me this fake ID that had a new name and date of birth so people would think I was an adult. She told me it was my father that blew up the clubhouse about a year after you dropped me there. She also told me that you didn't want me to know because I'd been through enough. She said you thought I'd run... I may have, if it didn't come from her. She made me feel like she needed me, so running wasn't an option." Damn, Nanna was smart, and she's right. Stasia craves people needing her, and to be independent at the same time. Dad just nods, willing her to say more.

"I remember a phone call she said was from you, which always put a smile on her face. It wasn't long before she noticed a car creeping down the driveway. She dialled one of her friends that came over from time to time. She told him to get here now. I still remember it like it was yesterday, she put the phone down and said, 'Pack that bag girly, today is the day you run!'" Stasia looks down at her thumbs and circles them at a mesmerising pace, like she is nervous to go on. Looking up through her lashes, she adds, "She reassured me that she will catch up and not to worry. I knew the drill and to trust myself. I had four safe houses to get to. Two of them had people Nanna Sally knew, the other two places would be empty. Which at the time, scared the shit out of me, but she was right. I was fine. She had a note for me to read. The note had instructions and money so I could get started." Again, she gazes down at her thumbs, their rapid movements serving as a distraction from the harsh reality of the situation.

"I was supposed to stop a town over from here, but when I got here, I couldn't leave. I got my job straight away, and met Sophie. We became fast friends, and I helped with Keata. I got my own place, and things fell into place easily." Her tears stream down her face. My dad is the first to comfort her.

"Okay, it's okay, Little Bird, you're doing great. Do you know why Nanna Sally never came?"

Shaking her head, "No, I thought it wasn't safe. Just recently, I was going to move again, but Sophie… I don't know, maybe I just needed a reason to stay. No, I don't know what happened. Please say she's okay!" Stasia sobs. I have a feeling she knows deep down, but she didn't let her thoughts go there. Dad squeezes her hand, and she looks up at him.

"Little Bird, Nanna Sally died protecting you. She left me a note saying that I should find you. But she didn't say where you would be. She also said to make sure you knew she loved you like her own and she would do it all again. Do not blame yourself, because she'll haunt your ass. The last thing she said in the note to remind you that this is what family does and don't you forget it!" Dad winks at Stasia, but her gaze remains fixed on the wall. My focus is fixated on her silent tears that continue to stream down her face. It's uncertain what Stasia has taken in.

She says nothing for a long time. After a bit, Dad says to her, "Talk to us, Little Bird. We need to know where your mind is at." She shakes her head and wipes her face, getting her breathing under control.

Looking at Dad, she responds, "I think I already knew in the back of my mind that she might be gone, but I didn't know for sure. It hurts too much to think about. I hate that you saved me to lose your mum. It's not fair." Her tears cascade uncontrollably, her body convulsing with sobs.

Dad just gives her a sad smile and tells her, "When you're ready and all this shit is dealt with, I'll take you to her. Where we laid her to rest, you can say your goodbyes, Little Bird, it helps. Trust me. I'm going to leave you with Drew so you can talk it out, or just process for a bit. It's a lot to take in, honey." He hugs her tight and stands to leave the room. She nods her head to no one and tries to turn away from me.

I whisper to Stasia, "I'll be back soon. Don't go to sleep."

Getting up, I hear her say, "Take your time. I'm going for a shower." Stasia gets up and moves to the bathroom, looking vacant. I follow Dad out. I need five minutes with him before I go make sure things are okay with Stasia.

Closing the door, I see Krip is leaning against the door across from my room. I glare at him but talk to Dad.

"Was that necessary, to tell her everything at once? Fuck." bringing my hands up to tug at my hair, trying to release some of the pent-up energy that's boiling inside of me. I need to continue trying to ignore Krip.

"Dad, she's been through heaps these last couple of weeks. She lost her place and… Shit!" Feeling more out of control and needing to smash the smug look off Krip's face, I decide, yep, this seems to be the best idea right now. Dad steps in my pathway, probably knowing what I'm about to do.

"Son, trust me. The straighter you are with her, the better it is. Your mother always told me that if I gave her enough time to imagine shit, I'd lose. But if she knew enough truth, she would process it better and we would fight less. So, I took that on. She'll be fine. We are all on the same side." I look past Dad to glare at Krip.

"Why are you still here? Thought you would have taken off. You've seen her now. Time for you to move on!" The smug prick shrugs and smiles at me.

"Not going anywhere, brother. She still means a lot to me, so I'm staying. You fuck up and I'm here to pick up the pieces!" Fuck this shit. I barge past Dad, but he pulls me back then looks at Krip.

"Leave it, Krip, she told you they are together, now drop it. Son, go be with her. She needs you right now. She doesn't need you two fighting. You both hear me? She means a lot to me as well, so let's work together. Yeah?"

We both give a chin lift, gritting our teeth. I'm not sure I trust Krip. I met him a few times when he came to our club with Dad and he's a bit of a ladies man. He better stay the fuck away from Stasia. I don't think he'll live if he doesn't.

Opening my door again, then locking it behind me. Fuckin' Krip can stay the fuck out. I walk straight to the bathroom. She's still in the shower, crying her heart out.

A wave of despair washes over me, causing my heart to plummet. Why did I leave her so long. I dealt with Nanna's death years ago. Made peace with it. My mind drifts to the day the new girl who came to Nanna's farm. I wasn't allowed near her because I was male and she had gone through some shit.. It pissed me off then. It still pisses me off now.

I strip out of my clothes and jump into the shower. She jumps out of her skin at my first touch, but I hold her. Telling her everything will be all right. She ends up sobbing into my chest, but eventually settles. She's so exhausted.
When I feel the water cooling, I help her out of the shower, put a towel around myself, and dry her off. I carry her to the bedroom, grabbing one of my t-shirts and pulling it over her body. I grab my boxers and put them on, and put both of us in bed. Stasia's body snuggles into mine. It's the best I've felt all day.

I stare at the ceiling, hearing her breathing even out. I relax, thinking she's asleep, but then she says, "I'm so sorry. I wish this never happened. I wish your dad never found me, cause then she would still be alive."

I grab her face gently with both my hands and make her look at me. Looking deep into her eyes I tell her, "Beauty, if none of this ever happened, then I'd never have met you. And I don't think I could deal with that. Nanna loved us all and I know she would do it all again, no matter what! So don't think like that, okay?" When she shakes her head no, I don't know where her head is at. She turns in my arms. I keep us as close as possible. Holding her from behind, I pray I get through to her, because I know I'm losing her right now.

Sienna Gypsy

STASIA

24

STASIA

I jerk awake in a cold sweat. All I can feel is filth all over me. I look at my hands, they're shaking. Grabbing a hold of my thighs, I push down hard to relieve the unease that's trying to make me sick. Rubbing them back and forth, I hope the feeling in my gut goes away. A drop of perspiration runs down the side of my face.

God, I need a shower. All I can smell is the last night I was at my father's house, mixed with the death I've just found out about. I can't believe Nanna Sally is dead. Oh God, a wave of nausea hits me. I bolt to the bathroom to heave everything up. I'm still dry retching when Drew comes up behind me. He pulls my hair out of my face and rubs my back. I feel him squat behind me, with my body now in between his legs. He has a wash cloth that he's wiping my forehead with.

"I got you Beauty, lean back." I lean back into him, expecting him to hold me there. He doesn't. Lifting me gently, he guides me to the shower and turns on the water before setting me down. I struggle to comprehend how to halt him or convey my discomfort as he begins to undress me. I'm numb. He unbuttons his jeans first. Reaching back with one hand, he pulls his shirt over his head with no effort at all. I couldn't help but think if I pulled my shirt off like that, I'd get stuck, or cocooned with no way of breaking free. I shake the thought away as he puts me in the shower and gives me my toothbrush with toothpaste on it. Following his simple, gestured instructions, I brush my teeth.

When I'm finished brushing, he takes my toothbrush and puts it in the holder. He whispers, "Talk to me about what woke you." Shit, I don't want to; I have to get away. I don't know if my father will hurt the ones that I love, like Sophie. Oh God, what if Keata gets hurt? I couldn't live with that.

Shaking my head, I tell him what I can.

"Just memories. Some old, some new, and what's coming. Drew, how do I fight this? I can't help but feel guilty. This is all on me, if anything happens to..." my eyes jolt to Drew's, "Oh God, Keata? What if he goes for Keata?"

"Beauty, he won't be able to get near Keata. Everyone in this club has a soft spot for her, and Bullet will kill anyone who comes within ten feet of her. Trust me, you girls are covered. I won't let anything happen to you! Neither will Dad, nor bloody Krip. I might not like him here, but he's on my side to protect you, so, Beauty, you're safe." I take comfort in his arms, which makes me feel better. He's rubbing my back with his arms wrapped around me. It feels good. He brings his hand up to massage my neck and it relaxes me even more. I close my eyes and get lost in the sensation when I feel his lips on my forehead. I move my head to the side. He takes my invitation and comes to my ear with his lips. He nibbles along the top of my ear, then down to the lobe, breathing me in.

"Beauty, you are tempting me here. I can't keep this up. You're pushing my limits." I moan a little louder than I expected, squirming a little. God, he feels so good. The hot water runs over our bodies as Drew touches me. He doesn't know what he does to me. His hands descend from my shoulder blades to the dip of my back. His thumbs circle above my butt cheeks. He proceeds to make a circular motion with both hands, caressing my entire backside while simultaneously seizing the opportunity to kiss me breathless. He deepens the kiss, his hands still massaging my ass. I can't help myself, I moan into his mouth. His hands reach under my ass, to my thighs, to pick me up, and my legs wrap around his hips. My arms are on autopilot, going around his neck, my hands combing through his hair. I feel his erection rubbing the lower region of my... "Oh, God," I move my hips, then stop suddenly, realising... Shit, skin on skin. He pulls back, staring me in the eyes. Looking like he was going to back away. I decide then and there that maybe I need this; maybe it's time. I've never been here willingly, so I tell him.

"I can't promise I won't freak out, but I want to try. Please, Drew?" Drew pecks my lips, still taking me in. He's thinking, I can tell, then he sighs.

"Beauty, first, I'm clean and I'm guessing you are as well because of what's happened in your past. I know you haven't been with anyone since Dad saved you. Second, we have our whole lives. You don't need to rush this. Don't think I don't want to. Fuck, I'm lacking control at the moment!" He comes in for another kiss and I take it.

Then, my back is up against the wall and I feel something break in Drew, in a good way, as he takes over. He's kissing me hard. Then, he's at my neck, sucking on it. Before I know it, because my brain is somewhere between cloud nine and never wanting to be on earth again, I feel him. The sensation of him entering me is slow. All my nerve endings feel like they're going to burn and explode in the most delicious way. He allows me to slide down to his base. Needing to rest there for a bit, I take a breath before I open my eyes to see that he is admiring me. He's giving me time to back out. Nodding at him with a strength I didn't know I had anymore, I give him my silent approval.

He leans in and whispers, "I'll take it slow, Beauty, but you gotta say if it's too much." He's panting, I can see this can't be easy, holding back like this. God, I want him to move. I decide it's up to me to reassure him by rolling my hips. He hisses in my ear.

"Jesus, babe, I'm gonna lose it. Stay still."

"Drew, I can't, just move. God, just move." He remains unsure, relying on me to guide him towards a way out. Maybe he thinks I'll change my mind, but I can't. I can feel something building in my lower belly, stronger than before.

"Fuck." Words slip from my mouth that aren't even English. I don't know what I'm saying.
I move with him in a rhythm that is so deep, it tears at my soul like it might set me free.
He's talking to me. But I'm oblivious, nothing's making sense but the feeling that's burning so sweet.
"Shit, shit, fffuuuuuuccckkkkk..."

As I drift in a haze of euphoria, the lingering impact of the experience surrounds me in a sense of tranquillity so peaceful that I lose consciousness.

I wake, finding myself lying on his bed, how the hell did I get here?

"Are you okay, Stasia? You passed out." Shit, did I? I smile at him, feeling lazy. I have no words yet, and by the look on his face, he gets it. Smirking at me.

"Beauty, you look drunk. I like this look on you." He rubs the back of his fingers down my cheek gently.

"Mmmm" that feels good. I'm experiencing an overload of feelings right now. Hypersensitive is a new feeling for me, and the exhaustion is strong. I'm falling asleep again. "Drew?"

"Yeah, babe?"

"We need to do that again. I liked it. But not now, I'm tired." I smile as I finish, so does Drew. He snuggles into my neck and sucks hard, causing a scream to come out of my mouth. I pull away, giggling.

He smiles big, "Night, babe, get some rest. We will pick this up in the morning." He winks before he pulls me in close so we can both sleep.

That wasn't the last time that night or this morning. We replayed, and added some more delicious memories for me to keep.

I'm in the bathroom freshening up. When I hear him.

"Beauty, I want to come in there with you, but you need to get ready. Prez has been waiting all morning. Come on, get out." He says this while holding out the towel. I turn off the shower and step out as he wraps me in the towel. I tremble with delight as I recall the memories of last night and this morning. The thought erupts warmth inside of me. When he kisses the mark he left on my neck,

I get lost in the sensation. The slap on my butt scares the bejesus out of me. Getting me to hurry, I rush into the room where he left some clothes on the bed. Sophie must have brought them for me because they're mine. Once I'm dressed, we head out together, with his arms around me, pulling me in tight.

Once we're out in the main area, I see that everyone is up, including Soph and Keata. Even Cobra and Krip. I run to Keata and give her a big hug. She cuddles me like a koala bear, so tight. I look at Sophie. She has tears in her eyes, so I pull her into me.

"I'm sorry, I didn't know that would happen, Soph. I'll move, I promise!" She hugs me back and tells me.

"Don't be stupid, Stasia, you're not going anywhere. I trust these guys to keep us safe."
I'm looking at her like she's lost her damn mind. She relies on no one. I'm not sure what has brought about this change, but she's trusting these guys.

She adds, "Bullet won't let us leave this clubhouse till it's safe, so get used to it. If I've got to deal, so do you!"
Now that's the Sophie I know. I can tell she's thinking of ways to leave, which I smile at. I hug Cobra, who kisses my head. Eyeing Krip from where I am in Cobra's arms, I know I need to go to him, so I run to him.

He wraps me in a bear hug, which causes Drew to walk over to us and say, "Get your hands off her Krip." As he's saying that, Krip is looking at the hickey on my neck and seems lost in thought. What's he doing? We've always been close, but he's like my brother.

Drew grabs me and wraps me in his arms, then stares at Krip, "OFF. FUCKING. LIMITS!"

Bloody hell, Krip must be playing with Drew's emotions. I'll talk to him later. We're close, but not like that.

"Beauty, you want something to eat?" I nod because I know that's the best distraction.

"I'm starving. Yes, please." He chuckles, then pulls me in the kitchen's direction, where there are masses of food. Bacon, eggs, baked beans with onions, and yummy toast. I'm drooling at the sight of it. Drew makes me coffee while I get myself food. Prez looks into the kitchen and says "Thirty minutes, my office." I nod, thinking he means me, and Drew must think the same.

I scarf down my food. God, I was hungry. Drew laughs, "Babe, did I give you an appetite?" He smirks at me, and I slap his arm. "Don't say that!" My cheeks heat.

Looking innocent, he responds, "What? That we had the best sex ever, and that I made you hungry?" My face flushes with heat, and I am certain it must be as red as a beetroot at this moment. "Oh, my God, SHUT UP! I can't believe you said that. What if someone hears you? How embarrassing!" Jesus, he can't say that out loud. He just smiles this sexy ass smile that makes me smile bigger. That bastard. I dip my finger in my coffee and then flick it at him.

"Oh, you want to play, Beauty?" He jokes, closing the distance between us. I think quick on my feet, sidestepping him. God knows how I make it free and try to run for safety. I end up running into that old guy from the other night, the creepy one. He holds me tight in his arms. Shit! I try with all my strength to pull away, but he holds me tighter. *Shit.*

"Spud, take your hands off her!" Krip steps up behind Drew, glaring at Spud, daring him not to listen.

"You better let her go, old man." Thank God he lets me go, but he shoves me hard and I fall from the force.

Drew catches me, "You okay, Beauty?" I nod, but that guy scares the shit out of me. Drew turns to Spud.

"Touch her again, Spud, and I will shoot you!"

Spud just laughs, "Bros before hoes, broth-" Before he can finish his sentence, both Krip and Drew lay into him.
Spud hits the ground. I pull back and squeal as Cobra grabs me and pulls my head to his chest, walking me to what I think is the office. Entering the doorway, I see Prez as he pulls a seat out for me.

"Have a seat, Stasia. We got a bit to go through." I nod, not sure how I'm feeling about what just happened. I feel stupid for loving them both for protecting me, but also sort of scared of how they did it. Cobra is behind me as I sit down. Bullet comes in, and not far behind is Krip. After a bit, Drew walks in and takes Cobra's place behind me, putting his hands on my shoulders. The others sit and stand around the office, then Prez grabs our attention.

"Right. Stasia, did you know the guys that grabbed you?"

Shaking my head, I say, "No, I didn't see anyone I knew. But my father had something to do with it. I heard the one that grabbed me say my surname." Drew's rubbing my shoulders soothing me.

Prez continues, "Who is your father, honey?"

"Everyone calls him Frazer, but his first name is Fred."

Cobra adds, "Not sure if you guys have encountered him. But he's a piece of work. I found Stasia about six years ago and saved her from her so-called father."

"Don't. Please don't. I don't need people to know, Cobra. Please." I shake. Memories are creeping in, and I can't seem to stop them. Cobra gets in front of me and squats down to my eye level.

"Little Bird, I'm not going into detail, but they need to know how bad, yeah?" I can't. I shake my head and then look at Prez.

"I can't. Ask me my questions, then I'll go. I don't want to hear it. It's too much for me."
Drew has me out of the chair and in his lap before Prez can speak. I bury my head in his shoulder and Krip is there for support as well, holding my shoulder.

"Ok, so, have you seen your dad since being here?"

"No."

"Any of the men that grabbed you, have you seen them before?"

"No. There was only one." There's more to say, like he covered his head, but I kept it short. I want out of here.

"What about the guy who held up the café?"

"No." Drew states.

"Prez, that's it. You got what you need from her. The rest, you can get from us."

"Hold on. Stasia, the men who work with your dad, any names?" I nod but look at Cobra.

He winks and says, "I've got that, Sam. She can go." I'm wondering who the hell Sam is, but then I realise it must be Prez's name.

Drew takes me and whispers in my ear, "Where do you want to go? To our room or...?"

"Take me to your room, but tell Sophie to come. And bring Keata. I need company, please." Drew nods and yells at Cory.

"Get all the girls to my room. Oh, and Cory, stand watch till I come back, yeah?"

I don't hear the rest. We head to his room, and he hugs me till my friends get there. Then, he kisses me on the lips and tells me he'll be back soon.

Sienna Gypsy

DREW

25

DREW

C losing the door behind me, I nod at Cory. Looking in the other direction, I see Knight coming down the hallway. I'm wondering what the fuck he's doing. I walk off, then think better of it.

Glaring at him, I ask, "What you up to?" He looks at me like I should know.

"Four girls in one room? What do you think I'm doing, Bro?"

"For fuck's sake, Knight, stay with Cory! Leave the girls alone!" Why do I keep thinking that one day he will just grow the fuck up? I can't believe he is fucking pouting. What the actual fuck? I glare at him as I walk down the hall to Prez's office.

I yell over my shoulder, "Cory, you're in charge!" Knowing that will piss Knight off.

Knight then yells back, "The fuck? He's a prospect! Drew... Man..."

I can hear Cory say to him, "Grow up, man." He's right, hence Cory being in charge.

Walking into Prez's office, I take a seat. Dad and Prez are already in deep conversation. Bullet and Krip are leaning against the wall next to the door as I walk in. Dad and Prez stop talking as I sit down.

Looking at both of them, I nod.

"Fill me in." Dad looks at me with uncertainty.

"Boy, what do you know about Stasia's background? How much has she told you and what do you remember back when she arrived at Nanna Sally's?"

"I know bits. I've seen scars, asked about a little, but I have heard her nightmares. I know it's bad, but that's not what we're trying to figure out, it's what Frazer is playing at! And why now and not before?" Dad nods. Looking at me like he's seeing me differently now. Then, Krip nods, too. They must think I'm going in blind. Fuck that! Krip speaks up next.

"I think he's just found out she's here. But how? Anyone you can think might squeal?"
Shaking my head, I think he's wrong, but how else? Since Izzy's been here, something isn't right. Prez nods and I say my piece.

"I hate that idea, but it's the only way. We've kept the pictures quiet, no one knows, but the people in this room,"

Bullet nods, "I'm gonna get PC on the pictures after our meeting. We need to get busy before shit happens. All these girls are a target, and that includes Mira, Prez. This will be our weak

212

link if we don't get the girls to cooperate. So, if we work knowing this, they should stay safe." Bullet, always looking at the bigger picture. I agree, looking around the room, so does everyone else. Prez is next to speak.

"You're right, Bullet, the girls need to be aware. I'm not risking Mira not knowing. She will be more accommodating if she knows. I think they all should know. And I don't care what Nova and Cory think, Izzy gets told. They are under club protection until further notice. Make that known, boys." We all nod in agreement, knowing we have to get our feelers out.

Dad adds, "No one is free from judgement. It could be a club girl, or even a brother who is pissed. We need eyes and ears open. I've already heard the club girls complain about Stasia and Sophie, so you boys need to straighten that shit out. The girls here need to know they're above those bitches in the club!"

Bullet and I both nod, and then Prez says, "Well, nothing else we can do yet. Keep your ears to the ground. We'll get PC involved quietly, and Krip and I will talk to the club girls, get what we can. Unless, Cobra, you want to join?"

"Nope. The bitches, you can have. Not single anymore and happy brother. All yours Sam." Dad says, with a big smile. My eyebrows automatically rise to the top of my hairline. Well, looks like Dad and I will talk later. Don't get me wrong, Dad loved my mum, and it killed him when she died, but it's good to see him find someone to spend time with.

Prez dismisses us. We all leave the office to have a drink at the bar first, then, I head to my room. I need my girl. Yeah, she's mine. There's no way I'm going to let her go now that we've been together! Fuck... she is something else. I've had sex with plenty of other girls, but with her, there are just no words. Everything about Stasia... Fuck, I sound like a sap.

Walking up the hallway, a few of the girls come out of one of the other rooms. Once they see me, they start their shit. Hips swaying, tits out. I'm thinking to myself, *not even close, bitches.* When two of them slide up to me, pawing at my chest, I step back, grabbing their hands.

"Don't touch! There is plenty out there," I say, pointing down the hall. They giggle like I said something funny, then Knight surprises me.

"Girls, you don't want him. Let me show you a good time." He takes them down the hall. One looks back at me like she's eyeing me for something.

I text Bullet to tell him which one to check out. Anyone and everyone, as we all agreed.

As I get close to where Cory is, he's shaking his head. I'm trying to figure out what's going on, but as I get nearer, I can hear them. They're singing some shit about black magic. One is pretty good. The rest are just giggling and singing. I can even hear Keata's distinctive giggle. I smile at the thought.

I walk into my room. No one notices me. I just lean against the door frame and watch. It's Stasia with the voice, she's good, really good, and she has Keata with her. They are a sight.

Stasia is letting everything go like nobody's watching. She's so hot, swinging and rolling her hips.

I have to smile at Keata trying to copy. They have such a bond, these two, it's awesome to watch.

Sophie spots me first, and stops dancing. Mira stops as well, but Stasia has her back to me and is still going. Keata spots me and reaches out to me. That is when Stasia goes bright red. Why? She's so hot. Shit, everyone needs to leave my room.

I turn the music off. The girls must decide it's time to go. Mira's the first to leave.

"Sorry Stasia, I need to check on the food for later. I'll come back before I go home, okay?" What she doesn't know is that she's staying here. They all are. Better protection for them all. They all decide to leave my room, heading out the door.

After the last one is gone, I close the door and turn to look at Stasia. She is looking at me, unsure of herself. I smile because I can see she's embarrassed.

She whispers, "I need to tidy up before dinner," and starts walking away. I follow.
As we both enter the bathroom, her first and then me, I stop at the doorway and lean on the frame. She watches me in the mirror. I smirk, but she's shaking her head.

"No, you don't!" I smile now. She's still shaking her head.

"No Drew, I need to freshen up." I nod and stay there. She stares at me a little longer and must decide that I'm going to stay put. She goes to turn the tap on, trying to pretend I'm not there. She hums that song again and I can't stop myself anymore. I move in and as I touch her hips, she squeals, I lean down into her neck. "I love your voice, and the light in your eyes when you play with Keata. It's something to see! It's beautiful, sexy as fuck, Beauty." She doesn't have a choice. I kiss her. I demand more from her now. I know her triggers. I'm mindful of them so as not to let her fall into her nightmares. I undress her, and I see when she decides she wants this too. She didn't have a choice when I saw her dancing, with her hips swaying, earlier. I groan just thinking about it. I know I will not last long. I want to be inside of her.

"Beauty, I'm going to fuck you this time. I might be a little rough. I promise you will like it. But same rules, babe, just say the word and I'll stop." I kiss her under her ear on her neck, then suck

215

hard. I love marking her skin. She moans now, so I'm thinking she must be on board. But that's not enough. I need her words.

"Tell me you hear me. You need to tell me first." She nods, but that's not good enough either.

"Words, Beauty. I need your words."

"Yes, d- do it," she stutters. "Promise I will."

I can't hold back. Grabbing her hand, I spin her around and put her on the bathroom countertop. I've already undressed her. I unzip my pants. Pushing them down, then rub my length along her slit. So smooth. Fuck, she feels good. As I push in, I can feel how wet she is, and I slide right in.

"Fuuucckk! You feel amazing, babe."

Then, I move in and out once, and the little minx looks at me with a sultry smile, "You said rough. This is not rough, Drew." She seals the deal by running her tongue over her bottom lip.

"Shit, I'm close, babe, I swear. Tell me to stop now or I can't hold back much longer!"
She moans at my words, and I decide to push in hard and fast. I watch her face change. Her jaw drops open and her eyes close.

I pull back, taking my time till the head of my dick is about to release from her, then I slam back into her. I do this repeatedly until I can feel her tighten around me. She is holding onto the counter, but I grip her hips. I'm using everything in me to not cum yet. I want to last, but as I'm about to slam into her one more time, I feel her cumming. And that's all I can take. Fuck. The tingling sensation at my groin spreads to my spine. White vision erupts, and my brain tingles. This feeling seems to only be with her. It's addictive. As I'm about to finish, I grab her chin and kiss her with everything I have. Fuck, she is beautiful. I study her intensely. She's smiling. "What has you smiling, Beauty?"

She responds, "You. You blow my mind. I didn't think I could do any of this, but… with you, anything is possible! Thank you." She leans forward and kisses me again. We're still connected, "Unless you're ready for round two, biker boy, get out the way, I need a shower." I slap her butt and leave her to it.

We got to dinner and that's when we decided to tell the news to the girls.

That they are all here for a while, under our protection.

STASIA

26

STASIA

I walk into the kitchen of the clubhouse to see if I can help Mira. There seems to be heaps of people here tonight, but she has lots of help. Girls I've never seen before are here. They hardly have clothes on.

Then, Mira sees me and tells two girls to take over for a bit. She comes and wraps me in a hug, "You feeling okay?"

Nodding at her, I ask, "You need some help?" I look around the kitchen and notice she probably won't. "Even though you look like you got it under control." I gesture towards the girls helping her.

She laughs, then says, "Yes, these bitches have to do something, other than laying on their backs. Most of these girls belong to the club. Sounds bad, I know, but it's not that bad. Some love the attention the guys give them and enjoy the partying, while others have nowhere to go. The club protects them. But don't pay them any mind. You might get along with some, but not all of them. I don't, there's plenty more Kim's in here, but Drew's never been with any of them, and Kim was a mistake because he was way too drunk." Okay, that was a lot to take in.

"Did you just word vomit on me?" I ask, to break the strange feeling in my chest. I hate that Drew knows these girls, and that Kim got to me.

She smiles, "Yes, I suppose I did!" We both laugh at the same time. One of the girls is scowling at us, she sashays up to us, "So, you're the new club girl they're all talking about?" I turn red. I don't even look or dress like them.

Another girl says, "I've got some clothes you can wear. They won't touch you looking like that!" I can feel my frustration building to anger. As Mira says something, I talk over her.

"I'm not here for your men. I have my own! You can have the rest!" Mira is glaring at the girls who are finding this entertaining, but that doesn't stop them. One, in particular, comes up to my face and tries to intimidate me. Pointing her pointy nail at my face, waving it around like it's a knife.

"You don't know how this club works, Girly! We are here to serve these guys in any way we can. That's why girlfriends come and go, but we stay. So have your fun. Drew will be with us later!" I clench my fists and try to mentally calm myself down. All I want to do is scream in her face and tell her to fuck off. I decide to go with not showing her she's affecting me.

"If he wants you, he can have you. I don't really care. But until he makes that decision, stay away from me."

Mira steps in front of me, spitting her words at the club girl. "Back off, Brittany, you know as much as I do, Drew doesn't touch you bitches. So, fuck off and go wipe the tables and set them. Shit needs to be done, and you're staying on table duty." She is still glaring at her, daring her to say something back. Mira's eyes don't lose contact with Brittany's as she pulls me away, dragging me through the kitchen doors. Taking me around the corner to the hallway away from Brittany, she spins me around and I hit the wall.

"Don't do that. Drew is with you, no matter what those bitches want. That's why they're in your face, because he's brought no one around the club, he never has! Don't let them take him away from you, because he will fight for you. Don't be the one to let him down." I'm not sure what she means, but I nod my head in understanding, even though I don't.

Taking a deep breath, I reply, "Mira, I didn't say I wouldn't fight for him. I only said that if he wants them, he can choose them and let me go. But I'll tell you this, Mira, I do care for him and probably more than I think I do. Because thinking about him with anyone but me, pisses me off." As I finish my sentence, I notice Drew is not only standing near us, but close enough that he can hear me. Shit, he's smiling from ear to ear. Damn it. Then, he walks closer. Mira says something, but I can't hear her. Drew is too close now, and Mira is gone.

He wraps his arms around me, placing his hands on my hips, drawing us closer, our bodies press against each other intimately. He then leans in, and nibbles at my neck, repeating my words, "So, you like me, hey?" I can feel his lips move into a smile on my neck before he nibbles again.

"Like, a lot?" Then his nose slides up to my ear and bites my earlobe. Shit!

"People with me piss you off, hey?" Then he sucks my neck, hard… the ass.

I try to pull away, but he squeezes me closer, "It's the same for me, Beauty." Then, he takes my lips in a soft and slow kiss with his tongue asking to be let in. I obey. Before I know it, I mould into him. My legs are around him, I'm up against the wall, and he's kissing me deep and heavy.

Only when he pulls away do I realise where I am. His sexy smile is dream worthy. I hate he has this effect on me. Damn it.

"You need to stop doing that. I keep losing my mind."

"That's because I'm your black magic, Beauty!" I freeze. Oh, my God, how embarrassing. I can't believe he used that song he walked in on me singing. I slap his shoulder, he laughs but lets me down gently. I'm so embarrassed I try to walk away, but he grabs me and kisses me hard on the lips again. When I open my eyes, he is walking off... asshole. I can't believe he said that, but then I catch myself. I'm smiling like an idiot. Argh! Bloody men.

After dinner, they take us girls to a room. It has a TV in it, some comfy chairs, a pool table, a coffee table, a kids' corner, and a jukebox. I go straight to the jukebox and pick some songs. I love getting Keata to dance with me. She can't hear them, but she watches me and follows my lead.

I pick Cyndi Lauper's'Girls Just Wanna Have Fun', Madonna's 'Like a Prayer', and a few other pop songs Keata loves. The last one is 'Wannabe' by the Spice Girls. By the time this comes on, I forget people are making their way into the room because Keata, Sophie and I are screaming out the lyrics. Well, Keata's mimicking the lyrics. She's so cute.

Once that song finishes, Bullet comes over and takes Keata. She goes readily. She has a huge soft spot for these men. I can't believe it. He blows on her hand, and she giggles and plays with the short stubble he has. She must like the feel of it. He walks to where Sophie is and whispers something in her ear. He kisses her temple and they both walk off towards the room they're staying in.

Sophie smiles at me, "He said he has books for her and is going to read to her, and for me to come and bathe her when I'm ready." Well, shit!

"How are you coping with giving up control, Soph?" I smile, knowing she's fighting herself to run to that room.

She shakes her head. "He has fifteen minutes, then I'm going in!" I laugh cause that is actually progress. We talk a bit longer before she walks back to Bullet's room.

Drew's walks down the hallway with his hand out, "Come on, babe, we need to talk in the room."

I follow him to his room, then once we are inside, there's a knock at the door. He opens it and I look behind me and do a double take again because Cobra and Krip come in. They both find somewhere to lean on the wall and Drew comes over and sits next to me.

"Beauty, we have put all you girls under our protection. This means that you go somewhere, me, Dad, or Krip are with you. No one else, unless you speak to Dad, me or Krip. You understand?"

"No... wait... why? Because of what happened? The other girls are going to hate me."

"Nah, they won't. They will hate us if we don't do this. Trust me, Mira will be on my back. Now, we don't know for sure if it's your father, but I'm not taking any risks, not with you. Krip is trying to find out if he's in the area, but no sign yet. You and Sophie can go to work, but one, or possibly two of us will be on duty. Bullet has also picked his own boys to watch over Sophie and Keata. You okay with this?" Jesus, Sophie's going to kill me, having no breathing space.

I nod, but say under my breath, "Good luck with Sophie." Cobra comes over and gives me a hug, and I ask, "Hey, do you still talk with Savie?"

"Yeah, I do, and she wants to see you. She can come soon. We need to make sure everything is safe here first, okay?" Nodding, I realise I miss her more than ever.

"Next time you talk to her, can I speak to her, please?"

His eyes flick in Drew's direction, "I talk to her every day, maybe twice a day. So yeah, if you're around, I'll grab you. Now get some rest and I'll see you in the morning." He gets up and goes to the door telling Drew they will talk later.

He nods, then Krip comes over, picks me up off the bed. Gives me a big bear hug till I squeal, then he laughs, "Night, Little Bird, talk tomorrow."

Drew is glaring at him as he struts out the door.

I hear him say, "Krip, don't make me regret letting you help. Keep your hands off my girl, Okay?"

"Yeah, Drew, whatever you say, man." He says, with a sarcastic smirk on his face. Yep, I'm gonna have to have a talk with him. He's riling Drew up on purpose. The asshole.

Once everyone leaves, we are curled up in bed with my back to his front, and I drift off to sleep quickly. Not even thinking about those bitches earlier today.

Sienna Gypsy

DREW

27

DREW

The next few days are quiet. We have been doing things like normal. I don't even think the girls have noticed the guys who are protecting them. My gut is churning though. I know that something's going to happen. Prez wants to have church today with the main patch holders. So, hopefully, he has some sort of news. I'm expecting him to have some sort of idea who the leak is, or maybe who else is involved.

Feeling my phone vibrate in my pocket, and thinking it's Prez with the meeting details for later today, I decide to check it later and finish lunch with my girl first. We are sitting at the back of the café where Stasia works. She's on her break. Eating together gives me time to check in with her.

Stasia has taken everything in stride. I really thought she'd run, but she hasn't. Last night she told me heaps about what happened to her growing up. The way her school treated her and how she was bullied. How her dad abused her, drugged her, and beat her. How Frankie scarred her like it was a game. Fury burns through my veins thinking about what she went through. The only thing that calms me, is knowing Dad saved her. As well as the things Nanna did with her to show her how to be brave and to have a plan to get away a second time. I'm so grateful to my grandmother, more than she will ever know!

If I ever meet this Frankie guy, he's dead. The same as her father. I've seen her scars, but never knew how she got them. The night she revisited her demons by telling me everything was bad. Her nightmares came back, and she needed shower after shower to feel clean again. It tore at my heart, watching her go through that. It might've been her idea to tell me, but I'd never put her through that again. I tried with everything in me to soothe her pain. She tells me I do, but I don't want her going back to a time where all her terrible memories invade her mind ever again.

Keeping the conversation easy. I talk about Keata.

"How long have you and Keata been doing your singing duo's?" She looks down at her food, picks up a chip and uses it to move more chips around her plate. I can see the words she wants to say and that we are having the wrong conversation.

She says in a whisper with half a smile on her face, "Since I've known her." When she looks at me, I know she's blaming herself on the inside for all that has happened. I also see how worried she is about her friends. As soon as her break finishes, Stasia takes our plates.

"I'm on kitchen duty, so I'll see you when I'm finished." She gives me a hesitant smile. "Only two more hours." she tells me in an uneasy tone.

Knowing she is worried, I nod, calling her name, "Stasia?" She stops and stands still. I stand and walk around the booth we were sitting in and kiss her on the lips, hoping to invade her haunted thoughts.

Releasing our kiss, I grab her behind the neck gently, keeping our foreheads touching, "I'll be just outside. Message me for anything. You hear me?"

She closes her eyes and breathes in a shaky breath. She takes a minute before responding, "I will." Then walks toward the kitchen. I watch her stride through the kitchen doors before I head out of the café to where Krip is.

He yells at me as I'm crossing the car park, "Got some news." I pick up my pace to a jog, eager to hear his news. Coming to a stop next to him, I wait to see what Krip has found out, but as I arrive, he asks, "She in front or out back?"

"Out back, Tommy's there, so she's covered." Krip talks about a guy he knows, that used to work with Frazer, and I listen till I hear a noise that sounds like a dog whining. Then it stops. We both look up at each other, not really sure what we are hearing. Somehow, I remember the text I got. So, I grab my phone from my pocket at the same time Krip speaks.

"Someone must have kicked a dog." I nod, but when my message opens, my blood burns. It's not a dog. As I'm looking at the phone, the message is from an unknown number. There are no words, just two pictures. One is of the back of the café, looking in through the back fly screen door. They must have gotten this when I was sitting with Stasia. The other one, that came through as I opened my phone, is of Tommy's surprised face. You can see the end of a cricket bat in the top right-hand corner. I curse, and we both sprint towards the café.

I rush into the front door of the café, and Krip runs around the back. Bursting through the doors, I storm into the kitchen. Skidding to a stop. The first thing I notice is the open flyscreen door. There are utensils scattered everywhere, like there was a struggle. I spot blood on the ground. It looks like whoever did this dragged someone towards the door. By the time I get to the door, I spot Stasia struggling to crawl over to Tommy. His head is bleeding profusely. I rush over, thinking this is where the blood was from. Then I notice Stasia has blood seeping down her left side above her hip. She has tears running down her cheeks. I change direction. As I get to her, Krip comes around the back. He sees Stasia and the look on his face is furious as he comes toward us, but I shake my head.

"Krip check on Tommy. Call an ambulance NOW!" He takes his phone out, starting to dial. I take off my jacket, then my shirt, scrunching it up into a ball, then pushing it into Stasia's side where she is bleeding. My head is whirling and spitting thoughts in every direction. How the hell did this happen? We had the place covered. It makes no sense. Tommy's good at what he does, we all know it. When he was in the Army, he was a force to be reckoned with. He's the one we call in to put the boys through their paces. That's how damn good he is. Damn!

I hear Krip say, "Yeah, there's a pulse, but it's weak. I have pressure there. Just hurry the fuck up!" He hangs up. I can hear the sirens in the distance.

Stasia keeps saying, "He found me, he found me!" Over and over. I think I know who she is talking about. It's not her Dad, it's Frankie. There's no sign that anyone was back here either. Fuck!

Everyone arrives at once, the ambos, my Dad, Prez and more of the club.

The paramedics load Tommy into the first ambulance. Another ambulance is here for Stasia. She's conscious but in shock. A paramedic tries to get her to speak, but she just keeps mumbling the same thing over and over: that they've found her.

I haven't left Stasia's side. Once we are in the ambulance, she makes eye contact with me.

I can see the confusion and terror in her eyes, "I'm sorry... He can't be here... I'm not his, I swear I'm not!"

Trying to calm her as best I can. I use the back of my fingers to feel the softness of her skin on her cheek, caressing them, calming her.

"No, baby, you're not. Stasia, look at me! You're not his! You're mine, all mine, you listening to me, Beauty?" I don't even know if it's what she needs to hear, but I need her to hear it. Fuck!

The medic nudges me out of the way and takes her vitals. He explains what I already know, "On the outside, she is okay, but she's in shock. She's also gonna need some stitches." Watching him examine the wound, he then adds, "The knife that was used must have had jagged edges. Which makes it look worse than it is. It looks deep, too, so the scarring is going to be messy." I nod, knowing that's exactly what Frankie, the sick fuck, wanted.

As the ambulance pulls into the hospital's emergency area, she remains motionless. Her eyes glazed over, as if she's looking to me for a solution to make this better. She seems to be preoccupied with something. Could it be hope? Shaking that thought away, all I want is to stay with her, to keep her safe. Not allow anyone from her past near her again. She's not going anywhere! Not even work! I don't care now!

Sitting in Stasia's room in the hospital, we're all waiting for Tommy to come out of surgery. Stasia's room looks small with Dad, Krip and me in it. Stasia's asleep at the moment. Doc wants her to rest, so he gave her something to help.

"Any word about Tommy?" I asked Krip, who got back from doing rounds.

"Nah, not yet, but your Prez wants to see you, and he told me to tell you, 'sooner rather than later.'"

"Not happening! He can come here. I'm not leaving her, not right now!"

"Drew, go! I got her, Son. I won't let anyone in here but us three. He could have something."

I shake my head, struggling to keep my cool with my dad. I point to the door and say, "I'm not leaving. When he comes, I'll be right there just outside that door, and nowhere else!" The thought of someone getting to her while I was so close just across the damn carpark it's eating me alive.

I get up, reluctantly, and kiss her on the lips, reassuring her I'll be back. Krip goes to the door. I scowl at him.

"Where the hell are you going?" I demand, glaring as he pushes the door open.

"Nowhere," he snaps back. "I'm standing guard right outside." Good. I start pacing, my frustration building, then stick my head through the doorway and bark at Krip, "Do something useful and get Prez—now!"

He glares at me but heads towards the waiting room. He's back before I know it, with Prez in tow. As I walk to the door, I can see Mira in the distance looking at what her father is doing. She turns, glaring behind her like someone is pissing her off. I'm not sure if it's because she was close to Tommy, or if she wants to see Stasia. As soon as Prez is close enough, he pulls out his phone and turns it towards me.

"I got these this morning. That's why I called church. They have eyes and ears on us, and I don't have a damn clue who is getting in this close to my club!" *Shit!*

Answering quickly, "Who else knows about these texts?"

"Just you. Bullet will know as soon as he calms Sophie down. She found out what happened at the café and wants to be near Stasia." Bullet wants her and Keata safe.

Wondering who the fuck is talking club business, "Who told Sophie? Any ideas?"

Prez shakes his head, disappointed, "No, we kept it quiet, but someone knew, and she's not telling us who told her. Mira was with me, but she knows the code, so I know she didn't tell." I'm thinking Mira might have. She's never had any girlfriends before, and these girls seemed to have formed a bond fast. I'll address it later because Mira won't let many know.

Looking at the pictures Prez has on his phone; they are way too close to not have been taken inside the club.

"We have to have some sort of breach. Someone inside the club is doing this. We need to find them... NOW."

Prez nods, then instructs me, "Only the top patches are to know anything. So, Nova, Knight, Krip, your Dad, Bullet, and Trigger. He wanted in." I nod, knowing he would.

Prez continues, "Trigger came to me. He's worried about Keata. I trust him. He has always been Mira's guard. You know he's safe." I nod, knowing all of this and thinking, *hurry the fuck up*. Prez snaps his fingers to get my attention.

"You listening?" his eyebrows hit his hairline, then he proceeds, "But I think that's it for now. Shit's getting bad with one of ours down, and Tommy's too good to be taken off of his assignment to guard the girls. Fuck," Prez brushes his fingers through his hair, he's stressed, "I even want him under guard. I'm sure he knew the attacker."

"Yeah, I was thinking the same thing. Anything else?" He looks back at Mira.

"Yeah, take Mira and keep her in eyesight! You think she and Tommy had something going on?" *Shit!*

"No, but who the hell knows. She's your daughter, the master of everything. You haven't even been able to hide your sex life from her, but she has her own locked down hard."

He growls back at me, "You think she has a sex life?" Fuck if I know. Shit!

"I don't know, but that's the point, and she's eighteen. What eighteen-year-old is a virgin, Prez?" Fuck, how the hell did we get here?

Deciding it's better to leave, I say, "I gotta go." He nods, but his eyes go in Mira's direction. I nod at her and point toward Stasia's door. She knows what I mean.

As soon as she reaches me and her dad is out of earshot, I tell her, "He's onto you. You better spill it!" I'm bluffing, but it's worth a try.

Shaking her head, she tells me, "Well, you're both wrong. Of course you both think I'm sleeping with him." Throwing her hands up in the air, she states, "I live with idiots, I swear." Well, fuck. My eyebrow arches, waiting for her to continue. She's still shaking her head, then tells me, "We have a friendship, but it's not what you think. He's trying to get his own life sorted with the girl he's in love with. I'm his sounding board, you know, like yours. I have my interests, but they're out of my league, Drew. So don't stress your pretty little head. Still a virgin here!" As she finishes the last bit, she is staring at Krip and he's staring back at her. She goes red and barges past him, walking through the door to see Stasia. I'm not sure what I just saw. But I'm glad he's not staying here long.

Because she's right, he is out of her league. Shit, if Prez knew, Krip would be gone now! Sent back no matter what my Dad thinks.

When we get in the room, Mira goes to sit next to Stasia, and Dad moves to the window, leaning against the ledge. I ease Stasia over a bit so she can curl up into me. Krip walks in and Mira doesn't make eye contact with him, but he's staring holes through Mira. Interesting. After a bit, he looks at me.

"Hear anything?"

"Nah. Not yet. Prez had some interesting photos. Too close to not be one of us. But that's what we're gonna talk about in church." Dad nods and Krip looks back at Mira, then back at me. Gesturing with his thumb in Mira's direction.

"She always present when you talk club business?"

"Not always, but her dad wants her in the know on this, so she's good. That way she's aware, but not everyone will have the privilege. We're compromised, so only top patch holders will be in the know, and that's limited too." We've been talking about strategies for a while. I feel Stasia move, but it's not good. She's dreaming, and she fights with me. I look at Dad, he gets what I'm suggesting, and gets everyone to leave the room. I call her name and gently stroke her head.

"Stasia, it's me, Beauty. Come on, wake up. I got you, you're safe," I repeat myself a few times before she wakes up. When she does, she is crying.

"Beauty, I got you. Don't cry, I'm not going anywhere." She tries to wipe her eyes, but I wipe them for her. She buries her head into my side, then puts her arms around me.

Putting my chin on the top of her head, I ask, "How's the pain? You still sore?"

It takes a bit before she answers, "I've had worse from him. The memories are worse than the pain."

Holding her tighter, I whisper in her ear, "You want the doc?" I feel her shake her head slightly.

"Nah, is there any news about Tommy? And does Mira know? God, this will kill her!"

"Hey, is something going on with her and Tommy?" Stasia lifts her head up to make eye contact.

"No, but they're good friends." She shyly changes her line of vision back to my shirt. The pain in her eyes is killing me.

"Babe, don't worry about the others, okay? Just get better, and then we can figure stuff out with Tommy, okay?" She nods her head.

"I'd rather know, keeps my mind active." I nod, then ask her more questions about the attack. She only remembers Frankie and didn't see anyone else. It's like we are missing something.

I spoke to the doctor. He says the brain will block out traumatic events, that in time she will remember when her brain allows her to. Which is shit for us. We need to know who's betraying the club.

Sienna Gypsy

STASIA

28

STASIA

Nightmares relentlessly invade my sleep throughout the night, despite the medication I've taken. I'm pretty sure the only thing stopping me from screaming the place down is Drew. He won't leave me, which is a relief! He calms me, but I still can't get the vision of Tommy out of my head. The blood... God, I hope they tell us soon. It's killing me that this is all my fault. Drew moves and pulls me closer. "How are you feeling now, Beauty?" the corner of my mouth lifts into a lopsided smile, not really conveying my feelings at this point. I do not know why he calls me Beauty. My scars have been the elephant in the room since the first day Drew saw them, and they are not beautiful. He hasn't asked any questions, but I see them in his eyes. I told him what happened to me, but he never pushes me for more. Drew only ever goes at my pace, never ever faster than I can handle.

Confusion is an understatement. My nerves and anxiety are hitting the roof. Just thinking about the fact that the man I've feared my whole life has found me paralyses me to the core. But now, he has found me, stuck a knife in my side and told me the things he wants to do to me! God, who will keep me from him? Things got foggy. But I remember what Frankie said to me. I remember him dropping me like a piece of dirt on the ground. I used all the strength I had to get to Tommy, but I don't think I made it.

His head was a mess. I remember the weird noises. That's when I ran out of the kitchen. Frankie had already locked the cook in the toilet outside and I knew Tommy was just outside the back door. Drew said Tommy would keep me safe.

I thought I was safe.

I was wrong...

Frankie didn't even need to hold me down, because seeing him froze me to the core. I couldn't have moved even if I tried! Everything Nanna Sally taught me went out the window. My mind can't configure the rest of what happened. It's like it's just out of reach. The doc has said that in cases like these traumatic events, the brain is complex. It protects itself and that I'll remember when I'm ready.

I reply to Drew's question, "I'm okay. Can you go find out some news please? I'll feel better when I know Tommy's okay." Drew rubs my back, snuggles into me without hurting me and takes a deep breath.

"God, you smell good, Beauty. Bullet will be in soon with Sophie, so we will find out then. And hopefully, Sophie will calm the fuck down." he says with a bit of humour in his voice.

"She's been driving Bullet nuts. He caught her twice, trying to get to you. Said he was going to tie her to the bed soon if she keeps this shit up!" I can see that Drew is shaking his head, amused. I don't know why he thinks this is funny.

"What? What do you mean tie her to a bed?" God, my mind is whirling. What if Bullet is like my dad, what if I'm wrong about everything? The blood rushes from my face as I lock eyes with Drew.

"Is Sophie, okay? Why would he say that to her?" I shout the next part. "Drew, she's my best friend!"

"Beauty, he's trying the only way he knows how to keep those girls safe. And he didn't tie her up, it was a figure of speech." Damn him and his controlling friend, this is going to push my friend away. Oh, my God, she's going to kill me. Shit.

After about an hour, the doctor comes in to check on me, saying I can go home. He stresses no moving around because the stitches will either leak or burst open. I agree with his terms, and the doctor goes to organise my release papers. Once he's gone, Drew's gaze holds concern as it locks with mine.

He clears his throat, "Beauty, I need you to listen, and I don't want you worrying about money or anything. Are you listening?" I nod, thinking he's going to tell me he's putting more men on me at work.

"You're not going back to work until we have this sorted. I'm not risking you or your friends." My head shakes no, before I even register what I'm doing. Why would he consider this acceptable?

"No. No, that's not happening. Drew?"

"Yes, it is. It's done Stasia."

"We have bills to pay. Rent and food. You might have your club, but I can't do this to Sophie. That's her place, and I need to work

Drew. It keeps me busy. You can't make me stop!" Anger burns in my gut. He can't do this. Sophie will kill me. Jesus, I need him to stop. He can't just make decisions this important. I'll never be able to support myself.

"You don't need to pay your bills, Stasia. They're paid."

"Wait, what?"

"You heard me."

Now I'm furious. How could he do that? "Well, I'm paying you back." I snap at him. He chuckles, not even caring what I'm saying.

I blurt out to him, "Sophie is going to kick me out anyway for bringing this trouble to her house!" Drew chuckles some more. I slid my fingers in my hair and pull, making some sort of noise at the same time. "Arghhh." God, he has no clue!

By the time Drew had me showered, yes, Drew, because a male nurse came to help me and Drew flipped his shit.I was almost ready to leave when the door burst open, and Sophie runs to me, giving me a hug. She is crying and mumbling something that I can't quite make out. I look to the door and Bullet is shaking his head at Drew. Sophie holds me and yells at Bullet, pointing at the door.

"YOU CAN LEAVE NOW!" My first clue that she's pissed. Next, her hands grab my face. "We are going to work this out," she is frantic, her hands and eyes searching for damage on me.

"How much damage did that asshole do to you? That idiot won't tell me!" Her eyes are roaming frantically, still trying to find my wounds. I'm glad I'm dressed right now.

The look she gives Bullet this time is deadly! She's pissed, but Bullet stands there, not caring at all. He actually looks like he's smirking. What the hell? Drew seems to be oblivious to these two fighting, he comes to me and kisses the top of my head.

"I'm going to check there's nothing else you need for when I get you home." He says, then walks out. Bullet stands there, leaning against the window ledge. What the fuck! I've got to be in an alternate world. Deciding to ignore the biker in the room, I turn to Sophie.

"Soph, I'm fine. I'm more worried about Tommy than about me! We still haven't heard anything?" She looks at Bullet for the first time with concern, then back at me, shaking her head. Something isn't right. They're not telling me something. I step away from her and stare into her eyes, looking for anything she could tell me, or what she's not telling me."Sophie... what? W- What is it?"

She's about to tell me something when Drew walks in, and he's not happy. He looks at Bullet, then shakes his head. I hear him grunt out, "Why did no one tell me?" The anger is radiating from him in waves. Bullet is quick to answer.

"You need to check your phone. We did as soon as it happened. He came out of surgery at 1 a.m., then passed away at 4:30 a.m.. Mira's a mess and the girlfriend wants us all dead. We need to make a move to get the girls back safely!"

A loud buzzing runs through my ears. Everything about Nanna Sally, her death, now this death. I can't believe he's dead... he didn't make it... I knew... maybe... Oh, my God. I shake my head. The buzzing won't go away. Is it buzzing? I'm losing my mind, hoping I don't lose it completely, right this minute. I hear something.

"Breathe, Beauty" I know that voice.

"Just breathe, Beauty. We will figure this out!" my head is back there. There, where I was a little girl. Where I couldn't help myself. The memories are flooding my mind.

I mumble to no one, "W- Why are they doing this to me? I-I was a child, now they want to... What? To rape me as an adult and kill people I know and love, just to get at me? Why? Didn't I go through enough? I can't... I can't let anyone else d-die because of me!" Drew is holding me now. I'm crying hard in his arms. He's holding me tight, calming me. I can't believe this is happening. And Tommy, his poor girlfriend,they were working it out.

"I need to see her!" Drew pulls me back to him.

"You're not seeing her till she stops threatening us! Just give her time, Beauty, then I'll take you there!" I nod, but I don't think I really know what I'm agreeing to.

The rest of the day is a haze. We get to the club; I pick at my food and do as I'm told.

After cuddling with Keata, I go to bed. I'm on some sort of autopilot, and my nightmares seem to stay at bay tonight. I don't know why.

I know Drew wakes me through the night for meds and my pain relief, but then I fall back to sleep. I know the guys have been in and out of meetings, but I don't know what they're talking about in them. When Drew comes in with coffee, I decide to have a shower to put space between us.

"I'm fine. I need to freshen up." Drew's eyes scan me suspiciously.

"Beauty, anytime I can have you naked I will. But when you're broken, I got you. Now, come on!" He gestures to the shower. He helps me with my top, my dressing needs changing, but he suggests, "I'll do it after the shower. The dressing will come off easier wet." I nod, knowing he's right.

In the shower, he is a complete gentleman and takes good care of me. He's not all innocent. He kisses my neck the same way that makes me tingle all over, and holds my body like he owns it, which I'm pretty sure he does now.

When we're finished, he changes the dressing and helps me dress, then walks with me to the kitchen. He makes, or rather grabs, my toast and more coffee and we find our seats. As I'm getting comfortable, I see Krip heading over to sit with us while we eat. He asks how I'm doing. He grabs my hand, shaking his head. I can see the sorrow in his eyes. I can't stand the pity I see in them.

"That was close, Little Bird, you scared the shit out of me. This ain't happening again, you hear me?" I nod, but my head isn't taking in what he is saying. I'm still lost in all that has happened. Drew snatches my hands back and glares at Krip as I am jerked from my thoughts. I don't think Drew enjoyed being kept in the dark. He also doesn't like anyone touching me. He's been brewing since yesterday, being the last to know about Tommy. I can see it eating at him.

Sophie comes in, "I need to get Keata's prescription. I don't have it. Stasia, can you come with me?" Still feeling like autopilot is running, I nod and stand. Drew and Bullet come as well; Mira keeps Keata for us. They have been drawing, and Keata wants to stay with her.

As we pile into the truck, an eerie silence envelops us during the journey home, broken only by the hum of the engine. Drew remains silent. I reach out, massaging his shoulder in an attempt to offer comfort.

"Honey, are you going to be okay?" I whisper in his ear. Then I lean into him. He smiles at me, nodding his head.

"You just made it better, Beauty." Then he pecks my lips. I don't know why he said that, but I hope no one blames me for what happened to Tommy. Bullet turns right, down our street.

As we approach, I'm startled to see some of our stuff on the sidewalk, then I look at Sophie, "Are we behind on our rent?"

Bullet answers, "No, you aren't," but he glances at Drew, then the road again. As we drive past, I know why. Someone has turned the place upside down. Everything from the house was thrown outside. It's all ripped into strips and chunks. Sophie's hand covers her mouth, tears streaming down her face as she trembles in fear. A sense of dread courses through me, chilling my bones with its icy touch. That buzzing noise is back, whooshing through my ears. Thoughts of my past are coming to the surface again. Using all the inner strength I have left, I repeat to myself, *I can't stay here*. I've wrecked her life. I've wrecked everyone's lives. They're never going to stop! This can't be happening. I've got to go. I zone out, not wanting to be here anymore.

We didn't stop. I'm in Drew's room, staring at the door when Cobra walks in with Krip and Drew. They look mad. I know it's my fault. They won't have to worry. I stand up and rub my legs a bit, hoping to warm them. It doesn't though, they're ice cold. I look at them and gather the courage I need right now, then clear my throat.

"I never meant to bring trouble here, and I didn't mean to put anyone at risk when I came here. I never thought he'd find me. Please believe me..." As I'm about to go on, Drew cuts me off.

"Stasia, he was always going to find you. It was only a matter of time." I'm nodding because I know what I have to do. I either have to submit to my father and accept my life, which makes me shake with fear, or run and hope he never catches me.

I'm about to say what I'm going to do. When Cobra comes to me and hugs me tight. He says into my hair. "Little Bird, you became part of my family a long time ago. We may have lost each other for a while, but I never gave up looking and I'm NOT giving up now. You're not running! You hear me?"

Shaking my head, I tell him. "Cobra, you mean everything to me as well, and your son means even more. But if something happened to any of you, even you, Krip, I-I wouldn't be able to d-deal!" Tears are gushing down my face. I'm crying, but I'm determined now, I have to go. I know it in my heart.

"Beauty, we have a plan. You need to trust us! You can't run!" Drew sounds stern. But he's not seeing how bad this is going to get.

"I don't think you understand Drew, I-I don't have a choice this time!" Cobra moves away and says he'll be back. The feeling of dirt and filth is gripping my body. The feeling is getting worse. I try to brush it off.

I grab at my skin again. Knowing what I need, I turn and stutter my next words slowly, "I need... space... I have t-to go... I... I'll be awhile. C-Can we talk later?"

Drew tells Krip, "I'll find you later." He leaves with a nod. Once in the bathroom, I jump straight into a hot shower. I scrub slowly at first, then memories flood my mind and I put more force behind my scrubbing. When I think I can't handle it anymore, Drew is there to help me. This makes me cry harder. I didn't even know I started crying.

"Why? I can't take it anymore. He needs to let me suffer. I need to not feel." I say to myself. I pull away and my stitches pull and hurt like a bitch. I yelp, "Shit! Don't, Drew, you can't anymore! You need to let me go."

"Like fuck! You are with me. Wherever I am! Beauty, you don't get to leave. You are mine as much as I'm yours, so don't get any ideas." he says this as a warning. Argh, he just won't listen, but I've made my decision. I need to plan a way to leave.

Sienna Gypsy

DREW

29

DREW

Stasia is going to leave. I know she is. I've seen it in her eyes. She has been on twenty-four-hour watch since the attack. If I'm not with her, Krip or Dad is. They both can feel it coming too. She thinks she can solve everything if she runs or goes straight to the lion's den, which will only make things worse.

We've been in meeting after meeting at the Club. Trying to figure out what to do and discuss what's needed to do it. Frazer has vanished and there's no word on Frankie. No sign or trail of him anywhere. We've checked everywhere and come up with nothing. PC is looking into flights and buses to see if he's gone back to Melbourne. Dad suspects he has gone back as well. He's pretty confident that he has and has a plan. But Prez, he's convinced that it won't work. He thinks by using this plan, we're moving the problems elsewhere, away from the club. I think Dad's plan will work. He won't be ready for what we have plotted out. When we take off back to Melbourne, he won't be expecting us. Dad knows

Melbourne inside and out, so Frazer will be easier to find. And when we find him, he's going to die a slow, bloody death. I swear on my Nanna's grave, he and Frankie are dead men walking!

We're in another meeting right now, and Prez is talking it out with Dad. Savie is coming down for Stasia, and then we are going to decide whether we drive or fly to Melbourne. I'm looking forward to Stasia seeing Savie. From what she told me about Savie, it's only going to help.

Focusing back on what Dad and Prez are talking about, I'm trying to grasp if Prez will see it Dad's way. Their debate is more about the safety of the girls, not whether it will work. Then, I observe Prez nod in agreement. Well, fuck me, he's going to let it happen. That's a start!

"Drew," Prez calls out my name to get my attention.

"What are you going to do if she goes to Melbourne? And what if she wants to stay there when this shit storm blows over?" The fuck if I know! I want her safe right now. Even the thought of her being near either of those scum makes my blood run cold.

"Prez, I'll want to be with her. Yeah, I know I'm needed here, but once I'm done here, I'm with her. Whatever her decision. She's been through enough. But she has Sophie here, so I'm pretty sure she will come back." Prez nods, knowing whatever happens, I'm with Stasia. I look around the room at all my brothers, knowing most of the guys in the room are oblivious to my decision. Krip nods at me. He must agree with my choice, not that I care. I want her safe.

Frantic knocking echoes through the room, and Prez gestures to open the door. Mira stands on the threshold, her expression anxious.

She scowls at Krip first, then she looks at her dad and states, "Dad, they're gone. Stasia, she's gone! I'm pretty sure she left first, on her own." Then her eyes travel over to Bullet, looking unsure how to proceed. She goes for gentle, "Sophie and Keata left as well." Her eyes snap back to her dad as she adds, "They wanted to look for Stasia! Shit. I told them to wait for you, Dad!" I'm up and storming for the door before she's finished her sentence. So does everyone else. Bullet has grabbed his phone and is ringing Sophie as he barges out of church. I know it's no use with Stasia. She made her mind up days ago. We all saw it. I hear Dad swear behind me and throw something at the wall.

He yells after me, "Drew, you go find her. Take Krip and Nova. I've got to head to Perth to pick up Savie. Shit! What the fuck was she thinking?"

I turn, mid-stride, and yell over the guys leaving the room, "Dad, you know what she had in her mind. She's been distant since Tommy died." As I turn, I say to no one, "I'll get her back. FUCK!" I'm going to smack her ass when I get her back safe! She better be safe.

Heading out back, I jump on my bike. Krip and Nova are behind me, getting on their bikes about the same time. We start up our engines together. Mira runs up screaming over the engine noise, "Hey, Bullet got ahold of Sophie. They're two towns over, in Yornup. She was heading to Bridgetown. She seems to think that's where Stasia will go." I nod. I'm not in the mood for small talk and I'm going to find it hard to rein it in when I get my hands on her. Fuck!

Before I take off, I decide to tell Mira, "Get someone to the house, and not you! I need to know if she got her car or not." Mira nods. I can't hear her over the engines now, anyway. She walks over to her dad. Bullet snakes out of the entrance with Knight and Trigger behind him. So, there will be the six of us, till we split up at Yornup. Here's hoping Sophie listens.

It takes fifteen minutes to get to Yornup, breaking speed limits all the way. Cops usually leave us be, but as we see Sophie up ahead, sirens start up behind us. Bullet doesn't slow down. He keeps going towards Sophie. Jesus, makes me more eager to get to Stasia, just to make sure she's safe.

The rest of us pull over. We turn off our engines and wait for the officer to come over. As he arrives, I get a text from Mira and Prez saying her car is gone. Scratching my head,I think, *how the fuck did she manage that*?

Looking up, I give the cop a chin lift, "'Sup, Officer?"

Eying our bikes, he steps in front of us, "Good. Any reason you men are in a hurry?" I nod, getting straight to the point. "How long have you been on duty today?" His response comes out cautiously. "Since 7:30 a.m. why? Are you looking for someone?"

"Yeah, she's in a Honda Civic, two door hatchback, and the car's probably about twenty years old."

He doesn't say much but, "She came through here a couple hours ago." I'm still staring at him, expecting more. I raise my eyebrows firmly, a silent demand. When he doesn't offer any more, I add, "Anything else?" The officer stands stern over me, his arms folded tightly across his chest. He glares at me, not sure whether to answer.

"And you guys want to know why?"

Not having much patience left, I spell it out, "She has dangerous company heading her way. We are trying to get to her first, before shit gets bad. You got me?" I clamp down my raging thoughts,

254

locking them away as I meet his glare with a fierce intensity, daring him to look away. The officer stubbornly holds my gaze, refusing to yield first.

I see his jaw tighten before he replies, "Might have been two and a half hours ago, but she was driving safely, not in a rush." He scrutinises us, taking in every detail, "Hope that helps boys. Now you guys try to keep your speed down, yeah? Especially in the town areas." I nod to thank him for his help, but I have other things on my mind.

Turning, I see Bullet and Sophie in a heated discussion, and I don't think Sophie's going to win this time. He's wild and I can see Keata in the back seat of the car.

Bullet turns his back on Sophie and then yells in my direction, "You go on. Keep in touch." I nod to him, knowing that Stasia and I are going to be in the same intense exchange.

As I start up the bike with Nova and Krip, Trigger says he's going to come with us just in case, I nod and take off. I know Bullet is fine by himself. Knight's skills are just as deadly. People underestimate him because he's always doing dumb shit with women.

It takes another fifteen minutes to get to Bridgetown. There's only one main road in these towns. The streets that run off of them, only leading to housing. All the commercial stuff is on the main road. There's a bank, a post office, and two pubs, but if you know where to look, there is a third pub as well. If she's here, someone would have seen her. Gotta love these little towns.

I head to the last pub, where I know an old fella who knows everything that happens here. Even if it's only a car passing through. Walking through the doors, I spot him at the pool table. As usual, it's just inside the front door.

"Hey Drew. What brings you up to these parts? No trouble, I hope!"

"Nah, old man, looking for my girl. She took off, scared. The cop in Yornup saw her car and said she was headed this way."

"Scared you say? What makes you think I'll tell you then, if I saw her and she's scared? What'd you do to her?"

Shaking my head, "Nothing old man, she's running from her past, and if I don't find her, it's going to catch her. You see her?"

"Yeah, black hatchback?" I nod for him to continue, "She stopped at the servo, and put more petrol in. Looks to me like she might drive some more." Shit, where would she go?

Staring outside, I'm trying to bring to mind what her thought process is. Tapping on the window brings my sight to Trigger. He peeks his head in, "Hey, who's that by the petrol station? He's been on our tail since we left Yornup, kept his distance, but definitely following us."

I squint across the road, trying to get a closer look. The man has his arm out, hanging low over the car, tapping the door with his fingertips. I've not seen him before. There looks to be a shadow, someone else in the back of the four-wheel drive. Could be somebody who works for them or it could be fuckin' Frankie. My blood burns. Before I know it, I'm almost out the door when Trigger grabs me by the arm and drags me back, slamming me against the wall.

"Drew, whoever it is, it's better he doesn't know we see him. Fuck's sake brother, I've got him in my sights, yeah? If he changes direction, I'll follow and give you a heads up, okay?"

"Goddamn it," I mutter through gritted teeth, my nod confirming that I'm hanging on by a thread. He seems to know as well, "You either need a shot of alcohol or a beer to cool down brother, Go, let me chat to some locals." Krip agrees with Trigger, we both watch him head straight to the bar. Nova leaves out the main door. He's heading towards the petrol station on the next corner to ask about Stasia. When I look in Trigger's direction, he's going the opposite way.

As I get to the bar, Krip passes me a beer, saying, "Let me tan her ass! That way you can still talk to her, or whatever!"

"Krip, you're not touching her ass, got me? But I'm going to have trouble keeping my cool. Fuck, I'm pissed she did this!" Krip shakes his head.

"We all knew she was going to leave. Fuck, we even stepped up the security on her. I blame who let her out! Put your anger towards them. She doesn't know that side of you." he says, staring at the air in front of him.

"Keep that away from her. She's seen too much bad in her life." Chugging back the beer Krip pushed my way, thinking to myself, I won't have a choice. My thoughts are going crazy sitting here, not being able to do anything. Raising my hand, I get the waitress's attention, asking for another beer. Krip does the same. I'm hoping the beer calms my brain as I know Stasia won't deal if I loose my shit.

When I'm finished, I'll head outside and see what the boys have found out. Swigging back the last sip, I spot Nova coming back in.

He approaches both me and Krip. "She's staying in the next town, filled up her tank and will be back later to meet the guy with the keys." *Fuck.* Anger curls in my gut at the possibility of the other guys tailing us creeps into my thoughts.

"If she comes back, the guys following us are going to find her."

Nova shakes his head no.

"Got the guy's number to the place she's renting. Told him to ring her and tell her to meet at the place she's going to be staying at. I've also texted Trigger to start a wild goose chase. So, he's setting that up. We're good, we got till 4 p.m., even got us a car to use." He looks toward the end of the bar.

"One of the staff over there said we could use hers, so we don't get followed." I turn and sit back, leaning on the bar, and look at him. He has this covered! Fuck!

He slaps my back and informs me, "We got your back brother, order lunch, have another beer, we will get her. I'll be back. Got some shit to set up!" He walks back out the door. Krip hasn't stopped drinking next to me.

"Brother, you going to stay sober?" he shakes his head. "Nope! I'm so pissed at her, so its best I drink a bit more. By the time we're back on the road tonight, I'll be fine, or I'll take that hot barmaid up on her offer!" Krip replies, his hand reaching for another beer she offers. His gaze lingers on the waitress, a hint of interest evident in his eyes.

3:30p.m. comes, and that's when Nova comes in with keys, pointing to the back of the pub. We head out the back. There's a car that's waiting for us with a dark tint, too. The beer has done its job, but I'm not sure if I trust myself for when I see her. I'm fuckin' mad! But I'm seeing why she thinks it would be easier this way. It's all I've done since sitting at the bar for the last few hours. If only she had no assholes after her!

Sienna Gypsy

STASIA

30

STASIA

The guy at the petrol station has contacted me and said he would meet me here at 4 p.m.. I have been sitting in this car since 1:30 p.m. I didn't want to, well, I didn't have anywhere else to go. So I stayed here. I keep thinking about if Drew even cares that I left. If he's even noticed. He hasn't even rung me yet. Well, maybe I did the right thing. Sophie keeps ringing and texting, but I don't read them. I can't put Keata in any more danger. I can't believe she thinks keeping me safe will be okay for Keata. She doesn't know what they're like. They will use anyone they can. Child, adult, they proved that with me and with Izzy.

Relief was clear on my face when Spud offered to take me to my car, even though he makes my stomach churn. He didn't sit still on the drive, looking sideways at me all the time, like he had another agenda. I put it down to him helping me escape and betraying Drew's trust.

Torture to Bliss

I took Drew's gun when he left for the meeting this morning. He's probably going to kill me when he figures that out. I don't care, though. I'm not going back to live the life I lived before! I've decided I need to fight! Fight to get my life back! If my father wants me back, then I'm ready to fight back this time. Frankie scared the shit out of me at the café. I'm determined to do something this time. Freezing is not an option. I know what a psycho he is. Well, I've known how psychotic he is for a long time, but I didn't think I would freeze. It could have been the shock, but this time I'm good, I'm sure of it. I've got Keata and Sophie to think about, and… well, maybe not Drew, but I want him safe.

I fell asleep for a while in my car. I wake abruptly, startled by a loud noise. It could have been a car or a truck, but as I glance around, I see nothing. I go to get out of the car, but before I do, I remember Drew's gun. Searching through my bag, it's at the bottom. I put my fingers around the handle, grasp it in my palm and pull it out. I glance over the gun to make sure the safety is on before I stuff it down the back of my jeans.

Stepping out of the driver's side, I notice movement near the front of the house. Like a low-hanging tree branch swaying more than usual. making me wonder if someone brushed up against it. Shaking it off, I try reassuring myself that the movement I saw could be a harmless cat. I look at my phone, seeing it's only 3:00 p.m., the guy said he'd be here at 4 p.m.. I walk the opposite direction from the moving tree, up to the top of the driveway and look around. The road is dead quiet. I'm in the middle of nowhere. I could scream, and no one would hear me. Shit!

Deciding to stretch my legs. I walk down the road a bit, thinking it'll calm my thoughts and I have to remind myself that no one is watching me. Reaching the end of the road takes about fifteen minutes. Looking around, I don't see anything that sets off alarm bells, so I decide to head back towards my car.

Sienna Gypsy

My mind's been in a mess since I left this morning. One minute, I long to be back in Drew's arms, but the next, well, I know deep down that I'm doing the right thing.

A truck comes into view in the distance. As it gets closer, I exhale, realising I don't recognise the people driving it. I keep walking, shaking my hands in front of me. Hoping the terror that's building inside will release through my fingertips. My mind races with the what ifs. It's hard to stop it from doing so.

As I get closer to my driveway, I hear another truck. As I turn, the realisation hits me. It's the same truck that passed before. He's slowing down. I watch him lean out the window and shout, "Hey, you must be new here. I live down the road. Come up for a coffee later if you're not busy and meet my roommates. I'm Jeff, by the way." Terror surges through me, bringing back bad memories.

I nod with a small, polite smile, "Maybe later. I've got a bit to do first. So might need a rain check, but I'll see how I go."

I wave goodbye, praying I don't see them again. Turning around and going back towards my driveway, I think to myself, I'm only staying for seven days. Seven days is a safe amount of time.

As I'm chanting this to myself, I look up at the front door of the house. It's open. My body goes still. I'm on high alert, scanning around the property. I don't see a car. My heart picks up a beat as I hear tyres crunch over gravel. I don't want to turn around. The crunching stops.

I focus all my thoughts on trying to control my breathing. Remembering how Nanna Sally taught me to focus breathing in through my nose and out through my mouth. I then look towards the house. My brows furrow. Is there someone in there? Breathing out through my mouth, I wonder if the truck that's here now, is the man with the key.

Shit! I hope it's the man with the key. I stretch out my fingers and then tighten my sweaty palms into fists. Then, I casually put my hands in my back pockets. Trying to get my hands close to the gun without it looking noticeable. I turn sideways so I can see both the door of the house and the truck at the same time. In my peripheral vision on the right, I see movement. I adjust my head to get a better look. The blood drains from my face as I see Trigger come out of the house. Shit, they found me. Then, strangely, relief hits me. I turn my attention to the guy that is now walking up the driveway from the truck. Wait. There's another guy still in the truck.

Shit, I bring one hand up to my back where the gun is, when I hear Trigger say, "Your home, honey! Come over here and I'll take care of these guys, see what they need." I smile, knowing I can trust him.

But the guy from the driveway says, "She was just telling us we could help her move. We didn't know she had company." He has a vicious sneer on his face. He's getting closer, and he's reaching for something in his jacket pocket. The man stretches out his arm. He points a bloody gun at me, shit! I decide it's now or never. The adrenaline that's bubbling in my body helps me point my gun at him.

The guy looks at me and spits out, "Well, I hope you shoot to kill, honey, cause if you don't, you will be a dead girl when I'm finished. Pity, I thought we could be good friends first." I have to fight the chill that runs down my spine. The other guy is next to him. I was too busy watching Trigger and didn't notice him get out of the truck.

He keeps creeping closer, "She also said, earlier, that she was going to come up for a visit! Didn't you, sweetheart?" My eyes are darting from one guy to the other, measuring who is closer to me. One guy winks at me like I'm on the same page as him. What the hell? I'm pointing my gun at the first guy and the other one is still edging closer.

I go to move my gun and hear Trigger warning the other guy, "I wouldn't, if I were you," he growls with his gun aimed on the second guy. Thank God. Maybe we will get out of this alive.

"Stasia, walk towards me, honey," he says with unwavering confidence. I don't. I know how dangerous this is and I'm ready to fight. So, I turn and plant my feet, as Nanna Sally told me to and make sure that my aim is good. I relax my shoulders, then lock my arms in place. Eying the gun, I flick the safety off. Everyone talks at once, but I block it out of my mind.

As I'm about to say something, I hear the second guy say, "You're going down just like the old lady did!" Something snaps inside of me. I move targets so I'm pointing at the second guy who admits to killing Nanna Sally and I shoot the first shot. It hits his right shoulder. I aim the gun again and I hit his left side. My legs feel weak and I fall to the ground, but I don't stop. I take one more shot. He was the one who killed Nanna Sally. No matter what, I will not be going back to my dad or Frankie again. I turn my head and see Trigger coming for me.

I smile, trying to tell him, "I got him."

He drops next to me, "At a price, honey. You should have let me handle it. Get your head clear. Drew and the boys will be here soon."

31

DREW

When we arrived at the house, all I saw was Trigger, pointing in Stasia's direction. He didn't seem worried. My gaze locks on Stasia and I notice the flinch her body gives from my look. I'm trying with everything in me to not lose my shit. I don't lose contact with her gaze while Trigger gives me a rundown of what happened. The last thing I remember was punching him. Nova and Krip jumped in and pin me to the ground till I calmed down. I'm not sure how long I'm there for before I hear her, "Don't hurt him." Her words repeat in my mind, I let them wash over my body but that still doesn't stop my anger. I breathe in and out a few times. Which brings me to now, my brothers still holding me down. I search their faces, trying to shove down my anger before I tell them, "I'm good." Nova, not as trusting as the rest, asks, "You sure?" I'm nodding my head, refusing to use my words. I'm still struggling with the rage inside me. I stand up and walk the opposite way from Stasia, trying to push this feeling of chaos away from me. How can she not realise how much she has hurt me? Why does she think it's okay that she just ran? And she shot somebody. She fucking shot somebody!

Pulling my hair again, till the pain soothes my fury, I wonder how the fuck she got a gun! How'd she get to her car when everyone knew the girls were on lockdown? She was supposed to be monitored. How the fuck did this happen?

My mind is whirling, how could I have changed things? Nothing other than tying her ass up is coming to mind. *Is that even legal?*

I turn back around and lock eyes with her again. I study her, she looks scared, and unsure. Maybe even sorry. She's biting her lip, I can truly say she's out of her depth of understanding of what's going on. She needs to understand that this can never happen again, she cannot run from me.

Raking my fingers through my hair, I take the first step, walking towards her. I make sure to take controlled breaths until I'm standing in front of her. I watch her gaze start from my feet; they glide up my body till we have eye contact. We stand in silence; I'm struggling to figure out what to say to her first. "I'm sorry, I didn't know this would happen." She says, her voice soft.

"Stop." I snap, "Of course you didn't know this would happen. You're not a fucking clairvoyant." Her body jolts from my sharp words. I fold my arms in front of me and try to relax my stance. In my head I am repeating, *breathe, calm down*, but I'm still out of my mind with rage. "Fuck, Stasia, what if you got hurt? What if you got shot? Did you even think that was a possibility? I bet you didn't! You were thinking about everybody else but you. Does how I feel not even come into the equation? I thought we were an us. Which means we're in this together, no matter what." I watch as a tear runs down her cheek. "And where did you get the goddamn gun?" She has nothing to say back to me, so I turn my back and walk to the closest bike to get on it.

"DREW!" she screams at me. "Don't you dare spit those words at me and not even wait for my response. I did think about everybody, including your club, and my friends, and Keata. What I was thinking is that if they got a hold of Keata or my friends I wouldn't want them to live with what I went through. To survive that, it took everything in me. And to even look at you and feel anything at all it took every last bit of strength I had left. Yes, you helped move my fears and helped me feel protected. But right now, you are not my priority. Everybody else is, and I thought I could take that away from them, and this was the only way I could do it. THAT IS WHY I DID THIS! AND THE GODDAMN GUN IS YOURS!" The last part, she screamed at me. Nova comes up behind her and pulls her into his chest to comfort her, I rev the engine. I say to no one, "I'll be back at the clubhouse." and burn rubber to get out of there.

I'm sitting at the bar, drinking. Drowning in my thoughts, not understanding what happened. Remembering her fighting back like she did, if I wasn't so mad, I would be proud of her. It's a while before I hear the doors open to the club. I turn my head to my shoulder and watch who comes in. Nova is first, keeping Stasia close. He has her hand and takes her towards the hallway heading to my room. He doesn't lose eye contact with me the whole time he walks her in that direction. I turn back to my beer and take a long drink. I've had two beers, and from the adrenaline that's been running through my body, it feels like I've had ten. I need to blow off some steam. I look for Knight, then give him a chin lift. He walks my way and we both walk to the gym.

Once we're in the ring, Knight asks, "Are we going to talk feelings?" I shake my head. He knows damn well we're not talking feelings. I raise my fists, "Come on, give me your best." And for the next hour I enjoy the punches, and the pain that comes with them. Knight's known for his fighting. It's something he is good at, and why I choose him to fight with, because he won't hold back.

Needing to clean myself up, I head towards my room knowing she will be in there. As I arrive at my room, Nova looks at me and gives a clipped nod, "You cool man?"

Am I cool? No fuckin' way! I flip him the bird, because of course I'm not okay! Fuckin' genius.

As I enter my room, my eyes connect with Stasia's like a magnet. She is looking at me with tears in her eyes. I shake my head at her. I'm mad as shit, but less than I was before.

I walk towards Stasia, until I'm by the bedside, her eyes haven't left mine. I reach out with both hands and cradle her heart-shaped face in my calloused hands, and stare into her eyes. I take a deep breath before I speak.

"You scared the shit out of me." Then I lean down till my mouth is next to her ear and I state firmly, "Don't run. Ever again. I lost my mind today. Fuck! Never do that again!" She grabs me by my shirt and pulls me into her, bawling against my shoulder.

She keeps mumbling and repeating herself, "I'm sorry, I'm so sorry. I thought it was the only way!" I pull back to get her attention.

I stare into her eyes to assure her, "It's not! Now it's time to trust me. Beauty, you listening?"

Nodding her head, she says, "Yeah, but Keata. Drew, they can't touch her." I grit my teeth.

"No one will touch her. Bullet is on top of it, Stasia. She has more protection than anyone!" Stasia takes a deep breath, and nods her agreement.

Stasia moves somewhat, giving me more room, so I sit on the bed next to her.

I get a call from Dad. I answer, "Hey, what's up?"

Dad's voice sounds drained as he asks, "She alright?" I'm nodding even though he can't see me before I respond.

"Yeah, shook up, but she's okay. She won't do it again, but we need to talk. The shit that went down, it's not good, Dad."

Dad sighs before saying, "Yeah, I heard, Son. Look, Savie wants to talk to her." Looking down at my shoulder where she's leaning into me, she is still sobbing.

"Nah, I will ring you back when we are good." I hear him explain to Savie that she needs to wait. He gives me his E.T.A., which is an hour and a half out. I say goodbye, turning my attention back to Stasia.

"That was Dad." She nods into my chest but doesn't say anything. I tell her, "I need to shower. I was sparring with Knight," her eyes connect with mine, still unsure. She nods and pulls back, curling into the pillow. I enter the bathroom door and stop. "Stasia, I know we have a lot to talk about, but me and you, this is it for me. You need to know that without you, there is no me." I turn and head in the bathroom and close the door.

After what must have been two hours, I get a text from Dad.

DAD: *Boy, u hungry? Sav is coming in now.*

ME: *Ya I'll have the same as you. All good*
with Sav, see u soon.

After a bit, there's a knock at my door. Stasia is asleep next to me, so I yell, "It's open." Krip walks in with Savie and I smile at her. I've met her a few times, but not as Dad's lover, just a friend, but I've always thought that something was there.

She greets me with a kiss on the cheek "You need to move. I need some time with her. Please let me hold her."

After what happened between us, I don't want to, but I begrudgingly move, "Fifteen minutes is all I'm willing to give, so hopefully that's enough."

She chuckles and looks back at me, "We'll see, Drew... we'll see!" I don't move far, but search out Krip, who's against the far wall. He hasn't even spoken to her yet, and we haven't even touched on her shooting someone. I still can't fuckin' believe that!

After a while, Dad walks in with some food and Stasia wakes as he enters. She looks around and I can tell she is wondering who's holding her. Because her eyes connect with mine, she looks up slowly. I'm not expecting her reaction. Her chin wobbles, and then she is sobbing, but Savie holds her tight. After a while, she says something to Savie, but I'm not sure what. She holds Savie tight before she goes back to sleep again.

It's quiet for a bit before Krip talks, "Trigger left no survivors, so we're not sure if her father was involved."

Dad nods, then says, "Sam seems to think one of our guys took her to her car but he's not sure who yet." I know Prez will butt heads together when he finds out who, and Mira will investigate her own way as well.

Then, the part that's been burning a hole in my head blurts out, "How the fuck did she shoot that guy? What was she thinking? Shit, why didn't Trigger stop her from going down that road? She's never going to deal with this, she has enough on her plate, FUCK!" Dad nods, but Savie's not shy about advising me what she thinks.

"Drew, until you guys talk, you won't know what she can handle. She's stronger than you think, but she is good at hiding shit in her mind. Trust me, but give her time and let her know you're there for her."

"We have already had words about her running, but she knows I'm here." Surely, by now, she knows I'm not going anywhere! Damn it. She's so wrapped around my heart that it doesn't beat if she's not here!

I can't stop looking at her. It's not long before Dad comes and grabs Savie and kisses Stasia on the head. He then informs me, "We're going to unpack and get settled. You good?" I nod, then give him a hug.

They walk out, but before they leave, Savie says, "Drew, give her time. She will trust you. But she is still learning to be a couple, remember that. Just let her place everything in her mind first, yeah?"

She winks at me as they walk out. As she gets to the door, she turns, "Then she'll show you her own rampage!" I smirk. Her rampage. Fuck, she showed me, and I loved it. I watch her leave, closing the door. Turning into Stasia, I curl up with her and turn out the lights, soaking up the knowledge that she is here and alive. The rest we can figure out later.

STASIA

32

STASIA

Drew's scent washes over me. His cologne and the feeling of his arms around my shoulders are soothing. His arms squeeze me close, causing me to open my eyes. I can't believe he's still into me after everything that happened, and me shouting at him. I couldn't control myself. It was like a poltergeist took over my body and word vomited everything that was building up in my mind.

The pressure in my bladder is uncomfortable. I need to get to the toilet. I try to get up, but Drew stops me by squeezing me slightly more around my shoulders.

"Where do you think you're going, Beauty?" he says with his gaze fixed on me.

I have trouble maintaining eye contact when I respond, "I need to go to the toilet. You need to move."

Drew moves and lets me up. I get up and walk to the bathroom. When I walk back into the room, I see Drew sitting on the edge of the bed, deep in thought. I'm still nervous about where we are. I have never been in a relationship before, so I don't know the rules. I sit next to him, and he grabs my hand tight, which causes my body to relax. I didn't even know how much I needed his touch. "Beauty, I meant what I said. You are it for me."

I nod and can feel his conviction. "I'm still processing, and don't know the rules for this." I point between us. "Do I still get to hold you when I want?" he chuckles.

"Yes! You will always have the power to hold me whenever you want."

I turn my head and look him in the eyes, "I didn't yesterday! I didn't like seeing the hate in your eyes."

His hand comes up and brushes a stray hair behind my ear, "I had no control yesterday, I was so far out of my mind with worry, I spiralled." I nod, needing his confession. I touch his cheek below where he is sporting a black eye, "Knight do this?" he nods. I lean forward and kiss his bruised eye. When I pull back his eyes are still closed. "Beauty," he breathes.

"I don't like you bruised, Drew. When you walked in yesterday, I couldn't even think straight. Looking at you and the swelling scared me more."

"I'll remember that, but, Beauty, you yelling at me was the hottest thing I've seen in a long time. Don't stop putting me in my place. If I'm out of line, you tell me. Deal?"

"Deal" I whisper, he leans in and takes my lips gently, which turns frantic fast.

His lips are all over my lips, neck, under my ear, and he stops. I'm all worked up, panting, wanting more. He pulls back and asks me "How are you feeling?" Well, a little riled up but I know he is not talking about that right now.

"I don't know. I don't care that I shot that guy, if that is what you're asking. But as for everything else, I'm confused." He's silent for a bit. I turn my head so I can see his face, he looks relaxed.

He responds, "About what?" I gather my thoughts and try not to confuse him with what was going on in my head when I answer him.

"Well, you're still here. I'm okay with the shooting, but I'm not sure why you're still around and why you care so much?" The last part is still a question that lingers in my mind.

As he kisses me again on the neck, he tells me, "Haven't you figured it out yet, Beauty? I can't seem to function if you aren't where I can see you or if you're in trouble. You've added yourself to my heart, and it's not whole without you. God, I didn't know if I was going to drag you to my room, cuff you to my bed, or spank the hell out of you for that stunt. But I've shoved those thoughts aside, for now. So, get used to it. Then we'll talk about cuffs and locks, yeah?" he chuckles.

"Oh, don't forget the spanking!" I giggle, not knowing if it's because I'm uncomfortable or if I'm curious. I'm going for uncomfortable right now. Drew raises a challenging eyebrow.

"Don't tempt me, Beauty!"

At 9:30 a.m., Savie knocks on Drew's door. A moment later, Krip comes in.

"I'm leaving. Need to follow a lead!" He says to whoever is listening. He doesn't even look at me. I hate that I've made him this mad. He's going to yell at me, I know he is. I can feel it in my bones. Krip leaves, and my eyes clock him till he exits the room. Trying not to think about it now, I turn my attention to Savie. I'm so happy Savie's here. It's like the weight of everything isn't there anymore. Same as when Drew takes me in his arms. Maybe that's what family is like, just like Nanna Sally always told me.

Savie comes over and gives me a big hug, and I smile at her. She sits down next to me. Drew must take this as his cue and heads towards the shower.

Savie grabs my hand and squeezes.

"He makes you happy, doesn't he, Little Bird?"

Nodding, "Yeah, he does, but I don't deserve him. At first, I thought, I can't be with him because he's a biker. And, well, my father and Cobra... I thought I'd be causing trouble for everyone. But Drew moved in, and I didn't even know how far he snuck into my heart till today!" Savie's smile beams from her face. It's so blissful. She has always been a beautiful woman.

"Oh, honey, he loves you hard. I can see it. He thinks the sun rises and sets with you, so don't lose him. Honey, guys like this only come round once. If you let them get away, you might not get another chance." Then she gives me a gentle hug and walks to the window, staring at nothing. I don't think she's thinking of her and Prez. Well, her husband from back when we met. She never really told me about what happened, but I think he treated her wrong and she regrets something from before then, or maybe I'm wrong. She won't tell me, anyway.

"Little Bird, as soon as you're well enough to move, we are going on a road trip!" I look at her like she lost her mind, but she turns to look at me and smiles.

"Don't worry, Drew is coming. He wouldn't leave you, anyway. Well, he was going to at first, but after you were in that shootout when you ran, he decided he ain't leaving you now."

"W-wait, what did you just say? He was leaving me?"

"No, no not at all, he was going to go and make sure things with your so-called father were finished. Then he was going to come and get you." Oh, that makes more sense.

"So, what now? Are we going?"

Savie walks over to my bed and sits on the edge, "You're coming home with me, we're driving, and the boys are riding." She claps her hands together, saying this like it's going to be the best road trip ever. I sit there staring at her. I'm not sure if this is a great idea or the worst one yet, but I've got two more days to process this. So, I decide that's what I'm going to do, and I'll talk it out with Sophie. I don't want her to freak, either. She needs me as much as I need her.

DREW

33

DREW

I haven't slept much at all, since Stasia was in the shootout. She is definitely keeping me busy. Ever since I met her, shit has been piling up and I'm powerless to stop it. Plus she killed a man! I sigh and look away, towards the door, trying to rein in my thoughts. She thinks she's going to be okay, but sometimes emotions creep up without warning. I pinch the bridge of my nose, trying not to think about the uncertainty. My gut pulls tight with unease. Hoping the thoughts will go away, persuading myself that we will cross that bridge when it comes.

Throughout these last couple of days, I've been talking to Dad and Prez about the drive to Melbourne, making sure we're all ready for tomorrow. We can't fly, so we are driving. I'm mapping out which way we're going, because we want to get there as fast as possible. We're going in a group of eight. That's me, Dad, Krip and Bullet on bikes, and Savie, Stasia, Sophie and little Keata in the car. Stasia doesn't know yet that Sophie and Keata are coming, but

I wanted that part to be a surprise. She's had so much shit so far. A bit of bliss will help.

We also have a group following of four and that's to make sure Stasia's father doesn't jump us. It won't be easy with Knight, he's bad enough on his own, but with Nova, Trigger and one of the other guys, Thump, it will be impossible.

Thump was the guy who helped me with bikes and anything else when Dad stayed in Melbourne. Thump is older than me, but not as old as Dad. He has a problem with trust. His background is something no one talks about. He seems to trust me, and the other brothers, unless it's one of Knight's scheming ideas.

There's a noise at my door and the girls burst through. I glare at them with a *what the fuck* look. At least they look half guilty.

Well, Mira doesn't give two shits, but Sophie and Izzy mouth 'sorry'.

Stasia looks at the girls with tears in her eyes and Sophie rushes to Stasia on the bed. Before I know it, she is in their arms, standing with them. "Oi, how about some privacy? This is my room, you know." I curse to no one because no one is listening, anyway.

Standing, putting on a shirt, I lean down and kiss Stasia's cheek. She moves away from the girls and wraps her arms around my neck. Putting her head on my shoulder and her nose at my neck, she inhales deeply, smelling me. I can't lie, I love it when she does this, it's my favourite thing she does. Well, one of them. I smirk, thinking of them.

As soon as I get to the door, I turn and look at them all fussing over Stasia, which hits the best part in my chest. I need to get her a vest. I've decided there and then, I'm not waiting anymore.

Walking down the hallway, I spot Prez and he signals to for me to head to his office when I'm ready.

Bullet's there with Nova, Krip, and Dad. I close the door and Prez gets straight into it. They already dealt with the two dead guys, and now are looking into more places where her father and Frankie can be.

"We've checked from Donnybrook to here, but nothing has come up. We're missing something. No hotel, bed-and-breakfast or campsite.... nothing!" Nova says.

I look at Bullet, saying, "What if we're looking in the wrong area? What if they know people down here, have a girlfriend, or the girl they've used before? Any ideas?" Dad nods his agreement and so does everybody else.

Nova then says, "I'll start looking at club girls, new and old, and hang arounds." We all agree to this. "I think going back and taking another look at the house and seeing if there is anything we can find is a good idea. Bullet and I can do that before the end of the day." I speak. We get chin lifts all around the table. Prez adjourns the meeting.

Our meeting took a good part of the afternoon. We are heading back towards my room. I notice the girls have moved to the main area, sitting in the chairs and lounges.

Stasia has Keata on her lap, all cuddled up. They don't look like they're letting go anytime soon. Bullet and I decide to go run some errands while they're all catching up. We need to check the house again for some clues and check to see if anyone's hanging around.

Arriving back, I head to the bar and grab a seat, just sitting back, watching. I feel a hand on my shoulder and another on my back, too close for my liking. I don't even bother turning.

"Fuck off, bitch, get your hands off me!" She doesn't take the hint.

"Oh, baby, you want me. She can't do shit for you! But I can sort you out." As she's talking, her hand descends from my shoulder to my chest. I grab it firmly and yank it away, intending to hurt her.

She laughs, "Oh, baby, I like it rough. What else you got?" Fury burns in my mind as I grab her by the throat, pinning her to the bar. "You put your hands on me one more time bitch, I will kill you, don't come near me or what's mine again!" I'm glaring at her with hatred washing off me. She is going red in the face and struggling to breathe.

When Knight comes over, he says to Veronica, "You need to fuck off and learn your place. Don't touch us unless we want it or fuck off and don't come back!" She's nodding, gasping for air. I throw her to the floor and don't even care. Having that skank touch me makes me sick. This is why I never touch club bitches! I drink my drink, then make my way to Stasia. I need her right now.

As I approach her, I stall to a stop, thinking maybe she will reject me, but she surprises me.

"Did you just take out the trash, honey?" I can't stop my mouth from curving into a smirk. Fuck, I needed to hear that.

"Something like that, Beauty. You nearly ready for bed?"

She shocks the shit out of me by kissing Keata and passing her to Sophie, "Yeah, honey, take me to bed." But she has a need in her eyes. Jesus.

She goes to stand, but I pick her up. Cheers go up around the room as I take my girl to bed. I'm thinking of all the ways I'm going to enjoy her, but as I get to my room, fuckin' Veronica is there, leaning against my door. Something is wrong with her head. As far as I'm concerned, she is out of the club now! I'm not having her near Stasia anymore. I go to tell her, but she talks first.

"Why her? What has she got? She can't even sort you out. She's damaged goods!" I go to respond, but Beauty beats me.

"It's called class and dignity. Not all men like slutty bitches. Maybe you need to take a step back, look at your self-worth, and realise that as women, we have more to offer!" I decided I don't want Stasia around her any longer. I storm past her to my room, but Veronica hasn't finished.

"Maybe you're right, but you won't be around long enough to see that!" She leaves and I believe Veronica knows something we don't. Son of a bitch! We get in our room and as soon as I put her on the bed, "Don't let that," I point to the door. "Ruin our night. But if you don't want me or you can't tonight, I understand." She pulls back and drops her gaze, and whispers, "I don't care what she says, but we can. I know we can. Because I want you, Drew. Now."

Jesus! The excitement this girl causes me is next level.

Stasia's sultry look is egging me on. Undressing her is all I can think about. "Beauty, take off my top." She scrambles towards me and reaches for my top, pulling hard over the top of my head as I bend forward. She looks back at me for my next instruction. Winking at her I say, "My turn, let's take your top off and your bra." I don't let her do it, I do it for her. My hands grasp the hooks on her bra from the back. I let my lips cascade along her neck and lick up towards her ear, watching as the goosebumps shimmer over her body from her excitement. Using my fingertips on her shoulders, I pull her bra straps down, letting her bra fall to the ground. I watch her beautiful breasts bounce ever so slightly, they're perfect on her body. Her nipples pebbling into hard points. My hand reaches over to her cheek, and my thumb brushes against her smooth skin, up to her ear. Then, my hand glides down to her neck and shoulder, where my thumb massages her collarbone. When I make my way down to her breasts and play with her nipples, I hear her gasp. I was too memorised in watching her breasts, my eyes dart back to hers. "You're beautiful, you know that, Beauty?" She brings her body close to mine so we're skin to skin, I can feel her hard nipples on my chest. When our lips collide, it's nothing but bliss. Hunger washes over both of us as we pull away the rest of our clothes. It takes me a minute, but I pick her up and put her on my dressing table, which is the right level. At last, I slide into her. I can't stop the feeling that is racing through my head of losing her. She is scraping at my back with her nails, which is driving me crazy. I swallow her moans with my mouth. "Drew, harder, harder. I need more." Her encouraging words cause a feral need within me. I pump in and out of her till we both cum. We stare at each other for a while before I give her one slow, sensual kiss. I help her off the dresser and we head to the bathroom to clean up.

Stasia's in bed and I'm lying there thinking about what happened before with Veronica. I grab my phone. Something Veronica said won't leave my mind, so I text Nova to tell PC to do some checks. He replies straight away,

NOVA: *On it, brother!*

Good, now we can sleep, if Stasia stops pushing up against me like she's ready to go again, the minx. "Babe, stop. I told you, get some sleep, or we will be at it all night." She huffs like a child and pulls away. I smirk, knowing she'll be back soon enough.

Sienna Gypsy

DREW

34

DREW

It was still dark when I got up this morning to get everything packed. Getting Stasia to sleep was the simple part. It's the unknown that bothers me. The prospects did a lot of packing last night, and I'm going over everything. But there are other things that need to be done before I see PC.

Once it's all done, I head to his tech room. I'm eager to know if he got any information last night.

As I walk into the kitchen to grab a coffee, I see Nova. He's there with Izzy, organising breakfast.

Pouring my coffee into my mug, I ask, "You talk to PC, brother?"

He juts his head towards the door, looking peeved, responding, "Yeah, follow me. You're not gonna like what we found out."

I grab my coffee and follow him to the tech room. Nova knocks once, then opens the door. PC looks up from his computer and gives a chin lift, then briefs me.

"Found out that Kim and Veronica live together, been friends for years before the club. Now what's interesting is the home phone has had calls to a private number. That's since all this shit's been happening, and more frequently now." *Well, Fuck!*

I reply, "That's not a coincidence. Fuck, you tell Prez yet?" PC is shaking his head.

"Not yet, got a meeting with him in ten minutes, but if Veronica got any word about the move, they will know." He looks down at his computer, hitting a few more buttons.

"Drew, I'm thinking a decoy, which I'm working on now, will work better," I nod and grunt my agreement. I tap my knuckles on top of his desk waiting because he seems to have something more to say. His reply is quick.

"So, who's the other mole, cause I'm thinking it ain't just the girls?" Dread fills me with him voicing it. Making it more noticeable because he's right. I nod.

"Yeah, I'm thinking the same. PC, Thanks for looking into this. I'll join you at the meeting. I'll get Dad, yeah?" As I walk towards the door, I pat PC on the shoulder in thanks.

PC and Nova both nod, and then I'm out into the hall, stalking towards Dad's room on the other side of the compound.

Knocking on his door, Savie opens it up with Dad's t-shirt on and she blushes. She throws her thumb over her shoulder and points at the shower.

"He's in the shower. You want to wait in here?" Shaking my head.

"Nah, all good. Tell him I'm waiting in the kitchen and it's important, yeah?"

She nods, "Will do, Drew."

Heading back down to the kitchen, a feeling hits me. I'm happy for Dad, but that's the first time I've seen him with someone else. I've known over the years, but I never saw it. He never allowed me to see that side of him, even as an adult. If I was there, no girls or women ever were. I've seen the others being stupid. Even guys cheating on their partners, but that's not on me and not something I believe in. Makes me appreciate the real thing more.

Sitting at the bar, Izzy gives me some toast and asks if she can go back to my room to see Stasia.

I tell her, "Go on back, I don't think she's awake, but if she is, tell her I'm in a meeting with Prez and will be back soon." She jumps excitedly.

"Yes, I will! Thanks, Drew." Then she rushes down the hallway towards my room.

Sitting near the kitchen waiting for Dad, eating my toast, I get caught up in my thoughts. I'm glad he was always an honest man with me. It showed me that mum was something to him. Which showed me how much respect Dad had for Mum, and how much I would eventually have for someone special.

I feel a slap on my back. I jolt from the sting, looking up as I realise it's Dad. He has his hand on my shoulder. Turning, I smirk.

"Hey, sorry, was daydreaming a bit." Dad chuckles, swinging his head from side to side.

"Son, I'm sorry you saw that. I've wanted to talk about this for a while, but I suppose now is as good a time as any. You know I always loved your mother. Even to this day. She was an extraordinary lady. You know that, right?" His voice is raw and emotional. I nod, knowing he needs to say this to me.

"Good. Yeah, well, Savie, and I have been dancing around each other for a while now, and I've finally caught her, so I'm hoping when I put my patch on her, you'll be okay with that." Wow, he is in love with Savie. I believe she'll be great for Dad. My chin descends automatically in a nod.

"Dad, I couldn't be happier for you! Mum passed years ago. Savie's not the first person you've been with since mum passed." Pausing, I turn more to make eye contact.

"Well, I wouldn't know, cause you never, not once put me through that crap. So, as far as a blessing goes, be happy. I am!"

That hand on my shoulder squeezes me, then he ruffles my hair saying, "Come on, we have a meeting to get to." I stand and turn. Dad smiles and pats my back, then he almost has me in a choke hold, hugging me from behind.

"Anyway... there's been some updates. We have a bit of a lead." Dad walks beside me. "Come on, then let's go see what's going on. So, you're good with Savie?" I can't help the smile that I have on my face.

"Dad, she's awesome, and my girl loves her like a mother, so I'm more than good. But are you okay with me and Stasia? I know she's your Little Bird, but, she's mine Dad. I love her." He looks at me knowingly.

"I know, Son. Trust me, we all do!" The look on his face is caring. I nod back at him.

Dad strides to the office door ahead of me. He opens it first, and we both enter, one after the other. My eyes observe where everybody is in the room. Noticing everyone is here, but PC. The room's not as full as it normally is. Only the high patch members are here. This update needs to be discreet. We are still not sure which member is our rat. I walk to where my chair is, while Dad walks around the other side of the long table, to the centre of the room. He leans against the edge of the wall nearest the window. As I take my seat, Nova begins the meeting by filling Prez in about Veronica and Kim. "PC thinks we should use a decoy, set them up so they think they're gone. We're not sure what they know and who else is involved." As he finishes talking, PC walks in with a big smile on his face. He eyes everyone at the table, then looks at Dad and takes a seat.

"I've made a decoy, Prez. But only the people in this room can know because I think I know who the mole is, but we will know for sure soon. So, everyone will be in the van as if we're leaving. You guys will take the girls into the shed to keep them out of sight and prevent any club members from accidentally overhearing their conversations. When it's time put them in the first van, but leave them there. Then the other van I've set up will head in the opposite direction from Melbourne. You guys are going through Albany, while the other van will head in Kalgoorlie's direction. They'll turn back once they get there; a wild goose chase. But I've made sure the whole club knows you guys are going through Kalgoorlie and that you boys are all in the van!"

Prez nods, "So, who do you think this mole in my club is PC?" PC taps his nose like it's obvious, then nods at the door.

"I reckon he'll be trying to listen. If not, he'll be around the bar seeing who knows what, but my guess is Spud. I've been watching him. I also know he's been Veronica's main screw lately."

My eyes meet PC's, anger storms through my veins. Fuck! Fuckin' Spud! Clenching my fist tight. I don't even notice the noise raising in the room, only the rage and white noise in my ears.

It takes a minute before I notice that the room has erupted in arguments and threats all around the table. Prez strikes his fist on the table a few times to quiet the room and looks at everyone.

"Leave him, for now!" his glare connects with PC.

"Any proof PC?" I can see the fire burning in Prez's eyes. It matches mine, but he will hold his cool, for now. I'm hoping I'm not the one to break the decoy by killing him.

PC replies, "Nah, no hard proof yet, but I'll get it soon. I set something up that will lead only to him if it is him." Prez nods.

"Right then. Let's play this PC's way. But be careful, there are more in on this than that lot, and I'm hoping Spud's the only one from this club!"

Disappointed that it's a brother, brotherhood is the wrong thing to cross. The club will not give him mercy!

Prez gives us some last-minute orders, like we are now leaving later tonight, so the first van is well on its way. If there's anyone watching the club, they will see nobody else leave. We all agree that the girls will hate being in the shed all day, but they'll understand. I hope. Shit! What a long day it's gonna be!

Sienna Gypsy

STASIA

35

STASIA

L ying in bed, my body still feels tender from last night's love making. Who knew sex was a workout. Thoughts keep going round and round in my head. I need to stop getting into trouble! I go to get up and hear knocking at the door.

I yell out, "Is it open?" The door swings open and Izzy's head peers in.

"Yep, it is. You awake?" The look on her face looks apprehensive.

Wanting to comfort her, I tell her, "Yeah, come in, tell me what's up. You okay?" The look on her face is as though she's weighing the pros and cons of what she has to say. Eventually, she blurts out, "Wanted to make sure you're okay. I've been worried sick, and when Nova told me he had to go find you, I didn't realise you took off. I thought someone took you! Why would you do that?" Izzy sighs, her shoulders slumping as she looks up with a contrite expression.

"Izzy, all I was thinking was that if I didn't get away, they would take you guys. I'm not sure what the boys have told you. My father is an evil man, so are his friends, and I couldn't let you or any of the girls go through what I've been through. I needed to stop them, but I didn't think it through. I didn't even think Drew would try to find me." I say the last bit, fidgeting with my thumbs.

"What? Why not? Are you kidding? That man loves you like crazy! He was like some crazed terminator. He just went straight to his bike and barked out orders, so he didn't backtrack. I don't think he even thought about anything either. You were his only priority!" I know Drew said this, but to hear from someone else makes it more real.

"Well, I'm not going anywhere now. He made some things clear, things like being handcuffed to the bed if I pull a stunt like this again.So I'm thinking, let's not!" I shrug the last part off, hoping that never happens.

"Good 'cause I don't want you to leave, I would miss you, and I sort of need someone who gets me, and you do. I think it's because of our... Well, you know." She says this with her head down, picking at the material on her tracksuit pants. I know something is bothering her.

"You still having nightmares? Are they getting worse... Or?"

"Stasia, I'm okay, you've been through enough. I'll be fine." And now I know we need to talk.

"You know, it will help me as well if we talk. My nightmares have been back and they're scarier than before. I think the knife incident brought them back, and now I have people who I care about that could get hurt. I'm scared now, more than I've ever been!" I'm hoping my admission to being scared will help her bring out her demons to me.

"I know what you mean. Before, when they took me, no one cared about me, anyway. But when they found me, Nova and Cory, I'm...," a single tear slides down her face while more tears pool in her eyes. She's trying to say more but can't get it out.

So, I tell her, "Oh, honey, come here." She comes to me, and I embrace her in my arms, tightly at first, then we both sit there in each other's arms.

When she can talk, she says, "I keep seeing them come for me. Then hurting everyone here, and the guys hating me for bringing it to their door!"

"Oh, honey, that will not happen. Nova thinks of you as his daughter, even though I know it's not been long, but he won't ever let anything happen to you. As for the club, they all feel the same way! As for Mira and me, well, we'd kick some biker butt. Well, I'd let Mira pave the way. She's a hell of a lot tougher than me! But hey, we'd do some damage!" She wipes away the tears streaming down her face. A sad smile breaking through as she lets out a small, hopeful giggle. I guess we both know I can't kick butt. Izzy looks up at me with a sombre look on her face.

"Please don't leave me again. I need you, and this." She squeezes me and I know what she means because it's what I craved and didn't get till Savie and Nanna Sally. We sit there for the next half an hour with her in my arms, listening to music and me giving her songs that helped me when my brain wouldn't shut off.

We both hear a creaking noise and look at the door at the same time. Drew's head appears around the door. He looks at us both.

"Everything okay?" I nod as Izzy gets off the bed and then looks embarrassed.

"We were just listening to music," Izzy smiles at me and nods. "I'll leave you both to it. I've got to see Cory. He wants to do some shooting practise today."

"Have fun! I loved shooting with Krip. We should have a shoot-off when you're more confident!" I say with a wink.

"Oh, you're on! I'll ask Cory if we can. That will be great!" She has the biggest smile on her face now, and I can see how pretty she is. I hope her smile stays there till she sees Nova. I think it would make his day knowing she is smiling like that. She's out the door and skipping down the hallway, Drew looks back at me, shaking his head.

"You think that's a wise idea, Beauty? I think the boys are going to kill me, putting ideas like that in her head." he chuckles. Meanwhile, I can't see the problem.

"Drew, you want us to use a gun and not be scared. Let us have a bit of fun and the scary factor will go away. Trust me, Krip did it with me all the time."

"Beauty, I don't know." Scratching his head with force, he adds, "We're leaving today, so don't make promises you can't keep." he strides over to his drawers next to the window and pulls out clothing. I'm staring at him, a little confused. He must feel my eyes on him because he turns his head slowly to look at me.

He smirks and then responds, "How's Izzy doing? Nova's been worried lately. She's not sleeping." I'm still annoyed at his bitter response to me making promises you can't keep. I try not to roll my eyes.

"Yeah, she's had a lot on her mind lately and me running off didn't help. I didn't think anyone would miss me." I halt my sentence and think about what we talked about. Feeling like I'm responsible for some of her pain, I carry on.

"She opened my eyes, though, and gave me a few hard truths!" And for the first time, I saw Izzy's true age, she has always seemed so much older till today. Gives me more reason to make sure I keep this promise. A thought comes to mind, and the fear of leaving this place behind hits me in the gut.

"Drew, we're coming home, aren't we? She has a long way to go, so I need to be here for her. I know I can help her!" I say desperately.

"Babe, whatever you want, 'cause I'm staying wherever you are, Beauty." His jeans hug his muscular thighs as he saunters across the room. A hint of a smirk playing on his lips, making it impossible not to watch him. Reaching down, he pulls me into his arms. He then leans in and kisses my lips, gently. Heat travels slowly across my face.

Drew pulls back, searching my eyes for an answer, then he adds, "I'm with you forever, Beauty, so where you go, I go. You got that?" I nod, feeling the warmth spread across my chest. He has done it again, unchained more of my past and made it better. God, he better not leave me! He keeps me wrapped in his arms for a bit before he pulls away again.

"Have you had coffee or breakfast yet?"

"No, I was just getting up when Izzy came, but I'll get organised now."

"No, you take your time, and I'll go get something for you to eat. Go have a shower and I should be back when you're finished."

"Okay, but don't be long. I want to get out and see Soph and Keata." He smiles, walking out the door like he's hiding something. God, he's so sexy with that smile.

I'm trying to hurry so I can go see Soph and Keata before we leave. I love spending time with Savie, but not being able to spend time with Keata will be hard, really hard, and now Izzy as well. I hope all this ends really soon!

Sienna Gypsy

DREW

36

DREW

W alking out, going to see what I can get Stasia for breakfast, I notice Krip, Prez, and Nova chatting as I enter the clubhouse's main area. I walk over and catch the end of Prez speaking, "Yeah, been thinking that since Stasia's gun shootout. That it might be the best place for all the girls." I look at all of them.

"What's up? What am I missin'?" the last part I say clapping my hands together once and rubbing them back and forth till my hand feels the heat. Prez looks at me miserably, and my enthusiasm drops.

"I've been thinking, and these two agree, that Mira and Izzy are going." Prez fidgets, then looks behind Krip towards the opening to the main room. His brows are knit together, and his jaw is clenched tightly. "After Stasia running, and the shootout, I'm not risking any of the girls. At least if they're on the road, with all of you boys, they're all safe." My gut's churning, but I agree.

"We might need extra guys riding with us, and two in the van with the girls. I agree the girls might be safer together, but something doesn't feel right. We still need to be on high alert!" Prez pats me on the shoulder.

"Cory already said he's in the van, and Felix, the new prospect, was told last night by Cory that he's coming as well."

"Good! Who is on the bikes with us?"

"Maverick and Helmet." I nod, knowing they know their shit, both ex-army so they can handle whatever comes at them.

"Well, what time are we leaving then?"

Krip answers me, "Seven tonight, on the dot. Plus, I got a distraction organised for the boys, local strip joint coming in. Should keep everyone who's not in the know busy enough from figuring out the plan, so make sure you're ready."

"No worries," I say as I walk off in the kitchen's direction to get my girl her coffee. Our decoy leaves in one hour, which Stasia still thinks is happening, and she will need to stay in hiding. And I'm hoping,' cause now all the girls are coming, she will be okay with hiding out. Well, I'm crossing my fingers, but the other girls won't be getting in the van till near 7p.m.. No one knows they're all leaving, which is wise. The boys won't expect them to be around because of the strippers.

As I enter the kitchen, I'm staring at the floor, thinking about the mess that is about to unfold, when I collide with someone. As I look up, my gut burns with hatred. It's Spud. He jumps like the guilty asshole he is. I try to master my fury.

"Spud, what are you up to?" He doesn't have food or coffee, so he's up to something. I know he is!

"Nothing, just finished my coffee and heading out for the day. What's going on here tonight? The boys are all excited about something." He's looking around guilty, not making eye contact.

"Prez organised the strippers tonight. You gonna stick around?"

"Yeah, yeah, will do. I'll be here. Sounds good! What's the special occasion?" I bet, motherfucker.

I nod saying, "Pretty sure Prez needs to let his hair down without Mira on his back."

"Yeah, yeah, sucks to be him, hey?" He says this and heads to the door. He turns and says, "See you tonight, yeah?" I nod. I'm not telling him shit. But I think he knows something. Watching his back as he walks away, I let my anger simmer, promising myself I'll have my revenge.

I finish making Stasia's coffee and hope it's enough for me to calm my mind when I return to my room.

Walking in the room, Stasia is getting out of the bathroom, still in a towel. My body stops still as my eyes undress her from that towel. As I sweep my gaze down her body and back to her beautiful heart-shape face, I can see the hunger in her eyes, and it's calling for me.

I reach over and place her coffee down behind me without looking, advancing on her, not being able to help myself. I want her in my arms, now! I don't lose eye contact. As soon as I'm close enough, my arms wrap around her firmly. I bend down and kiss her hard. Using my tongue to entice her to open her mouth so I can taste her. It doesn't take long for Stasia to kiss me back, just as hard, with her tongue fighting mine for dominance. When she moans, something snaps inside me. I can't stop now. I pull her towel off and throw it to the floor. She grabs my t-shirt. Pulling it over my head, her hands slide into my hair. She pulls me back to her lips, where our mouths clash together again. My hands are roaming her body while we are kissing. Her skin feels like silk. My hands glide over her ass, then up to the middle of her back.

Stasia's hands are at my buttons, she mumbles, "Off. Get them off." We both take my jeans off in a rush. We fumble, stepping towards the bed. As I'm about to push her on the bed, I realise I may hurt her.

Fighting my inner self, who needs inside her, "Babe, are you okay?" I try to slow myself by sucking her neck and nibbling as I go down to her shoulder. Her breathy response excites me more.

"No, but don't stop, Drew... please," That's enough for me.

I think for a second with a smirk on my face, Then I ask, "On top or under, Beauty?" She's looking at me full of need and wanting, God, I love her like this, "Back!" Is all she says, and before I know it, I'm on top of her. Her legs wrapped around me, pulling me into her ecstasy.

We lay there for a while before Stasia says, "I think my coffee's cold now!" We chuckle softly as I pull her into my arms, rolling over.

After a bit, I nuzzle her neck and tell her, "Beauty, we have a change of plans. We are doing a decoy. A van will leave, but you won't be in it. It's going a different way, but we're leaving tonight at 7 p.m.. The boys will go on a fake run as well. So we'll leave about 6:50 p.m., and you girls will be right behind us." I run my hands up and down her bare back while I'm talking. I love feeling her so close to me.

Her response is almost a whisper, "So, me and Savie are going to be hiding? Will we be okay?" I kiss her on her forehead to reassure her.

"Yeah, babe, I'm sure. It will be you and Savie to start with, then when we leave, all the girls will be with you" She looks up at me like it's Christmas.

"You mean all, like, as in all of them..." she sits up and is looking at me as if I hold the answer to world peace.

"Yeah, Beauty, like, all of them. Mira, Sophie, Izzy and Keata." I sit up and kiss her, then go to get out of bed. She pulls me back and kisses me hard.

When we finish, I ask her, "What was that for?"

"For being you, and being my knight on a shiny motorbike!"

I chuckle, "Beauty, I'll always be that knight for you, and you, alone. You hear me?" She nods and I kiss her gently this time and when I finish, I slap her butt.

"We need to get ready. The people who know, know you leave soon. Come on, let's get dressed."

We both get organised for what's coming and I'm praying that it all runs smoothly.

STASIA

37

STASIA

"**W**hy did they think this was a good idea?" I ask not only myself, but Savie as well. We've been in this shed far down the back of the compound with a van in it for a while now. We are ready for when the other girls come. Which won't be for a while. We have most of the day left.

Savie and I have been playing cards. A game called Last Card. She taught me when I was younger and we're making it interesting by betting stuff like food for the trip. Savie looks at me, shaking her head.

"Well, honey, it's a better idea than leaving without a plan and getting killed." I can see her searching my face for understanding. I need to remember that this could turn bad at any moment. I'm bored and want this done already.

"I know, I know. What else can we do? I'm over cards. I already owe you too many lollies and I need to find a way out of that karaoke thing you sprung on me!" She'd come up with me singing at a karaoke bar, then I did a double or nothing and guess what? It's two bloody songs now. We need a new game; one I can win.

I suggest eye spy, but Savie laughs at me, "Girl, we are not playing that! You always cheated when you were younger." Well, I was still going to cheat, for the record. I put some music on my phone with my earphones in. I share the other earbud with Savie, so we don't bring attention to where we are. We sit, listening to music, in the room's silence.

We hear some men talking and we both freeze. Savie gestures with her pointer finger to her lips, signalling to be quiet.

Then we hear Cobra's voice, "Over here, Cory. Put all that stuff in the back." We both sigh in relief as we watch Cory put two more bags in the back. They must be Mira's and Izzy's stuff. I look at Cobra, wanting to hurry up and get out of here already.

"Are we going yet?"

He smiles, shaking his head in a no, "Little Bird, an hour and a half and we're out of here, okay?" Still smiling at me, he bends down, kissing the top of my head, then he points to Cory.

"They're staying now, so get organised. So, when we ring you guys, you leave. Stasia, this is Felix," he nods at me, no shaking hands or anything, so I smile.

"Nice to meet you."

Savie says the same, then she states, "Great, new people, let's get the van done, then play Last Card," I hear Cobra grunt.

"Dear, you better play nice!" Then he whispers in her ear, she slaps his shoulder, saying, "Of course, I wouldn't bet for that. That's only for you!" She kisses him and then looks at me.

"Come on, the quicker this is organised, the quicker we can scam these boys!" she says the last part with a wink. Both the men are looking at Cobra.

He shrugs his shoulders, "Good luck." He marches towards the back, where he came in.

We've been playing for a while, and I have one more card left in this game. I'm praying that they don't change suit. I have the last card and its hearts, but Savie looks like she knows. I think she had been counting cards. As I'm about to have my shot, Cory's phone rings.

As he takes the call, he gestures for us to pack up, then nods, "Yeah, we're on our way!" He grabs the cards, passes them to Felix and tells us girls to get settled.

"What about…?" As I'm about to ask, both girls enter and walk in on their own, no chaperone. Mira leading them.

They jump in the back of the van with us, and Mira tells Cory, "We're picking up Sophie and Keata from the café down the road. Bullet and Krip are both with them."

Both Cory and Felix nod and start the van up. I look at Savie nervously, not sure we are about to do the right thing. I take a deep breath as Cory presses a button from the front seat and the doors slide open. The van slowly exits the garage and leads us into the night's darkness.

After six and a half hours of driving, we pull up to Nanna Sally's house. We didn't stop much, us girls only got one pee break. I was tired, hungry, and begging for the toilet. I missed Drew, we hadn't talked at all throughout the trip. Every time we stopped, he didn't. And when he stopped, we kept going. Then he'd catch up. Looking at him through the van window was making me clench my teeth hard. The annoyance was getting to me, I wanted him!

He must have felt the same way 'cause when he opened the door, his eyes were only on me. "Cory, you're sleeping first, then you're on lookout duty and Felix is driving tomorrow. We are leaving here at 7:30 a.m., sharp. So, if you're tired, get the rest you need now, and find a room inside. Dad has already opened up. Let's move!" He grabs my hand and pulls me out of the van, being careful at the same time. He strides up to the entrance of the house. My mind slows down and I'm not ready for the surge of memories that overwhelm me.

Nanna Sally, all our fun, arguments, and tears. And the day she said I needed to go. She said all of this with determination, like it was all going to be okay. Dread washes through my soul, causing me to stumble. Drew halts and looks back at me. I see the realisation hit him.

"Beauty, shit, I didn't even think this would bother you." His arms engulf me. He holds me firm with one arm around my waist and the other in my hair on my scalp, keeping my head to his chest.

I feel his breath on the top of my head as he says, "You tired? Let's go get you sorted." We head toward the attic, which I was not expecting. It is the one place I never went near. 'Cause it was his, and I always felt like he was none of my business. I thought it would be small, but the space runs the length of the house. It isn't just a bedroom, there is an entire bathroom as well. Everything still looks neat, like someone stayed here recently. Drew must've read my mind because he answers my thoughts.

"Dad comes here a lot with Savie and with the club on runs, so he keeps it sorted, and this has always been my room. Didn't you snoop when you were here?"

Shaking my head, "No, not after what I went through. Back then I was so scared of your dad." He laughs.

"Dad would not have cared, you could have. Anyway, I have a shower up here and a toilet, so we only have to go down for food. So, go and clean up. The next part of the trip is something I need to figure out. I'll talk to the guys and be back."

I walk towards where the shower is when I hear Drew say, "One more thing, Beauty." turning to him, I'm amazed at how close he is. He reaches me and dips his head to crush his mouth to mine. The feeling of his mouth soothes my uneasiness. When he pulls back, he winks and says, "Have a good shower and get some rest. I'll be back soon." He pecks me on the lips one last time, then leaves the room.

DREW

38

DREW

I walk down the stairs to where Dad should be. I need to know if there are any updates, and grab our stuff. I bump into Krip, who is holding our bags, and I grab them from him.

"Thanks, I'll take it in."

Krip smirks at me and then leaves, but yells over his shoulder, "Yo. Ya know, she's a sister, bro. Never been anythin' else."

I feel my jaw clench, "Yeah, I get it, but I still don't want you to be close to her. Oh, and stay the fuck away from Mira, Brother. I am not blind. I see shit starting there!" I glare at him.

He turns and walks backward, "Not going there, Brother! Too young and naïve for me!" And when I think he's finished, he adds, "And she couldn't handle my kind of fuckin'."

"Just stay the fuck away from her, got it?"

He throws his hands up in defeat, "Will do." Then turns and leaves. But I know there's something going on. Mira is acting crazy, and Krip's good at hiding shit, but he ain't that good!

Carrying all our bags and other items for Stasia, I barge through, into the room, and Stasia's on the other side of the door as I step through. The shocked look on her face is priceless.

"Oh, I was just coming down to get that!" She says while pointing at our bags. I pass her stuff to her and enter the room.

"Yeah, thought you'd need a change of clothes, but I have a t-shirt you can sleep in." I say as I pass it to her. Leaning in and giving her a quick peck on the lips. Then I leave again.

As I close the door she yells back, "Don't be too long!" I turn my head and wink at her. Heading to where all my brothers are, I want this meeting done.

The meeting has been going longer than I wanted it to, it seems someone saw Spud leaving after us. No one knows where he's gone, or if he's on his own.

Dad explains to us, "Prez said he left in the same direction as us, but that means nothing. We still need to keep ourselves on high alert." He points outside.

"We have Felix outside on patrol at the moment, but I want more guys out there. So, sort ya shit, and get to where you're needed."

We gather around and finish talking about who's on what roster so we can get some rest. Krip, Felix and Bullet are on the first watch. Then me, Dad and Maverick, and last is Helmet, Trigger and Thump till we leave. We do have a small army with us, but that was the plan.

I set my alarm to make sure I get up in time for my shift. I'm glad we're only doing short shifts so we can all get some sleep. We still have a large distance to cover tomorrow and we're leaving early. I head up to my bedroom. Stasia passed out. I jump in the shower, and then get into bed with Stasia. Her body must know when I'm around, because she curls into me and snuggles. She's rubbing her nose on the side of my chest like she's smelling that it's me. It's not long before sleep pulls me in as well.

Waking up to my alarm, I scramble to turn it off before it wakes Stasia. I want her to sleep. She's still not healed properly, and she needs rest more than anything. Sneaking out the door, as I hit the bottom of the stairs, I see Dad doing the same thing. He nods at me and we both head to the kitchen.

He puts the coffee pot on, "You sleep much?"

"Yeah, fell asleep fast, but I'll have a coffee."

"I received a text from Prez in the last hour. They found Spud; a drunk driver ran him off the road. But he was heading in our direction, so we're positive he's involved." Clenching my jaw, I find it hard not to think up ways to kill the bastard.

"Yeah, he was in the kitchen when I was talking about our plans in the hall, but I don't know if he heard anything. When I asked what he was doing, he lied. So good job, drunk driver. Pity they didn't do more damage. Fucker deserves it!" Nodding, Dad passes me my coffee and we head out to relieve the first group. Felix comes up first.

"It's been quiet, nothing out of the norm."

Dad replies, "Good, go get some rest. You're driving when we leave." He nods, and then goes to where he's sleeping. Krip and Bullet come over from a dark spot, they were under a few different trees and bushes, way out of sight.

They both say, "Nothing yet" and head inside. Maverick comes out at the same time the other two go in, giving each other a chin lift. He passes us doing the same. Maverick doesn't even make conversation, and heads straight to where Bullet was. I head to where Krip was and take up camp with my coffee. Dad sits in the dark spot near the corner of the house. Camouflaged in the dark.

After about an hour, I see four lights, two cars. They're driving slowly down the long driveway. Alarm races through me. It's way too late for one car, let alone two at the same time. Dad flicks something at me to get my attention. I shake a branch to signal that I'm aware of the cars, so is Maverick. I pray they keep on moving. Someone turns a light on inside the house at the same time the cars stop and park just out of sight from the window. Shit!

The car lights are off. I'm hoping that whoever is inside the house doesn't come outside. The people in the car are now out and crouching down with weapons. Fuck! I can't think of where to look. I've got my gun aimed at the dude near the fence. But my head keeps turning back to the entrance of the house.

Maverick has his gun aimed, and Dad has his rifle ready. Just as the guys hide at the tree that's closest to me, Stasia walks out with a coffee. I do a double take. Why the fuck would she come outside? I send a prayer that she doesn't get shot. Fuck! She's gonna be the death of me! Dad must get her attention. She sits in the shadows and whispers something to him. I can only just hear her. Dad must have told her to move back inside, but to keep in the dark, because she nearly makes it.

Then a voice yells out. "Best you turn around and come with us, or we'll shoot down the house and none of your friends will survive!" I become motionless, cursing to myself. Stasia stops in her tracks. Although I can't hear Dad, I know he's coaching her on what to do. She turns around real slow. Turning, I make sure I can take out as many as I can, 'cause Dad will fire the first shot to signal us to start. I've got my guys in sight. They're easy prey. I just hope Dad gets in front of Miss Hit-the-Dirt before she hits the fuckin' dirt again.

Shit, why didn't she stay the fuck inside? I gather myself and concentrate on where my gun is pointed. I can feel the sweat at my temple pebble.

Stasia calls out, "Why are you after me?" Dad fires his first shot and connects with his target. We all start shooting, mine go down fast, so do Maverick's guys. I get one from the other car, but I think I only nip him. I hear Stasia cry out. When I turn to look at what's happening, I see it's Krip pulling her inside. I turn back to get this done. Looking at Maverick, he's out of position, heading towards the car that has more guys shooting at us. I aim my gun and fire, giving him cover, then follow him. He covers with gun fire for me. Dad's still shooting. More guns go off behind us. Once we get close, there's only one left, and Maverick has him by the throat. I do a quick search and yell "Clear." Dad comes over.

"Krip is back, go check on Stasia. I got this!"

Then another gun goes off and the guy Maverick has by the throat has blood leaking from his chest. We all turn and point our guns in the shot's direction. Bloody Mira, she is there with blood on her. I stalk to her, but she's glaring at the guy who's on the ground. Krip swears, then glares at Mira.

"What the fuck you doing, Mira? Get inside! He was our only go-to guy for info! FUCK!" his hands scrunch in his hair, and he pulls and growls into the sky, then glares back at her. He's pissed, but he didn't see the look on Mira's face. Something's not right.

Mira smiles at Krip, "Oh, you're welcome. But this guy over here is still alive, asshole!" She turns and storms up the front steps and swings the front door open, slamming it shut behind her. What the fuck just happened?

Sienna Gypsy

STASIA

39

STASIA

I feel a strong hand wrap around my upper arm and pull hard. Before I know it, my body is being pulled without my brain telling it too. I look up and Krip is dragging me. He drags me inside the house, I stumble behind him. He dragged me inside. I can't believe it. Without him getting into my personal space, I would not have gone. I open my mouth to tell him this, but I feel his powerful hands pick me up as he throws me over his shoulder. My breath leaves my lungs. He winded me.

Gasping, trying to catch my breath, I notice we are heading down the hall to where my room is. He goes up the stairs. As he spins around, I see the bed. He puts pressure on my hips and I'm moving as he throws me into the air. My arms are flapping, and I scream. The pure shock was that he didn't do what I was thinking. I'm freaking out, scurrying, trying to land without hurting myself. My body jolts and the pain travels from my ass to my mid-back. What the hell? Fuck, that hurt. I glare at him wanting him to feel the pain I'm feeling right now. I have no words! My anger is boiling. He just glares straight back at me. Krip is pointing his finger at me.

"STAY THE FUCK PUT TILL DREW COMES IN!" He then turns and slams the door shut behind him. I'm still staring at the door, wishing he'd vanish. That's fine with me, asshole! Like I wanna be where people are getting shot at! Rolling my eyes, I try hard not to think about how sore I am and how fucked up this is.

I sit for a bit on my bed, still glaring at the door, wishing I could lock it. I'm so lost in my thoughts when the door bursts open and Mira comes in looking like a hot mess as well.

"I'll be back. Just stay here, okay?" I watch her go to the corner of the room, grab something out of a bag, and then walk back out the door. I look at her confused, like I've really got a choice in this! When she leaves, my head's still swimming. What the hell is she up to?

Why the hell did I go outside to check on Drew? He hadn't been back to bed since I was in the shower. Even though the bed smells like him, it's like he wasn't there. So, I went to look for him and all hell broke loose.

My brain has been fuzzy since this mess started. I can't seem to think straight. I feel like I'm gaining some control again when Mira bursts back through the door; that did not lock with my mind's powers. Shaking my head, I realise I'm delirious. I try to focus on Mira and notice the blood on her face. She walks over and sits on my bed next to me. She has no idea she has blood on her face. Why the hell is blood on her?

She starts to rant off to no one, "What an egotistical pig of a man he is. He better stay away from me. I hate him. I'm over his 'I'm too good for you' bullshit!" She's lost it. Is she talking about Drew?

I opened my mouth to ask her who she was talking about, but she was not finished with her tirade.

"He can't even see past the fact... Argh!" she pulls at her hair. "I just hate him. The asshole thinks I'm so young. No one in my dad's charter talks to me like he does! Who the hell does he think he is?" I see her arm move as I look. She picks up the water bottle I didn't notice and throws it against the wall. Water sprays everywhere.

I'm still staring at the water as it runs down the wall, using a quiet voice, hoping I don't set her off again, I ask, "Mira, honey, what happened?" She looks at me and I see her register that I'm still in the room, she opens then shuts her mouth, then opens again to tell me.

The door swings open and hits the wall. Scaring the absolute shit out of us both. Krip barges in, looking like he's going to kill someone. Drew storms in behind him, not looking any calmer.

Krip is the first to yell, "MIRACLE, WHAT THE HELL WERE YOU THINKING? THAT," he points toward outside. "OUT THERE WAS CLUB BUSINESS! Who... and when are you allowed to help, and why the hell would you? FUCK!" He spins around and paces, pulling at his hair. He looks like he has more to say, but he glares at Mira.

She glares at him and spits, "My name, to you, is Mira! And what I do and don't do, is none of your concern! I'm not having this conversation with you or anyone, not now or ever! Oh, and fuck you, too, asshole!" I can see Mira's face flush with rage. I try to change the subject, but she is up and out of here. I glare at Krip. He's never talked to me like that, or anyone I know. I think he's lost his mind. I go to tell him, feeling I could be the voice of reason. I open my mouth to begin, but he puts his hand up in front of my face, "Don't, Stasia, I haven't even said what I wanted to say to you. I'm still fuckin' mad at you for running when I told you not to, so shut it!" I blow out a breath in defeat. I've let him down by running, and then tonight, getting in the way of club stuff. I knew he hadn't talked to me for a while now, but I realised he was waiting till he had calmed down.

I look at the floor when I hear Drew talk next. "That will be the last time you talk to either of them till you find some damn respect." Drew gets right up in his face and shoves him into the wall with his hands fisted in his shirt.

"Stasia might be a sister to you, but you need to remember she is my woman! And let me make it clear, brother, talk to her or Mira like that again, and you won't be walking! Got it, brother?" Drew spits back and shoves him once more, hitting the wall again. I expect Krip to fight back, but Cobra walks in and tells Krip to move, and go back to the shed, where he's needed. Drew's still waiting for a fight. He's holding Krip to the wall. Cobra ignores the obvious and ushers Drew into the room further.

Once Drew's hands let go of Krip. He walks backwards till he hits the doorway, keeping both his eyes on Drew. They both keep eye contact as Krip reaches the door entrance. He is standing aggressively still ready to fight. The look in both their eyes says they're both not finished.

I actually thought Krip was going to charge at Drew, but he points his finger at him and says, "Later!" Drew nods, and Krip leaves. He stalks out of the room, slamming the door.

Cobra comes over to me and sits down, distracting me from what just happened with the guys. He puts his arms around me and squeezes me, and I feel safe, like the day he saved me as a little girl.

"You good, Little Bird, did you get hurt?"

"I'm good, but what's going on? I'm confused. Who were those guys? Why do they want me and what the hell's wrong with Krip?" Cobra shakes his head.

"Pretty sure the guys work for or with your dad. And as for Krip, he doesn't handle girls near danger that well, and you running off before put him in a bad space. He's struggling with that, and now Mira's fighting him. He'll deal better once we get to Melbourne. Now, stay here. We have stuff to fix. I'll go check on Savie and if she's awake, I'll bring her here, yeah?"

Nodding, he kisses my forehead, then gets up to leave. He passes Drew and demands, "Fifteen minutes, then, in the shed. See you there." Drew nods. Giving Cobra the confirmation he needs, he leaves the room. Drew then looks in my direction.

"You good? Sure you're not hurt?" Drew walks over to me and takes me in his arms. It's not the same feeling I get with Cobra, but it has the same effect. Safety and protection. He runs his hands all over my body, searching for any other damage. I'm soaking up the feeling that erupts throughout my body. That feeling of calm and home.

"Why the hell did you go outside, Beauty? With everything that's going on, if you got hit again, shit, you need to take more care. Promise me?"

"I thought we were safe. I didn't know, or I would have stayed inside. I really thought that we were safe here."

Drew's not impressed, "We're not, so unless I'm with you, stay indoors." Glancing at me, he adds, "Any idea what Mira's story is? She talks about anything to you lately. She's a bit on edge."

"No, she just had a breakdown in here before, but I know nothing. It was a bit out of left field."

"I've got to go. If Mira tells you, and she's in trouble, let me know. Something's going on. I hope it's not too big." He kisses me on the forehead the same as his dad did, and I watch him stride his fine ass out the door.

Taking in all that happened, and praying to the God Almighty that this was it for tonight. I can't deal with any more drama. I go to look for Mira. She has some explaining to do. I hope she'll tell me. As I walk through the door, I hit a body. I look up to see it's Savie. She touches my face.

"Hey! Are you okay?"

"Yeah," nodding my head in the direction I think Mira is in, I say, "Come with me. Mira did something and Krip lost his shit. So did Mira, so let's go." I say, deciding it's best to take the focus off of me. She follows me down to where I think Mira is, but she's not there. So, we go to the kitchen and she's in there with a bottle of Scotch. Okay, this is serious!

"Mira, you okay?" She looks up, but just shakes her head, then throws back another shot of Scotch.

She shakes it off and goes for another, then Savie says, "Girl. Share. If you need it, then we're gonna need it as well, so pass it around."

She nods, then says, "I'm not saying shit to either of you. But if you wanna drink with me, let's do it!" Savie goes straight to the cupboards, grabs more shot glasses and grabs three tumbler glasses. She turns to the walk-in pantry, goes in, looks around and comes back with vodka and sprite.

She looks at me saying, "Ice is in the freezer. Grab it, Stasia, and let's go where no one will find us for a while." I go to the fridge and open the top part where the freezer is, still thinking, *where's a place no one will find us*? Savie winks at me and nods to Mira.

Sienna Gypsy

"My room, girls. Let's go!"

Arriving at Savie's room, I'm the last to walk through and Savie says, "Lock it, Stasia, we have some drinking to do!"

Thank God Bullet had put Sophie, Keata and Izzy at the back house in a granny flat, sort of out of the way. So, they're probably still asleep. Looks like we are going to be trashed.

After about an hour, we are still bitching about men, laughing at ourselves and dancing to music. I'm feeling free, like nothing has happened. Mira and Savie are holding up well, like they haven't even had a drink. I'm feeling lightheaded, with no thoughts running through my mind. The fact that I don't drink often is the reason I'm so drunk now. I'm waffling on about how yummy Drew is, and they don't get it.

"He's like..." I'm flapping my arm around trying to explain, but those bitches are laughing at me.

"You two are switches or whatever fat word is!" Am I slurring? I throw my arms up in the air, but someone takes the floor from under me, and I knock my head on the ground and moan. Trying to rub it better, I eye the girls but there are now four in the room, and someone is banging on the door. I think Savie and Savie's twin get the door. Cobra and his twin walk in. He takes one look at me and shakes his head at the girls, they just laugh again, Mira and Mira's twin... maybe it's just Mira, tries to pull me up but we both fall again.

I hear Cobra say, "You do this?"

I put my hand up like I'm in school shouting, "Yes fanks 'tis me!" He is now shaking his head and yelling out to Drew. I hear him and get excited. I push Mira off of me, she falls on her ass and bursts out laughing. I'm licking my lips and patting my hair down,

Mira's laughing harder. I glare at her. "Shut up, I need to look good for my hottie!" Savie shakes her head.

"Yeah, this might be on me, shit!" I'm pissed. Nope, not just pissed. Really, really pissed! Because suddenly I'm upside down.

I pick my head up, "Wow, why are you all upside down and the ground is moving?"

Then I hear my honey's voice, "Babe, I've got you." He chuckles and then slaps my ass.

"Mmm, yes you do, baby," I hear him laugh as we are walking out of Savie's room. I'm swaying with every step. I feel like I'm being rocked to sleep. My eyes grow heavy. I try to keep them open. It feels too good to even try to open them again. When my face is snuggled into a pillow, sleep drowns out the night.

Sienna Gypsy

DREW

40

DREW

We head back to our rooms after setting up the hostage in the shed. Entering the rear of the house, I stride toward my room to get to Stasia. I reach the top of the stairs and see my room is deserted.

Dad's voice calls out behind me, "Drew." Hearing the girls chuckling, I turn in his direction. They're creating a racket. The noise sounds like they're falling all over the place. Next, there's an excessive thud.

"Shit." I hurry to check that Stasia is okay. I pass Savie, she smiles at me. When I'm looking at them, I have no words. They're drunk. I move straight to Stasia, bend at the knees and throw her over my shoulder.

"I've got you, babe!"

"Mmm, yes you do, baby." I laugh and carry her to my room and put her to bed. She is semi-awake while I'm trying to change her. She mutters promises and who she trusts.

I'm one of them, "Glad I'm one of them, babe." She's none the wiser about this conversation. Once she is in bed, she cuddles into the pillow I had before the shit hit the fan. I go wash up and grab her pillow to sleep.

An annoying buzzing wakes me. Reaching over to the side table, I turn off the alarm before it wakes Stasia. I only wanted a few hours before I head back out to the shed.

Getting out of bed, my mind is trying to put together why Mira took that guy out. Krip and I have had some heated words, and that fucker is getting on my nerves. I have to head out to the shed with Dad to plan what to do with the guy who's still alive. We all want answers, and need to get as much information as we can.

Bullet is there as I enter the shed. I give him a chin lift. I go to Bullet first, 'cause I'm still pissed at Krip.

"Your girls good, brother?" he nods.

"Yeah, they're asleep. Hope they stay that way for a bit!" Nodding, I wish Stasia, Mira and Savie didn't drink, but I figured it would happen after Mira did what she did.

"Yeah, I'm hoping that Stasia stays asleep." Running my hands through my hair, "I will not be in a good place after this." Bullet nods and walks over to where the hostage is sitting, tied up with rope. Nova has Thump, Felix, Cory and Trigger outside, dealing with the dead bodies. Dad has strapped his knuckles on and Bullet has his tools out. We're all ready to do some damage. Dad is in front of the guy, slowly pacing back and forth like a lion teasing its prey. He waits for the perfect second throwing a punch right when the guy least expects it. "Who are you workin' for?" Nothing but silence. Dad waits for a bit and stalks around him, watching the hostage carefully.

"This could be easy or hard for you, mate. I suggest you tell us. I'm a very patient man." He looks around at all of us, thrusting his thumb in our direction adding, "But, these guys aren't. You are after one of their girls. Now, that involved us, so, last chance mate, who you workin' for?" The hostage shakes his head. He makes eye contact with Dad and spits blood from his mouth where Dad punched him. It lands on the floor near my boot.

"Can't tell you shit. But what I can tell you is ..." he looks from Dad to all of us, then back to Dad, he spits out, "There are more coming, and it's bigger than you think it is!" I look at Bullet. We both know what's next. Dad nods at Bullet. Bullet picks up his bat and places it on his shoulder. He looks at the hostage one more time before he swings his bat across the hostage's knees. The scream is instant. Bullet then swings one more time at his abdomen area.

Then he pulls back, "Just a name, it's not like you're gonna live through this, asshole, but I can go all night, so can my brothers, up to you." Bullet shrugs like they're in an easy conversation then puts all his weight into the next swing and hits his thigh. Which causes the guy to scream out again. The guy is crying and moaning in pain, as saliva and blood are dripping out of his mouth.

I add, "You could make this quick, or you could make this last all night." The hostage's head is hanging while he's trying to catch his breath.

I nod at Bullet to go again. He groans first before saying, "The p-person you think is b-behind this, it's not him. Frazer thinks it's all h-him… but it's b-bigger than him. You can thank Frankie for that."

He then glares at Dad, "Now do as you p-promised!" I look at my brothers, then Dad, he nods, so I get down close and grab my knife, and point it at his kneecap.

"You got more, motherfucker, now spill. We have all night!" The hostage's breathing is rough. He's struggling with everything Bullet has done so far.

He won't last much longer, but he answers the last question, "No, y-you don't, 'cause they're c-coming here. You probably have an hour, tops, maybe two, but they're coming!" I stand and put my knife in its holster, watching the relief on the guys face, then think better of it. I grab my knife back out and slam it into his leg. He is silent for a minute before he fills the room with his screams. Stepping back, I pull out my gun, aiming right between the eyes, sick of his screams. I pull the trigger and watch the blood run from the hole in his head.

Dad glances around the room, then points at me, "Grab his phone, see if there are any messages or phone numbers we can use." Dad walks out but turns back and says, "Son, we will need to burn this place down." Seeing regret on his face with these words, I know he'd only do this if he didn't have another choice.

Thump has the guy's phone, scrolling through. "He's lying, they were supposed to hold us here until lunchtime tomorrow. What's the plan now?"

"Same plan. I got insurance on this place, so we burn it, but only after the girls are on their way. We'll leave a message for the assholes, see if we can find out who this other player is." Dad points to Helmet, Trigger and Thump.

"You three are on till morning. We leave as early as we can."

Stretching out my arms, I look at the clock, it's 6:30 a.m., but Stasia is snoring up a storm. Well, not loud, but loud enough. I get up to see what is happening. Stepping into the kitchen, I see Dad is cooking. "The girls are going to need food."

I nod, but Krip comes in, "Why can't we grab something on the way?"

"Nope! They got trashed, really trashed. Stasia's still in bed. Where's the Panadol? She's gonna need it." Dad points to the cupboard above the sink. I walk over and grab it, then go back to my room to give it to Stasia.

Sitting down next to her, she moans, "Why would you do that?" I smile, knowing she is going to be fun today. But I'm guessing Mira will be on fire after yesterday. After a lot of complaining and a shower, all with me helping, we walk into the kitchen. Mira and Savie walk in together. Krip, the asshole, decides at that moment to bang the pots like a fuckin' child. I glare at him, but Mira just points at him, "I will stab you! Argh... Cut it out!"

Krip laughs, then puts the pots away, "Got a headache, girls? Maybe next time you will wait till we get to a safe place!" The smug smirk on his face makes me want to punch it off. I go to tell him to shut it, but Savie beats me.

"Krip, I'll kill you myself. I don't care how much my man needs you! You listening?" He smiles at her, knowing she means it.

Grabbing his coffee saying, "I got it, but..." Savie raises her hand and stops him dead in his tracks.

He shakes his head, grumbling, "You women are taking over the damn MC!" And storms out of the kitchen. Mira hugs her in response to Krip leaving and goes to get coffee. Stasia is still moaning; in a split second she runs out of the kitchen towards the bathroom. We can all hear her dry retching. I follow her and help her when she vomits into the toilet.

After we all grab our stuff and pack the van, we end up leaving later than we planned. We found a few more messages that came after the first texts we saw. Which confirmed for us we don't need to rush. Stasia's still sick, but doing better. I haven't had time to tell her that Nanna's house is being burnt down. I'm not sure how she will take it, so I organise, for the first leg of our trip, to be in the van and Cory happily takes my bike.

As we are leaving and getting to the end of the road, I see the smoke in the distance.

I turn to see confusion on Stasia's face, "Is that fire? Drew. Drew, turn around." She hits the back of the seat in a panic.

"There's a fire at Nanna Sally's house."

Turning, I try to console her, "Beauty, we had to. Dad gave the order. This makes it impossible to find out any more, since more people were coming." I see the battle in her eyes as she realises this is happening. Her head nods but her expression is vacant as she watches it go up in flames. I climb into the back seat and hold her. I knew this would be difficult. She turns and leans into me. She rests with her eyes closed until exhaustion pulls her into sleep.

Our first stop will be at Norseman, which is a couple hours away, so I get comfortable. Stasia is curled up tight next to me. Keata is trying hard to get my attention, so I get her out of her seat. Sophie shakes her head at Keata who is smiling so big. She shows her a slight hand gesture and I pull her on to my lap. She curls up with Stasia.

Just before Norseman, I wake Stasia up. Her drinking last night helped with her sleeping today.

"Hey, Beauty" I shake her gently, "We're stopping for a quick feed. We are filling up the spare fuel tanks we have with petrol so the bikes won't run out for the entire trip. We're having a meeting as well. You girls can eat, get drinks and snacks for the van, yeah?" Nodding, she wipes the sleep out of her eyes while stretching out, then looks back at me.

"Is Cobra, okay? I mean, it's his mum's house. I'm sorry!" My stomach tightens at her words. I run my hand over her hair and tuck the loose strand behind her ear so it's out of her face.

"Dad's fine, it was his idea. He says there's insurance on the place, so it's fine." The expression on her face changes, she's thinking, I can tell.

"I'll help him rebuild it, maybe the inside, would that be okay?" I look into her eyes. Excitement building as I realise her expression means she isn't going to run. She's thinking of our future, and hell yes, that makes me feel alive.

"Yeah, babe, I'm sure Dad will like that." I say, pressing a kiss to her head.

We pull to a stop at the servo, and we all get out to stretch out our legs. The girls go inside, and we fill the extra tanks and stand in a group for a bit of a meeting. Dad talks first.

"I want us in two groups. We know they're not ahead of us right now, so the girls and four bikes go first, then the rest of you can dawdle behind. That way, if something comes up behind us, you lot can give us a heads up. If people are following us, we need to choose option B. Nova and Krip know these roads well, so you two split up. Krip, you are in the first group to lead them if we need a getaway. Nova you are in the second, knowing we need to get to this destination here." He points things out on the map on his phone. Everybody nods in agreement.

Krip comes in saying, "Our next pit stop is a long way off, Caiguna. It's about six hours away. Now, if you need petrol, stop, fill your bike and move on. We want a straight run for the van and only stop if needed."

Everybody seems good with this, then Nova jumps in saying, "So if we get separated, we head to Adelaide. I'll text everybody that checkpoint Cobra showed us on the map. If this plan goes to shit, we meet there!" Dad seems happy with that; I watch everybody nod as well.

"Right, let's head inside, have a feed and hit the road as soon as we can!"

The girls are all sitting together, chatting like schoolgirls. At least Stasia looks better than before. As I sit down next to Stasia, Bullet and Nova take their seats nearby. We sit in silence while the girls chat away.

Sophie's phone goes off, but she doesn't answer it, she looks at no one. I hear Bullet ask, "Who's that?"

Sophie's back straightens, her eyes darting from Bullet to Stasia. "I'm not in town and everyone I know in this world is here, so it's no one I know."

Looking back at Bullet, she adds, "Probably a wrong number." A text comes through after, followed by another one. She checks it then turns her phone off and continues to eat as if nothing happened. I'm watching Bullet. He hasn't taken his eyes off Sophie's phone, as if it is a ticking time bomb. Something's not right. Stasia notices too, but she stays quiet, finishing her drink, eyeing Sophie.

Bullet stands abruptly, grabs Keata off Sophie's lap and passes her to Stasia. He grabs Sophie's wrist and pulls her out of her seat. They walk off. I only hear the beginning of what he says.

"Talk! I know it's somethin'. I can't fix what I don't know, Soph!" I'm looking at Stasia ready to ask her, but she beats me to it.

"I don't know. But if she tells me, and it's private, and can't put us in any trouble, then I'm not saying anything to you." Shit. I kiss her temple, hoping that she lets it slip, anyway. As we are walking to our bikes, Bullet pulls me over in his direction. "Four days in a row, same number, but she won't answer it and won't tell anyone!"

I turn my head and make eye contact, "You ask PC about it yet?"

"Nah, I want her to tell me. But I might flick him the number. Fuck! Why do they make shit so damn hard?"

Brushing my fingers through my hair, "Fuck knows! We will keep our eyes open." Bullet stalks to his bike and swings his leg over the seat and sits. We both start our engines and feel the power of our bikes through the revving engine. Once everybody is in the van, Bullet and I are the first out of the petrol station, tearing up the gravel. Letting the wind and the open road take away the stress that's building.

STASIA

41

STASIA

Everyone has been on edge since the first hour back on the road. We've been driving in the van towards the next destination. Sophie even pulled out a movie on Keata's iPad, which helped mostly everyone.

Izzy isn't making any small talk. She isn't talking at all. I can sense how scared she is. The silence is doing my head in. I would sooner rip my hair out than listen to the noise of the wind coming through the window right now.

"Mira, you gonna spill about the other night?" I ask to distract myself. Mira looks up at me, then leans her head back near Keata's, "No! I need to get my head straight. But I will tell you in time." Her answer surprises me. My cheeks warm as a smile spreads across my lips. The next words slip out without thinking.

"You promise?" She looks at me for a moment before she answers.

"Stasia, I promise."

Mira looks at Sophie and asks, "What about you Sophie?" The look on Sophie's face tells me she won't say anything to anyone right now.

She deflects, "I'm fine, worried about everything. Stasia, you're worried for us. What about you? What we're going through is nothing compared to what you've been through. Between losing your house and moving in with me."

"Hey! That worked out great when my stubborn ass gave in." I shrug to myself, thinking back on the memories.

"Yeah, Stasia, it worked out great, and we love having you. The gunshot wound you got at work, then the stabbing... should I go on?" I roll my eyes.

"Jesus, the way you put it, it's like I'm a magnet for this!" Savie burst out laughing. I look at her like she's lost her mind.

"S-Stasia, gee girl," she's pointing her finger at me, "She nailed it on the head!" Laughter erupts through the van. "Since the day I met you, you've been in trouble, even at Sally's house. She'd ring Cobra all the time and tell him the clumsy shit you'd do. Girl, you're Murphy's Law. If it can go wrong, it most likely will!" She's slowed her laughter now. My face goes red as the heat of embarrassment rises.

I turn my gaze to her, "Well, when you put it that way." Savie looks at me with sympathy.

"Honey, it's not that bad, but we gotta focus on balancing you out a bit. That's where your girls come in. We watch out for you, and hopefully..." She leans into me now, "And it is hopefully; stop you from falling." She turns and studies all of us now.

"And that goes for all you girls in this life. You need us, so don't lock us out."

Mira replies, "Knew I should have grabbed more alcohol, great toast Savie! I've got a confession though." We look at her, expecting her to tell us stuff from the last couple of days.

"I've been alone for years and had to fight Dad and his brothers all my life. Actually, the brothers have been good, but not having any girls around was hard. But finding you ladies and knowing that you girls have my back is awesome! Stasia, I'm glad Drew ran your ass over, cause if he didn't, I wouldn't have you girls now." Sophie screeches, pointing her finger at me hysterically.

"Yes, that's another thing, you got ran over!" We all look at each other and then burst out laughing at her outburst. Yeah, I'm a klutz. A warm fuzzy feeling washes over me, knowing I have found my people.

"You guys are my family. Growing up as I did, then finding Nanna Sally, helped me see what family is. Now I have it!" We all welcome the silence. Most of us carry on watching the movie, the rest of us listen to music after our sister moment.

We pull into our last stop to fuel up. Piling out of the van, we head inside. I'm starving, and I predict everyone else is as well. The guys aren't here yet. I can't see Drew anywhere, but Nova comes over.

"He's only twenty minutes out. Go eat, he'll be here before you know it."

I smile at him. "Thanks, Nova. You want me to get you something?"

"Nah. Hey listen, how's Izzy been? She, okay?"

I reach out and touch his shoulder, "Good. Quiet, but good. Izzy has enjoyed being with the girls. She's slept and has had no nightmares so far. So, that's something." I think for a minute and add, "Nova, just so you know, I've got her. We talked the other day, and she's in a better place. Her road is still bumpy, but she will have smooth spots coming." I wink at him as I head to the café inside the servo.

After I get my food, I look for Sophie. I can't see her anywhere. I grab what I want to eat and find Mira, she has Keata with her, "Hey, you good with Keata? I'll be back in a minute."

"Sure!" She shoves her burger in her mouth and does one of those full mouth smiles. I laugh out loud.

"You're so gross!" She laughs and shoos me away. I head to the toilets. They are outside and around the back of the servo. Bravely, I go in, still on edge from the week we've had. Hearing Sophie talking to someone on the phone, I listen carefully.

"Stay away Jay... I'm not scared of you... She doesn't know you. .. No, I'm not... leave us alone..." she hangs up. I watch as her shoulders round and she hunches over, crying into her hands. I come up behind her and wrap my arms around her. Her body jolts at my touch. Turning her in my arms, I secure her tight. She buries herself in my embrace, hugging me back.

I sigh, "What's going on, Soph?" I ask her, as I stroke her back. She sniffs a few times, then says, "He wants us back. Reckons he's had his fun and it's time to settle back down." She draws in a shaky breath. "Like I was waiting for him or something. Stasia, I'm not going back. Even if that means I need to go far, far away, where he can't find me!"

"Hey, you're not on your own. I'm here and Bullet won't let you go without a fight, so don't think about him, okay?" She nods.

"I'm not going back there. Keata will hate it, and I just can't, Stasia." I nod, wondering if this will be a threat to us all.

Then she says, "Say nothing, please. Promise me. This is my problem, Stasia, no one else's!" her facial expression turns serious, waiting for my answer.

I agree. "Only if he's not dangerous, and Keata or you can't get hurt."

She nods, saying, "Deal." Not sure if I believe a word she's saying, I gesture at the sink.

"Okay, now wash up, your eyes are red. Then we'll go eat. Mira has Keata, so she's already eating, okay?" Hugging her once more, I leave the bathroom hoping I'm making the right choice.

Finishing up my food, I hear some bikes driving in and turn to the window. I see that he's here with the rest of them. They all go to the counter when they come in. Standing, I notice Drew is still outside. I race out the door and rush to Drew, colliding with him, wrapping my arms around him tight, holding him.

He holds me back and dips his head to my ear, "You good?"

"Yeah, wanted to feel you." He squeezes me tight again, and lifts my chin with his pointer finger. In the next moment he leans down and gives me a soulful kiss that causes goosebumps to erupt all over my body.

Drew notices, "You cold?" with a smirk forming on his lips.

Shaking my head from side to side, I respond, "No, I'm good." His smirk turns into a smile, knowing damn well why.

Then whispers in my ear, "When we get to Adelaide, Beauty, we can have some downtime, okay?" He kisses me again and heat fills my body from the core. God, he makes all my insides melt.

Walking away, I shake it off. When I get to my chair, Izzy looks at me weird.

"What are you doing?"

I blush, then say, "Nothing."

Mira notices, "She's just shaking all the goosebumps away, aren't you, Stasia?" The warmth I was feeling has turned to red hot embarrassment. I put my head down and let my hair cover my heated face. I grab my frappé and put my lips around the straw and suck, hoping the ice-cold drink will take away the heat from my face.

I can't even look at Mira as I say, "Shut up Mira! I was…" Needing to search for the word because the embarrassment is fogging my thoughts, I go with, "Cold."

They all laugh, and I hear, "Sure you are." around the table. I need a subject change.

"So, Mira, are you going to tell us soon or what?" She looks at me, knowing what I'm doing, she just shakes her head no. Well, that went well!

Nova comes over and tells us, "Good news ladies, we're resting up here for the night, then getting back on the road."

Drew comes over, saying, "You want to ride with me to the motel, Beauty?"

Excitement races through me, "YES! OH, MY GOD, YES!" I can't wait. I'm bouncing out of my seat. Going on the bike would be great.

I'm sitting behind Drew on his bike. He gives me these crazy looking glasses and a bandanna. My nose scrunches, "I'm not wearing that!" he chuckles, "Suit yourself." I grab the helmet and put it on. He said the place is close to here. As we hit the road, I let out a squeal of excitement about being on his bike. No wonder he loves the wind in his face. Then, out of nowhere, something hits my face. It hurts, and I grunt. Then something smashes into my eye, I scream in frustration. Drew turns his head and chuckles. I go to say something, and I swallow a bug. I'm coughing, spluttering and dry retching. Shit!

We pull into the motel and Drew looks at me and laughs.

"Babe, the bandana and glasses are not for looks. They're to stop that shit from happening." The feeling of heat in my cheeks creeps up fast. I didn't put it on because I thought it was a staunch thing. "Well, fuck that, I'm gangsta now!" I blurt out, "I'll be buying my own so that doesn't happen again!" He can't help it, he laughs. I do too, but mine seems to be half-hearted with bugs still stuck in my throat. Bloody nature!

We check in, but we're not in our own room. Drew and I have some alone time. We spend it talking and enjoying each other's company. But there are two double beds in the room I'm in. All of us girls are together, and the guys are out doing patrol stuff or meetings.

The next day runs smoothly. The trip is just as boring. So, we girls annoy Felix and Cory by asking twenty-one questions. Like, who was their first girlfriend? Which Felix says he never had one, but

Cory had a high school sweetheart that he says didn't last longer than six months, which is better than nothing. Izzy brings up a relationship with a boy, but from what she has told us, it was innocent. I'm glad she's talking about the pleasant memories in her life that had happened before all of this, it tells me she is healing.

"Izzy, can we set up the competition we were talking about when we get to Melbourne?" She looks at me and her face flashes with excitement and I'm not the only one who notices.

Cory asks, "What comp are we talking about?"

"A shooting comp, us girls need some more practice and some fun. You reckon you can help us out, Cory?"

He's still looking at Izzy's face through the mirror. He shakes his head, "If it gives Izzy that much happiness, then yeah, I'll organise it." Izzy and I squeal in excitement.

Mira and Savie say, "We're in," and Savie adds, "There are a few other girls who will be interested at home as well. What about you, Sophie?" She looks up.

"Maybe, I'll see."

"Okay, done. I'm counting on you, Cory!"

He smiles and says, "No problem!" I hope it happens 'cause we all need a little fun! Izzy is shining through her darkness, which makes me smile. The smiles and excitement stay in the van the rest of the way to Eucla.

We arrive at Eucla with time to eat, stretch our legs, and let Keata run around. Bullet has been playing with her, Sophie is nowhere to be seen. Deciding to explore a bit, I spot her behind the building where we had lunch, on the phone again, telling whoever it is to leave her alone.

"Just don't come near us. We're happy now. Leave us alone." I can't hear him, but I hear Soph. She is covering her mouth trying to stop herself from crying. Her last words are, "You will never find us. I'll make sure of it!" She hangs up and looks around. I stay where I am and give her some time, but she walks the opposite way of me. I go back to where I came from. I hope she knows what she's doing. Drew's words come to mind. There is no way Bullet is going to let anything happen to them. I'm hoping that he can keep his promise.

DREW

42

DREW

T he next leg of our trip is to Streaky Bay. It's along the coast and off the road. By the time we get there, I'm stiff, sore, and can't wait for a hot shower. We're staying longer here. Eight hours, maybe more.

Most who search for us will assume we're taking the quickest path to Melbourne, oblivious to our hidden route. Only half of us are at this hotel, the rest are down the street in the motel. We are going to the bar to have a drink and relax later. But I wanted to stick around with Stasia, curled up, and spend a moment together on our own. But she has other plans. Craving a steak feast and dessert, she reckons.

As we get to our suite, Stasia places her stuff next to the bed and grabs out some clothes. It's a white dress with some sort of lace on it.

She sees me observing her and beams, then declares, "I need to get cleaned up. How long do you think we're here for?" Swaggering forward, following her to the shower, I imagine all the ways I can change her mind about the steak dinner. We have twenty minutes before we need to be at the bar. Eyeing her, I decide a joint shower is happening.

As I get to the shower door, Stasia asks, "What are you doing? You mentioned not till Adelaide?" I interrupt her from speaking and kiss her deep and tender.

Pulling back and staring into her eyes, I say, "Beauty, we need to shower quick, then get your tush to the pub. Unless I can persuade you to stay?" I smack her ass for effect and observe her jump in surprise. A mischievous smile plays on her lips.

"Well, you can't come in with me then, because I'll get distracted." She is struggling to keep it together, but I can sense her excitement.

"Beauty, you don't have a choice today, because I missed you. And my body sure as hell misses you." She gets all embarrassed and turns the shower on. I go up behind her and help her get undressed. She turns in my arms, I observe as her lips turn up into a smile as she runs her fingertips down my face, along my jaw to my lips.

We stare into each other's eyes for a few seconds, "Well, biker boy, you best hurry then!" she whispers. My lips crash with hers, my hands in her hair, trying to pull her face even closer, so there is no space for air. I know I can suffocate in Stasia's taste happily. My hands slide down to her neck, where my thumbs massage under her jawline. My fingers wrap around her nape, tenderly keeping her head where I need it. I pull back somewhat and Stasia moans softly from losing the feeling of my lips. I grin as I run my eyes over her to explore her face as she gives me a knowing smile. Gently, I nudge her towards the shower while I lean back in and kiss her again.

"Ready?" Not waiting for her reply, I slam into her as I suck on her neck and listen to her pleasure. Holding her firm around her hips, keeping control, I draw out slowly, all the way to the tip, savouring the feeling of her tight centre. Then I slam in harder. I pick up my pace, uncertain if it's her moaning anymore, or me. Stasia contracts around me. This happens so quickly that I'm not ready for my own eruption inside of her. I keep moving, slowing my pace as the ripples end. I drop my forehead to Stasia's back between her shoulders, trying to recover my breathing.

Stasia giggles, "I can't move. I'm done." I kiss her on the neck where I left a mark of passion. It makes me feel possessive of this gorgeous woman. I encourage her to turn around in the shower as I wash us both, enjoying the just fucked look on her face.

As I exit the shower, knowing we are about to be late, I smile, "You best hurry, Beauty, we are late."

Once we're ready, we head out of the hotel room, to the pub. Everyone's already there as we walk through the front door. The guys hoot and holler as we stroll past the bar. Stasia smirks at them, then leads us to where Sophie and Keata are. I follow. Lucky for me, Bullet is at the same table. Smirking to myself, I realise it wouldn't matter if he was here or not, because I need to be close to Stasia right now. It's an urge I can't shake. I don't like it when I can't touch her. As we sit, the girls chat. Bullet and I just sit and have our beer. After a bit, Savie comes to the table and looks at Stasia.

"Right, your first bet takes place tonight. They have karaoke starting soon, so, girl, you're up!" Stasia's face flushes.

"No, why here? I'm not even drinking, shit, Savie, why?" Savie smiles big time.

"You're singing, so have a few shots and get ready. There are three people before you!" I get up and get her some shots.

I hear her say, "Hey, but one was for you to join me, so, I pick today as well!"

She looks proud of herself now, but Savie says, "Fine, but I sing one song with you and then you're on your own!" Stasia gets up to get herself a shot of something, so I yell over the noise. "I'll get it! Be back in a minute." After I get a tray full of shots, I come back. Stasia looks worried.

"Babe, drink some of these for courage, and you'll be fine."

I get in close and whisper, "I've heard you sing. You're good, so don't worry."

She smiles, then says, "It's not that. It's all the people, I get nervous, but with Savie up there I should be good!" She drinks four shots in a row and sips on a beer that I got. Her cheeks are slightly pink, so she should be feeling a buzz right about now. They call her and Savie up to the stage.

Stasia shrugs with her arms in the air, "I don't even know what we're singing!" she mouths.

'Sober' by Pink, comes across the speakers. I look at Dad. He's watching Savie with a smile. The girls sound very similar. Their voices are husky as well. God, Stasia looks hot! Once the song finishes, they are both smiling and laughing. Stasia says something to Savie, and she nods. Savie goes to the DJ and speaks to him, then she stands behind him, not too close, but not far away, either. Then the next song comes on, which is 'Scars to Your Beautiful' by Alessia Cara, and I can't take my eyes off her. I don't even know if anyone is talking, I'm transfixed on her. Dad comes over and bumps me with his shoulder when she finishes.

"Well, she's been hiding her talents. That was awesome. Maybe the girls can sing again sometime?" Hell yes, I'd like that, but only if Stasia wants to. Shit. I'm lost for words. I don't even answer Dad. The girls are back, everyone is talking to them. The other girls, Sophie, Mira, and Izzy are raving about how good they sound together, but I've had enough. I don't have any words to show her, so I pick her up, straddle her over my lap and kiss her hard. I can hear the guy's whooping and hollering, but I don't give a shit. She is mine, and fuck everyone else.

She pulls back, and looks at me, smiling and a bit flushed, saying, "So, you liked it, hey, biker boy?"

"Yeah, I did, and you only get to do that when I'm around,' cause, shit... I don't even know why... just, only when I'm here!" She giggles, enjoying my loss of words, and rests her head on my forehead.

"You got it, honey, anything for you." I kiss her again till everyone tells us to get a room.

All I say back to the guys is, "Lucky we have one tonight!"

Dinner comes, we're all eating and are in a good place. Even Sophie is enjoying herself, and Keata is in Bullet's arms, giggling. I notice Sophie's phone is absent. Maybe she left it at the hotel, I'm not sure, but at least she's happy.

It's 11:45 p.m. once we all head back to our hotels. Dad has told everyone that we will leave by 10 a.m. at the latest tomorrow. But he's also told us to stay on alert, 'cause we are staying longer. Taking the longer route, we could collide with the enemy coming into Adelaide.

We eat breakfast and stretch out, then we get back on the road to Adelaide. It's a three and a half hour trip. We get to stay at Haidie's clubhouse. It's not one of our own, but a fellow club that's been with us for a while. The Prez before Dad and this club's president were friends for a long time, and Dad kept the alliance going. They have a big night planned for us, but I won't be joining them, and neither will half the guys. The young ones might, but I'm on edge, have been since Esperance. Been waiting for intel on this other guy, it's looking like he's a big player in this.

As we walk into the clubhouse, I pull Stasia close. I notice Nova has Izzy close, and Dad does the same with Savie. Mira walks in with Krip behind her this will be interesting 'cause the guys are seeing she's the only one on her own. But Mira can handle herself, that's for sure. I feel sorry for some of these guys already. She'll be respectful but won't take their shit. All of us will be right behind her, which is what gives her an edge.

The president of the club walks in our direction and introduces himself to those of us who don't know him. He goes through who's staying where while we get the younger members to sort out the bags. Then, we head to where there's food and drinks. What I don't like is that there are club girls everywhere, and none of us are interested. I keep Stasia close as we get our food and find somewhere to eat, Bullet follows us to our table.

"Sophie refuses to bring Keata out here. So, I told her I'll be back with her food and not to let anyone in."

Nodding, I ask, "Her phone, she still has it?" Stasia looks at me, then goes back to eating.

"She says it's in her bag, reckon everyone's here so she doesn't need it out." I nod, but Stasia fills her mouth like she might say something without being asked. She knows something, and she's protecting her friend, just like she said she would.

"So, you heard anything from home yet?" He shakes his head.

"PC has nothing, but he will, just needs time. And Prez is trying to figure out who this big player is, we need some idea what we're up against!" Nodding with agreement, I change the subject.

"So, you riding back or what?"

Shaking his head. "Not sure, but if we are, I want to make sure we can do some sightseeing, show Soph and Keata around properly. I'll cross that bridge later, though." Knowing what he means, with all that's going on right now, I agree. We finish up our chat and he goes to get Soph and Keata some food. My gaze connects with Stasia knowingly; she knows something and I'm going to find out.

"Spill!"

"No, you said that if I think it's not dangerous and no harm can come to her, then I don't have to tell you!"

"Yeah, Beauty, but at the moment, we have enough on our plate, and not knowing can cause more problems! So, spill!" Looking around, she's trying to find a way out of this.

"She hasn't told me much yet, but I know she needs a new phone and a new number that won't connect it to her, then her problems will be gone." Stasia whispers the last part. She looks down at her fingers and plays with them, not looking like she believes herself. Fuck. Running my hands through my hair in frustration.

"Beauty, for someone who knows nothing, you know a hell of a lot!"

Stasia looks at me, eyes wide, saying, "That's all you're getting. She will kill me, and possibly kick me out of my new home if I say anymore!"

"Babe, when this is over, you're moving in with me, so I don't care!"

"No, I'm not... I can't move in with you. I moved in with Soph, and I'm helping her with all her bills, so you're out of luck, biker." She gets up to leave, but I stop her.

"Babe, we have a meeting with the guys, so make sure you stay in our room. Lock the door, okay? I know these guys, but not well enough to trust them with you. Keep Mira with you too because I don't need her causing shit tonight!" She nods and gets up to find Mira. I watch her until both Mira and Stasia are heading to our assigned rooms. Our discussion is not over, even though she thinks it is.

Dad organised to use their meeting room. Just as we're about to start, their president walks in.

"You don't mind if I sit in, do ya, Cobra?"

Dad nods, "We're going to chat about where we're at, Dozer, but you're welcome to sit in. It's your club." I don't like this and neither does Dad. Which is why we are only talking about things that are common knowledge. But when Dozer asks questions that are more confidential. Dad stops the meeting and tells us we're dismissed.

Then Bullet comes to me, "Brother, your room, now!" I shake my head.

"The girls are there." He looks at Trigger and then at me.

"His room, let's go." Once we're there, Krip is behind us as well. We all enter Trigger's room, but I notice that we have a spy. Trigger does too, and tells him to get lost. Once we're inside, Trigger puts his music on with the speaker he brings everywhere with him. He heads to his bathroom, gesturing for us all to follow. We all know he's trying to drown out the sound. Bullet talks first.

"Something's not right, we need to leave soon. Send Cory to fill the van now, and the tanks of the bikes, that way we have petrol. We need to leave pronto. I'll get Cobra alone soon and tell him, and I don't want Keata here, let alone Soph, so be ready to roll as soon as Cobra says." Bullet and I make eye contact. We both know shit is about to happen. I can feel it in my gut.

STASIA

43

STASIA

Mira and I are in mine and Drew's room. She's pacing in front of the door. I'm sitting on the bed, my fist scrunches the bedding into my hands, wondering what is going on.

My gut tightens as I ask, "What is it?"

Mira doesn't even look at me when she answers, "I don't trust this place. Something's off!"

"What? What do you mean?" Mira stops pacing and looks at me. Her facial expression changes and softens slightly.

Slowly, she comes to sit next to me, saying, "I hope the boys have the same feeling too, but this club… Something is not right! I can sense it."

"Okay, maybe you're just feeling off. The shit between you and Krip..." She snaps her head to me.

"Stasia, there's nothing going on between me and that scumbag, and this is way more important. I gotta ring Dad." She dismisses me, and looks in her pocket and pulls out her phone. She dials, then looks again at her phone and tries again, "Try yours, mine's not working." I pull mine out and try to ring Sophie, but nothing.

"Mine's not working either! Shit!" She nods as if she might be onto something.

"Okay, I need my bag. I have a gun in it. They put me in a room with Izzy and that's where my bag should be. I think Izzy is with Sophie and Savie at the moment. Shit, I hope Savie picks up on this." She's rambling. Jesus. Have we walked into a trap?

Staring at my hands, I whisper, "Mira, what are we going to do?"

"The main thing is to stay together until we are out of here, don't, and I mean don't, go anywhere by yourself, Stasia. That goes for all us girls. We need to stay together." Nodding, I agree, thinking about the guys. My stomach tightens. Damn my father!

When Drew comes in, we both jump, not sure what to expect when he barges through the door. Mira talks first.

"We can't use our phones, and I want my gun. It's in my bag in Izzy's room. Drew, something's not right!" She says all this in a whisper, which Drew nods and then points to the bathroom. We follow.

He turns the shower on and whispers, "Yeah Mira, something's up, but we're not sure what yet, so don't get jumpy. And what do you mean, your phone's not working?" I jump in so he realises it's not a coincidence.

"Mine either. I tried to ring Soph, but it's dead, and Mira tried to call her dad." he blows out a harsh breath. Looking at us both, he reaches for my phone in my hand and hits some buttons before giving it back.

"Shit, I have to let Bullet know! But I don't want to set alarm bells off either. We need a distraction." As he says this, Krip walks through the door and winks at us girls. He nods his head towards the door, then looks at us mouthing, "Follow my lead."

"Mira, what the fuck you doing out of my room? When I tell you to wait there, you wait there!" He points at Drew, signalling to keep talking, while he writes on a piece of paper. Drew goes with what is going on.

"I've warned you once, now I'm warning you again, brother, stay the fuck away from her!" Drew then looks down at what he's written.

The club is not safe. Bullet knows phones are down and you need to leave. Leave me and Cobra here, use Mira as an excuse. Let's do this. We need to fight but take it to the main room. Mira, kill this note. Take Stasia to Bullet, pretend you're getting him.

He hand-gestures to all of us and nods, making sure we all understand.

"Yeah, well, I'll do what the fuck I want! Now, Mira, move!" He nods at Drew like he's telling him, 'come on, hit me'. Drew flies at him. They go through the door and are punching each other hard. They're heading to the main room and Mira has already eaten, yes, bloody eaten the paper, and pulls on my arm.

"Come on, let's get Bullet. Hopefully, Drew will kick his arse." As we head to where Bullet and Sophie are, one of the other club guys says, "Where are you two going?"

Mira answers without missing a beat, "Getting our Sergeant of Arms! Krip's been pushing me around for weeks now, and Dad gave him strict orders on what to do!" She says this, pointing in Krip's direction. He nods, then lets us pass. Thank God. As we get to Bullet's room, he pulls us in and closes the door, putting his finger to his lips to quiet us. Then grabs his gun and heads out of the room. He gets to the door and waves for us to follow.

What the hell is he going to do? I look at the girls; Sophie, Keata and Izzy. They look as scared as me, but Mira and Savie look like it's game time. They both shrug like it's no big deal. We sneak out to the main room where Drew and Krip are still in a fight. Everyone is too focused on the fight. Drew has blood coming down his lip, and Krip's eyes are swelling. I see Cobra is with the other president and he gives a slight nod to Bullet, which was so slight that if I wasn't staring at him, I would've missed it, and what happens next scares the ever-loving shit out of me!

Bullet aims his gun at the Drew and Krip fighting, then he pulls the trigger.

Drew lands one more punch into Krip and gets up, then he says, "You're lucky the bullet wound is only graze, motherfucker. Stay the fuck away from Mira and everyone else." Then he turns to his dad.

"This is your second in command. I thought you changed, Dad. Well, fuck you!" He grabs me and Mira and heads to the door.

Some of the other club guys go to stop us, but Cobra yells, "Let the little bitch go! I'll deal with him later!" Savie has a determined look in her eye and looks at Cobra.

"You okay with this?"

He looks at her and tightens his jaw.

"Yeah, and if you're not, leave!" Savie stares at Cobra. I grab her arm and pull her towards the exit, hoping this has to be a show for the other club.

Savie is still looking in Cobra's direction as we make it to the exit. I can't believe we all get to leave. Savie turns and looks at Drew before she hurries us to the van that Cory has already started.

As we get in, Drew says, "We'll talk soon, keep your heads down and stay safe, okay?" I nod, knowing he has to go on his bike. The girls are all in the van, so is Felix, and Cory is driving. We're down the road and heading away from the club. I'm anxious and finding it hard to breathe when we all hear a pop sound. We all look around, but we can't see anything. I'm looking up at the stars feeling sleepy. When I try to fight it, I see everyone is fighting it, and then there's darkness.

DREW

44

DREW

I close the door on the van, hoping like hell we get the girls to safety. Striding to my bike, I throw my leg over the seat and settled onto my bike. Resting my hands on the handlebars, I peer at all the guys that are with us. Maverick, Trigger Thump, Felix, Cory, Nova, Bullet, Helmet and me, having to leave Krip and Dad. This is hard for all of us, but hopefully Dad has a plan, and if he doesn't, he's been in worse situations. Getting into a fight with Krip was what I needed. Once I laid the first punch and he hit me back with the same force, a burst of relief washed over me. The urge to hit each other was mutual. I have been on edge with him since he showed up with my Dad. Krip, however, has been wanting a fight since he walked into the club for the first time. He must have figured we can burn that energy in a fight. We both realised it was inevitable anyway, because of Mira. But Bullet shooting him? I can't see Krip being happy about that, let alone dealing with whatever he has to do here at Haidie's club.

I keep repeating to myself that we need to get to the next checkpoint. Fuck, I hope like hell no one knows where that is, and Dad gets there with no trouble. Bullet starts his bike up first. We all rev our engines, enjoying the power of the engine that rumbles through our bodies, calming our thoughts. We all roll the throttle and head out of the clubhouse. Following in the same direction as the van, hoping like hell that we all get to our next destination.

Settling into the journey, keeping our eyes on the van ahead of us, and the road, for kangaroos. I notice the van swaying. I signal to Bullet, who is next to me. He notices. It pulls back to the middle of the road. Bullet signals for us to catch up to it when it sways to the left this time. We both speed up to see what's going on. Suddenly, a police car flashes its lights, and signals for us to pull over. Fuck, I pray the van keeps going. I go to pull over when another cop car pulls out in front and signals for the rest of the bikes to all pull over. I'm glad we have guys in the van with the girls.

We're all watching the van in the distance. It sway's again with the brake lights coming on and off.

Everything that happens next is in slow motion. They hit the sign and then the curb. The van is in the air and lands on its side, sliding along the ground till it stops.

I go to start my bike again, but the cops bring out their guns, saying, "We have called the ambulance, so let us do our job. After that, you can go." I glance at Bullet, who looks like he's going to explode. He gets off his bike and sprints towards the accident. I'm right behind him. My thighs burn from the speed. The cops are yelling at us, their voices fading in the distance as our legs pound into the ground. Nova is keeping up with us till more cops pull up. As we get close, they have a barrier up to stop anyone from getting through. We're halted by the barrier, three police on each of us. We are all standing there wondering what the fuck just happened!

372

I figured we were home free. I assumed that if I got the girls out the door, they would be safe, and so did most of us. Now, all the girls have been in a car crash, including little Keata. I'm hoping the car seat we put in for her might be what saves her.

If we could have gotten near the van, we might have saved the girls, but as soon as it all happened there were police everywhere.

It's like they were waiting for us.

I go to Bullet, "We need to get over there, brother." Both of us look at the barricade that's stopping us. He nods at me and then whistles to get everyone else's attention. All the brother's nod and move forward. We get close, but another cop stops us.

"Sorry guys, it's too dangerous for…" He doesn't get to finish his sentence because we all push through him, none of us caring right now. I noticed two ambulances coming on site, that was fast too. I'm not complaining if it's legit, because the girls could be in danger. We hang back, closer to the crash, waiting for an opening to get through. The ambos do their stuff. I study one guy, and he looks like a guy from the club we just left. We need to get in there now! I see the ambos pulling them out and no one is conscious. There were three ambulances. Bullet and I push through the next lot of people to get to the girls and Nova was right next to us. We have all got our eyes on our own girls and watch for any clue as to how they are. They don't seem good.

The ambo yells to us all, "Look, you need to meet us at the hospital. We need to get them there, now!" I'm staring at Stasia. I've frozen on the spot, like ice is running through my body.

I listen to Nova say, "Good, but we're going in the ambulance, so make room!" He jumps in with Izzy, so I follow and get in with Stasia. Bullet does the same with Sophie and Keata. We are all trying to process what just happened.

I signal for the guys to head to our next checkpoint, and they all nod. I grab my phone and send out a group text so I know Dad will get the message about the accident and where the checkpoint is for everyone. My first text back is from Prez.

PREZ: *I'm on my way. I got Mira's text 2 minutes ago saying shit hit the fan. I'll ring soon for an update. How many do we need? Is Mira ok?*

ME: *Van flipped. Girls are all unconscious. Hurry! I think the big player is Haidie's club. We were there when shit hit the fan!*

PREZ: *ok, on our way. Flying in. Should be there in 3 hours. I hope we have some answers by then.*

Next, a message comes from Dad.

DAD: *Boy, these guys are in on it. Break contact. I'm killing this phone. Keep the girls safe and tell Savie I'll be home soon!*

Did he not get my message about the accident? Shit, scrubbing my face with the palms of my hands, I'm in the ambulance, hoping that the girls are going to be safe. The ambo closes the doors as I'm staring at the floor of the ambulance, tugging at my hair harder. How the fuck shit get bad so fast? Stasia looks so peaceful. I'm holding her hand, waiting for the ambo to get in the truck. There is a popping sound. I try to explore to determine where the sound came from, but as I stand, I feel groggy. I go to open the door, but I'm fighting to keep my balance. Grabbing the sides of the ambulance, I try not to fall as my body fights sleep. This was all a trap. I grab my phone, still fighting to stay awake and delete everything, hoping that no one can trace it. Prez is on the way and with Dad's last text, I'm hoping he makes it out. I try again to open the door. Falling to my knees, scrapping the door with my nails, and trying to hold on as long as I can, the last thing I see is Stasia. Then darkness.

Waking up to sounds near me, I slowly peer around. I don't know where I am. There is banging, like somebody is thumping on a wall or shed door. Struggling to get my bearings, I sit up. God, my head hurts. Placing my hand on my head, I rub my face, feeling disoriented. The banging is louder now. It sounds like it's coming from two different directions. I can't get up yet, so I drag my body, and crawl to where one sound is. Placing my ear to the wall, I can pick up a voice. Shit, that's Nova.

I bang and yell at the wall, "Hey, you okay?" he hears me, I yell telling him, "There's someone else over to the other side." I drag my body back to the other side and check. Putting my ear to the wall, and it's Bullet, fuck.

"What the hell happened?" I yell at both of them. "Where are the girls?"

Nova yells back, "It was a trap from the beginning. I overheard one of the so-called ambos before I blacked out, I hope the guys figured it out beforehand." He's right, shit, the cops were there too early, and to pull us over... who the hell is behind this?

I yell back, "Agreed. Bullet's on the other side. See if you can find a way out!" I go to the other side. Bullet decides the same, saying it's a setup and now we're all looking for a way out, a weak spot in the room. The only thing on our side is that they did not tie us up. So, if someone comes in, we all have that advantage.

After what feels like three or four hours, Bullet yells "Car, look alive!" I bang on Nova's wall and repeat the same thing. Now, if these guys have done their homework. They will realise they have three highly trained soldiers locked up, but if they haven't, then that's on them and we are out of here. I sit in the dark and pretend I'm asleep. The lock clicks. I turn and watch the door creeping open. In walks a man I've never seen before. He walks in with confidence, but he doesn't appear to be armed. I stay still, waiting.

"I know who you are, Drew. But what I don't know is why you have what's mine?" I'm struggling to not answer him. I want him to believe I'm asleep. He walks closer and gets down at my level, not too close, but close enough that he would take notice if I'm asleep. I take a slow, deep breath and let my head drop a bit. He seems to have bought it. He walks out and calls to someone else, which is what I wanted to know. How many men are here? Two more guys come in, from what I can tell. I listen to them talking.

"I thought he'd be awake by now."

The other guy, with long hair placed in a pony, says, "Yeah, let's go check on the other guys."

The first guy talks again, "We only need to hold them till we secure the other package, then we leave these guys here. Come on, let's check on the other two." Hearing my door close, I hope Bullet has the same idea. A gigantic crash and thudding noise comes from against the wall, close to the door. Things go quiet...

I notice Bullet opens my door then goes to Nova's door and says, "Well that was too easy, idiots didn't even tie us." Agreeing, I push through the door, "They said they only had to keep us till another package is secured." Peering at Bullet, I try to inform him without stating it.

Bullet nods, saying, "They have Keata and the other girls.. I'll get some answers from these idiots. You two go see what vehicle is here."

Turning back to Bullet, I ask, "You think they will give you something?"

"Drew, I'm not playing this time. What I did to the last survivor we got info from, will seem like child's play. I'll get what we need!" The dead expression in his eyes confirms that this is going to be one fucked up interrogation!

Coming outside, there are no more men, which makes little sense.

There is one car, and guess what? The keys are waiting for us. Again, way too easy! As we check the area further back, there is nothing and the area we are in isn't that far from the club we were at. We both head back to where Bullet is. He has made a fuckin' mess. Two guys are dead, but the main one got away. Bullet got the intel we need. The girls are at Flinders Ports, and they need to keep us out of action for twenty hours till the boat leaves.

As we get to the car I say "Nova, any phones? We need to get ahold of Prez and find out his E.T.A. and see if there's anything on their phones that can help us."

"On it,"

Starting the car, we head off, with only an idea of the location and the knowledge that we only have twenty hours to get the girls back!

DREW

45

DREW

T he best place to go is the checkpoint. When we get there, we are relieved that everyone is there. Trigger meets us at the front gate. The checkpoint is a farm of sorts, on about five acres. It's one of our old member's homes, who ended up retiring here with his wife. He still keeps his hand in with Cobra. When trouble's around, we try to stay away and he knows we wouldn't put him in danger unless we had to.

Trigger greets us with open arms, saying, "Jesus, brother, I was worried we wouldn't see you. Well, standing, anyway. Prez is here. Come on, let's go!" We return to the car and drive towards the house.

There are loud cheers when we walk into the house. I suppose we look good for what could've happened. Prez is the first to greet us by slapping us on the back, a one-armed hug from everybody else follows. It goes to show how close we are to our club.

After all the greetings are done, Prez calls us all around and asks, "What do we know?"

"There's about nineteen hours left to find the girls and that they're at Flinders Ports. The guy Bullet interrogated told us they're in a container."

Connecting eyes with Prez, "Have you heard from Dad?"

Nodding, "Yeah, he's good at the moment with the way you guys set it up. He's told me his boys from Melbourne will join us in about..." looking down at his wrist looking at his watch, "An hour. So, manpower will be strong!"

Nodding, "Good, we will need it. Haidie's club isn't huge, but they have enough guys. Now we've got our twelve, plus... How many of the Melbourne charter is coming?"

"Ten, Cobra sent out a high alert, so Bear contacted me at the last stop they had. We got plenty!"

Bullet asks next, "What about Cory and Felix, any word?"

"No. Nothing. We're hoping they're with the girls." We do some planning while PC prints out overhead maps of the place, and Prez organises us into groups.

The hour seems to drag, and so does my temper. Every time I glance at my phone, the time hasn't moved. Fuck!

Bullet comes over to me, "PC got me some info about that number, but Soph killed it and dumped her phone on our last stop. The number seems to belong to a Jason Simpson, you heard of him?"

"Nah, I noticed Stasia was worried though. Let's get them back, brother!"

"Yeah, I'm going on a killing spree and if I think about what they're going through... Fuck, Drew!"

"I'm hearing ya. If those other guys are here, we should get ready to roll."

Once the guys from Melbourne arrive, we organise the plan going forward. Bear tells us more info that Cobra had gotten to him, we have more of an idea about where the girls are supposed to be. They could also be held at a different location with the plan to bring them at the last minute. We need to hurry, the sooner we get them, the better!

Prez gives the word that we are ready. We all get our guns, weapons, and anything we can think of to get our girls back. We all head to Flinders Ports.

STASIA

46

STASIA

Waking up, I pull at my arms. They're tied, and my legs are tied as well. There's something in my mouth. Where the hell am I? All I can hear is silence. I look around the room, hoping to understand why I'm here. Then, bits come back to me, saying goodbye to Drew, him closing the car door and us thinking we were all good, until we were fighting to stay awake.

My head is really sore. It must have been the stuff they knocked us out with. Where are the other girls? I try to look behind me, and see a single door.

After a bit, I hear a commotion, I just can't sense the direction that it's coming from. The sound is getting louder.

I hear a female voice screaming, "Get the fuck away!" The exit that's behind me bursts open, then closes. Two girls are thrown to the floor, I'm still not clear who it is, but I'm sure one is Mira. She pulls herself up and goes to bang on the door. The other girl scurries herself to the side wall, shit, that's Izzy.

She is shaking so badly. I can't even ask her if she's all right, 'cause my mouth is gagged and Mira is beating the shit out of the door. I'm pretty confident that it won't help us, but who knows at this point.

After Mira notices I'm in the room, she comes to me, takes off my gag, and turns my chair around so I'm facing the exit. "Oh, my God, are you okay? I didn't know where you were. Savie, Sophie and Keata aren't here either. Do you know where they are? What are we going to do?"

I glance at Izzy. "Are you okay? What happened to you?" She trembles more, not answering me. I stare at Mira; she runs over and drops to Izzy's side. Izzy jumps.

Her nerves must be a mess, then I look at Mira asking, "Did you two get separated?"

Nodding, Mira replies, "We just met up." Shit, what happened to her or what did she see? Mira tries asking her, but she can't stop herself from shaking. I'm wondering who has us when my father makes his grand entrance and everything falls into place for me. My father took Izzy, and this is how I got found. I can't stop staring at him as he comes into view.

"Well, well, well, it's taken me a while to find you, Anastasia. Why would you run from what you had? It was your calling. The same as your mother's!" I feel sick. *Not him!* I take deep breaths, trying to gain some of the courage that Nanna Sally pushed me to have, but I'm still tied to a damn chair. Shit. I gather as much inner strength as I can to talk to him. Before I get to speak, Mira runs at him, ready to knock him over, but he sees her coming and punches her in the mouth. She doesn't have time to find her balance. She hits the floor. I'm not sure if she's still conscious, till I hear her moan in pain.

I look straight at my father and say, "Let them go, plus the others, I'll come with you, no complaints. I promise!"

Shaking his head, he replies, "It's too late for them. We have plans for you all, even…" He kicks Mira in the stomach hard and she groans. "The club's princess, which I must say, what a great surprise!" Oh, God this won't be good, I can feel it. Shit, do the boys even know where we are? Then Cory and Felix come to mind.

Looking in the door's direction, Felix struts in, looking too smug. Oh, my God, no. He can't be. Was he in on it? Did he do this? As he saunters over to us, my father puts his arm around him. Great work, Son! The world around me slows. What? Son? C-Can't be, shit!

My head spins, and my father says the words I've been thinking, "Anastasia, meet your brother, Felix. Felix, meet your sister!" I stare at him for what seems like forever. I forget who's here. Hearing Izzy startles me back to the room.

"Where's Cory? What have you done to him?" My father laughs, he laughs hard, like this is the best joke he's heard in a long time.

When he can speak, he replies with, "You'll have to wait and see. I had plans to kill him, but I don't have the last say this time. You will meet the man in charge soon enough. Be patient, or maybe I'll let your brother get properly acquainted with you and move these girls and give them some of what's coming for them." Oh, God, no. If he finds out Mira is a virgin, she's... God no. I start to talk, but someone comes in the door. This guy is tall, bald, and probably Cobra's age, but he looks mean. Oh, God, I don't even know who he is.

"No one touches them yet! My father will be here soon!" He points to something, and two other guys come in and tie Mira and Izzy up, but they don't gag us. When they finish, they leave the room, but not before my so-called brother says, "See you soon, Sis." A chill falls over my body as I stare at him. I'm still in shock. I have a sibling, and we are all captured.

Mira's the first to speak, "God, I didn't know he wasn't good. Dad will kill him for turning on the club, let alone doing this shit. We need to get out of here."

We sit in silence. Mira and Izzy may try to find a way out, but I've gone blank. Looking at Mira, I see they split her lip, and she has some dried blood around her mouth. My body's shaking 'cause I'm cold. I know this is it and I've brought this to these girls.

Mira must sense what I'm thinking, because she shakes her head then says, "Get that shit out of your head. We are getting out of here. We might get a few bumps along the way, but we're getting out. Are you both listening to me?"

Izzy nods. I look away. I'm mortified that this has happened. Having a brother and then him having to live through... Oh, God, did he grow up by himself or did my father have two different lives? It's not like we are that different in age, and I left. Maybe I could have changed him, made things easier. I don't even realise I'm sobbing until I hear my name, then I hear it more clearly, it's Mira trying to calm me.

"Shhhh, Stasia, we got this, yeah? I have your back, you hear me? Now, and after all this shit is over!"

"Oh, Mira, it's not just that I failed my brother, it's what he had to live through, it's what I got away from, I would have stayed and protected him... God, he must hate me!"

She shakes her head, saying, "You can't think that way. And if you ask me, it's too late for him! He's bad, Stasia. He's going to kill us or hurt us, so don't feel that way, not for him or anyone! Now focus, we need a plan."

"We do, but what are we going to do tied up? At least if they untied us, a plan might happen." She shakes her head.

"I know, Stasia, dammit, Maybe we can convince them to untie one of us. I think we need to cause some problems, maybe one of us could start vomiting or some sort of other commotion?"

"Let's try to get these off first, then go for the commotion." I say, while pulling at my ropes. We all agree and fall silent, trying to undo them.

STASIA

47

STASIA

The girls and I have been pulling at our ties for a while now. I think mine have loosened, but I'm not sure.

"What do you think is going to happen to us?" Izzy sounds so lost, so absent. She's staring at the floor, and her face is vacant. It's scaring the shit out of me.

"Izzy, we're going to get out of this. You need to think positively, and remember, we're here together!" She looks at Mira with no emotion on her face at all.

"Mira, I will not be the same after this. You don't know what they're going to do to us. I lived through it once. After Nova and Cory, who until now, I didn't know how much they meant to me, I'm not going to... I won't be able to come back from this." She continues to show no emotion. She is correct, but I want to assure her. If my father gets his way, we won't be the same.

I'm deep in thought when the door opens again. Someone we don't know comes in with something to eat. I can see Mira wants to eat, but Izzy and I know better. We're best at trying to make it look like we ate and fake being asleep.

"Eat, then I'll be back later to collect!" He gestures his head towards the food.

"We can't eat if we're tied, you need to untie us!" Mira says this with a resolute voice.

"I'll untie one of you, so when I leave, she can undo the rest of you, but when you're finished, you need to retie each other. If you don't, there will be consequences, so don't get any ideas!" He unties me, and leaves.

As soon as he's gone, I go straight to Mira and whisper, "Don't eat the food, it could be poisoned, okay? We need to make it look like we ate some of it though."

She looks at me like I'm stupid. "Why would they do that?"

"Because that's how my father works. If he can't get what he wants, he will drug you." Looking over to Izzy, she nods with understanding. When she's untied, she picks up the food to smell it.

Mira says, "Jesus, they're not hiding it, I can smell it... shit!"

"Yeah, now we're untied so let's make a plan." Izzy rubs some food on top and at the corner of her mouth, good idea, I do the same but just on my chin.

Mira looks at us like we're talking code. "If they notice we have food on our face, they will think we ate some of it, hopefully, anyway!" Mira nods.

"How long do we have before this stuff should work?"

"I don't know, but like any aspirin or chemist drug, about thirty minutes, so he will be back soon."

Mira nods, then says, "I'll tie you back up, so he has to tie me up." We all agree as she starts.

"This is the part you need to make sure you're out of it; if they kick us or touch us, you can't flinch, but let's hope they don't." I tell the girls. I nod, but I'm not positive this is going to work. I know I'll be ok. But Izzy, she was a mess when she came in, and I'm still not sure if they did something to her. I hope we get through this next bit.

After a while, we all hear the door, so we go limp and close our eyes. I hear people come in and they're talking among themselves. Soon I feel my ties loosen, then I'm being picked up and dropped on the floor. I hit my head, and it hurts like hell, but I don't make a sound, and I don't think the girls do either. I stay as relaxed as I can, hoping like hell they don't notice we're still awake. I'm being moved again, but it feels like I'm being put on a stretcher, or something that might be easier to move us.

As I'm put on it, I feel someone push my hair back out of my face, "This one is going to be worth a pretty penny!"

Then another voice. "Yeah, whoever gets to tame this one over here, will have a job on their hands, the boss already hit her, must be feisty!"

"Yeah." Then nothing but silence, until they move us to a van. I don't even think we are all together now. I hear and feel him move me into the van, but I don't hear anybody else. Then, I can feel someone over me, looking at me, close. I can feel their breath on my face, then down my neck. Chills run down my back. This will not end well. I chant in my head, *please don't*, over and over again hoping like hell this won't happen. I feel a tongue lick my face. I'm holding on by a thread. If I move, he will know. Oh, God, please! His hands are on my shoulders, then he runs them down my body.

When I'm going to move, I hear another voice saying, "She's secure? We're leaving in ten."

Then the guy above me yells out, "Yeah, ready!"

Then he whispers to me, "Won't be long and you'll be mine, bitch!" When he's gone from earshot, I let out a deep breath.

I hear the van start up. We are on the move. There are others around me, I can feel it. But I don't think my girls are with me. God, I hope they're alright.

Then I hear someone say, "You think the boss is going to let that other girl go? He seems to want her for himself."

I wonder who they're talking about, then the other one says, "Yeah, after those bikers took her off him!" Jesus, they're talking about Izzy.

"Yeah, he's talking about making her pay. The new boss seems to think something else is happening, that's why we're going to Flinders Ports." Why the hell are we going to a boat port where containers are put on big ships? Oh, God, Drew's never going to find me, this is it. My brain is imagining the worst, everything I left behind, and everything I shoved to the bottom of my mind is slowly surfacing. This can't happen.

Stuck in my own thoughts, I don't realize the van stops until I'm pulled out. I'm being carried somewhere else, but I'm cold. I can feel the wind, then I hear a metal door open. A few people are already here, all men, then I hear my father.

"They should wake up soon. So, what's the plan?"

"Put them in these four containers. The other two are already where they're supposed to be." What is that supposed to mean and who do they mean? As they're still talking, a door closes, and their voices sound muffled now. They must still be outside. I'm still wondering who they're talking about. Please let Sophie and Keata be okay! God, everything is wrong. Am I going to be able to live with myself if I can't see them, and if something happened to Keata? *Shit.*

After a while, I hear a scream, then silence, then another scream. Then, the door opens, and I open my eyes. There's a man with my father and Felix, just standing there. The words rush out of my mouth before I can stop myself.

"What's going to happen to everyone? And where's Sophie and Keata?"

My father chuckles and Felix sniggers. "Don't worry, they're fine, back where they belong, which is none of your concern." Back where they belong? Where's that? Shit.

Felix looks smug with his answer, but I need to know more, so I ask again, "Where..." and out of nowhere I'm slapped hard across the face, and as I recover, I see a fist coming for my face. The impact snaps my head back. Then, I'm forced forward when I'm hit in the stomach. I try to tighten my body, ready for the next blow before I pass out. He stops. My head's throbbing and ringing. When I try to look up, I get one more in the eye, which knocks me out.

STASIA

48

STASIA

Someone is standing over me. Drops of water land on my eyes, nose, and mouth, causing me to wake. At first, I'm not sure what it is. I'm about to shake it off and take a breath, but as I breathe in, my mouth and throat fill with the water he's pouring over my face. He empties the whole bucket on my face as I struggle for air. The water is in my lungs. I cough and splutter everywhere, trying to get my breath back. I hear chuckles from above me.

"Damn, you didn't choke to death. Maybe next time." I'm still coughing when my eyes open and I look in the voice's direction, I see it's Felix, my brother.

"What did he do to you? I'm so sorry I wasn't there to help you. I would have stayed to help you. Why are you doing this?" He laughs at me. I was hoping for... well, I'm not sure what, but not him laughing.

"Dear sister. You think I care what happens to you? Do you think I cared if you stayed? If you stayed, he wouldn't have found us, and I wouldn't have known him. He changed my world, and my drug-fucked mother, who didn't feed me, well, he kept her away from me. So, you leaving did me a favour, Stasia." The look on his face is something of relief. I sit still, thinking he will change his mind, but then his face contorts into something scary.

"But you also ran from what our father made you for, since your mother couldn't hack it, and guess what? Now you won't be able to hide, 'cause this time will be worse, and you have no one to save you." Oh, God, he's the same as my father. How do people think like this? It's not normal. How am I going to get out of this? Trying to concentrate on my breathing, not wanting to know what's next. I see his fist clench, the look in his eyes, oh, God, what's he going to do? I feel a sting on the side of my face as my head whips to the left. My entire body tenses. I slowly look to where the force came from and see the horrible look on Felix's face. Fear races through my body. I pull at my restraints, letting the burn of the rope ease my fear. Allowing my mind to drift to a place of peace, where no one can hurt me.

I'm so sore. My face feels like it's going to explode, my ribs are sore as well. I feel sleepy and my head droops. Without warning he punches me. His fist connects with my chin and my head snaps back. The chair I'm in hits the ground, and so does the back of my head. Pain radiates through my head and my body. I'm fighting to keep my eyes open. Everything is blurry. I can feel warmth at the back of my head. I'm still tied up. My eyes lose focus. I blink and see a figure standing over me. I see Felix's mouth moving, squinting my eyes tightly closed and opening them again. He must be talking to me, but I can't hear him anymore. I can't hear anything at all. I'm fighting to stay awake.

Sienna Gypsy

DREW

49

DREW

W e're making our way to where the girls are supposed to be, but I have a sinking feeling in my gut. I hope we get there in time, before anything happens to them.

Heading into the outer harbour, Prez signals to come to a stop. We pull over where we can't be seen and hear what he has to say.

"Okay, stay in the four groups I put you in. We will surround the six containers. From what PC says, they are next to each other or nearby," he shows us on the map and points to the spots he wants us in.

"So, Bear, your crew is here. Bullet, yours here. Drew, yours is on this side. And me and my crew on the right bottom. Wait for my signal before we go in. Got it?" We all nod. Then Prez slaps his hand down on the van.

"Right, twenty minutes, boys. Make sure you're all in position. Let's go!" We all head out. I nod at Bullet as we do. My crew is over from his. As we start the van, another vehicle speeds around the corner. It takes off in a rush towards the entrance where we came in.

Trigger is an extra in my group. He looks at me and says, "You don't need me, do ya, V.P.? Let me follow that van. It could be nothing, but I could also get a lead."

I nod, "Yeah, go. Take your gun and be careful." He's already heading to his bike on the other side of the street. I look back at my crew, hoping we all get through this. I take one more look over my shoulder and he's gone.

As we arrive at our position, we look around. I can see the containers they're talking about. They're only guarding four of them. God, I hope they're all there.

There are about fifteen men that I can count, which keeps us with the higher numbers. Prez flashes a light, and that's our five-minute warning. We all get down lower and head closer to where the containers are. Right on five minutes, Prez fires the first shot and takes out the first guy, then the place turns into chaos.

So far, none of our guys are injured. We're making some ground, but Bullet's group has extra men on them, shooting from behind. Bullet signals to me that there are more coming in, and to check my own ass. I do and he's right; we have three on our tail that we didn't clock earlier. As they're closing in, I hit one in the leg, and one of my guys shoots him with a headshot. One down, two to go. Then, Nova takes out the other one and I get the last one. I look at my guys, none of them have been shot, so we keep moving forward.

As we get closer, I see one of ours go down. It's a shot to the shoulder and it's one of the Melbourne boys. Bear is right next to him, after he kills the guy who shot him. He wraps up his arm and puts him in a safe area that has cover, and then keeps moving towards the containers.

There are four guys left, and Prez yells out, "You're outnumbered, why don't you give us the girls?" Then, a guy walks out who looks like Frazer... Hang on, it is Frazer.

"You guys won't live through this, you should just leave to live another day!"

Prez smiles, then answers, "From what I see, you're outnumbered, and we want what we came for. Now, hand over the girls or we'll take them by force!"

Frazer says, "Tut, tut, tut. I don't think you're in a position yet to demand anything. You need to see what you're up against!" As he finishes talking, I hear the roar of engines coming behind us. Looks like Haidie's Club has arrived. Turning, I see Melbourne's president, my Dad, with Krip riding next to him. Looks like they think Dad's turned. I wonder if Frazer will agree.

DREW

50

DREW

A s they pull up and turn their bikes off, Dad looks around at everyone. No one is holding him or forcing him to be there. Same as Krip. Frazer looks at them, but doesn't seem fazed. He looks right at me, then at Prez, and smiles.

"You didn't know, did you, that the man you trust and look up to, works for us, did you?" I say nothing, and neither does Prez. The only thing on my mind is to get the girls out. In a hushed voice, I tell my guys to get ready to make a move. I see Bullet is talking to his guys too. Looks like we are on the same page. Prez looks at me and gives a slight nod with a warning look, telling me to be ready to move and not before. Bullet gets it, too.

Prez negotiates, "So, you have the Melbourne charter Prez and his V.P.. I have his crew. What is it you want? And what is so damn important with the girls that you have to do this?"

"Unlike you, I know where my men stand, and as for the girls, their destiny was always this. Your V.P. just delayed it a bit. But all is well now, won't be long before you will meet her owner. He bought her years ago, don't worry about your little heart, Drew, they will keep her alive. Now, why don't you guys move back so we can do our job?" Over my dead body. Prez glares at me, probably knowing what I want to do, that mother fucker needs to die. I chant that over and over in my head. I need to direct my attention to what's going on around me. Watching everyone's body language, which intensifies as we wait.

When Bullet says, "not asking again Frazer, get the girls or we are going to war right fuckin' now!" Frazer turns to talk to Bullet. As he does, Prez nods at me and I make my move. As I get to some cover, guns start going off again. My crew gives Prez and Bullet's crew cover, then we try to work our way to the containers. It takes a while before I see an opening to make another move. With the determination to do or die trying, I head to the first container. As I get close enough, I squat down, searching and staying alert to see if anyone is watching me. I don't see anyone yet.

I pull the door open and there's no one there. But someone was, I can tell, It might have been Keata cause there's a toy on the floor. I go to pick it up and look at it, then go looking for other evidence that Sophie was here, but I come up with nothing.

I'm about to head out and go to the next one when someone shoots at me, and misses. I duck down and find some cover. There's not much in this container but a chair and a table. I hide behind the table and throw the chair as a bit of a distraction. It hits its target, and I stand to see it's one of Haidie's crew. I shoot to kill, then the guy behind him comes through and I don't waste any time. I shoot again with the same result.

Staying focused, I make my way to the next container and see a shadow coming around the corner. As I'm about to shoot, Nova is there, "All clear, brother. Let's go!" We advance towards the next container.

I can smell smoke, but I'm not sure where it's coming from. As I get closer, I can see smoke nearly all around us. I look at Nova.

"We need to move. Do you know where the smoke is coming from?" He shakes his head and keeps moving.

As we get to the container and open the door, I see it's Savie. She's unconscious and not moving. I rush to her. When I get near, I drop to my knees and feel for a pulse. It's there so I untie her.

Nova picks her up, saying, "I'll get her to van one and get them out of here. You keep going, I'll catch up or send someone to help, yeah?" I nod as we head to the entrance of the container.

Keeping out of sight, I make it to the next container without too much risk. As I get to the door, I can hear someone in there. I listen longer and I can tell there's more than one person in there. There are a few, maybe three or four. Before they notice I'm close, I need to get in. Someone comes up behind me. I turn on full alert, but it's Knight.

"Wait two minutes, Brother. Bullet and Nova are coming. What we looking at?" He asks this so quietly that I nearly missed it.

I point into the container and say, "We need to get in there, get cover, take control, and get whoever is in there, out!" Knight nods, then he points a finger over to where the boys are coming in. He relays what I told him while I make my way inside.

I still can't determine who they're holding yet, but when Nova gets in position, I signal to take them out. One guy is hiding behind whoever they're holding there. We're making ground, the smoke comes into the container and it feels hotter in here. The container is on fire. We need to step this up, quick.

405

As I get closer, I get a look at who's in there. It's Mira, and Krip is with her. He's the last one left of the group. I watch from where I am as he's about to pick her up. He whispers something in her ear and kisses her on the temple. She means more than he's been saying she means to him. The emotion on his face is raw, but as he sees me, it's gone. As he gets closer, I point my gun at him.

"Pass her over, now!" He gives her to me, and I see Knight, Nova, and Bullet standing behind me as I turn around.

Before he lets go, he mumbles, "Keep her safe, Drew, and don't let her come after me. Only you guys will know, I'm still Angels of Fury, yeah?" Jesus, he's not coming back, I nod.

"Will do! Stay safe, brother." I breathe out, still pointing my gun at him.

He then looks at Bullet, "Make it a surface wound brother!" Bullet nods, then shoots him without thinking about it, and walks out after me. As I exit the door, I look back and see Bullet skimmed his arm. He looks like he could kill someone right now, and I'm not entirely sure whether it's his arm, or that we took Mira from him.

Mira is unconscious, too. I take a bit to get in the clear, then Knight takes her from me and takes her to the next van, to where it is safe.

I see the guys are still in a gunfight and the containers are on fire, mainly on the outside, though. There are still two more to check, but I don't know if it's going to be Sophie and Keata, Izzy or Stasia.

Bullet's already at the container, and I'm still moving in and out of the war zone. He's almost ready to push through the container door when I get to him, with Nova and Knight right behind me. Once we get in, Nova sighs in relief, because it's Izzy. She's out of it, but still breathing. He makes quick work of grabbing her.

"Go to the last container. I'm going with her." And he heads out. Knight follows him. Being his cover, Bullet and I head to the last container, which has flames everywhere. The door is already open. As we rush in to see Felix picking up an unconscious Stasia, he smiles at us, and I nod to tell him we'll help him get her out. I need her in my arms, though, so I rush to him. When I'm nearly there, he points a gun at me. I skid to a stop.

"What the fuck?" He's still smiling at me.

"Oh, you didn't get the memo, well, let's see now... Stasia here is my sister, and she has a place where my father and I need her to be." My body freezes and I'm unable to get my words out. I'm staring at him, and if he's the reason the girls were caught... Fuck, where the fuck is Cory?

Bullet yells from behind me, still pointing his gun at Felix, "Either you put her down, or pass her to Drew. You're gonna get shot either way." Felix laughs, proving he is just like his father. Bullet shoots him in the shoulder that's not covered by Stasia. As the bullet hits him, he drops Stasia. She hits the dirt hard. She lets out a moan. I run to her and pick her up. Her eyes connect with mine, as I stand. Pain rips through my arm and I run for the door. When I turn, I see Frazer with a gun. It's aimed at us both. Stasia whispers "No." She moves around me, grabs my gun from behind my back and shoots him. It happens in slow motion and the pain in my arm doesn't allow me to stop her. More guns go off, I need to get Stasia to the van. Looking behind me, I see Bullet's there, covering me.

Once he's in the van, he says, "The other two aren't there. Fuck, I hope Trigger has something for us!" We both jump in the van and take off. Looking behind me, I see the fire has gone wild in the distance. I can hear sirens coming.

Looking at Bullet, he looks defeated. I ask, "Where are we going now?"

He says, "Melbourne charter, but if the girls are bad, we hit the first hospital we see!" He's staring out the window, looking at nothing. I might have my girl back, but nothing is going to be ok till we get Sophie and Keata back!

Sienna Gypsy

STASIA

51

STASIA

Hearing voices wakes me. My vision is terrible, dark and blurry. When someone touches my forehead, I moan a bit. I pull away. Well, I try to, but it hurts like a bitch. Then I hear Drew.

It can't be. A whisper escapes my lips, "Felix?" but I can't be sure yet if I said it or if it's in my head, but then I hear Drew again.

"Beauty, I got you, shhh. Where does it hurt? Talk to me, babe."

Then I hear another voice say, "Hospital it is, we will get to the one closest to Melbourne. We're far enough away from these guys."

"I'm so sore, my h-head hurts b-bad." I choke out. Drew kisses me and reassures me that we are going to the hospital. I nod and close my eyes again, letting sleep take me. I hear Drew in my dreams saying he loves me, and he won't live without me. It feels so real, but I'm sure it's me dreaming.

I wake, and everything is dark. The pain is better now, a dull throb. I think I'm in a bed. It smells clean and feels firm, not like where I was before. I try to move my hands, but someone is holding one of them.

I'm about to pull it out of their grasp when Drew's voice stops me, "Beauty, it's me. Rest, you're safe now." I look down to our hands and try to smile. "Y-you saved me. W-where are we?"

"A hospital. Your head was badly damaged. I didn't notice it till we got you in the van. You were sleeping a lot when we got you to the van. You said you were in pain. Your face is swollen. The back of your head had a deep gash on it. How are you feeling now, Beauty?" I don't even think I register half the stuff Drew says. I was mesmerised by his hand and fingers gently rubbing mine. When his hand comes to my cheek, gently caressing downwards with his index finger, it makes everything right. So, when I murmur "mmm." he replies, "Beauty, how you feeling, babe? You want the nurse for some meds?"

Oh, he asked me something, shit. It's then I notice he has his arm in a sling, "No, I feel good. What happened to you?" He is still touching my face as he replies, "It's a scratch, a bullet skimmed the side of my arm." Still, the thought of him being shot is upsetting.

After some silence, I ask what I need to know. "Drew, did you get everyone out? They split all of us girls up. I saw Mira and Izzy for a bit, but no one else."

He doesn't answer me straight away, but tells me, "Beauty, you okay if I get in bed with you? I need to hold you, babe." Drew pulls me close to him after I move for my answer.

I have the cheek that is not so sore on his chest, while he ever so gently touches me near my wounds. He whispers, "Beauty, we didn't get everybody, but we are making plans as we speak, to get them back. And we will! You need to trust us on this."

I know who he's talking about before I even ask, but I ask anyway.

"Who?" Drew stays quiet for a long time. Tears fall down my face, 'cause the thought of not seeing my girl and doing the things we love to do together is killing me. She can't defend herself. I know her mother will die to protect her, but at what price? Before I know it, I'm sobbing, and Drew knows who I'm thinking about.

"Yeah babe, it's Sophie and Keata, but we have a lead, and Bullet is on a warpath that no one can stop, not even Prez. We will get them back, I promise you."

I bury myself in Drew, sobbing till I run out of breath. Even if I tried, I couldn't say anything. After a while, I must have drained myself of all the energy I had. I've been saved from one nightmare only to relive the new nightmares in my mind.

I wake in a cold sweat. I'm seeing visions of things that happened to me as a child, but with Keata's face, not mine. I can't believe we know nothing. I feel movement next to me. Drew is still next to me. He rubs my back.

"You okay, Beauty?"

"Yeah, just a nightmare. I'm scared for Keata. God, I hope they don't hurt her. Drew, we need to find them!"

"Beauty, we are already on it. Bullet got a call before we found you about the phone calls she was getting. We are thinking they are behind her going missing. Did you ever meet a Jason Simpson? He's the guy that's been texting and talking to her."

"No, but I know that it's her ex, Keata's father. He left them when she fell pregnant, then he came back, and her life turned to shit. She never said the words, but I'm pretty sure he beat her, but I'm not sure about Keata. But she got away when Keata was two. I'm not even sure where she was from, originally."

Feeling Drew's arms embrace me brings a peace I can't explain.

"That's great, Beauty, it's more than we had. I'll let Bullet know in the morning. He'll be by at 9 a.m. We should be ready to leave then."

"Good, where are we going? Where is Felix? They said he is my brother. He is just as bad as my dad. I can't believe he hit me."

"Yeah, he's been taken care of. As for your father, what do you remember?" my thoughts are clear.

"I shot him. When I saw him, I knew you had put your gun in the top of your jeans. I needed to shoot him. He needed to be gone. I have no regrets." Drew looks concerned, searching for regret on my face. But there will be none. "I'm good, actually more than good. I know he is gone." He pecks my lips and smiles, "Yeah, Beauty, he is gone." He pulls me closer and makes eye contact with me. He looks like he's about to cry. I don't take my eyes off him.

"Stasia, I went to hell and back with you being taken and I didn't think I was going to get you back." He swallows, then kisses my swollen eye gently. "When we got to the containers, I didn't even think what I'd have to do to get you back, I just did it. All my focus was on you, and when I saw you unconscious... My heart stopped. You are everything to me, Stasia. I don't think you get it. You are my morning sun and my sunset, my everything." I have more tears burning down my cheeks, 'cause if I'm honest with myself, he was my main thought as well. I needed him so badly, and hearing that he feels the same. God, that feels...

He's stirring up feelings in me I can't explain. "Beauty, I'm saying that I love you, more than you will ever know. And when you'll let me, I'm making it real. You are mine and that's forever, so when we get back, you're moving in, and we are getting married!"

I'm sobbing, laughing, and squeezing him all at the same time, but when I say, "Yes!" He smiles, then leans in and takes my mouth in a much needed kiss. One that promises more than tomorrow, more than my life. The fact he can unchain all of my heartaches, my pain, and allow me to love again, shows me that this is the man for me.

I pull away, with tears still coming down my cheeks, "Drew you are my everything. I've never loved anyone as I do you. God knows I tried to hide from you, and push you away, but this," I point to my heart, "Doesn't work right without you. The love I have is unexplainable. It cuts deep, so deep that it broke the chains that slaved me, and all that stands in there now, is you, and I know with all my heart, that I'm where I'm supposed to be."

EPILOGUE

Today's the day. The day Cobra and Drew are taking me to see Nanna Sally's grave. I have a mix of emotions running through me. I'm still not sure what I'm going to say to her. My mind has been a mess, and if I'm honest, everything I've lost since leaving Nanna Sally has crumbled. My thoughts are always thinking about Sophie and Keata, wondering if they're okay. Are they still alive? Does Jason have them? It's all too much to process. As I finish doing my face, Drew walks in. "You nearly ready, Beauty? Dad's waiting out front." We were on our way home and stopped in Esperance. We've even been back and looked at the house that's been burned down and talked about the plans to rebuild. Cobra wants me to be a part of it, which makes me happy. I put all my toiletries away and take one last look in the mirror. "Yep, it's now or never." I say, walking towards him. He kisses me and wraps his good arm around me, his other arm is still sore. His kisses are always so magical, he always makes me forget what we're doing. When he pulls back, he says, "Let's go." Damn him, and his magic.

We arrive at Nanna Sally's grave and I'm silent for the most part. I listen to Drew tell her about us, how much I mean to him, how he would die for me. I have my eyes closed while I'm listening to his words. When I open them, Drew is on one knee with a ring box in his hand and asks, "Stasia, will you marry me." Tears leak from my eyes before I say anything. I look to Cobra, and I know this will be the last time I see him because he is undercover at the other club. He smiles at me with approval. And I nod. "Yes, Drew! Yes I will marry you." He stands up and puts the ring on my finger and then kisses me hard. We must have been like that for a while because I hear Cobra clear his throat and we both smile and pull away. I turn to both of them and ask, "Could I have a minute alone, please?" They both nod and leave me with Nanna Sally. I don't talk at first, I glance at her grave site and look at the fresh flowers.

I get on my knees and play with the grass as I say, "Nanna Sally, first I want to say thank you. You didn't have to take me in or fix me, but you did. I didn't get to the last destination but looking back now, I realise that was because it was destiny. I met your grandson. He showed me a whole new world. Just know that I will always take care of him and love him forever, I hope you're okay with that. I've said yes to marrying him, he is my everything." Wiping the tears away from my face I stand up. "Oh, and Nanna Sally, I will visit often and tell you our stories whenever we come back to Esperance." I start to walk back towards the car that Cobra and Drew brought me in, and I smile. Because they are my future.

The End

I hope you loved Torture to Bliss. I loved writing it and became very involved with the characters!

Sienna Gypsy

ANGELS OF FURY
2
ILLICIT ROADS

PRELUDE ...

SOPHIE

I wake to my head bumping against something hard. I can't see anything yet. It's like my eyes refuse to adjust and I have a headache from hell. When I try to sit up, I notice I'm tied up, but something is in front of me, not sure what it is though.

After a while, my memory comes back to me. I remember everyone in the van all struggling to stay awake. I remember grabbing Keata and holding her to me, and then the darkness came. Jesus, Keata! Oh, my God... What has happened?

Movement in front of me startles me, so I try again to open my eyes. There is a small shape in front of me. I don't have clear vision yet, but I'm sure it's Keata. God, I hope she stays asleep longer.

Where are the other girls? We were all in the van. I remember Bullet saying, 'Hang tight won't be long now.'

I lay there till my eyesight slowly comes back to me. I keep looking at Keata, hoping she'll be ok. When the car comes to a stop, I hear someone get out, but there's no talking, it's footsteps. The person must walk away from the car, because the footsteps are fading. Keata isn't even stirring. God, I hope the gas that we inhaled isn't too much for her little body.

After being in my head for a while, I hear the footsteps again, then the car takes off, slowly this time. We seem to turn, like, maybe parking, but I'm not sure. Once the car stops, I hear the person get out. They must walk away from the car for a bit again.

Then I hear them coming closer. Closer than before, I get ready, 'cause I'm sure they're coming to where we are. I'm positive now, that it's the boot of a car. After a bit of time and silence, the boot pops open. I see a gun first, it's pointed at my head, then I look to see who my kidnapper is. I can't talk, I can't think, but he can.

"I told you I would find you, Sophie!"

Sienna Gypsy

Music in Book and Songs I Listen to While Writing.

Black Magic

Girls Just Want to Have Fun

Like a Prayer

Wannabe Spice Girls

Sober by Pink

Scars to Your Beautiful

The book is in Aussie language with a little slang.

The book is based in Australia.

AUTHOR BIO

S ienna Gypsy is an author whose passion for storytelling was sparked in school, where a compelling story she wrote led her teacher to encourage creative writing. Despite facing challenges with dyslexia and a processing disorder, she continued to pursue her love for writing. Now, as a business owner, she supports people with disabilities in finding meaningful employment, reflecting her belief in empowerment and resilience. A former dancer and lifelong horse lover, she enjoys the company of her two cats and two dogs. Always ready for a challenge, she channels this drive into her writing, creating stories that inspire and resonate. Stay connected with her journey through Facebook, Instagram, TikTok, and Goodreads.

Milton Keynes UK
Ingram Content Group UK Ltd.
UKHW040836300924
449047UK00001B/152